Also by Phyllis Moore

People of Akiane Trilogy
Pegasus Colony
Storm's Coming
Jessica's Mission

The Destiny Series
My Haunted Bed & Breakfast

People of Akiane
Book Three

Jessica's Mission

Phyllis Moore

Myth Rider
Publishers

Novels are a ride into another world.

Moore, Phyllis
Jessica's Mission / by Phyllis Moore — U.S. ed.
First Edition

Summary: The People of Akiane are blinded by their past. They must overcome generations of mistaken beliefs in order to see their future.
Lieutenant Jessica M. Hewitt must confront the demons of her past if she is to find the home she desperately seeks.
Together they will change the future of Akiane.

ISBN 978-0-9907091-4-5 paper book
ISBN 978-0-9907091-48-3 e-book
1. Science Fiction — Fiction.
2. Science Fiction Colonization — Fiction.
3. Strong Female Character — Fiction.
4. Jessica's Mission — Fiction.
5. Character Driven, Science Fiction — Fiction.

First published in U.S.A. 2021
Typeset by Cheryl Barr
Printed by Amazon KDP

MythRider Publishers

Cover image from IStock
Cover design Phyllis Moore
Book jacket design Cheryl Barr

Acknowledgments

It is said that writing is a lonely profession. That is somewhat true. There are many long hours of writing and rewriting, but without the help of beta readers, proofreaders, and editors, books would never come into existence.

Because of Alistair Phillips, I completely rewrote the beginning of this novel.

I rewrote smaller sections because of comments made by; Cheryl Barr, Jan and Jim Daire, Georgia Haug, and Judy Comstock.

The overall story came together thanks to my editor Patricia Morris.

Special thanks to fans who make long hours worthwhile.

Phyllis Moore

Chapter 1

Akiane Historical Chronicles
First Day on Akiane

Earth Standard Year: 2144
Akiane Date: Day One

IT WAS to be Earth's greatest achievement, establishing the first galactic colony in the Pegasus Constellation. Using folded space technology, World Space Coalition sent three spaceships, *WSC Eagle, WSC Hawk,* and *WSC Falcon,* to transport a total of 2,035 settlers to their new home planet, Akiane. More ships were scheduled to bring a continual supply of goods to help support the settlers until they were well established on their new home planet.

Twelve years on a spaceship seemed an eternity. Children born on the ship had never felt a star's warmth, seen blue sky, or run barefoot in the grass or jumped in a puddle of water. They'd never played with their own kitten or puppy. Parents were looking forward to introducing their children to all these new experiences.

WSC Eagle arrived first, but did not land. Its orders were to gather information on the star system, its planets, and their moons. *Eagle* launched probes to gather

1

information on Akiane's air, soil samples, and take digital recordings. Data was sent to the other ships and to World Space Coalition Moon Base. From that information, the settlers would choose the best location to build their settlement.

Each ship carried DNA for livestock, seeds for crops, and settlers.

WSC Eagle carried the bulk of the DNA and the colony's power source. Once it had completed its mission, landed, and delivered its cargo, *Eagle* would return to Moon Base.

WSC Hawk carried the most settlers. It was their mission to choose a suitable landing site for their new colony. The ship was to be disassembled and used to build the first city in the new Pegasus Colony.

WSC Falcon would be the last to arrive. Its crew would support the colonists while they settled in, then return to Moon Base.

The colonists on *Hawk* were excited to walk the land of their new world in the light of their new star. They selected one of the landing spots suggested by a probe and would temporarily set up camp before sending shuttles to explore other possibilities and determine the best site for their permanent home.

During the journey, couples married, families grew, and lifetime friendships formed.

Nadira and Pavel met on *Hawk* as teenagers, grew up together, and married. Now within two weeks of giving birth to their first child, they let out a sigh of relief as the ship landed. They'd made it. Their baby girl would be one of the first born as a citizen of Pegasus Colony.

The captain's voice came over the intercom. "It's cold outside, folks, but it's a clear day. We have searched the area and all seems fine." After a slight pause, he said, "All personnel on duty, please remain on board. Those off duty and all civilians are welcome to disembark, but please stay close to the ship for the time being. Don't forget to dress for the cold."

Their good friends, Marianna and Havi, joined Nadira and Pavel in their cabin eager to explore the planet together.

Pavel was about to help Nadira into her winter jacket when she felt a sharp pain.

"What?" Pavel worriedly asked. "Not time. Have two weeks."

"*Nyet nyet*, not time, my one and only love," Nadira said. "But not feeling good. Is best to remain behind."

Pavel hung her coat in the closet.

"Sit on couch," he said.

"*Nyet nyet*, bed," Nadira said.

Pavel commanded, "Computer: bed."

A queen-size bed appeared from the wall with blankets, sheets, and pillows. The bed smoothly descended as two legs slipped out of the end of the bed frame and settled on the floor.

He placed the cushions from the couch on the bed then propped the pillows against them. "You more comfortable in your nightgown?" he asked.

"*Nyet nyet*, help me out of snowsuit," she said.

Nadira sat on the edge of the bed. Pavel helped her out of her boots and snow overalls.

Once she was settled, he started to take his coat off. "I stay with you."

"*Nyet nyet*, love of my life," she said, "I be all right. Have need to rest. Our parents and the others are waiting. You go. No disappoint."

He stopped with his jacket half off, undecided. The expression on his face said he was torn between going outside and staying with his beloved wife.

"I will stay and be *compañía* for Nadira," Marianna said. She took her winter jacket off and handed it to Havi, then sat on the edge of the bed.

Havi hurried to help her take her snow boots and suit off.

Then she comfortably settled on the bed next to her friend.

"Me feeling *bajo el clima* (under the weather)." Marianna rubbed her swollen belly. "Carrying *un niño es* hard work." She was disappointed at missing their first adventure, but she was also glad for the excuse to stay behind. She was only six months pregnant, but there were days when she felt she had been pregnant 20 months. This was one of those days.

"Havi and I stay," Pavel said. "We go when you feeling better. We explore together."

Havi hung Marianna's things in the closet and had started to take his jacket off.

"*Bien*," he said as he reached for another hanger.

"*Nyet nyet*, please don't," Nadira said. "No company. Go."

"But you don't . . ."

Nadira interrupted Pavel. "Rest best if you not here. Go."

"What about Mari?" Pavel asked.

"We talk and nap," she said as she patted Marianna's leg. "Leave, now. Tomorrow you show us."

Marianna knew the little boy in Havi was excited to explore their new planet, but the responsible husband wanted to stay with her.

"Go, *mi amor*," Marianna said and noticed how tired she sounded.

Reluctantly, the men left.

* * *

Hawk had landed in the late afternoon on a large snow-covered stretch of beach between the edge of a crater and the ocean. Mounds of snow had been sculpted by the wind into statues of abstract art.

4

The settlers dressed for the below-zero temperature and either snowshoed or cross-country skied across the snow.

Pavel and Havi chose to cross-country ski. They were in awe at what looked like an alien scene painted from an artist's imagination. The reality of the situation was surreal. They were actually standing on a planet in the Pegasus Constellation.

Two overhead full moons looked like they were about to eclipse each other. The planet's star hung in the late afternoon sky but would soon drop behind a giant gas planet rising from behind the mountains in the west. The planet was covered with angry orange, brown, and gray storm clouds.

The day would quickly darken. They had little time to explore.

Akiane's snow-covered landscape reflected the colors of the gas planet's clouds. As the clouds moved across the giant planet, their reflections swirled in the snow, moved down slopes, over the beach, around boulders, over the ship, then stretched onto the frozen ocean. Some of the settlers skied with the movement of the reflections. Others suffering motion sickness, sought the quiet of the shadow under *Hawk's* belly.

Pavel and Havi greeted their parents, siblings, and extended family members as they skied up the crater's slope to get a bird's-eye view of the beach on one side and the crater on the other side. They stood in amazement at the size of it, for they could not see across the crater's edge.

The snow-covered crater also reflected the gas planet's clouds.

"Not Kansas, *mi amigo*." Havi laughed.

"Beautiful, but not like Siberia," Pavel agreed.

Having grown up in Mexico City, Havi was not used to snow. "When spring comes?" he asked.

"After years of winter, will take long time for spring to take hold, comrade," Pavel said. "

"Years of winter is as difficult to comprehend as years of spring. How hot do you think it get?"

"Not like deserts of Mexico, I guarantee," Pavel said.

"I already miss Mexico summers."

"I not miss Siberian winters," Pavel said and sighed. "Yet, I fear winter here worse than homeland."

From among the western mountains, rose ominous dark gray, almost black plumes of smoke that held flashes of furious orange fires and bright flashes of lightning.

"Not look good," Havi said. "If wind bring here, ash suffocate."

"Trouble first day, *da da*(yes)," Pavel said.

"*Lo siento*, sorry." Havi said with a sheepishly smiled. "Volcanologist in me. We *suerte*, lucky, not closer."

"Should we warn others?" Pavel asked, concerned.

"No. If big explosion, we know," Havi said. "Now, *disfrutamos el dia*, we enjoy the day."

There was a bright flash of light in the sky, which quickly faded.

"What?" Pavel's mother asked.

"My dearest love, not know," his father said. "Perhaps a meteorite."

"Will be another?" she asked.

"Unsure, my only love," he said.

Havi leaned toward Pavel and softly said, "*Eagle* exploded."

"You sure?" Pavel asked.

"Meteorite across sky. That explosion."

"Havi, those people."

"*Sí*, and our power source."

"Where *Falcon*?" Pavel whispered.

"*Dos día*, two days behind." Havi shook his head.

"Tell others?"

"Nothing can do," Havi said. "Best to let the captain speak."

"*Da da,*" Pavel agreed.

The joy of landing on their new home planet was now marred by worry for their future.

Pavel and Havi skied down the slope toward the beach, riding the reflections in the snow. They slipped between boulders, around the ship, and along the beach near the frozen ocean with their families to join their friends.

The first earthquakes were so slight only a few noticed and realized what they were. Soon everyone felt the quakes.

Those on shore should have immediately gone back inside and the captain should have moved the ship further inland.

However, according to the information they'd received from *Eagle's* probes, they were not in an earthquake hazard area, and thought they were feeling the aftershocks of a faraway epicenter. All seemed safe.

Seismic waves came more frequently. Avalanches of snow and rocks fell from the edge of the crater.

Planetary geological scientists set up their seismic equipment to monitor the planet's geological event. The size and closeness of the gas planet's gravity was having an effect on Akiane's gravity and causing the earthquakes. There wasn't just one epicenter; the quakes were happening everywhere. The scientists hurried to the ship to warn the captain.

He promised to take it under advisement. He then retreated to his ready room to study the situation.

Astronomers hurriedly assembled a telescope to photograph the gas planet and moons. They too returned to the ship to monitor the event from their computers in the safety of their work area.

Oceanographers worriedly watched the frozen ocean. The same random land quakes were also happening on the bottom of the ocean. If the ground shifted along fault lines, or dropped, the ocean waters would create tsunami waves and, no matter how thick the ice, those waves would break through.

They tried to warn people that it might not be safe to be outside. Some listened and followed the oceanographers back to the ship. Most did not.

* * *

Marianna and Nadira reclined on the bed, leaned back on their pillows, and chatted for a while before they dozed off.

Though Nadira didn't notice the barometric pressure drop, her body did. She let out an agonizing moan as a spasm seized her.

"What?" Marianna woke with a fright. She sat up so quickly she almost had a spasm.

"*Rebenok prikhodit!*" (Baby coming!)

"Nadira, no. She not due for two weeks."

"My baby comes," Nadira said louder.

Marianna pushed herself off the bed, moved as quickly as she could to the Civilian Communication System, slammed her hand over the button, and yelled "Medical!"

"Medical here," a calm voice answered.

"Nadira is having her baby!" Marianna shouted at the intercom.

"So are 15 other women," the voice answered. "Prop her up with pillows. Keep a watch for the baby . . ."

"*¿Qué?*" Marianna demanded.

She didn't need instructions; she needed someone who knew how to deliver a baby.

"Can't come right now. No one can. Remain calm. Get clean towels. Call as soon as you see the baby's head crown. Be prepared to catch the baby yourself. If she comes before we get there, wrap her in a towel and place her on her mother's chest. Wipe her eyes, nose, and mouth. Medical out."

Marianna stared at the CCS intercom. She couldn't believe it. They were going to leave her alone to deliver the baby.

* * *

As predicted, ocean waters did become turbulent. The sea ice wobbled as it rose and fell awkwardly. Ice popped and cracked as if a thunderstorm within raged.

The expanse of ice covering the ocean rose and dropped with a horrific sigh. Then with deafening sonic-like booms the ice shattered into billions of pieces.

Everyone on the beach watched in bewildered fascination to see what would happen next.

Earthquakes increased to such intensity and frequency, people screamed as they lost their balance.

At the same time, angry waves rose like geysers, throwing giant ice floes aside as if they were tiny bits of ice. Waves shot upward, reaching for the sky. Gravity refused to release them. Waves crashed back into the ocean like giant waterfalls, chewing up more ice floes. The ocean became like a boiling pot of water.

"Maybe we should have stayed on ship with our wives," Pavel said.

"*Sí,*" Havi said, "too late now."

* * *

Mighty swells became mightier waves that swiftly inundated the beach. When the first set of waves retreated, only *WSC Hawk* remained. The beach had been swept clean of all snow, rocks, and people. Not one person made it back to the ship.

Hurricane winds assaulted *Hawk* from every direction.

9

Billowing dark gray, yellow-green, and black clouds formed with the speed of a time-lapse film, producing heavy rain, blizzard, and hail the size of baseballs.

Waves washed over the land threatening to drag *Hawk* out to sea.

The captain started the engines, but was forced to move before the engines were fully charged. Able to rise only a few meters, *Hawk* started toward the crater's edge. The captain had hoped to move inside the crater where the waves couldn't reach them, but the engines failed. The huge ship collapsed near the bottom of the crater's edge rattling everything and everyone in the ship.

At last, the ship was safely beyond the waves' reach.

* * *

Marianna tried to move back to the bed, but the ship was shaking so violently she had to cling to the counter to keep her balance.

Suddenly the ship jolted, then dropped so fast Marianna was left hanging in mid-air. Nadira was floating above her bed. Both women screamed, then fell.

Nadira bounced on the bed, her legs, and arms wildly flinging. "Oh, oh, oh," she cried.

Marianna's feet hit the floor. Her legs gave way, and she crumpled. Momentarily stunned, she lay on the floor unable to breathe. Her baby objected and kicked aggressively, then became quiet. She fared for her baby's safety worried.

Was he all right? She rolled onto her back and waited until she finally felt movement. *"Gracias a Dios,"* she whispered (Thank God).

Marianna remembered her friend.

*"¿*Nadira, *estás bien?"* With great effort, Marianna rolled over and heaved herself to her hands and knees. "Nadira, you all right?"

10

Nadira, was half off the bed, trying to pull herself back onto it.

"Aaa."

"What?"

"MY WATER BROKE!"

Marianna crawled to her friend, rose onto her knees, and with all her strength, pushed Nadira onto the bed. Then she crawled onto it next to her friend.

Both women let out a sigh of relief.

The com crackled. Marianna hoped it was Medical saying they were on their way.

It was the captain. "We moved the ship farther inland. It's not as far as we'd like, but we are out of the worst of the waves. We should be safe until this passes."

"That no help," Nadira said with a weak laugh.

"Waves?" Marianna asked. "What he talking about?" Their husbands were outside. "Why does the ship need to be safe?" *¿Dónde está* Havi? Marianna's thoughts shouted. *¿Por qué no está aquí? ¡¿Donde está?!* (Where is Havi? Why isn't he here? Where is he?!)

"Come." Nadira was having difficulty speaking and gasping for air. "Do as nurse say . . . pillows . . . prop up."

Marianna gathered all four pillows on the bed and arranged them so Nadira could lean back at a higher angle.

"Better." Nadira started to say, "Towe . . ." but finished with a primal roar as she began panting.

By the time Marianna returned with several towels, Nadira's knees were up. "*She's coming! Prikhadit.*"

Marianna couldn't look. If she saw the head, it would be her responsibility to deliver the child. She didn't know how.

"Mari!" Nadira demanded.

She looked. "The head," Marianna squealed.

"Tell Medical. Hurry, no stop her." Nadira gritted her teeth as she strained with the coming of her child.

"Medical, Nadira's baby is coming."

"Okay. Is she pushing?" the voice from the com asked.

11

Unable to speak, Nadira bobbed her head up and down.

"Yes," Marianna frantically yelled.

"Okay, remain calm and position yourself to guide the baby as the shoulders emerge. Don't bother about the placenta or the umbilical cord. There is no hurry for that. Someone will be right there. You catch the baby, wrap her in a towel, and place her on her mother's chest. And don't forget to clean her eyes, nose, and mouth."

"No can," Marianna squeaked. She wiped sweat and tears from her eyes.

"You can."

"What if . . .?"

"MARI!" Nadira held a towel in her hand. "HURRY!!!"

Marianna took it.

Nadira gave a mighty push, and the head emerged. On the next push the baby turned and one shoulder slipped out, then the other.

On the last push and the baby slipped out onto the towel in Marianna's hands.

The baby girl was slimy, red, and ugly. *Is this what* mi bebé *will look like? Bebés supposed to be beautiful,* Marianna thought. She placed the baby on the bed and tried to clean the child's nose and mouth and eyes with a tissue, but it wasn't working.

"Mari, is something wrong?"

"No."

"Why you look sick?"

The baby gasped and then let out an ear-piercing wail. Marianna was so surprised, if she had been holding the child, she might have dropped her.

"*Lo siento,* sorry." Marianna picked up the baby and placed the child and towel on Nadira's chest.

Nadira enveloped her arms around her newborn and let out a long satisfied sigh of relief. She became so still Marianna thought she had fallen asleep.

She took a step away from the bed. She knew there was more to be done, but Marianna didn't know what to do. What if Medical was too late and the baby died? Would Nadira blame her? No, she had done what she was told, but was it enough? She knew it wasn't.

Nadira opened her eyes, smiled with the luminous joy of a new mother, and said, "Thank you, my ever faithful friend. Never I can do this by myself." She closed her eyes, still smiling.

Within a few moments, a nurse arrived, pushing her medical cart. She took the baby, cut the umbilical cord, cleaned her, expertly wrapped the baby in a pink baby blanket, and handed her to Marianna while she took care of Nadira.

The baby slept. A little fist covered her mouth as she sucked on it. Marianna's eyes traced her little nose, long black eyelashes, and a full head of curly black hair. "She's perfect." Mi *hope* mi bebé *boy is as perfect.*

Once Nadira was cleaned, dressed in a new gown, her bedding changed, and was back in bed, the nurse said, "Sorry, I can't stay longer, we have more babies on the way. You are our twelfth. We have at least five more coming, but there could be even more than that."

Marianna handed Nadira her new baby girl, then placed a hand on the nurse's arm and softly asked, "What is happening? Why did captain move ship?"

The nurse was suddenly overwhelmed with emotion. Without looking at Marianna, she shook her head and quickly left.

Something was terribly wrong. Marianna feared for Havi's life.

"Oooooh, love of my life. My heart sings joyfully." Nadira whispered to the sleeping infant. "I sorry your papa not here to greet you. Such a surprise upon Pavel's return."

I hope so, Marianna thought, but fear overwhelmed her. She dropped to her knees and prayed.

* * *

The gravitational storm created by the gas planet was so horrific the settlers named it *The Storm*, for there was no other storm like it.

Akiane had shaken with such force that parts of the mountains had crumbled and new mounds of rock were forced upward. After The Storm, the surviving settlers parked *Hawk* and *Falcon* side by side in what they learned was not a crater, but a caldera created by The Storm.

If they were to live on Akiane, they needed to build a city that could withstand the violent influence of a giant gas planet's gravitational force.

With the help of a shuttle, the settlers found a nearby inactive volcano in the mountains. They pulverized the lava into a powder and mixed it with a chemically designed, self-healing polymer.

From the mixture, they made hexagonal blocks to construct a dome around both ships. The dome was to protect them from severe winter years. Once the dome was finished, they planned to use the ships for material to construct the city they would build inside the dome.

They named their new home Endurance for they would endure much but would persevere.

While under construction, the beauty of native trees, bushes, flowers, and grass flourished over the caldera and inside the dome. The dome became a permanent garden.

They would need a glass ceiling so the star could shine through and nourish the planets and that could withstand The Storm.

They followed a lava river from the mountain volcano to the ocean. When hot lava hits ice-cold water, the lava becomes obsidian glass, which is extremely brittle.

The settlers melted the glass, then genetically altered the fragile obsidian making it self-healing and sturdy enough to withstand The Storm. Their garden benefited from the star's daily nourishment.

They named the star *Kahair*, Arabic for good because of the warmth it brought.

The glass ceiling allowed them to enjoy the night's view of the stars. To their surprise, they were also able to enjoy the Aurora Borealis that came before, during, and after the arrival of the gas planet that created The Storm.

They named the gas planet Loki after the trickster god of magic and fire, who caused more trouble than he was worth.

The aurora they named Freya after the most beautiful goddess.

Both names came from Norse mythology.

* * *

When Nadira and Marianna learned they were the only ones left of their families, they decided to live together to console each other, and share in raising their children.

Nadira named her daughter after her husband's mother, Abir.

Abir was one of 21 babies born that day.

Three months later, Marianna gave birth to a boy and named him after Havi's middle name, Rico.

Rico and Abir grew up as siblings but eventually their love deepened beyond adopted brother and sister, and they married.

When Abir was 27 years old, she unexpectedly became pregnant with her fourth child. That child changed the history of the colony.

Chapter 2

Akiane Historical Chronicles
Governor Faris Assetti

Akiane Date: Year 27
Endurance: Medical Lab

"OPEN IT," Governor Faris Assetti commanded. *Bismillahi! Ya Raab Ahhdeenee!!* She prayed in Arabic that she was doing the right thing.

"I don't think we should," Dr. Evan Beasley said.

"We will not know unless we try," she insisted. Her stomach cramped as if she'd eaten spoiled meat. She knew it was wrong, but she had to prove to the others—the child was human. It deserved to be loved and nurtured as any member of the Community. The child did not deserve to be rejected just because it was born in a cocoon.

"The mother," he objected.

"Abir has already abandoned her child," Faris assured him.

Two Weeks Earlier

"Ah, Faris, I am enjoying my retirement." Beasley was sitting against a large rock reading his favorite book on his

16

tablet. Faris suspected it was for the hundredth time. That was what Beasley missed most about Earth, new authors. He'd read most of the books in the library database many times, and had not read anything new in decades.

"I am in need of your service, my old friend," she said.

"You have said more than once how magnificently I've trained the next generation medical team. Why do you need me now?"

"I'm not sure I said 'magnificently'." This was not a social visit. Therefore Faris did not sit. She wanted Beasley on his feet.

"Hmm, I am not senile yet. I still have an excellent memory," he teased.

"I want you to examine Abir."

"Abir is 27 years old. After three children she thought she was finished. It's not unusual for a new baby to come unexpectedly." He smiled. Faris didn't smile back. He grimaced. "What about her pregnancy bothers you?"

"She is only three months along, but in a matter of days she has doubled in size."

"What's the medical team's assessment?" Beasley closed his tablet.

"They are baffled. Every test says she and the baby are normal. There is no reason for the sudden growth."

"I must admit, this could very well pull me out of retirement." He rose to his feet as if he were still a young man.

Faris rarely found the time to exercise, probably because she hated it, something she was beginning to regret. Today she felt more like 110 instead of her 61 years.

She knew Beasley didn't like retirement. He'd stepped back in order to give the new medical team room to grow and learn without his meddling. She also knew he would be interested in the prospect of a medical mystery. And if his good friend Faris asked for his help, how could he refuse?

After a thorough examination, Beasley came to the same conclusion; Abir and the child were healthy. There was no medical reason for the sudden growth.

Beasley had said this day would come, but Faris, like so many others, chose to ignore the possibility as long as possible. Not because she didn't believe him, but because of the trouble it would cause. People did not like change, especially one as monumental as this.

The doctor had noted the slight physical changes of children starting with the second generation born and raised on Akiane. No matter the pigment of their skin, every one of them had a hint of maroon in their coloring. Within twenty years, the children began to have raven hair and lava black eyes.

Dr. Beasley did a methodical examination of their DNA and concluded that all the children born on Akiane had a new mutation. He didn't have the expertise to explain how or know why it had happened.

He did say, "This planet is changing our children. One day there will be a new generation who will reflect the full impact of that change."

No one had listened. No one had *wanted* to listen.

How were we supposed to prepare for a woman giving birth to a child in a cocoon? Faris wondered.

When Abir saw her baby, she screech in terror. She thought her insides had come out along with her child.

It was wrapped in a thin membrane filled with amniotic fluid. The umbilical cord fell off. The covering was a light shade of ivory and was just transparent enough to see the shadow of the baby inside as it moved. The soft casing gave way when the child pushed against it.

Beasley tried to ease her fears by saying, "It's not your uterus. It's a cocoon."

He was amazed at the miracle of a new kind of birth.

"Cocoon?" Abir asked in disgust. "I don't understand."

"This child's birth is no different from the way our dogs are born," Beasley said, in the hopes that he could reassure her that her baby was well and healthy.

Instead, she became hysterical.

"I am not a dog," she shrieked. "I am a good Jew. I am made in the image of Yahweh, not a DOG!"

"No, that's not what I meant." Beasley again tried to explain, but Abir was too distraught to listen.

She continued to wail in grief, "I have been cursed by Yahweh. What have I done to deserve this?" She started to leave the birthing room.

"No!" Beasley stopped her. "We must clean you up."

"I must leave!"

"If you leave you might get an infection," Beasley said. "Let us take care of you. You should rest, so we can observe you, and make sure all is well." He paused. "It will give you time to think about your child. You'll see you're not cursed."

She would not be consoled. Abir turned her head and lay crying as the nurse cleaned her up. As soon as she was finished and Abir was dressed in a clean gown, she ran from the room without looking back.

It didn't take long for word to spread. Soon people filtered into the medical lab wanting to know what had happened. They walked in without knocking or asking for permission. Some came with genuine concern; most came to gawk. Those who couldn't squeeze into the room crowded the hallway.

"I don't believe it," one said.

"It can't be true," said another.

"This is not how humans were meant to be born."

Then the questions came.

"Will it live?"

"Will the child suffocate in that thing?"

Then came the speculations and arguments.

"It must be opened at once before it dies."

"No, the baby must finish growing," Beasley said.

"How will you know when it is ready?"

"I say let it die. It's unnatural. Unholy. Let it die and be rid of the thing."

"No, the child deserves a chance."

"Yes, I agree."

"Let the cursed one die."

"How can you say that?" Faris bellowed. She knew the doctor had not meant to insult Abir by comparing her birth to the way dogs were born but the damage was done. As governor, it was up to her to pick up the pieces. "The child has a right to live."

"Why?" a man called Fintan said. He never had a problem expressing his opinion, and didn't care if he was right or wrong as long as his voice was the loudest.

He was of Irish descent, and his family was famous for two things: their hospitality and their love of horses. Fintan's father, Connor, had planned to bring both to Akiane.

He was so overjoyed at the birth of his first-born son, Fintan, he threw a three-day party to celebrate.

As a child, Fintan had been like his father, gentle and fun-loving but as an adult he'd become a bitter man who freely expressed his opinions without regard for another's feelings. This time, Faris feared his voice would become the popular ruling.

"The child is human," Faris said. "It has a right to live."

"Why? Because you say so?" Fintan demanded.

Maalekkkk!! What is wrong with you! Every member of our Community has a right to live," Faris insisted. She was shocked and frustrated that there was even an argument over the life of a child.

Fintan took several steps closer, his usual bullying tactic to tower over another, which usually worked.

Faris was not easily intimidated. She had been the commander of a spaceship for 12 years and governor for

20

27. She stood her ground, stared up at him, and fearlessly said, "You cannot arbitrarily decide who lives and who dies."

"If this child has been cursed by God, it has no rights," the so called good Catholic man said.

This was a futile argument. There was only one way to prove to him, and the others who agreed with him, that the child was not cursed.

"Open it," Faris said.

"I don't think we should," Dr. Beasley said.

"We will not know unless we try," she insisted. "Open the cocoon."

She was sure the child would live and would disprove the lie of a curse. Faris planned to bring the baby to Abir, hoping that once she saw her beautiful, helpless, little one she would change her mind. How could any mother reject her newborn? Faris wanted to prove that neither the mother nor the child was cursed.

Beasley hesitated. "Opening the cocoon before it's ready will kill it. We should place the cocoon in the vines and allow it to harden. Then the child will kick its way out." He abruptly stopped speaking.

Faris knew he was going to say, "Just like the dogs."

The others in the room whispered among themselves.

She heard her daughter softly ask, "Why not do as Beasley says?"

Fatimah, Faris' best friend and second in command, answered, "That would mean placing the child on the ground beside the puppies, which would emphasize the fact that the baby was no better than a dog."

Faris' chest constricted. She had difficulty speaking. "Open it." The words came out less intense than she'd intended. Breathing became laborious. Each breath was cut short by the pain in her chest.

Yee LahhWee!! Am I doing the right thing? For the first time in her life, Faris doubted her decision.

21

The medical team stood by, ready to treat the child as if it was a premature birth. Faris feared she might need the team herself.

Father Joseph Striken handed Beasley a small silver scalpel.

"You're a Jesuit priest," Beasley pleaded. "It could kill the child."

The priest leaned in close and whispered, "Even if we did wrap the child in vines, someone might make sure it was dead by morning. Placing a guard over the child would loudly declare that no one is to be trusted. This is the only chance the child has to live."

Beasley reluctantly gave in. He carefully cut the thin membrane. Liquid seeped out. As it deflated, the cocoon collapsed onto the child, suffocating it. The child squirmed and kicked in an attempt to free itself. The doctor quickly pulled the membrane away.

It was a girl—the first to be born in a cocoon. At 14 weeks, she was and larger than a newborn and already fully formed. Her skin was maroon and a fuzz of black hair was matted to her head.

Those in the room stood in a circle around Governor Faris, Father Joseph, and Doctor Beasley. They moved closer to get a better look. Someone in the hallway asked, "What happened? What do you see?"

Faris heard murmurs but she concentrated only on the child.

The baby girl opened her ebony eyes. She whimpered as newborns do. Several times she tried to catch her breath, then became quiet. Before anyone could respond, she died, just as Beasley had predicted.

"Sometimes, I hate always being right," Beasley said.

Faris knew he was angry, his comment was an accusation toward her.

She closed her eyes, and prayed, *Allah, have mercy on my soul.*

"God has decided," Fintan said unsympathetically.

The death of the child confirmed his belief in the curse.

Sachi said, "I agree. It is not Buddha's will for our children to be born as dogs. This child was of the evil one. Even its color is evil."

"No!" Beasley heatedly addressed the group. "This child was not cursed. If we had wrapped her cocoon in the vines, the child would have lived. This is not Allah or Buddha or God's will. It happened because this planet is changing us. It happened because too many of you have small minds and even smaller hearts."

"We will not be insulted by the likes of you." Fintan and his followers turned and left.

Beasley tenderly picked the child up. He studied her for a moment then whispered, "I'm so very sorry."

He had not look at Faris during his outrage. Nor did he look at her when he and his medical team exited the room.

He blames me for the child's death, and rightly so, she thought. *I have murdered the child by forcing him to open the cocoon too soon. I should have listened to him.*

She knew Beasley would never forgive her.

How could he when she could never forgive herself.

SubhanAllah Al Aatheeem, she prayed for Allah's benevolence and forgiveness.

What right do I have to call on him when I have murdered one of his precious ones? she thought.

Faris knew the medical team would perform an autopsy to learn as much as they could. Most of the Community would see the importance, but some would adamantly object. For their sake, Faris should stop Beasley, but it was too important.

The Community needed to know.

The others slowly filtered out of the small room, leaving only Father Joe, Fatimah, and Faris.

Faris wiped the beads of sweat from her face. It didn't help. Her hands were clammy. She wiped them on the front of her shirt; it was soggy from sweat.

"Maybe next time we will listen," she said. "We will give this child a proper burial and then we will prepare for the next one. We need to find a better way to care for the cocoons than to lay them on the ground with dogs. Fatimah, find someone to build nests for our children."

Fatimah nodded. "As you say."

* * *

Faris remembered the day she said goodbye to her father just before her ship launched for Akiane. She had assured him that she would return in 24 years. He tried to hide his disappointment at her leaving him.

He gave her a small, furry white dog, Harrie the Spitz, to keep her company during the trip.

This surprised her since he, like so many traditional Muslims, believed dogs were unclean. She tried to turn him down, but he'd insisted it was by Allah's will. She doubted the validity of his explanation, but her father was a good Muslim, therefore he must have had a good reason to give her the dog.

He let out a sigh of relieve when she accepted his gift and visibly relaxed. It was as if he knew she would not be returning, and for some reason, it was important that the dog went with her.

Faris requested a prayer closet to be built in a corner of her private quarters so she could pray in the room without the contamination of the dog.

It had taken time for her to get used to sharing her cabin with a dog.

But Harrie the Spitz soon became a comfort and a welcomed companion on the trek to Akiane. Now she wondered if her father had been right all along.

Even though Harrie was the only dog on the planet, she gave birth to a litter of puppies not long after they landed. The puppies were all born in individual cocoons, but because no one knew what to do with the cocoons, the first litter died.

By the second litter, Harrie and Father Joe had figured out how to use native vines to nourish the cocoons. He carefully wrapped one vine around each cocoon several times. The vines leaked a milky substance that kept the cocoon's membrane moist and fed the pup inside.

Future dogs gave birth among the vines where their owner or a passerby would wrap the cocoons for them. When the pups were mature enough to kick their way out, the cocoons hardened into a brittle shell. The pups came out fully formed with their eyes open. And like their mother, Harrie the Spitz, they were covered in white fur. Within an hour, they were standing and making squeaky barking sounds.

As they grew, some remained all white, but others changed to different shades of peach, red, or maroon. Sometimes their fur was spotted or had large patches of different colors. But over the years, the color of their fur never varied from white, peach, red, or maroon.

* * *

Faris wondered what would have happened if Harrie had not been the first on the planet to become pregnant and give birth all those years ago? As unwilling as some were to accept the truth now, how much more unprepared would they have been without Harrie's puppies?

Now she believed her father gave Harrie to her as a gift from Allah.

As the Christians were so fond of saying: *God works in strange ways.*

This day more so than any other, Faris thought. *Ya Ameen* (Magnificent One) *you knew what you were doing, after all.*

Joe placed a hand on her shoulder. "Allah does not blame you for this."

"I sacrificed the child's life to make a point that she was not under a curse. I should have listened to Beasley. I should have fought for her life. Instead, I let her die." Faris' voice broke with emotion.

"You were trying to defuse a bad situation," he said.

"Father …" She hesitated. She had not called him Father in a long time. Their close friendship had permitted them to use first names. But for what she had just done, she no longer deserved the privilege of calling him Joe. "Father, that little girl will never walk or talk, sing or dance. She will never dream of becoming—I don't know, anything. She is dead because of me." Was she confessing to the priest?

Was a Muslim seeking absolution from a Catholic priest? she wondered. *Perhaps.*

"Allah forgives you," he said. "This is not your fault."

His words carried no meaning.

Beasley had tried to convince Faris she was wrong, but her belief in the goodness of people would not allow her to believe the worst. She'd miscalculated the strength of fear and hate. Instead of bringing hope, she'd encouraged the belief in a curse, which would cause more problems.

Faris closed her eyes. She felt lightheaded. Her brain seemed to be floating in her head. She swayed.

Her faithful friends, Fatimah and Joe, helped her back to her quarters.

"Lie down and rest," they said.

She found no rest. Her chest hurt. Her sleep was restless. She felt as if she was the one cursed. Perhaps she was. She'd killed one of Allah's precious little girls.

Faris knew deep in her heart, *Alkaatala la yastahaloun alrahma!* (Murderers deserve no mercy.)

Chapter 3

A'Dumie
Love Lost

Akiane Date: Year 300
Endurance: Gardens

PETRA RAN toward him.

What is so different about her compared to the others? A'Dumie wondered. *What is it about her that makes my heart rejoice every time I see her?*

She was the same size as the others, same black hair, black eyes. And yet there was something about her that made her different, like the way she popped into his thoughts and stayed. There were times when he was having a conversation and suddenly he realized he was not listening. He was thinking of her. He became sad and disagreeable when he tried to force her out of his mind. But when Petra was comfortably secured in his thoughts, he was at peace. It confused him.

Petra ran along the garden path and stopped in front of him. "Something extraordinary has happened." Her hands flew up, her eyes were wide, and she could barely stand still. "A'Dumie, we have heard from our home world."

Of all the things he might have expected her to say, it certainly was not this.

"What? After 300 years?" he asked. "Why now? How?"

"I do not know. But, A'Dumie, they have sent us a message."

"What did it say?"

"Testing Communications," Petra said.

"Strange message," A'Dumie said. "What does it mean?"

"Perhaps they check to see if we would answer."

"After all this time, Petra? No, there is something else going on."

"Jecidia says it is a divine moment of the Holy One's providence."

A'Dumie nodded. Yes, of course he would believe such a thing, but it was not his place to contradict the high priest.

"Then it is so, since that one speaks for the Holy One," he said.

"Jecidia has answered," Petra spoke as if sharing a secret.

Of course he had. "What did he say?"

"We are here. Where are you?"

Abandoned for 300 years, the people of Akiane had come to expect nothing from Earth, but suddenly they sent two words: "Testing Communications." Why? What did it mean?

A'Dumie did not believe it was to their benefit to answer. He had an uneasy feeling that difficulty was on the way.

Years passed before Community received Earth's response. They did not realize the delay was because of their 300-year-old outdated equipment. It took twelve years for their message to reach WSC Moon Base, but only twenty minutes for the new updated World Space Coalition message to reach the people of Akiane.

Akiane Date: Year 312

After three centuries of believing the Pegasus Colony was a failure, World Space Coalition was delighted to learn of the colony's survival. *WSC Britannia* and its crew were sent across the Milky Way to reunite Earth with its colony.

"They call us their colony," A'Dumie said when Jecidia brought him the news.

Under the belief that they had been abandoned, Community had declared their independence centuries ago.

"It has been many years, many generations. Perhaps those of World Space Coalition wish to make amends for discarding us so long ago," Jecidia said, hopefully. "When they come, we will greet off-worlders with the same grace the Holy One has taught us to give to all."

Priest A'Dumie bowed in reverence to his high priest but he knew better. World Space Coalition did not come by the Holy One's providence; off-worlders came to take possession of that which was not theirs, the people of Akiane.

Akiane Date: Year 314

Petra greatly desired to have a child, but she wanted a child with A'Dumie.

"Touching is forbidden," he had repeatedly objected.

She had been patient but persistent.

After many requests and long nights thinking about it, A'Dumie's resolve was weakening. The thought of having a child with her thrilled him. Still, he could not bring himself to say yes.

And yet, somehow, Petra knew of his change of heart. Perhaps it was because he no longer turned from her when she spoke of it, and no longer loudly objected as he once had.

This time, he softly said, "No, we should not."

Endurance's lamps had been turned off for the night. She led him to a secluded area in the garden on the far side of the habitat, away from the main buildings where only starlight shone through the habitat's glass ceiling.

"No one but us will have knowledge of this night," she said. "Not even tell our child."

It pained his heart to know that his daughter would never know he was her father.

He watched as she took her thin green glove off her right hand. He knew he should stop her but he did not want to. She took his light green glove off his right hand.

She pressed her palm against his. They wrapped their fingers around each other's hand. Petra leaned in and placed her head against his chest. His other arm held her close as he rested his cheek against her head.

It felt good to touch and be touched by her. No one had touched him since he had turned nine years old and had become an adult.

"I can hear your heart beating," Petra said.

"I can feel you breathing," he said.

At that moment, their hearts and breaths synchronized.

Once finished, Petra sighed in satisfaction. His arm dropped as she pulled away and let go of his hand. She replaced his glove, then pulled hers on.

"It is done," she said. "I will go to the Blood Vines and build a nest."

He stood, remembering their touch but knowing they would never touch again. *How could such joy be so dreadfully wicked?* The thought confused him.

Life-givers were permitted to touch their children, but only while they were young. A'Dumie would never be permitted to touch his child, much less acknowledge her as his. If he did, all would know what he and Petra had done. Grievous shame would come upon his daughter. She would become an outcast. What would she think of him if she knew he was willing to being her forth as a product of his sin? Would she welcome him? Or hate him for making her an abomination?

What they had done was against nature. Life-givers gave birth. Another's help was not needed or permitted.

No one will know, she had said. He knew. She knew. The Holy One, whose law they had just transgressed, knew.

The elation at having a child faded as the shame of their sin swept over him.

* * *

The disease first appeared in Cecelia. As her pregnancy progressed, her black hair turned gray and began to fall out. Gray blotches covered her face and her skin became thin. She died while giving birth to her cocoon.

Jordyn's hair became streaked with only a few gray hairs. The blotches on her face came after her birthing. She died months after her child came forth from her cocoon.

Petra became sick soon after she birthed her cocoon. She lacked the energy to eat and became too weak to rise from her cot. She withered and became half her size. The blotches started on her face, then quickly spread over her body, making her skin seem translucent.

Despite the progression of her illness, she was determined to visit her cocoon every day while in its nest.

"You will feel better if you rest," A'Dumie said. "I will watch over your cocoon for you."

"Priests do not watch over cocoons, A'Dumie," she said. "The sickness comes too quickly. This is the only time I will have with my child. I want her to hear my voice. I want her to know how much I love her even though I will not be here with her as she becomes an adult."

When the time came for Petra's child to come forth, the cocoon's soft membrane hardened. Once the child

31

understood that her movements were restricted she would kick her way out.

Because of the illness, a special dispensation was given to priests to carry sickly life-givers to their nests. When A'Dumie learned the cocoon had hardened, he quickly went to Petra. He wrapped her in a blanket so he would not physically touch her, and carried her to her nest so she could watch her daughter come forth from her cocoon.

Word passed quickly. Several members of Petra's family community joined them to witness the event.

Little feet kicked as little fists punched their way out of the brittle membrane. A'Dumie remove the larger pieces.

The baby girl lay on her back, kicking at the air, waving her fists, and enjoying her freedom.

Her yellow eyes were open and darted around looking at those who had come to greet her. She had a head of white fuzz instead of black hair. And like all children, she would be walking and talking within an hour.

Petra spoke, "Welcome, my little one."

Recognizing her life-giver's voice, the girl stopped moving. She searched for the one to whom that voice belonged.

"What a lovely child," one of Petra's sisters said.

"See, she is healthy," another said. "It is a good sign."

"Welcome, little one."

The child listened to each voice, but did not respond until Petra again spoke. "I rejoice at your coming forth." Her voice was soft and frail but the little girl squealed with delight as she lifted her arms for her life-giver to pick her up.

Petra was too fragile to comply.

A'Dumie steeled his emotions as he lifted his child. This would be the only time he would be permitted to touch her. He placed his child in his love's arms.

Petra glowed with joy, too tearful to speak. She had lived long enough to meet, greet, and hold her child. Her daughter nestled her head into the crook of Petra's neck, a perfect picture of love.

The next morning, Petra lay dead on her cot. A life-giver and good friend from another family unit took the child and raised her. Petra would never tell their daughter the truth of her parents' love. A'Dumie would never be able to acknowledge her as his. For their mutual protection, he turned his heart away from her.

The illness spread mostly through life-givers. They would become too exhausted to walk or eat. One day the sick one would lie down to sleep and not wake up.

Children started to die before they became adults. Those who reached adulthood never gained their full strength and died far too early. Then children began to die in their cocoons.

Bringing forth life made the illness worse and hastened death. Many life-givers stopped having children.

It was named the *slow dying illness* because the length of suffering was different for each person. Some lingered in agony for years, some died within months. Only a few blessedly died within days.

There were those like A'Dumie who did not become ill. No one knew why.

It was thought the disease might be contagious. The sick were quarantined but the illness continued to spread and their population dwindled. Whole family units died off.

They were many Community discussions about what to do and many Community prayer meetings.

Nothing stopped the slow dying illness.

From the moment he learned of Petra's affliction, A'Dumie called out to the Holy One with all his heart. He prayed and fasted, not just for her but also for the entire Community. His prayers went unanswered. He confessed every sin multiple times, not just the sin of being with

Petra, but every disagreeable thought, every misplaced word. He worshiped and praised. The more people who became ill, the more fervently he prayed and prayed and prayed.

Nothing moved the Holy One. All prayers throughout Community remained unanswered.

The day Petra died was the day A'Dumie's heart shattered. He stopped referring to the Holy One by his intimate name of gentle and loving Father. Instead, he thought of Him as cold and hardhearted. From that time on, he referred to the Holy One as God.

A'Dumie's name meant vitality or fullness, one alive with hope and possibilities. *That was another person,* he thought. Another life when Petra lived and A'Dumie had been alive with the possibilities of hope.

The simple removal of the apostrophe and Adumie changed the pronunciation and the meaning of his name changed to void, empty, and hopeless, for that was what his life was without Petra.

Akiane Date: Year 326

High Priest Jecidia was not impervious to the disease, though it took him more slowly than most. He eventually stepped down from his duties. After much prayer, he declared Adumie his successor.

Adumie believed it was their original contact with Earth, all those years ago that had brought this curse upon them. His becoming high priest was a sign that it was his duty to stop those from Earth from coming to Endurance.

He sent messages to *WSC Britannia*, telling those aboard to return to Earth; they were not wanted on Akiane. Captain Norris insisted the ship could not turn around, which Adumie knew that was a lie. If a ship was powerful enough to travel across the galaxy, he had no doubt it was capable of turning around.

As *WSC Britannia* drew closer, the arguments between Adumie and Jecidia became more frequent. To the same intensity that Jecidia's enthusiasm grew, Adumie's anger and frustration deepened.

"The first settlers on Akiane came with a Jesuit priest. Perhaps this ship also carries one who speaks for the Holy One." Jecidia spoke with hope, for he believed the coming off-worlders brought deliverance from the slow dying disease.

"You presume those of Earth are holy," Adumie said. "Do not say God has told you so. He has not spoken to me. Therefore, I will not welcome them nor will I ask for one of their priests." He believed off-worlders came to take ownership of their home and of their lives.

"I believe the Holy One is with any who call on Him."

Adumie refused to answer.

"One should request a Jesuit from *WSC Britannia*," Jecidia said.

Adumie turned and walked away.

Jecidia took it upon himself to make contact. He knew Adumie would be upset but Jecidia desired to communicate with one of their priests. Surely the ship could spare one.

It was a long walk to *Falcon's* control center. Jecidia had to stop several times to rest. When he did finally sit at the monitor, he was so tired he was unable to focus on the panel of buttons. When he saw the word "RADIO", pushed the button and spoke.

Jecidia's words of request for a Jesuit priest passed though the 300-year-old monitor, flowed through space, and arrived at *WSC Britannia's* radio distorted.

* * *

WSC *Britannia* received a garbled radio signal from Pegasus Colony's antiquated communication system. The ensign on duty would have preferred confirmation, but transmissions from the colony moved so slowly through space, the ship would arrive before confirmation reached him. He took a hand-written note of what he thought the message said to Captain Norris.

"Pegasus Colony requests Jess Hewitt as ambassador to Pegasus Colony."

Captain Norris doubted the validity of the request; there must be some mistake. How could anyone from the colony know Ensign Hewitt was aboard?

He listened to the message himself. It was too garbled to be clearly understood, and came to the same conclusion as the officer on duty.

He passed the request, along with his concerns, to WSC Space Force.

World Space Coalition was under civilian authority and wanted first contact to be established by civilians only, which was why all scientists aboard WSC *Britannia* were civilians. Space Force military was to be enforced as a last resort to reclaim the colony.

No one at Space Force cared why the ensign had been requested. It was an excellent opportunity to include one of its own as part of first contact. The ensign was promoted to Lieutenant Jessica M. Hewitt and commissioned as WSC Space Force Ambassador to Pegasus Colony. The captain relayed the orders to Jess Hewitt.

She was stunned, bewildered, and definitely not happy.

Chapter 4

Jessica Hewitt
Renewed Life

Earth Standard Year 2468
WSC Britannia

Akiane Date: Year 328
On an Island Somewhere in the Ocean

I NEVER wanted to be Lieutenant Jessica M. Hewitt, Ambassador to Pegasus Colony. I didn't even want to set foot on the alien planet. Why would I? For seven years, Akiane was literally a frozen planet, not just the land, but most of the oceans as well. Summer didn't exist. The warm years were actually six years of spring.

The only reason I was on *WSC Britannia* in the first place was to get away from everything and everyone back on Earth. I wanted time to clear my head. I know it was a bit drastic leaving Earth for Space Force and moving to

WSC Moon Base, but I wasn't thinking clearly. Which was why I needed to get away.

It had taken the original colonists twelve years for a one-way trip to Akiane, but with improved Folded Space, it would take more that thirteen years for a round trip from Earth to Akiane and back again. That should have been plenty of time to get my head together and start over when I returned home.

And yet, this is my life we're talking about. And in my world, things do not go according to plan.

I couldn't get a satisfactory explanation as to why I was chosen to remind Pegasus Colony they still belonged to WSC. I was under orders and was expected to follow them.

Once I arrived, I quickly learned the people of Akiane wanted nothing to do with WSC, its people, or me—especially me.

WSC didn't acknowledge the colony's independence. They wanted their colony back by any means, even if it meant a military takeover.

The only way for me to gain the colonists' trust was to accept the challenge of a religious quest called Woden, which meant I had to trek across the frozen planet and return alive. The "alive" part was problematic; the odds were against me.

Nevertheless, that was how I came to be standing on a beach, on an island, in the middle of the ocean, with two colonists and a pack of dogs, hundreds of miles from the colony's habitat.

We had survived a gradational storm the colonists called *The Storm*, as if it was the only one of its kind, which it was. There's nothing else like it—the alignment of two planets, two of Akiane's moons, and one star that shook Akiane as if the star system was resetting the planet's orbit.

Before The Storm, the ocean had been under meters of solid ice.

During The Storm, the gravitational pull of planets, moons, and star stirred the ocean with such ferocity that horrific waves shattered the ice like delicate china.

It took weeks for the waves to settle into gentle swells that moved smoothly over clear blue-green waters. But close to shore, the sound of new ice crystals forming foretold of the ice reclaiming its dominance.

Ice crystals had been forming into odd shapes of pancake-size ice pieces with smaller bits of ice between them. The pancakes and smaller bits froze together to form larger puzzle pieces, the size of kitchen tables, with bits of ice between them, which would eventually freeze together, creating larger ice floes that would eventually freeze into small city-size floes.

From the beach, I saw lots of open water with pieces of ice as small as my hand to as large as a hovercraft.

Ice was the most dangerous when it was thin and translucent. As it thickened, it became white and mostly safe to walk across. But there were still plenty of weak spots where one could easily take a wrong step and end up in the frigid ocean.

Cameron, the leader of our little expedition, was testing the ice by taking slow careful baby-like steps while looking for a school of fish passing by. He had the strength of a grizzly bear, the nature of a teddy bear, and his baby steps were the length of my regular stride.

Nu Venia was the third member of our expedition.

When we first met, I thought Cameron was her father. Turned out she raised him after his mother died. And yet she was the submissive one.

They had a strange relationship.

Ice cracked under Cameron's weight warning that it was not ready to hold him.

Nu Venia and I caught our breath. If he fell in with the additional weight of his winter suit and boots it would be almost impossible for him to resurface. With the conditions of the ice, we could fall in and drown while trying to save him. And yet, we couldn't let him drown without trying to save him.

His chovis, and best friend, Nella, barked a warning. Cameron stopped and waited while she carefully inspected the ice by sniffing it. Then she quickly herded him back to the safety of land.

Nu Venia and I let out sighs of relief.

"After The Storm, ice does return but not to its former thickness until winter years return, nor will it fully cover the ocean," Cameron said as he dropped his fishing net at his feet. "All will soon become open water. For now, ice is precarious. One must be careful where one steps."

"Won't it take months for all this ice to melt?" I'd lived next to water both in Baja, California, and my home state, Minnesota. I was well acquainted with how air and water influenced one another. On Akiane, both were far too cold to help warm the other.

"No," he said. "Weeks."

"Weeks?" I asked. "How is that possible?" Once winter released the weather to spring, it took no more than a couple of weeks, at the most, for Minnesota lakes and rivers to completely thaw. How could it take only weeks for an entire ocean to thaw? Something else had to be going on.

"It is unknown," he said.

"So we have to wait until all this melts?" Frustration was apparent in my voice.

He eyed me. "The path set before us must be fully appreciated."

Cameron often made statements like that that made no sense. But this one, I understood. He was referring to the night we got drunk.

The Storm had produced hot springs on the island where we were camped. They thawed the surrounding land enough for us to dig a series of holes for the water to drain into. The original springs were too hot to sit in, but as the water flowed from one hole to the next, it cooled enough to create our own private hot tub to sit in, drink enough to get slightly drunk.

I know it wasn't professional for a military officer. I'd never been much of a drinker, but after we survived The Storm, we deserved it.

Once drunk, I spilled my guts to two people I didn't really know or particularly like.

Everything that had been bottled up for decades tumbled out of my mouth into their ears. From their mouths came the truth of my life: none of it was my fault. It was a stunning concept, one I'd heard before, but never dared to believe. And yet, when they said it, I believed.

The anger and self-hate I'd lived with for so long disintegrated.

It was the first time in decades that I'd felt such peace.

I was excited about the next chapter of my life. I wanted to sing and dance as if I was in an idyllic musical. Everything in my life was brand new, the air fresher, the skies clearer; a gentle breeze and warm sunshine promised a new beginning.

Cameron told me the sharing of feelings meant we'd made Community, which meant we were now trusting friends. I wasn't completely ready for the "trusting friends" part, but if it meant we could end Woden and head back, I was willing to agree to anything and be happy about it.

But, I wanted to start our return trip immediately, not in weeks.

I was tired of camping in temperatures so cold that I had to eat fish to keep my blood from coagulating. I was tired of sleeping on the ground bundled in fur blankets. I was definitely tired of sharing a tent with a bunch of chovis.

The colonists called their dogs chovis, and, as I learned, they are impressive animals. Worthy of being called chovis not dogs.

Chovis only eat fish, which was why Cameron was on the ice.

But, like Earth dogs, chovis wanted far more attention than they needed or deserved. As in, they wanted to lick my face. No!

One chovis, Essal, had decided that I was hers. It took a while before I was willing to concede to the fact that she was also mine. Amazingly, she gave birth to a litter of puppies by herself, without a mate, just to please me. I didn't want four puppies, but they made her happy. What choice did I have? I accepted them.

That's when I realized I'd made Community with Essal and, for the most part, with the rest of the chovis. I knew each by name. I trusted them and now cared for their needs, such as checking the condition of their paws, feeding them, and watering them before human needs were met.

On occasion they were also a source of food. That took a bit of getting used to.

At first, I refused to eat. But I quickly realized that when you're traveling literally in the middle of nowhere, where there are few food choices, you eat what's put in front of you or you starve. Starving wasn't an option. I swallowed my objections and ate.

As much as I'd come to appreciate chovis, I was tired of smelling them, of being licked by them, and having a 25-kilo dog push me out of her way.

I was tired of all of it.

I wanted a normal life. Well, as normal of a life as I could have living on an alien planet. For me, normal would be returning to the habitat where I could sleep in my own bunk, take a hot shower, and eat something other than dried tupilak meat, dried fish, or dog stew. I didn't want to wait several more weeks before heading back.

My new happy life was slipping away as the reality of my situation settled back into place.

"Ice will soon be solid before it all completely melts," Cameron confidently assured me. "We travel south over ice to find open water, but such a path is dangerous. It is best if one knows where to step."

Open water meant we would be inflating the folded plastic boat we'd brought with us. There would be no more sitting on a hard folded tent while riding on a sled or standing for hours mushing a team. We could comfortably sit in the boat and motor our way back.

What a lovely thought.

Cameron knelt before Nella and held her face in his hands. "Wandering ice is disagreeable," he said. "We are in need of the safest route to open water. You will find such a path."

Nella vigorously wagged her tail in agreement with her new orders.

"Go," he said. "Fresh fish will be waiting upon your return."

She yelped. Translation: "I will not let you down."

She was off, running at full speed.

"What if Nella miscalculates, falls in, and drowns?" I was surprised that I was worried for her.

"Nella will not misstep," Cameron said proudly.

For a long time, he watched as his white-furred friend ran, sniffed blue-gray ice, changed directions, then ran on.

Standing on our little island, on the beach next to Cameron, reminded me of another beach I used to visit.

* * *

I hated the cold, snow, and ice of Minnesota winters. As soon as I could, I moved to Baja, California. I loved the year-round warm weather with lots of sun, beautiful beaches, and perfect waves.

How I missed those hot Baja days with the sun beating down on me.

Happy memories of long walks with my fiancé along those Baja beaches flooded back to me.

Chad and I used to walk hand-in-hand along the water's edge in ocean-soaked sand. Ripples of waves washed over our feet. Sand squished between our toes. We were enveloped in love as we dreamed of our future together, which did not include Minnesota winters.

Dad had been reluctant to visit Baja, but when he did, he loved it. The hot sun warmed his bones and, of course, he loved being with me. I loved having him around and didn't want him to leave.

On that fateful day, Dad and I had taken a walk to the concession stand for ice cream cones and a lemonade drink for Chad. The sand became too hot for Dad's bare feet, so we walked in the water. I'd asked him to stay in Baja and move in with me. He agreed. We were both in high spirits and were giggling like teenagers.

I left him standing ankle deep in the Pacific Ocean and ran across the sand to Chad. I waved to Dad as I reached our blanket. I knelt, handed Chad his drink, gave him a quick peck on the lips, picked up Dad's shoes, stood, and turned. Dad wasn't there.

In the moment that I'd looked away, the ocean grabbed my father and seventeen other people and refused to give them back.

Chad and I frantically searched along the beach while lifeguards methodically searched the water for him and the others. They concluded that a riptide had caught them, and because Dad was older and frail, he had been easily swept out to sea. My father and seven others were never found.

* * *

Dad's death so traumatized me that I was unable to function.

I blamed both myself and Chad. I felt as if I'd neglected my father for my fiancé. I sent Chad away, quit my job, joined WSC Space Force, and moved to the Moon Base.

I thought it best to get as far away as possible from everyone and everything, but mostly I wanted to get away from me. I volunteered for the Akiane Project and a trek across the stars. I thought the farther away I got from my life, the better.

It didn't work.

It took surviving a night of terror, a bottle of homemade alien liquor, and a couple of aliens to truly clear my head.

I never planned to set foot on Akiane, and yet there I was, standing on an island in the middle of an alien ocean watching a chovis select my path across treacherous ice. I was entrusting my life to a dog, and I was okay with that. That's when I realized I truly was a different person.

I'd left Earth to get away from me. Twenty-seven light years from home, in the coldest temperatures I'd ever experienced, surrounded by more ice and snow than I'd ever seen, I had survived a storm that tried to kill me, and survived.

I'd accomplished my goal. I'd found me, and inner peace.

Chapter 5

Olivia Zeller
Time to Wake up

Akiane Date: Year 328
Endurance: Scientists' Quarters

OLIVIA ZELLER was the first one up for the new day and *she* was on a mission. As lead oceanographer, it was her responsibility to keep her research team on course.

She'd wanted to be on the ocean directly after The Storm, but Larry Gino had other ideas.

As Head Project Manager, Larry Gino had insisted that all scientists help with the cleanup of their dorm rooms, work area, kitchen, and dining area, and then help the colonists clean and repair as much as they could of the damage The Storm caused to their habitat.

In Olivia's mind, all of that could have waited. Research was far more important. She would have disobeyed his orders and headed for the ocean anyway, but her team rebelled against her. Peggy and Eric climbed on top of the habitat to help clear the glass dome of muddy volcanic ash. Henri was the official hovercraft driver and mechanic. He refused to give her the ignition key, holding her captive at the habitat.

As of yesterday, the cleanup was finished. It was time for Olivia and her team to head for the ocean, and nothing was going to stop them.

With no regard for the other thirty-five women sleeping in the dorm room, she pulled Peggy out of her bunk.

"What?" Peggy woke from a deep sleep with a fright.

"Get dressed. We're leaving," Olivia roared.

Several women loudly complained. Several pillows came flying at Olivia, all of which she ignored.

Once dressed, she entered the men's dorm, walked along the rows of bunk beds until she found Eric and Henri, and roughly shook them awake.

"Get up," she said none too quietly.

Larry Gino was furious. "What are you doing in the men's dorm?"

"I'm getting my team ready for the day," Olivia yelled. "What's the big deal?"

Olivia made sure her voice made up for her size. She hated being overlooked because of her small stature. But when she was angry and yelled, everyone heard, ducked, and ran, all except Larry Gino. *He* was not afraid of her. *She* hated him for it.

Even though everyone else called him Gino, she always thought of him as Larry.

"'What's the big deal'?" Larry yelled back. "If I walked into the women's dorm room, you'd call me a dirty old man."

"I would not."

"You would so, Olivia, and you know it," his voice boomed.

"We'll be gone in a matter of minutes." Olivia screeched louder.

"What about breakfast?" Henri asked, calmly wiping sleep from his eyes.

"You ate yesterday, you can eat tomorrow," Olivia said.

47

Eric groaned, flopped back onto his cot, not voicing his objections.

"I don't think so," Henri said, pulling his pants on. "Want me? Breakfast first."

Now all the men in the room were wide-awake. None were happy about the early commotion.

A pillow hit her in the back of her head, followed by "Get out."

More unpleasant comments and more pillows flew at Olivia.

Now she was aggravated. She caught the next two pillows and hurled them at the nearest person.

"Stop," Larry commanded before there was a riot.

The pillows stopped.

Olivia turned to Henri. "You work for me!" she again shrieked.

"I drive the hovercraft," Henri retorted calmly.

"You and your team will have breakfast before you leave," Larry bellowed.

"Just because you're head team manager, does not mean you're God."

"As head manager, I'm telling you, stand down, Olivia."

"I'm not a child," Olivia yelled. "You can't talk to me like that."

Lowering his voice, Larry said threateningly, "Then stop acting like one and get out of here." He pointed at the door. "You will wait until Vong is ready to make breakfast."

"It's okay." Vong yawned. "I'm awake."

Olivia stood fuming. This was one argument she was not going to win. She reluctantly left.

The untidy oceanography crew ate breakfast alone and in silence, but the tension among them was thick with resentment.

Olivia's grooming routine consisted of running her fingers through her thick orange curls.

Peggy had haphazardly pulled her bright-pink-and-blue streaked hair, with long dark roots proclaiming her natural hair color, into a lengthy ponytail.

Eric was in desperate need of a haircut and seemed to have permanently lost his comb. He wore a WSC cap backwards to keep his hair out of his eyes.

While still on board *WSC Britannia*, Henri had the ship's barber give him a military buzz before he debarked. He was the only one of the group who looked ready for the day.

On their way out, Vong handed them two small backpacks full of lunches, snacks, and drinks.

As soon as they were gone, Vong let out a long sigh of relief. Even with the others drifting in, the dining area was suddenly peaceful.

Their scientific survey hovercraft could just as easily slip over ice and water as it could glide over rocky land and up the side of the caldera's edge. It stopped for an overview of the ocean. The beautiful mounds of snow and wind-sculpted ice that had graced the shoreline and ocean were gone, leaving behind a completely barren beach.

Docile waves washed onto shore.

Just to the north, steam still rose from where lava flowed into cold ocean waters.

Henri moved the hovercraft south from the poisonous steam and along shore until he found a good place to slip onto the water. The height of the impenetrable black plastic skirt, or air cushion, kept the hull above the waves. Once he'd passed the waves, he set the propeller and engine at the back of the hovercraft on idle.

"Three drones, now," Olivia commanded.

Eric and Peggy lowered three underwater drones, each with a digital camera and a 180-degree lens that recorded everything in sight, into the water. They were meter-long cylinders, painted bright orange and white so they could be easily seen.

Olivia entered the cabin and sat down in front of a panel of buttons and levers that controlled the hovercraft, drones, and computers. She could have just as easily spoken and the computer would have obeyed, but she liked pushing buttons. It gave her the feeling of control.

She programmed one of the drones to travel south along shore; one headed north to the lava flow; and the third moved farther offshore into the ocean. She watched one screen at a time.

Before The Storm, the waters had been crystal clear and teeming with marine life. Now the waters were filled with silt and seemed devoid of any life, leaving only seaweed behind.

This did not help Olivia's mood. If she could have, she would have spit fire. Instead, she grunted a very annoyed, "Hun."

Henri stood in the cab doorway, smiling. "What?" he asked, seemingly innocent.

Olivia knew better. He'd come to watch another rant. He was the only one other than Larry Gino who wasn't afraid her. AND Henri was *taller* than her. She hated him for that too.

Without looking at him, she said, "Stop smiling."

She programmed the images into one long holo-screen to appear on deck.

As Olivia pushed past Henri to the deck, his smile had disappeared, but the humor on his face hadn't. She rolled her eyes.

Eric and Peggy had moved to one side of the deck, pretending to look overboard.

"You two stop cowering and get your gear."

They rushed to grab their orange backpacks crammed with research equipment.

It wasn't that she liked yelling; she just wanted people to do what they were supposed to. Unfortunately, people didn't know what to do unless she told them—loudly.

"You're staying here, on shore, and manning the underwater drones. Take one of Vong's lunch packs. Henri and I will return before Kahair sets," she said.

Olivia ignored Eric and Peggy's relieve at being left behind.

Henri maneuvered the hovercraft near shore.

The holo-screen on deck disappeared and reappeared on shore as a life-sized three-dimensional screen so she could get a full view of the area. Not one fish anywhere.

Peggy and Eric walked through the image as they moved onshore.

The image disappeared as Olivia released the underwater drones to Eric and Peggy's computers.

"Eric, take the north drone and inspect the underwater lava flow." Olivia pulled a multi-rotor out of a storage box, programmed it to Eric's computer, then released it. "Have this follow the lava flow as far into the mountains as you have a signal. Send a copy of everything to Spago. Oh yes, also send one to that old coot, Larry, while you're at it."

"Peggy, search the area south of here and farther into the ocean. See what you can find, if anything." Olivia started to turn a way, but stopped. "I also want you to digitally map the area."

"We already mapped this area," Eric said.

"Yes, I know, but we just experienced world wide earthquakes. I want a record of any and all changes for future reference." Then she ordered, "Henri, launch Turtle."

Henri maneuvered the hovercraft further offshore, stopped, and released the controls to launch Turtle.

Olivia unlashed the onboard crane and lowered Turtle, the Autonomous Underwater Vehicle (AUV). Turtle was a long cylinder-shaped bright yellow robot with fins on its sides, a rear propeller, and a camera on its nose.

"Where to, boss?" Henri asked.

Olivia sat next to him at Turtle's controls. "I don't know."

He did a double take. "So unlike you to be indecisive."

"Since you're so smart, where does one go when searching a deserted ocean for marine life?" she asked.

"North," he said.

"Why?" she asked.

"Why not?"

Olivia frowned. "Why not." She set the autopilot. Turtle turned north.

Henri set the hovercraft's autopilot to followed Turtle.

Chapter 6

Olivia Zeller
Marine Life

Later that Afternoon
On Akiane's Ocean

AFTER AN hour of watching the computer screen Henri said, "Nothing."

"Nothing."

"Try the ocean bottom," he said.

"Why?"

"Maybe fish went to the bottom to get away from the worst of the ocean's turbulence," he said. "Maybe they're still there."

Turtle slowly dove and traveled along the bottom of the ocean. The sediment became thicker, which hampered visibility. No sign of marine life.

"Nothing," Olivia said.

Turtle rose to three meters below the ocean's surface where it had better sight.

"It's as if the ocean is deserted," Henri said in wonder. He stood.

"Where are you going?" Olivia asked.

"Sometimes the old ways are best," he said. "Turtle can't see everywhere at once." He opened an overhead bin and pulled out a pair of binoculars. "I'm going to scan the ocean with bionic lenses."

On deck, he set his lenses on full force and began searching. He could almost see to the horizon. Blue skies. Blue waters. It would have been a beautiful and relaxing day, but they were searching for marine life, which made this a dissatisfying day. With the flip of a switch, he could see below the surface.

Two and a half hours later, Olivia stood on the opposite side of the deck from Henri, scanning the waters with her bionic lenses. They had not seen one fish.

"Time to take a lunch break." Henri retrieved their lunch pack.

Olivia would have objected just for the sake of objecting, but what was the point? There was nothing out there, and she was hungry. She'd never admit it to anyone, least of all Larry, but she was glad he'd forced her to eat breakfast. And she was thankful Vong had provided lunch.

She knew from experience that hunger pangs would have made the day even worse and would have soured her mood even more.

They sat on seats that ran along the gunwales and ate, talked, and stared at empty waters.

If Olivia couldn't learn what had happened to the marine life, her research project would be over. What then?

Fish couldn't have all died during The Storm, could they? How would they repopulate to the abundant life she'd witnessed before the event? Could they have laid eggs before The Storm, so they would hatch afterword? If so, when had they laid them and where were they?

A beeping came from Turtle's computer. The hovercraft turned northwest.

"Computer, Turtle's holo-screen," Olivia commanded.

The holo-screen appeared on deck showing a series of numbers.

Henri checked the screen. "Those are radio tracker signals." He picked up his bionic lenses and scanned the area where the robot was headed.

"What's that?" Henri pointed to a shadow in the water.

Olivia focused on the spot. "Not a rock," she said thoughtfully. "It's moving."

They readjusted their bionic lenses and saw a school of fish moving just below the surface. Turtle was heading toward them.

The beeps increased as Turtle picked up more radio signals. Olivia muted the sound.

"Computer, show download from those trackers," Olivia said.

They watched the download.

"Look at this." He pointed at the coordinates. "All the fish are coming from the northeast."

"Did you put a cam on any of those larger fish like I told you?" Olivia asked.

"Yes, boss," Henri said. "Let's see how lucky we are. Computer, are there any cameras besides Turtle in the area?"

A new holo-screen appeared with a list of cameras in the immediate area.

Henri tapped the screen on "AK-296."

The holo-screen showed a camera's view of several schools of fish swimming in the same direction.

"Computer, back up four hours," Olivia ordered.

The screen blinked then showed mostly empty water with a few fish.

"Back four hours from new coordinates," she ordered.

The screen blinked and reopened with footage of fish swimming into a swarm of unidentified red marine life. They were similar to leaves with a fat primary vein down the middle. The leafy, or lamina, part of the leaf rippled as if it was swimming.

There were thousands of fish in all sizes and colors. Some were small, sleek, blue-silver fish. Others had scales that seemed three-dimensional and changed colors as the fish swam.

There were larger predatory fish that should have been eating prey, but they weren't. The prey fish weren't even afraid of the predatory fish. None of the fish seemed afraid of the tupilak, a polar bear-like sea creature, which should have been feasting on all of them but, like the fish, it was only interested in whatever it was that created the red stream.

Red wasn't completely accurate. They were maroon, just like the people of Akiane.

How was that possible? Olivia wondered.

"We saw a red river just like that when we were flying over the planet," Henri said.

"Yes. It was similar to a river frozen in the ocean ice, but it's not liquid and it's not plankton. What is it?" Olivia asked. "Has the tracker given us a location?"

"Yes, but we can't get there."

"Why not?" Olivia whined.

"It's too far away. We'll have to wait until the next transport returns," Henri said, "and ask if they'll loan us a shuttle."

"I'll see to it," she said.

"I bet you will," he said with a grin.

"Computer," Olivia said, "return to live feed."

Two screens hovered before them, one from Turtle following the fish. The other was a view from a fish's point of view.

The hovercraft came to a halt.

"What happened?" Olivia asked.

"I stopped Turtle."

"Why?"

"Coral, similar to a colony of polyps." Henri pointed to the screen.

Polyps, tiny starfish-like creatures, clustered together on stems with branches that looked like trees. The "trees" created a forest of coral called sea whip because of the way they whipped back and forth within the current.

"Also known as *leptogorgia virgulata*," Olivia said. "But the water is too shallow."

"Apparently not on Akiane," he said. "But why are they all white?"

"Lack of sunlight under the ice," Olivia speculated.

"But what about the color in the surrounding coral?" he asked.

"I don't know," she said, annoyed. "This is an alien planet. I don't have all the answers."

"Think the sea whip-like coral will change color now that they have sunlight?"

She sighed. "We'll have to keep an eye on them and see, Henri."

The sleek, small, blue-silver fish gathered around the sea whip. At first there were a couple of fish, but soon there were so many they might have completely devoured all the polyps on the coral. But in the next second, they scattered as larger blue-and-orange-striped fish swam in to eat them.

"Biodiversity," Olivia said. "The predatory fish is the keystone to any ecosystem. In this cast, the blue-silver fish keep the polyps from overtaking the area, and the predatory fish keep the little fish from completely wiping out the polyps." She wasn't telling Henri anything he didn't already know. She was audibly observing the situation.

"There's more coral over there," he said.

"Let's not speculate on names until we take a closer look," she said. "They might look similar to what we know, but they're more likely completely alien to us."

"And we get to name them," Henri said with a laugh. He scanned the ocean. "We've been paying too much attention to the holo-screen."

"What are you talking about?" Olivia lifted her head to see. "Oh my."

Before them were kilometers and kilometers of low surface islands.

"This is huge," Henri said. "It might be as large as the Great Coral Reef off the coast of Australia."

"No. That's 3,890,000 acres," Olivia said. "Fish live in coral; they don't swarm to it."

"Maybe they're returning to it," Henri said.

"From where?"

"That red-river line," Henri said. "I bet they're here to spawn."

"That's the stupidest thing I ever heard," Olivia scolded.

"Oh, Olivia, I'm sure you've heard worse."

"Not from you."

"Was that a compliment? I'm flattered."

Henri's good humor annoyed her. It didn't matter how loud she yelled, scolded, or insulted him, it never bothered him. He was always in a good mood. It was so irritating.

"What are you doing?" Olivia watched him as he pulled a multi-rotor out of storage.

After he set it free, he spoke into his wrist computer. "MR-5, fly west for one kilometer at 500 meters high, record all dimensions and transmit data to computer."

The multi-rotor obeyed.

The data would allow them to classify the islands: continental, tidal, barrier, oceanic, coral, or artificial. They could also classify coral reefs: fringing reefs, barrier reefs, atolls, or patch reefs. All information gathered helped to determine the habits of fish. If the classifications were similar to Earth's it would give them a place to start their research. Depending on how different they were, Olivia's team could name them and start Akiane's classifications.

"Computer, show holo for MR-5. Have screen match MR-5's image size at 3D."

MR-5's screen extended beyond the hovercraft's deck.

"The colors are so vivid," Henri said. "A rainbow of every imaginable color of fish and coral."

"This is pristine biodiversity, completely untouched by humans," Olivia said.

"Until now," Henri chuckled.

Olivia refused to respond to such an obviously brainless comment.

Schools of fish passed through and around each other. Some stopped to nibble on coral and each other.

"This is a migration." Olivia realized. "They're returning to their individual breeding grounds."

"This reef isn't anywhere like the size of the Great Reef. It's so much larger," Henri said, in awe.

"But why are they all coming at the same time and from the north. What's up there?" Olivia asked.

"That red line." Henri reminded her.

"Right, but *what* is it?" she asked. "Can we send a multi-rotor or Turtle there?"

"We don't have radio range, Olivia."

She stood in deep thought. "I want a closer inspection of the reef," Olivia said.

Henri commanded, "MR-5, drop to one meter above the water, return to the hovercraft. Move in a zigzag pattern. Continue scanning and recording."

Olivia stepped up to MR-5's holo-screen and studied the scene as it slowly changed.

"If they are mating, I don't see fish changing colors. There isn't any kind of mating dance. I don't think they're mating, Henri."

"But they are spawning." He pointed to an open sandy area and touched the screen. "Computer, enlarge. MR-5, hover." The image enlarged. "The fish are making circles in the sand; they're nests."

"Pufferfish sires make nests to attract dams. Do you see any females?"

"No, but I do see them laying eggs." Henri touched the screen so they could get a better look.

Olivia touched another place on the screen and said, "These fish are making nests among sea whip. And here are some making nests from rocks and shells."

"The fry will feed on the sea whip when they hatch," Henri said.

"And fry next to those coral will eat that coral," Olivia said.

"Predator fish will eat prey fish," Henri finished. "Not so alien after all."

"Why spawn all at the same time? It doesn't make sense," Olivia said. "None of them are mating. How are the eggs fertilized?"

"Maybe the sires fertilize the eggs later."

"All the fish?"

"I don't know, but it would explain why we couldn't find sires when we first arrived," Henri said. "Maybe there aren't any male fish."

"Lu and Rona were also having trouble finding male chovis," Olivia said thoughtfully.

"I thought they found some," Henri said.

"Puppies. I gave them radio trackers so they could follow the few male puppies they did find."

"And?" Henri asked.

Olivia turned from the holo-screen to look up at Henri.

"Adult dogs mate with bitches, then leave for the ocean."

Henri stared at her. "What? How did I miss that?"

"Because you're an idiot."

Henri contorted his face to look like an idiot.

She rolled her eyes. "The bigger question is why is life on this planet predominantly female?"

"Not all life," Henri said.

"What do you mean?" Olivia asked.

"The colonists are male and female," he said.

"How do you know," she asked. "They're all similar in size. There is little variation in they way they dress or the way their fix their hair. All the fish seem to be dams. According to Lu and Rona, their dogs are mostly female. We are an alien planet, how do you know the colonists are male and female?"

"It's only logical," he said. "The colonists are human, after all. We came here from Earth."

"You're assuming, Henri," she said. "And you're not *that* big of an idiot."

"Was that another compliment?" Henri grinned.

"I admit nothing." Olivia almost smiled, but caught herself in time, and hoped Henri hadn't seen.

"It was a compliment. I'm growing on you, aren't I?"

"Assumptions cloud the mind, then mistakes are made."

"You're not going to acknowledge it, are you?"

"Assuming the gender of colonists could complicate things."

"How so?"

"I don't know, but I'll bet something about gender will brew a whole host of trouble." Olivia turned back to the screen. "We need multi-rotors to stay and record this area."

"It's too far," Henri said. "No satellites, remember?"

"I'm not waiting for the next WSC transport to arrive," Olivia said. "Program the last underwater drone we have to scan the area, then have it follow us home on a different path than Turtle."

"Keep scanning? Even over open water?"

"Yes."

Olivia would get every bit of information she could about the area and its marine life, catalogue it, and give a presentation unlike any other WSC Science Board had seen before.

She paused and gave a heavy sigh. Her team's names were also listed on the project, right under hers. She'd have to share.

My team and I will give a presentation like no other and we will share the Nobel Prize together, Olivia reluctantly conceded.

Her thoughts returned to the fish. It was wrong to assume all fish were female. They had to prove it. For all they knew, fish mated at the red river. But . . .

"How are the eggs fertilized?" she asked, thinking out loud. "Do they change sexes during mating season?"

"On Earth, there are over 500 species of fish that changed sexes during their lifetime," Henri said.

"We still have to prove it," Olivia said.

Henri held a scoop to collect eggs in one hand and a storage container for the eggs in the other. "Let's find out."

For the first time since The Storm, Olivia smiled, and this time she didn't care if Henri saw.

She couldn't wait to get back and tell everyone what she'd found.

"Launch the dinghy."

"Paddles?"

"Less invasive."

"Turtle?"

"Autopilot. Let him roam and see what he finds," Olivia said.

"I'll disconnect the hovercraft from Turtle and anchor it here," Henri said. "I'll program Turtle to turn around in an hour and come back to us by a different route."

They dressed in their neoprene wetsuits, packed their oxygen tanks and specimen containers into the dinghy, climbed in, and launched.

Chapter 7

Larry Gino
Changed Landscape

Akiane Date: Year 328
Somewhere in the Mountains

"WHAT?" old man Larry Gino hoarsely growled.

Younger Spago Jorgson stared at him and said, "It's just that I've never known you to be speechless."

"New to me too." Gino chuckled.

As head project manager over all the WSC scientist teams and project team leader of the planetary geology team, Larry Gino worked closely with Spago Jorgson, leader of the planetary volcanologists. While on the transport ship, they had become good friends, almost like father and son.

"Must admit, I never imagined a gravitational storm could produce this much change," Gino said. "Of course, I've never experienced anything like it before."

He'd come close to death before, on Mars, when he was young and thought he was invincible. Despite the danger, he knew if he trusted those in charge they'd deliver him safely back to his family. They had.

At 82 years old and having just been through a terrifying storm, this time was different. Larry had faced death, saw his mortality, and it scared him. If that had been his last night, he'd never see his boys or grandchildren again. That didn't sit well with him.

The colonists named it The Storm. *Appropriate,* Gino thought, *since it's one I never want to experience again.*

Spago turned back to the scene before them. "Too bad we didn't get the chance to witness the event firsthand."

"What we experienced was firsthand enough for me," Gino said.

"You know what I mean," Spago said. "I can't imagine what those first settlers must have gone through the first time they experienced The Storm."

"I can't imagine what it would be like to endure that every eleven years for the past 328 years," Gino said.

Spago wasn't listening; his thoughts were on the research they missed out on. "Gino, if it wasn't for Adumie locking us in our living quarters, we could have collected some amazing data. Now we've got nothing to show for an experience unknown to the natural scientists. Imagine what we could have learned."

The earthquakes had been so severe that the floor in the habitat moved with the ripple of the ground underneath it. Each quake only lasted minutes, but they were so numerous, it seemed like one continuous quake that lasted the entire night.

The scientists had feared their living quarters would crumble down on top of them. The walls, floor, and ceiling repeatedly cracked. But thanks to the self-healing materials used to build the habitat, just as quickly as they appeared, the cracks disappeared.

As terrifying as it had been, the scientists were extremely disappointed that they'd missed the opportunity to safely prepare their equipment to capture The Storm firsthand so they could study it later. All the equipment they had set up earlier had been destroyed.

The only warning they'd had that it was coming was when they found the bay door to their living area closed and locked. They had no idea why until they felt the first earth tremors and heard the explosions of an erupting volcano.

After The Storm, Gino approached the colony leader, Adumie, and offered to help the colonists clean up the volcano ash and melted snow that had left a muddy mess all around and on top of their habitat. Gino had hoped that by extending an olive branch, relationships between the two worlds might ease.

High Priest Adumie declined the offer, but an older priest, Jecidia, who appeared to be an advisor, reminded the high priest that many of their people were too ill to work. The cleanup was too big a project for the few of them who were still able to work. The high priest accepted the help with great annoyance and greater reluctance.

Earthlings and colonists shoveled mud and cleared the steps leading into the habitat's five tunnel entrances. The sixth entrance, Gino saved for Olivia Zeller.

Olivia had refused to help. She wanted only one thing, to be on the ocean with her team. But Gino recruited her team before she had a chance to pack up and leave. She was irate.

"If you don't help clean up, I'll delay your research for a week," Gino threatened.

He knew how badly she wanted to object, but her team had already abandoned her. If they continued to side with Gino it might be a very long time before she got back to her ocean. She gave in, but she did not go down quietly.

She fumed, complained, and loudly cussed as she worked, which was why Gino had her work alone. Anyone working with her would have been miserable.

It was the first time those of Earth and Akiane worked together. Even so, instead of being thankful, most of the colonists refused to engage in conversation with the off-worlders.

Once the cleanup was finished, the scientists were eager to return to their research projects.

Olivia and her team headed for the ocean.

The astronomers spent the day picking up the pieces of their Very Large Telescope (astronomers are not known for their imaginative names), and reassembled another VLT, so they could continue their study of the cosmos from the Pegasus Constellation.

The botanists were the most surprised.

Endurance had been built near hot springs where there was little snow. But the rest of the caldera had been covered with it. When the snow melted, a forest emerged.

The dominant trees had long narrow trunks, similar to palm trees, but were only half as tall with short thin branches. Just as Earth palm trees survived hurricanes by swaying with the wind, the scientists theorized these trees survived gravitational storms by swaying with land quakes.

Gino, Spago, and their teams headed to the mountains.

To everyone's astonishment and delight, the mountains, hot springs, and caldera were completely different.

Boulders had toppled over and shattered. Sides of mountains had crumbled, and new rock outcroppings had thrust upward through the ground.

One of Spago's four multi-rotors, VG-1, slowly flew up and down the same side of the mountain that he and Gino and their teams were studying. VG-2 and VG-3 were programmed to stay in the caldera and survey it. Multi-rotor VG-4 was somewhere in the mountain range searching for the volcano. All of them were taking post-storm images of the mountains, caldera, and forest to compare to the images taken when they'd first arrived.

The multi-rotors recorded at many levels, 2D hardcopy, and 3D holograph; 4D provided the ability to smell and taste an object; 5D recorded data down to the molecular structure. The two sets of images would be unbelievably different, as if they had been taken decades apart.

The scientific teams at WSC Moon Base will not believe it, Gino thought, imagining the excitement the images would cause.

Just as excited, Gino couldn't wait to start his comparison research.

"Sure made a mess of the landscape," Spago said as he checked his image pad. "Once my multi-rotors are finished with this flyover of the caldera, I'll program two to hover over the forest and video the transformation of spring."

"Excellent idea, my boy," Gino said. "You continually amaze me with your brilliance."

"Thanks, old man," Spago said with mock sarcasm.

He tapped his pad and a holo-screen appeared showing digital images sent from his multi-rotors.

"The caldera is larger than when we first arrived. And the new rock outcroppings are amazing."

"So much for a supervolcano creating all of this," Gino said.

A hardy belly laugh burst out of Spago. With great confidence he'd declared that a supervolcano had produced the caldera.

Supervolcanoes were the largest and most dangerous of all volcanoes. They imploded, destroying everything in the area, leaving behind a monstrous crater called a caldera.

The gravitational storm had proved him wrong.

"That kind of spectacular explosion would have been considerably milder compared to what we just experienced," Spago said.

"Speaking of volcanoes, where is the VG-4?" Gino asked.

"Still searching." He checked his pad. "Wait, we may have found it," he said. "VG-4, show image." The holo-screen obeyed.

An image of a volcano appeared before them. The top of the mountain had been blown off. They saw the signs of the lava lake receding inside the mountain. Only one of the many volcanic vents on the mountain still showed signs of pyroclastic flow, fast-moving river-like volcanic matter, was headed toward the ocean.

All other lava flows were dormant and were already cooling.

"Can the hovercraft take us there?" Gino asked.

Spago moved the image and followed a path back to where they were standing.

"I don't think so," he said. "Terrain is too rough."

"Doesn't look like we can walk it either. Too bad," Gino said. "We'll have to wait for the next transport. Maybe the captain will loan us a shuttle before the ship leaves."

"That's disappointing," Spago said. He studied the holo-screen. "I finally have my volcano and I can't get to it."

"Patience, my boy, patience. You'll get there," Gino said. "You still have plenty of data to keep you busy."

"Thanks, old man," Spago said. "I like that nothing about this planet is what we expected."

Gino scratched the back of his right arm. He was always scratching something—his arm, the back of his head, his lower back. It had become part of his thought process.

"Guess we'll have to rewrite the book on interplanetary geology and volcanology," he said.

"I'm going to make a recommendation that there be flybys after each storm so there are digital records to compare," Spago said. "Once WSC places satellites to orbit Akiane, we'll be able to monitor the entire planet. You can be sure there *will* be a new interplanetary book."

"I see a Nobel Prize on the horizon for you, my boy," Gino said.

"One for each of us, hey old man?" Spago patted Gino on the back.

"A Nobel Prize would be a nice way to end one's career, but not if it means enduring another gravitational storm," Gino said. "That's not something I ever want to experience again. I plan to be long gone when next it comes around."

"You'll only be 93 by then; you have plenty of time for a few more storms," Spago said.

Gino let out a light chuckle. "I don't mind living to 150. That's why I took the treatment in the first place, but I don't want to go through that storm six or seven more times."

"But now that we know what to expect, we'll be better prepared for it," Spago said.

"Not even one more storm," Gino said emphatically.

"I don't understand, Gino. Don't you want to study the geological changes?"

"I'm 82, Spago. I've got nothing to prove by surviving another storm."

A wide slow grin spread across Spago's face. "You're kidding, right?"

Gino didn't have the heart to tell the boy that he wasn't kidding.

For the first time in his life Gino was glad that Karen had not been with him to experience The Storm.

* * *

Thinking of Karen brought back fond memories.

The road trips had started soon after they married. They would set out one morning, chose a road they had never been on before, and take it just to see where it went.

When Gino was offered an internship to study lunar science and move to Moon Base, he asked Karen, "Would you be interested in taking the ultimate road trip?"

With a broad smile, she'd said, "Yes, of course."

When he asked if she wanted to take a road trip to Mars, she gave another enthusiastic, "Yes."

Mars became their home, and the birthplace of their two sons and grandchildren.

He and Karen had planned to extend their lives to 150 years so they could spend more time with their family.

Gino took the treatment first, a series of shots.

Karen became sick before it was her turn and was disqualified. She died too soon. Any time would have been too soon. Had he known beforehand, Gino would not have taken the treatment. He never wanted to outlive his best friend. Without Karen, this "road trip" was not only different but lonely.

Neither of his boys had followed Gino into planetary geology. However, his granddaughter, he'd nicknamed Sunshine, was interested in her grandpa's adventures. Maybe, someday, they'd go on adventures of their own.

When WSC offered Gino the Akiane Project, he accepted, hoping it would distract him. It had been another adventure of a lifetime, and at times, it had been a welcome distraction, but not today. Today he wanted to be on Mars with *her* at his side, not Spago.

If he returned to Mars, he'd resign from the Akiane Project and someone else would get the credit for what he started. Did it really matter? He had credit for the moon research and a Nobel Prize for his time on Mars. What more did he need?

He already had it all. Was it really worth leaving his boys and grandchildren for another adventure? No. He missed them too much. He'd been considering returning home on the next transport.

The Storm confirmed it.

* * *

"It'll be interesting to see what Olivia learned when she returns this afternoon," Gino said, shaking himself from the past before he became too emotional.

Before The Storm, Olivia and her team had found round pockets of soft ice just offshore. They'd sent an underwater drone with a cam and discovered five small volcanic vents along a fault line. It didn't take long before the heat expanded those small circles and melted everything for eight meters on either side of the fault. It was a sign that something was happening under the ocean floor. Now they knew it was a prelude to The Storm. It would be interesting to learn what had become of that fault and how many other fault lines had similar vents.

"Yesterday I heard a rumor and checked to see if it was true," Spago said. "I was amazed to see Olivia shoveling mud from a tunnel entrance. That's not something I ever expected to witness."

Gino's whole body shook with laughter. He took a perverse pleasure in seeing to Olivia's lessons in compliance. She was headstrong in her belief that the world revolved around her and her needs.

"I threatened her," Gino admitted.

"How so?"

"No helpie. No researchie."

Olivia followed the chain of command, and as much as she hated it, she'd bowed to Gino's authority as team leader and had shoveled mud.

"She must have thought you were serious, Gino."

"I did my best to make her believe it, and you did see her shoveling."

"I certainly heard her complaining," Spago said. "You know, when Olivia's unhappy, everyone's unhappy."

"That's why I had her work alone." A mischievous grin spread across Gino's face.

"You're an evil old man." Spago laughed. "But whatever you're expecting Olivia to find today, I doubt she'll be willing to tell you about it anytime soon, not after that blowup the two of you had this morning."

"She'll get over it," Gino said. "She always does."

"We are speaking about the same Olivia? Olivia Zeller? The feisty little redhead with a furious temper?"

"She's not that bad, Spago," Gino said. "She does have her glowingly good moments."

"You think too highly of her, Gino. I'm telling you, she's not going to give you any new information that she may have learned."

"Spago, she won't be able to help herself."

"Why?"

"Ice is melting too fast," Gino said.

"Have you also considered space weather?" Spago asked.

"Space weather caused by bursts of radiation, or solar flares?" Gino asked.

"It doesn't take much for the sun to affect a planet's weather," Spago said. "Even a small amount combined with the planet's wind, water, and temperature will have a major affect on Akiane's climate."

"Even so, Akiane's weather isn't warm enough to melt oceans of ice. And yet, ice is melting," Gino said.

"You're thinking planetary motion?" Spago asked. "As in Loki's influence on the planet's orbit."

"Here's my hypothesis—I think Akiane's core is also affected by the event." Gino let that bit of information sink in before he said, "I'll bet there are far more underwater volcano vents warming the ocean waters than we suspect. The same vents Olivia found along her fault line. They melted a good amount of ice by themselves. Just imagine if there were vents like that all over the ocean floor."

"That would mean there are hundreds of thousands vents," Spago said.

"That's what Olivia will find on today's outing. She'll be so excited, she'll tell everyone about her findings when she returns," Gino said.

Spago thought for a moment. "Makes sense. But she came to study marine life not underwater vents, remember."

"I am never wrong, my boy," Gino said. "You should know that by now."

"Right, old man." After a moment's silence, Spago asked. "Do you think Jess survived?"

"This planet is mostly ocean," Gino said. "If Jessica found land, she survived."

"Think she found land?" Spago asked.

Gino thought about it. He wanted to be hopeful, but what were the odds? He shook his head. "Probably not."

Chapter 8

Jessica Hewitt
Sea Creature

Akiane Date: Year 328
On an Island Somewhere in the Ocean

ONE WOULD think The Storm was the worst event of this Woden, but no, long tedious hours of waiting for the right conditions so we could continue our journey were the worst.

Here I was again with no book to read, no computer game to play, no friends to playfully annoy me. Instead, I was enduring another bout of monotony while waiting for Nella's return, with no idea as to when that might be.

Sitting wasn't an option. I'd had enough of sitting, so I set out on a mission of my own. Essal, who was always at my side, stayed behind with her pups. Her good friend, Imos, accompanied me instead.

If we had been on the ocean when The Storm hit, we'd be dead by now. Somehow, chovis knew what was about to happen and managed to find an island where we set up camp in a small cave.

It turned out that the cave was sitting over a volcano vent. Very warm mud started to flow from underneath our bedding. We evacuated and moved to higher ground.

The volcano melted the cave, then gave us a beautiful show of fireworks, which would have been far more enjoyable if not for the terror of the rest of the night. Lava flowed to the ocean waters. It wasn't until the steam cleared and the waves settled that we saw how much the island had grown thanks to the lava.

Too bad I didn't have the means to record the event. Spago would have loved a recording.

Many of the WSC scientists desperately wanted to join us so they could better study Akiane. Cameron gave them all the same answer: "No."

The only member of WSC allowed on Woden, and who adamantly did not want to go, was me.

As a consolation, I promised to bring back samples of what I found, which hadn't been much since most of our trip had been on a frozen ocean.

I did manage to find a few of Olivia's radio trackers on the fish we caught. She'd be upset because I didn't note the exact time and location where I found them. But there were no satellites for GPS and the people of Akiane didn't care about time. They simply moved from one day to the next.

The Russian astronomer who discovered this planet named it Akiane, Russian for "ocean," because there's more water on Akiane than there is on Earth.

Once we stepped off the land onto ice, we didn't step back onto land again until we reached this island. And when we leave the island, chances are we won't see land again until we reach Endurance. That is, if we can find the land where the habitat resides.

Cameron assured me he'd be able to find it. "Follow stars," he said.

I didn't care what method Cameron used as long as we returned safe and sound.

During my exploration of out island, I found a few plants just beginning to sprout and bagged them. I gathered a nice collection of algae for Jorge, colorful rocks for Gino, and samples of freshly cooled lava for Spago.

Gathering samples made me less lonely, and gave me time to think of the relationships I'd let slip by.

I was surprised at how much I missed my friends back at Endurance. On Earth I'd had few friends. My ill temper too easily ran people off, but not WSC scientists. I'm not sure if it was because they actually liked me or because we were stuck on the same ship with no way off.

When my orders changed from communication officer to ambassador to Pegasus Colony, I was moved out of the military quarters and into the civilian quarters.

Space Force thought it would be best for me to become acquainted with the people I would be living with on Akiane before we landed. I was the lone military Space Force person among the WSC civilian scientists.

I was ordered to move in with Rona Montgomery. It took a while for us to become friends. Unfortunately, we were not as close as we could have been because I didn't truly make the effort. I mostly tolerated her; it was easer than fighting.

The biggest surprise was Olivia Zeller. I'd disliked the little redhead's know-it-all superior attitude. It was fun pushing her buttons. It wasn't as much fun when she pushed mine.

Now, I missed our bickering.

Jorge Krause. Tall, blonde, amazing smile, intense blue eyes. He made my heart thump.

It hurt to think about how much I missed him. We could have become romantically involved while aboard *Britannia*, but I was afraid he would reject me once he got to know me. It was easier to ignore him.

We didn't really connect until I was about to begin Woden. Our first kiss was a goodbye kiss. I remembered everything about his lips—they were soft, tender, and passionate. It was as if I'd never been kissed before. He didn't just hold me, or give me a bear hug, he folded around me as if we belonged together and he would never let go.

But he did, so I could go on Woden.

It had happened weeks ago, but the memory was as fresh as if it had happened just this morning.

He said he'd wait for me. Oh how I really wanted *that* to be true.

Then there was Larry Gino. In many ways, he was everybody's mentor. He watched over the civilians as if they were his children. I think he had plans to adopt me as well. But I didn't take to his fathering. I didn't need a father. I'd had one.

Rejecting him might have been one of my biggest mistakes. I could have used some fatherly advice.

I'd have more than a few bridges to mend when I returned to Endurance.

By the time I returned to camp, the ice had hardened enough so Cameron and Nu Venia were on it looking for the shadow of schools of fish under the ice. After I'd safely stored my samples, I joined them.

We'd started Woden with 32 chovis, but their numbers had dwindled to 12, just enough to pull one sled. We'd eaten a few. Others had left us for the ocean.

Adult chovis that weren't pets or weren't caring for pups often heard the call of the ocean.

It was similar to the myth from the days when all ships sailed the ocean. Upon hearing the song of a siren, the crew turned their ship toward the song, thinking beautiful mermaids were calling to them. But it was monsters calling them to their doom. The wooden ship crashed on the rocks, stranding the sailors, and leaving them at the mercy of the sirens.

Chovis that answered the ocean's call swam so far out they were unable to return and drowned.

At least that's what Cameron and Nu Venia said, which made no sense. Why leave only to drown? What was the point?

Chovis only eat fish. If we didn't feed them, they'd desert us for the ocean looking for fish and never return.

When WSC scientists and I first arrived, we learned that the colonists rarely ate fish. Fish did two things to the human body. In small amounts, fish gave colonists the ability to endure Akiane's extreme cold. Twice on this trip, I'd almost died of hyperthermia. After a bowl of fish stew, I recovered nicely.

But when eaten in large amounts, over a long time, fish changed people's biological chemistry. My companions made it sound like the change wasn't good. I wasn't sure what that meant. I didn't ask for an explanation. I didn't want to know.

As I stepped off land, Cameron warned me to stay on the larger pieces of white ice.

In some cases, I took a small jump over open water, from one piece to another. Just walking across the ice could cause it to buckle and creak. Water bubbled and gurgled into small pools of water on top of the ice.

While we risked our lives for their next meal, chovis watched us from the safety of shore. Not even Essal was with me. Cameron said she would not leave her pups. I think it was because she was too smart to be on the hazardous ice.

Jorge had said snow and ice weren't just white. They were textured with reflections of blue sky, violet shadows, gray indentations, and yes, crests of white. At that time, I didn't believe him.

Woden had changed my appreciation of the landscape around me. I saw delicate shades of white, blue, violet, and gray, which fashioned an immense splendor. I pivoted to get the full panoramic experience of the beauty of the frozen scene.

Less than a meter in front of me, a small explosion sent bits of ice flying.

"What the . . . ?" I stopped dead in my tracks.

A huge red-furred tupilak head, the size of a baby bear cub, popped up, and looked directly at me. It had a black spot on the side of its bright pink nose.

Chovis went crazy. I heard Essal above the rest. She snarled and howled with such fury I looked past the sea creature to see her abandon her pups and leap off the island as if it were on fire.

I'd never seen a live tupilak before. Even though I didn't know what to expect, I knew something was wrong.

Cameron turned to see what the commotion was about.

"Run!" he yelled.

Tupilak, the king of the ocean, were hunted for their meat and fur. This was my first encounter with the creature. I didn't really know what to expect. But I did as was told. I turned and ran as fast as I could, not caring where I stepped.

My bulky fur boots were not made for running. I seemed to move at a snail's crawl. The ice buckled with each step. I looked back to see if I was out-distancing the creature, or how soon it would be upon me, and almost fell over my feet.

The monster was gone.

I stopped.

My head ached. My heart thundered. My breath was fast and deep. I gulped for air as I took a good look around. Where was the tupilak? Had it given up? Or maybe, I wasn't in any real danger after all. Maybe it wasn't hungry and had just popped up to say, "Hello."

Essal and the rest of the chovis were madly yelping and still speeding toward me.

Cameron and Nu Venia were capable of changing sizes at will. I didn't know how they did it.

Depending on her mood, I'd seen Nu Venia do it several times.

But this was the first time I'd seen Cameron become bigger than his usual large self. And it was the first time I'd seen him without his shirt or gloves.

He ran with a spear in one hand ready to protect me from this monster.

Nu Venia was running close behind him. She too carried a spear, but had not grown in size and was still fully clothed.

They yelled and motioned for me to come to them.

That's when I realized I had been running away from them. I was farther from shore than I should be. I retraced my steps, but at a slower, more careful pace.

I assumed the tupilak had returned to the ocean and I was safe. I was confused as to why everyone was still so excited.

A dark shadow drifted under my feet, circling me. With a sick feeling in the pit of my stomach, I realized the tupilak was tracking my shadow. It wasn't gone after all. It was biding its time. I picked up my pace.

The shadow swam ahead, to a small area of open water. Its head ominously rose up in front of me. First the pink nose with the black spot, the deep red muzzle filled with fangs, and finally its black eyes focused on me.

I skidded to a stop. We eyed each other for one long, heart-thumping second.

It glanced around and saw bloodthirsty chovis and an angry Cameron coming to my rescue. It casually returned its gaze to me. It was calculating its chances of success and didn't seem worried.

I didn't wait around to see what it had in mind.

I raced in a large arc around it toward Cameron, trusting that he would kill the sea creature with his spear and we'd have it for dinner.

Ice screeched behind me. I turned to see the animal, the size of a bull, come flying out of the ice with the grace of a penguin, and land lightly on all fours. It was coming for me.

I froze in mid-step, tripped over my feet and landed hard on my rear. Water seeped up around me.

Head down, eyes locked on me, the tupilak moved aggressively toward me. Ice vibrated with each step. Drool dripped from its sharp teeth in anticipation of ripping into me.

Acid fear paralyzed me in place.

The pool of gurgling water gathered around me. I feared the creature and I would collapse under its weight and we'd go down together where I'd become an easy meal.

As it neared, the tupilak slowed to one purposeful step at a time. Its nails clicked, clicked, clicked on the ice.

My time was running out. I swear it smiled in satisfied triumph. It knew it could take me.

Something white flew over my head and hit the creature full in the face.

Essal! Ever faithful and loyal Essal had come to my rescue. She was small in comparison to the sea monster, but she was fierce.

The creature rose on its hind legs, and I understood why Cameron had become larger. The tupilak was huge.

Essal clawed at its face and eyes. The tupilak grunted in aggravation. Essal fought with the fury of a mother grizzly. One good shake of the tupilak's oversized head sent her flying.

Even before her feet hit the ice, her legs were racing back with the fury of a Tasmanian Devil. She leaped onto the creature's underbelly and dug in like a cat on a tree.

The monster howled in pain. Essal's teeth ripped at fur. She was going for its innards. Blood darkened the tupilak's burgundy coat and splattered onto the ice. The tupilak reared its head and wailed, incensed.

"Get him, Essal," I yelled at her. "Rip him apart. We'll have him for dinner."

The monster doubled over, its teeth grabbed Essal by the scruff of her neck and yanked her free. Bits of fur went flying. Dark blood seeped down the creature's belly.

Essal's white muzzle and belly were also smeared with blood. I hoped it all belonged to the tupilak. Snapping her teeth, snarling, and howling angrily, she twisted and clawed mid-air trying to get back at my attacker.

The sea creature whipped her back and forth. She went limp. With a snap of the tupilak head, Essal went flying and landing hard, she skidded to a stop.

I started to go to her, but just as I was getting to my knees, the tupilak's two front paws came down heavily onto the ice, centimeters from my feet. The ice vibrated with such force, I sat back down. I thought we were going to drop into the ocean. The tupilak must have had the same thought. It rose again, probably with the intent of breaking through the ice.

Two chovis hit the tupilak's underbelly.

The tupilak defended itself by swiping at them with his paws. One chovis let out a painful yelp, hit the ice, and immediately attacked the nearest hind leg. Four more chovis jumped the monster, then two more. Eight chovis in all attacked. There were too many for the tupilak to deal with. Three more chovis joined the assault. The tupilak wailed in pain and aggravation, and turned to escape, leaving a trail of blood behind.

Chovis ran alongside, still attacking. One chovis clung to its leg, teeth buried deep in muscle.

In desperation the tupilak continued toward a hole of open water and the safety of the ocean. There were sounds of teeth gnashing, wailing, snarling, angry and pitiful yelps of pain from the tupilak and its attackers.

The sea monster reached the edge of the ice sheet and dove in headfirst. Chovis fell away as it slipped into the water. One chovis almost ran head on into the water after the tupilak but, at the last second, she turned and trotted away.

Chovis stopped yelping and circled the hole, sniffing it. They soon moved away, satisfied that all was clear.

With a sigh of relief, I lay on my back gasping for air and closed my eyes.

A shadow passed over me and I almost jumped out of my skin. Had the monster returned?

I opened my eyes to see Cameron with spear in hand, and Nu Venia at his side, standing over me.

"Is it gone?" I asked.

"The tupilak will not return," he said.

"Not this day," Nu Venia agreed.

I was safe, and for the moment, that's all I cared about.

Chapter 9

Rona Montgomery
Qorow Low

Akiane Date: Year 328
Endurance: Scientists' Quarters

"I'M NOT staying behind," Lu objected. "I have just as much right to meet the mother as you do, Rona."

"Lu, this is the first time a colonist has talked to either of us and she barely talked to me. If you come she might run and we'll never get another chance like this again," Rona said.

Rona Montgomery and Chow Lu's Genome Project was to research the direct effects on human DNA while living in an alien environment. It wasn't until they saw the colonists that they realized the significance of the project.

The colonists were extremely similar in appearance. They were one of two sizes, tall and taller. All of them had jet-black hair and most of them had jet-black eyes. It would be exciting to discover how humans from Earth could have change so dramatically in only 328 years.

Rona and Lu's plan shifted when they learned the colonists were dying of a strange disease. But when they tried to make contact, no one was interested. Until now.

Rona had encountered a colonist named Qorow Low. She thought the encounter was an accident, and expected the woman to run, like every other colonist she'd met.

This was no accident. The woman was a mother trying to save her child's life and had purposely sought out Rona.

Underneath her winter jacket, she had a baby strapped to her chest. The child was too small for her age, and her coloring was bluish gray. Rona had a sick feeling that the child was be dying.

Qorow Low was fearful that she might get caught talking to an off-worlder, so they stood in the thick of the garden by the lake and spoke quietly. She would not allow Rona to touch her or her baby, but she did agree that Rona could scan them and take a sample of their blood.

Rona returned to her work area and, with Lu's help, had prepared a medical bag. Now Lu was being difficult, insisting that she come along. Rona was trying to impress upon Lu the importance of her going alone.

"If she sees you she might rabbit."

"Rabbit?"

"She'll be as nervous as a rabbit and run away."

"I'm as much a part of this Genome Project as you are." Lu refused to give in. "I have just as much right to meet her as you do."

"Lu, she came in secret so the other colonists wouldn't find out. If they do, she'll be in a lot of trouble. Be patient."

"Who am I going to tell?" Lu asked.

"She won't even let me touch her or her child," Rona said.

"Why?" Lu asked.

"I don't know," Rona said.

Lu thought about it.

Rona held her breath, did Lu finally understand?

"I don't care. I'm going."

Rona opened her mouth, but Lu cut her off. "You can explain it to her. Make her understand."

"How, Lu?"

"I don't know," Lu said. "I don't want her to just be a set of numbers. I want to meet her in person."

"I'll tell you everything, Lu."

"It's not the same, Rona. What if you miss something?"

"Are you calling me incompetent?"

"Rona, no, of course not. I'm saying, four eyes are better than two," Lu said. "I'm not staying behind."

Why was she being so obstinate? Why won't she listen?

They didn't have time for this. If they took too long, Qorow Low might not be there when they returned.

"Fine." Rona finally surrendered, against her better judgment. "But if she is upset, you *have* to leave. Agree?"

Lu rolled her eyes, but reluctantly conceded, "Agreed."

She finished packing a hand scanner, syringes, and vials.

"How many vials are you bringing?" Rona asked.

"Twelve."

"Twelve? That's six apiece. The mother won't let us take that much blood," Rona said. "We'll be lucky if she lets us have one vial each."

"You never know," Lu said.

Rona shook her head. *She depends too much on feelings instead of reason. She'll be disappointed when the mother refuses.*

Qorow Low was still on the exact spot where Rona had left her.

Lu stepped forward, extended her hand, and said, "Hi, my name is Lu. I'm . . ."

Qorow Low stiffened, let out a soft cry of alarm. "You promised no one would know." She turned and ran.

"Wait," Lu reached out to stop her.

Rona grabbed her arm and roughly pulled it back.

"Don't touch!"

"What? Why?" Lu asked. "What's wrong? What did I do?"

"You don't listen, that's what's wrong," Rona said. "Stay here and I mean it."

"What? No!" Lu said. "I'm coming too."

Rona stood in front of her. "She's running from *you. You* stay here."

"But . . ."

"Stay or I'll put you on report. Do you understand? If I can convince her to come back I will. But you must wait here," Rona insisted.

"Okay, I'll stay," Lu said. "I'll wait here."

Rona took the shoulder bag of equipment from Lu and ran. She didn't call out for fear someone might hear. Instead she followed the sound of Qorow Low moving through the thick foliage.

As soon as she saw Qorow Low's back, Rona said, "I'm alone. Please wait." She spoke above a whisper and hoped no one heard.

Qorow Low slowed down, but kept moving. She'd heard and was considering Rona's words.

Soon they'd be out in the open and Rona wouldn't be able to follow her.

"Please," Rona said. "Lu is my partner. She only wants to help. I need her. I can't do this without her."

Qorow Low stopped and turned to face Rona. "Explain."

"Lu and I each have different kinds of knowledge of how to save your child."

"Each has a job," Qorow Low said.

"Yes, we each have a job,s" Rona agreed, though she didn't understand why a work-related relationship would make such a significant shift in attitude.

"You work together to finish a job."

"Yes, we work together," Rona said.

"I am with understanding. Community is the same. Each has a job. It is how we survive." Qorow Low thought for a moment. "You are trustworthy?"

"Yes, yes, you can trust me. I promise."

"You trust the other?"

"Yes, I do."

"There is no time to make Community," Qorow Low said.

"I don't understand," Rona said.

"There is no time to make Community," Qorow Low repeated. "Sharhr is dying. There is not time." She bit her lip. "I must trust. I will come."

"Thank you." Rona was unsure what had changed her mind or what she meant by Community, but at least she was willing to meet Lu.

Qorow Low was so desperate she was willing to let them take as much blood as they wanted. Now, thanks to Lu, they had six vials of blood from the child and six from the mother.

They were finally able to start their study.

* * *

On the day they first arrived, the scientists were surprised that their living quarters were one long empty room with 103 bunk beds sitting side by side in five rows. There were no individual offices, cubicles. No chairs, or tables.

Before *WSC Britannia* left orbit, the captain ordered the 3D imaging crew to make divider walls to separate the dorm in to more rooms. Then they made chairs and tables for their dining area and more for their work areas. But there wasn't time to make enough for everyone.

The scientists set up chairs and tables in the dining area first. Some people used the dining tables as their workspace between meals. The rest of the tables and chairs were used to set up as many workspaces as possible. Some, like Lu and Rona, volunteered to set up on the floor. It wasn't ideal, but they made it work.

* * *

With the most advanced tests available, Rona and Lu were able to use less blood for more tests. Lu purposely saved three vials each, from mother and child, for future use.

The tests covered all the usual physical examinations such as heart, cholesterol, liver, kidneys, but tests also went deeper into the circulatory system, the endocrine system to study their hormones, and mapped their DNA.

It took days, and sometimes weeks to receive test results in the past. It used to take a decade to map DNA. Today it took only hours. Some test results were available almost immediately; a few came after dinner; the rest would be processed by the next morning.

Rona and Lu's computers were synchronized to receive the same information at the same time, and transmit the information to their shared holo-screen.

Three days later, they were still trying to unmuddle the information.

They sat on the floor of their work area surrounded by their equipment, with their holographic computer screen before them. They leaned into the screen studying the results from the blood tests.

Rona held a vial of the child's blood and studied it. It lacked luster. She tilted the vial from side to side. The blood was too thick to flow smoothly from one end to the other. Not good. She opened the vial and sniffed—sour.

The mother's bright red blood flowed easily, and smelled metallic, signs that she was healthy. If the mother's was healthy, what did the blotches near her hairline really mean? According to Qorow Low, they were the beginning of a "longtime illness."

The little girl was listless, barely breathed, and didn't respond to sound. According to her mother, she spent most of her time sleeping and rarely ate.

"Not only will we check for diseases, but we'll also check DNA for new anomalies." Lu's eyes narrowed. The tip of her tongue peeked out from between her lips, a sure sign she was thinking. Her tongue disappeared. "We have all kinds of wonderful mysteries to solve." Her mood turned serious. "But right now, what's most important is figuring out this disease." Her head nodded once to emphasize the importance of her statement.

"That's why we're here," Rona said, feeling the pressure to help the mother and child. She was team leader, which meant, they were now her responsibility; they depended on her. If she failed, they would die. She couldn't let that happen. Yet she feared she and Lu might be too late to save the child.

"I came because my government sent me," Lu said.

"What?" Rona asked. "What are you talking about?"

But Lu was the one who was surprised. "You said, 'That's why we're here.' You made it sound as if I had a choice. I didn't. I thought you knew."

"That you grew up in a Chinese government's school institution? No, Lu, you never talked about it. You only talk about your family."

"Rona, there was no *institution*. It was a home and a privilege," Lu said defiantly.

"I'm sorry. But, I thought your mother raised you," Rona said. "I mean, since you never talked about it, I just assumed."

"I lived with my family until I was seven. My *muqin* was unwilling to give me up," Lu said. "I was small, so she was able to hide my true age, but the neighbors became suspicious when I was five years old three years in a row."

"Someone told," Rona said.

"We were never sure, but yes, we think it was a 'good citizen' who reported me to the authorities."

"Did your mother get in trouble?"

Lu's face stiffened. "I think the government is used to overly protective parents." She didn't elaborate.

"So what happened?"

"*Muqin* said I was special and I believed her. She helped me learn to read and write and do math by the time I was three, but it didn't take long for me to surpass her. She had trouble finding educational material for me," Lu said. "The Ministry of Education of China had me tested. I wasn't special; I was extraordinary.

"*Muqin* was limited on how much she could teach me, but the Ministry opened a whole new world for me." The expression on Lu's face didn't match the excitement in her voice. She seemed both sad and happy.

"Did you ever see your mother again?" Rona asked.

"Oh, yes." Lu brightened. "Twice a year I was allowed to return home for a two-week vacation with my family."

Rona caught her breath. She couldn't imagine growing up in an institution and only seeing her family a couple of times a year.

Lu's smile broadened like an excited child. "On the ship, I talked to my *muqin* every day."

"I'm glad." While on the ship, Rona had also spoken daily to her mother and sisters, but not her father.

"My father was so upset when I moved to the Moon Base, he stopped talking to me," Rona said. "I thought he was angry with me. Now I know he was too emotional to deal with the possibility of never seeing me again. If I'd known, we might have worked it out. I could have assured him that I would return home." She hesitated. "On my last day aboard ship, Mother convinced him that it might be a long time before we spoke again. Through tears, he told me how much he loved me and would miss me.

"If I had still been on the Moon Base, I would have quit the project and returned home right then," Rona said. "I feel like a traitor for leaving the family. Now with the lack of communications between Akiane and Moon Base, I don't know when I'll get to speak to any of them again."

Lu's smile disappeared. "Tech Terzo says the solar flares to settle before communications to the Moon Base are online again."

Terzo the Tech Guy was their computer geek with little to do since everyone's computer was working just fine. He spent his time designing virtual computer games.

For the last few weeks, he and Lu had been heavy into some sort of conspiracy. Rona wasn't sure what they were up to. Whatever it was, Lu wasn't talking. Rona didn't press.

The astrophysics team confirmed that the gravitational storm produced intense high-energy radiation eruptions, sunspots. The flares disrupted communication between Akiane and the Moon Base. They would have to wait for the next transport to send their reports to their WSC project managers and speak to their families.

For fear of crying, Rona pretended to stare at the holo-screen. She desperately missed her family, especially her father. More than anything, she wanted to go home and run into his arms.

* * *

Rona's grandmother had repeatedly told her not to forget her heritage. "We come from Africa," she'd said. "We were a proud people, but we were betrayed by a neighboring tribe and sold into slavery to white merchants. No one from that time could ever have believed that it would be possible to travel to other planets in our solar system." Grandmother's eyes sparkled with gratification. "But now you, a proud, beautiful black woman, will be the first in our family to travel to another planet in our galaxy."

"If I could, I'd take you with me, Grandmamma," Rona had answered.

"And I would go," her grandmother had said with wonder.

* * *

"I'm here because of my grandmamma," Rona said.

"What? Rona, I thought Olivia convinced you to stay," Lu said.

"The last time I went home, Mom was so sad, I just couldn't bear it. I returned to the Moon Base with the intention of resigning," Rona said. "Olivia convinced me I had to live my own life, not my mother's or my father's expectation of my life."

"Olivia can be such a pain, but she does have her moments," Lu said. "How does your grandmother fit in?"

"I left home because I didn't want to work on the family hydroponics farm. Grandmamma was the first person to tell me to follow my path," Rona said. "My parents and sisters wanted me to stay and never leave. My oldest sister married a man with a degree in hydroponic agriculture. He loved the idea of joining the family business. She tried to set me up with one of his friends in the same field." Rona dropped her head, remembering. She'd liked the guy, but the thought of spending the rest of her life with him had scared her.

Rona lifted her head and said, "If not for Grandmamma, I would have given in. She convinced me to apply for the Akiane Project."

"She knew if you stayed on the farm you'd wither."

Emotions welled up. "Even so, I miss them so much, I would return home today if it were feasible." Rona took a deep halting breath.

"Your grandmother knew you had to get as far away as possible. That's why she encouraged you to go off-world," Lu said. "If you had returned home, you might never have left again."

"Lu, I could die here and never go home again."

"Yes, but here you've traveled to another star system. You and I are about to make a scientific breakthrough. How would you feel if someone else had taken your place? You and I would never have met and I'd be sharing a Nobel Prize with someone else. How would you feel then?" Lu asked.

"You're right, I'd feel so bad I . . . I don't know what I'd do," Rona said.

"If you returned home, your spirit would die long before your body died. That's no way to live, Rona," Lu said supportively.

"I dearly love my family, but I felt so . . . so . . ." Rona searched for the right word. ". . . suffocated."

"I know," Lu said. "That's how I felt. I dearly love my *muqin*, but she was unable to meet my mental needs. At home, I was intellectually stunted. The Ministry of Education opened my mind to unlimited possibilities. If not for them, I'd be married, a mother, and working for the government instead of being here with you saving Earth's only galactic colony."

Rona sniffed, wiped her nose with a tissue, and smiled. Lu was right. She was better off here on an alien planet instead of being stuck on the family farm.

"Well, when you put it that way, I'll have to send The Ministry of Education of China a thank-you note for giving me the best teammate on this side of the Milky Way."

"Well," Lu mimicked, "if you're going to do that, I'll have to send a thank-you note to your grandmamma."

"Do it secretly. If my father sees it, she might never receive your thanks."

It felt good to laugh.

This was everything she had been working for. Every setback and delay had been a steppingstone across an impossible river. Thanks to Qorow Low, a bridge may have been built. Now it was time to get to work.

"Let's get to it and find the cure," Rona said with a big smile. "After all, that's why we're here, right?"

Phyllis Moore

Chapter 10

Rona Montgomery
RNA Messenger

Akiane Date: Year 328
Endurance: Scientists' Quarters

"YOU BETCHA." Lu's laugh was light, easy, and contagious. "Let's get at it. Sequencing the mother's DNA will help us discover how the retrovirus attacks her cells and . . ." As per her nature, Lu was eager and excited at the prospects, and verbalized her thoughts out loud.

There were times when it annoyed Rona, but after the last couple of months they'd just had, Lu's enthusiasm heightened Rona's expectations.

They'd come to Akiane thinking they had great opportunities and new discoveries in genetics, only to be rejected by the colonists. Without a project, Rona had become disheartened, but Lu's enthusiasm had kept them going.

Lu decided to study the colonists' pets. They learned that the dogs, Olivia's fish, and the tupilak had the same retrovirus that had killed one of their own and infected another. Thanks to Qorow Low, they were finally starting their WSC Genome Project.

". . . We'll have the colonists cured in no time," Lu finished.

Sounded good, Rona thought, *but too easy.*

WSC's scientific community was eagerly waiting for new discoveries from Akiane. It was hoped that the new discoveries would shed light on old theories and inspire fresh ideas. Rona was at the head of the chain of those new discoveries. She'd worked her entire life for this, and had hoped to be counted among the greats: Gregor Mendel, James Watson, and Rona's inspiration and teacher, Laura McKaffey. This was her one chance to get it right, which meant it was her responsibility to keep Lu on track.

"Don't count your crocodiles before they hatch," Rona said.

"What does that mean, Rona?"

"Mother crocodiles lay their eggs in a secluded area, in the sand if it's available, but when she returns to the water, predators come and eat the eggs. The mother doesn't know how many, or if any, of her eggs survived until they hatch," Rona said.

Lu sighed, and said, "Research takes time and is painstakingly slow. I know. But sometimes I wish it moved along a little faster."

At least they were not at the beginning of their research thanks to their studies of the dogs. They now had a human subject. But they wouldn't have all the information they needed unless they expanded their test numbers. Two subjects were no more that a tease.

Stay on the brighter side, Rona reminded herself. Two were far better than the none they'd had before. And they were now able to begin the study, and would finally have something to send to WSC.

The Hand Held Medical Scanner (HMS) had been inconclusive. It didn't register any disease in the mother or child. HMS had detected the retrovirus in Zhoa, but Rona and Lu had not been able to analyze his blood in time to save him.

Zhoa died during the night of The Storm. He shouldn't have died as quickly as he did.

Lu and Rona hypothesized that the stress of The Storm raised his adrenaline, which hastened his illness.

As unfortunate as Zhoa's death was, his autopsy and the subsequent research did help Lu and Rona find a cure for his brother Vong when he too became infected while butchering a tupilak.

He no longer handled raw meat barehanded.

Rona was able to develop an antiviral, which sent new instructions to the retrovirus, telling it to stand down.

Lu programmed thousands of microscopic nanorobots to carry the antiviral to infected cells. She inserted the antiviral into the nanorobots, placed them in a saline solution, injected Vong in his palm, near the infected area, and cured him.

Rona left Lu to study the incoming test results and took a short break. She returned with two cups of coffee in one hand and a small plate of cookies in the other. She sat down and placed everything on the floor between them.

Lu frowned as she stared at the holo-screen.

"What?" Rona asked.

"According to this, neither the mother nor her child are ill." Lu picked up a cookie. "There's no infection." She absentmindedly took a bite and chewed slowly while she continued to examine the information.

Rona picked up her cup, and one cookie, and dunked it in her coffee. "That can't be right." As she studied screen, she forgot about the cookie and placed her cup on the floor.

Lu put her cookie on her knee and pointed to the screen. "According to these readings, there's no infection. Their white blood cell count is normal."

That didn't make sense. The retrovirus killed Zhoa and it would have killed Vong. So why aren't the mother and child affected in the same way?

"We saw blotches of the illness along the mother's hairline. Her baby is limp and dying." Rona couldn't wrap her head around it. Nothing made sense.

"I know, I know, Rona, but the HMS says the child is healthy. Computer," Lu commanded, "show the images of the mother and child's retrovirus, and Zhoa and Vong's retrovirus."

They had promised Qorow Low they wouldn't tell anyone who she was. Therefore, Lu and Rona decided they would only refer to them as mother and child and labeled their files accordingly.

Four separate images appeared with their file names under each, but the images looked exactly alike.

"They all have the retrovirus," Rona said.

"That's because the retrovirus is the problem." Lu picked up her cookie and took a big bite.

"Theorizing too soon, Lu, will cause us to misdiagnose," Rona said. "There's more to this than we realize."

"Rona, every time we turn around, it's the retrovirus." Lu used the cookie to help emphasize her words. "What else can it be?"

"Computer," Rona commanded, "show all four subjects' white blood count." Her instructions were immediately obeyed. "According to this, Zhoa and Vong were infected, but the mother and child are not."

"Computer, show only the retroviruses," commanded Lu.

Seeing the image of the retrovirus by itself presented an astonishing revelation.

"How is that possible?" Rona asked.

The retrovirus didn't have a complete ribonucleic acid (RNA) to properly recode its host's DNA, which caused the host's DNA to become defective.

A normal retrovirus replicated quickly, but the defect RNA stalled the replication and created a jumbled mess.

"This is confusing," Lu said. She finished her cookie in one more bite. "The dogs have the retrovirus and they're not having problems," she said with a mouth full of cookie.

"We need more information," Rona insisted. She reached for her cup of coffee, but it was full of soggy cookie crumbs. She put it down. "I thought it a misuse of our time when you first suggested we study the colonists' dogs."

"I know," Lu said.

"But now we have a pattern. We just need to unravel it. Computer," Rona commanded, "display the retrovirus genome for the tupilak and dogs."

The women studied the screen.

"The retroviruses in the tupilak and dogs appear dormant. Their white blood count is normal. There's no infection," Lu said. "If the retrovirus is normal for them, it confirms the scanner's diagnosis of the mother and child."

"*But* the retrovirus is not affecting the mammals in the same way it's affecting humans. Why?" Rona asked. "The retrovirus wasn't dormant in Zhoa and it killed him."

"Maybe there's something wrong with the scanner," Lu said thoughtfully.

"No, there's something wrong with our conclusion," Rona said. "This is why we need more information."

"Computer," Lu said, "bring back the genome images of the mother and child. Keep present images." The screen grew larger to accommodate six images of mammals and humans.

Rona touched the screen. "Lu, there's a mutation variation in the tupilak and dogs' genomes, that is not in the human genome." She sucked in a breath. "Wait it's not a mutation that's the problem, it's an incomplete retrovirus. In humans the retrovirus is missing its enzyme that's why humans are having problems. But the retrovirus in mammals has the enzyme and they don't have the same genetic problem. Why the difference?"

The retrovirus *was* alien, therefore things *should* be different from an Earth retrovirus. Like any scientific mystery, it could take years, even decades of research and experiments, and conferring with scientists on Moon Base before they clearly understood the problem and were able to find a cure.

The mother didn't have years. The baby had no more than a few days, if she was lucky.

Somehow, Rona doubted luck was on their side. She was feeling the pressure of their extremely limited amount of time before things literally turned deadly.

Failure is not an option, Rona decided. *We have to figure this out.*

"Rona, this is the same thing that killed Zhoa. We treated Vong, and he's alive and well. If we do nothing, the baby will die. But we might be able to save her," Lu said. "We have to use the same nano-technology and antiserum we used for Vong. We cure the mother and child, the colonists will come to us for a cure, and everyone will be happy."

Once again Rona knew it sounded too good. There was more to this illness than they knew or understood. Every new bit of information brought more confusion. Still, Lu was correct, they had cured Vong; therefore, there was a good chance they could cure the child and mother as well.

Why was she hesitating?

"Do you need more convincing, Rona?" Lu asked. "Computer, is there anything about the colonists that is significantly different than those from Earth?"

Because of the closeness of workspaces, computers had been muted. The word "YES" appeared on the screen.

"Show us," Lu said.

The holo-screen disappeared. A smaller version reappeared with an image of one protein.

"There are 20,000 proteins in the human body," Rona said. "Computer, what is the significance of this protein?"

UNKNOWN

"Computer, to whom does this protein belong?" Rona asked cautiously.

COLONISTS: FILES FOR MOTHER AND CHILD

"Define protein," Rona said.

PROTEIN UNDEFINABLE

"These people have a protein that no human on Earth has," Lu said.

"An alien protein, Lu," Rona said in frustration. "Why not?" Here was another piece of the puzzle that didn't seem to have a place in the puzzle.

"Where did it come from?" Rona asked. "And what does it do?"

"It's only logical that it comes from the retrovirus," Lu said.

"It's logical, Lu, but where is the enzyme that produce the protein?"

Questions flowed between them.

"If the retrovirus isn't the cause of the disease, perhaps the protein is the problem," Rona said.

A new protein should have been electrifying. Instead it brought more confusion to an already confusing problem.

"The real question is how did the protein originate?" Lu asked.

Rona didn't like the tone in Lu's voice. She turned to her and asked, "What?"

"The dogs and tupilak also have it," Lu Said.

"That's *not* possible!" Rona said.

"Nevertheless."

"Lu, how do you know?"

"I asked the computer the same question when we were researching the Canini Project," Lu said.

"You never mentioned it," Rona said.

"We were so busy following male puppies, I forgot," Lu said.

Rona gave her a *"How could you forget?"* frown.

"At least I thought of it now," Lu said in her defense.

"Why wait until now to remember?" Rona asked. "Why not mention it when Zhoa died? We could be so much further ahead if we had started with this."

"Too upset over Zhoa's death," Lu apologized.

Nothing makes sense! Why does nothing make sense? Peoples' lives are at stake, Rona silently screamed.

Lu ate another cookie while Rona thought.

Rona leaned back on her hands. "You were right to study the dogs."

"I know I was," Lu said with a hint of humor, "but what changed your mind?"

"The colonists and dogs originated on Earth," Rona said, thoughtfully. "Maybe the problem isn't with them, but with us. We're the aliens."

"What do you mean?" Lu asked.

"There are so many female dogs, we had difficulty finding the elusive adult male dog," Rona said.

"That's why we put trackers on male puppies," Lu said, "to learn what happened to them."

"The dogs and tupilak are too similar," Rona said. "I think when adult male dogs leave land for the ocean they become tupilak."

"How so?"

"Akiane dogs stay the size of a large dog because there's not enough room for something the size of a tupilak to live in the habitat," Rona said. "But once in the ocean where they have unlimited space."

"They grow to the size of a polar bear," Lu said. "At least they don't become leviathan."

"The retrovirus is natural to the planet. But it's foreign to us because we're the aliens," Rona said. "We're studying this as if it's from Earth. But the dogs are now native to the planet. They become tupilak with the help of the retrovirus. Humans here are now native to Akiane, but the retrovirus is affecting them differently. Why?"

"We need to change our way of thinking," Lu said. "So we can determine the answer."

"Which is easier said than done, Lu, since we don't yet understand the retrovirus."

"Because we're the aliens," Lu said. "It would help if we knew its origin."

"There had to be something the colonists and their pets came in contact with when they first landed," Rona said.

"If so, why didn't they die off then?" Lu said.

"Because, Lu, there were medical teams back then, just like now. Someone must have figured out what was going on."

"Then it should be in the medical logs," Lu said, enthusiastically. "I'll talk to Tech Terzo and ask him to search *Falcon's* data files.

At the mention of his name, Tech Terzo looked up from his computer.

"We have a project for you," Lu said.

With a smile, he nodded and said, "Anytime."

"I'll let you know what we find," Lu happily said to Rona.

Which would be fine, if the files had not been corrupted because of three centuries of neglect, Rona thought. She was in no mood to start a long debate on Terzo's ability to find those logs. Best to keep her thoughts to herself. *Stay on topic.*

Rona again picked up her coffee, remembered the melted cookie, put the cup down, picked up a new cookie, but instead of eating it, she held on to it as she pondered the problem before them.

Once again, Rona saw failure slapping her in the face. Her resolve rose—she wouldn't let mother and child die. *Not on my watch.*

"Do we have fish genome?" Rona asked.

"No. Why? You think there might be something there?" Lu asked.

"They're native to Akiane."

"I'll email Olivia," Lu said.

Seconds later, Olivia sent two files. One marked, "Before Ice Melt." The other read, "After Ice Melt."

Lu opened "Before Ice Melt." They examined it in detail.

"Nothing new there." Lu closed it, then opened the other file.

They studied it.

It was a long while before Lu said, "It can't be that easy."

"Oh Lu, I think it can."

"But how?" Lu asked. "Were did it come from?"

"I don't know, but there it is," Rona said.

They reexamined the file, and squealed in delight. They bobbed up and down as if dancing. They hugged, high-fived, and screamed with joy.

The WSC scientists were a small group of people who knew what the others were working on. Therefore they understood when Rona raised her arms as if to hug them all, and said "We may have found the cure."

The room cheered, clapped, and shouted in triumph.

Chapter 11

Jess Hewitt
Cameron

Akiane Date: Year 328
On an Island Somewhere in the Ocean

I LAY on the ice and thought about how cold and wet I was, and how glad that I was still alive. A nice hot relaxing bath would have been just the thing to finish my day.

None was available. The hot springs we'd used to make our hot tub had evaporated. My warm fur bedding would have to do, with ever-loving Essal and her pups snuggled all around me for more warmth and comfort. I used to hate it when she tried to snuggle next to me, but she never gave up. Now, I was glad she hadn't.

In my moment of fear for my life, I'd forgotten about Essal. I expected her to come and see how I was. Where was she?

I sat up to look for her.

Why wasn't Essal here with me? I wanted to give her a big bear hug and a proper thank you for saving me from being eaten alive. When the tupilak had thrown her, she'd skidded across the ice and had been too dazed to move, but she should be over it by now. Where was she?

I stood up.

Chovis were gathered around something. Essal should have been among the pack of red-and-white-furred chovis. And should have been easy to spot with her one red ear and her all white fur coat. But I couldn't find her.

Cameron stood among the chovis. He was still shirtless and gloveless, but had shrunk back to his normal size. He seemed sad. Why wasn't he overjoyed with our victory?

I took another look around.

"Where's Essal," I asked.

Cameron looked away. Something was wrong. His shoulders slumped. He was about to do something he regretted.

The fear I felt at that moment was worse than the fear of being attacked by a tupilak.

My legs were suddenly shaky on the slippery ice, but I kept my balance.

Nu Venia understood my fear because she said, "Essal has given you honor."

Her words chilled me.

"What does that mean?" I asked, fearing that I already knew the answer.

Her expression said she wanted to offer comfort, but didn't know how. I didn't want comfort. I wanted Essal.

Chovis backed off as Cameron knelt next to the fallen chovis. One red ear lay on a the lifeless white face. Essal seemed to be sleeping; one good shake and she'd bounce up and come running.

My thoughts said, *Cameron is going to wake her.* My heart knew better.

Nothing on Akiane is wasted was a saying on Akiane. The colonists had few resources; therefore they wasted nothing, not even a fallen pet. Cameron planned to skin and gut her. My beloved Essal would be our next meal.

"No," I yelled as loud as I could. "She's not dead."

Cameron rose to his feet and walked a couple of meters away.

Why so far away? I wondered.

He called the chovis to him. They backed away, giving me room, but stayed close.

I'll never forget the sound of my boots squishing across the ice.

I kneeled beside Essal. Her blue eyes stared at nothing. Her bright pink nose had faded so it was almost white. Her one red ear lay on her forehead. She smelled of blood and the morbid reality of death.

She had been so determined that we become friends. She had taught me how to love.

It wasn't fair. It wasn't right.

It wasn't.

It just wasn't.

Nu Venia said Essal had given birth to puppies to please me. We were supposed to raise them together. We were supposed to go home together. She couldn't be dead. This wasn't the way things were supposed to end.

"Essal." I placed a gloved hand on her side and gently shook her. She didn't respond.

One of her pups nudged her. Another lay next to her. Two placed their heads on her back and whined pitifully. They already missed her. I didn't want to let go. I'd already lost so much.

"Essal," I said softly. I shook her again, a little more vigorously. "Please, wake up."

Nothing.

"No," escaped my lips like the wind foretelling of a coming storm brewing in my heart. Essal couldn't be dead. She'd just saved my life. She deserved a victory hug.

"NO!" I said with more fervor. She was my *friend.* I wanted her back. I needed her. I was not willing to let her go. Not now. Not yet. Not ever.

No matter how loud I said it or refused to believe, Essal did not respond.

For a long time I sat, not knowing what to do. I closed my eyes as reality oozed into my brain.

I took my thick fur gloves off, then the thin green liner gloves for one last loving touch. My hand passed over her head. I scratched behind her one red ear. That ear set her apart from the others. My hand passed over her muzzle now smeared with frozen tupilak blood.

I'd been afraid that I might not survive Woden. It never occurred to me that she might not survive.

"Why did you do it?" I asked. "We can't be friends anymore." I'd wasted precious time. Now it was too late. Why had I been so stupid?

In my mind, I heard Dad's voice say, "Crying won't bring her back." Mom had abandoned us, me. I wanted her to come home, but no amount of tears brought her back. The pain hadn't gone away, but the tears had. I moved on as best a broken-hearted little girl could.

What tears that might have come for Essal had dried up long ago. It was just as well. Tears were a waste of energy. They didn't bring Mom back. They wouldn't bring Essal back. No matter where I was or how hard I tried, some things just never change.

I stood, and just like that little girl, turned away.

All at once, chovis began to howl. I thought they were mourning Essal.

I was *so* wrong.

They pranced as if the ice was blazing hot. They howled not for Essal, but at the ice as they madly ran around.

"What's wrong?" I asked Cameron.

"I don't know," he said, just as the ice under his feet exploded. He flew forward, landed hard on his forehead, and lay stunned.

Why had he walked so far away?

Huth, Essal's mother, bolted at full speed. She leaped into the open water and disappeared in a froth of foam.

I was too stunned to think, move, or speak.

Nu Venia caught her breath in surprise.

Why had Huth jumped in?

The churning water quieted.

We anxiously waited for her to reappear. She didn't.

Chovis continued to bark and snarl. They gathered around Cameron. Nu Venia and I should have joined them, but it happened too fast.

With a groan, Cameron rolled over onto his back. One foot dangled over the hole.

A fretful cry came from Nu Venia.

"Cameron," I yelled, realizing what was about to happen. "Move your foot."

He was too dazed to understand. He bent his right leg. It was his left foot that hung over the water hole.

A bright, pink nose with a black spot slipped out of the water, followed by a deep red muzzle and a full set of sharp teeth. The tupilak was reaching for Cameron.

Suddenly I recognized that nose. That was Addle's nose.

Addle had been a bothersome chovis and had killed one of the lead chovis in order to become second in command. Her next goal was to take down the lead alpha female, Huth.

At the first sign of trouble, instead of leading her team to safety, Addle proved herself to be a coward. Afterword, the team rejected her and refused to follow her. Cameron demoted her by putting her farther down the line of the team. We woke the next morning to learn Addle had deserted us.

That tupilak couldn't actually be Addle. But how could a tupilak have the same exact nose as her?

No matter whose nose it was, it was on a snout with teeth that was about to grab Cameron.

"No! Stay away from him!" I screamed.

Nu Venia and I ran for Cameron.

White teeth delicately took hold of his pant leg. As the snout sank back into the water, Cameron's foot slowly slid into the hole with it.

"CAMERON!" Nu Venia and I yelled in unison.

Chovis circled the hole, howling frantically. Several grabbed Cameron's fur suit and struggled to keep him from going into the water. He kept sliding away.

Cameron finally came to his senses as his boot disappeared into the frigid water. He tried to roll over, but the chovis were in his way.

"Move," he yelled.

They backed off.

He managed to roll onto his stomach and grabbed at the ice, but the ice was too slick and fragile. His fingers couldn't find a hold and when they did, the ice crumbled.

I dove for him, landed hard on my stomach, and slid toward him.

He reached his hand out to me. I grabbed it, my bare right palm to his bare right palm. All touching was forbidden among his people. But in this instant, we had to make an exception. His big hand tightly gripped my hand and wrist.

My left hand clamped over his large wrist. I sank my fingers into his skin as tightly as I could.

I was not letting go.

Cameron continued to slide backward, taking me with him. He kicked at the water and at the tupilak.

Nu Venia landed on top of me, knocking the wind out of me. Her extra weight slowed us, but couldn't stop the inevitable; the three of us were going in.

Suddenly, Cameron expression changed from fear to relief. "I am free. I hit the tupilak in the nose. It has released me."

Nu Venia scrambled to her feet, straddled me, grabbed my waist, pulled me to my knees, and then to my feet.

I added my strength to hers as we pulled Cameron out of the water.

Chovis yelped madly, making it difficult to think.

"Stop it!" I shouted.

They didn't.

Cameron was coming out. He placed one knee on the ice, then jolted backwards, landed on his belly, and almost pulled me down with him. Nu Venia held on to me. We were literally at a standstill.

"Aaaa." He screamed in agony. "My foot. Tupilak—foot."

The sea monster must have released Cameron's pant leg so it could get a better grip on his foot.

"Cameron, does he have your foot or your boot?" I asked.

"Boot," he grunted.

"Shake your foot loose!" I said. "Nu Venia, keep pulling."

She pulled.

I firmly planted my feet and also pulled.

"No!" Tears of pain slipped down his face.

The colonists had the ability to changes sizes. I'd seen Cameron and Nu Venia do it. But could he change just one body part?

"Make your foot smaller," I yelled.

He wiggled. "Working. Pull harder."

Nu Venia and I pulled with all out strength as he twisted loose.

"I am free!" he exclaimed.

Once Cameron was released, Nu Venia groaned as she heaved us away from the hole. I put my full strength into helping her. With his free hand he hoisted himself out of the water. But just as he placed one knee on the ice, he fell onto his stomach again. I jolted forward.

Cameron was sliding back into the water.

Nu Venia lost her hold on me. I lost my footing and landed on my stomach and found myself sliding with him toward open water.

"Nu Venia," I yelled. Once again she landed on top of me, but the tupilak was too strong. It was pulling the three of us in.

"No, no, no!" I yelled.

"My foot," he groaned.

The tupilak had grabbed hold of his bare foot. The pain must have been unbearable.

"Can you make it smaller," I asked.

He could only shake his head.

"Pull harder," I gasped to Nu Venia.

Her grip around my waist tightened. She stood and pulled with everything she had.

Cameron still had my hand.

The tupilak still had him and it was winning.

Cameron was sinking deeper. We were playing tug of war with the sea monster at the expense of Cameron's foot. If only the tupilak would chew it off, but it was holding fast.

"Ahhaaah," Cameron cried. Tears streamed down his face.

"Jessica, let go," he croaked. "Not drown with me." He released his grip.

"NO," I screamed. He was my friend. How could I let go? He could live without that foot. Nu Venia and I could not live without him.

Nu Venia was unable to stop us from sliding toward the open water. The ice was too slick, the tupilak too strong.

Suddenly, we were now both on our knees, too close to the hole. Cameron was chest deep in the frigid water. Still, I would not let go. I'd go in with him if it came to that. We'd fight the tupilak together.

Nu Venia mournfully whimpered in my ear, "Jessica, let go. Cameron is lost."

How could she say that? As long as I still held his hand there was hope. There had to be hope.

"No! I will not let go!"

Something bit my right palm. Involuntarily, my hand jerked free. My left hand still held his wrist, but his wrist was too big. It became bigger. He was trying to make me let go. I squeezed as tight as I could.

Cameron's hand slipped from mine.

Nu Venia and I fell backwards. We became entangled. I struggled to free myself, but she held on.

"Nu Venia, let go of me, I have to go in after him."

"No!" She was adamant. "I cannot also lose you."

Even though he knew he was already lost, Cameron wildly grabbed at the edge of the ice.

"I love you both," he said in desperation. "Stay true to each other. Remember your calling."

The ice gave way and he was gone.

No splash. No thrashing. Just ripples. Then nothing.

I stopped struggling. Nu Venia eased her hold on me, but did not let go.

Bubbles. The last of Cameron's air. Water stilled.

Chovis let out a mournful whine.

Nu Venia buried her face in my back and sobbed.

I heaved as if to cry. Wails of grief tried to rise from deep in my belly. But tears would not come. For far too many years, I had not allowed my feelings to surface. I'd forgotten how to cry.

All I could manage was a disbelieving moan.

Chapter 12

Jessica Hewitt
Nothing Wasted

Akiane Date: Year 328
On an Island Somewhere in the Ocean

THE PITCH of chovis' soft whimpers became ear-piercing barks.

Tupilak!

No, this was different. It wasn't the chovis' deep growls of warning. I looked around to see what was bothering them.

A white furry lump was floating in the hole where Cameron had just disappeared. Huth. Ice was quickly forming around her.

Chovis didn't eat tupilak. And it seemed tupilak didn't eat chovis. Was that some kind of mutual respect? Could they attack and kill, but not eat each other? Why?

"Help me, Nu Venia."

Nu Venia sat like a stone stature, staring at nothing. Tears streamed down her face.

Lost in my own disbelief, I hadn't noticed what she was going through. I'd known Cameron for a few weeks. She'd known him her entire life. She was in her private world grieving her best friend.

I wanted to join her and disappear into a fantasy world and never return to reality, but where would I go?

When I was a child, I used to play in a virtual fantasy game where I was a fearless dragon girl. Mom shattered my pretend life, and my real life, when she left. I never found peace in that game, or in my life, again.

Would I return to Baja? WSC Moon base? *Britannia*?

There was no part of my life that I wanted to revisit; each held bad memories.

Just a few days ago, I'd dealt with the demons that had haunted me. I'd resolved those issues. This was supposed to be the next phase of my life. I was supposed to be starting over, brand new.

This was a horrible restart.

Sitting and staring at nothing would mean imminent death. I wasn't going to die like that and I wouldn't let Nu Venia die either.

As unpleasant as it was, I shook her back to reality.

"What?" She blinked several times as if she'd forgotten where she was. She didn't wipe the tears away.

"Cameron." She moaned.

"Huth," I said.

Nu Venia looked around, expecting Huth to be trotting toward us. When she saw her floating in the hole, she started to retreat back into her private world.

"Nu Venia, no." I pulled her to her feet. "Help me get Huth. The water is freezing around her, but it's new ice. I don't want to fall in as I pull her out."

She nodded.

I stretched over the unstable ice. Nu Venia held onto my legs. My fingers just reached Huth's tail. I grabbed it and pulled her toward me. Ice cracked as it released her

Nu Venia pulled me to safety.

I hauled Huth onto my lap.

Ignoring the pain of my cold hands and a new itch on my right palm, I gently ran my fingers over Huth's wet fur.

116

She'd given her life in an attempt to save Cameron.

Few people would give their life for a friend. Most people ran the other way. I'd never thought about what I would do if a friend were in danger. I knew now.

I'd been willing to be pulled into the water and die with Cameron. Where had that come from? In my entire life, I'd never been heroic.

Maybe I would have been willing to die in an effort to rescue my father. If I'd seen him in the water, riptide or no, I'd have gone in after him. I would have held onto him, and possibly died with him. At least, he wouldn't have died alone.

If I had died with Dad, I'd never have come here. Cameron would still be alive at the habitat. He wouldn't have been on Woden, and Nu Venia wouldn't be stranded out here with me.

Cameron wanted Woden so we could get to know each other without the influence of my admiral or his high priest.

They each had their own agenda; one wanted to reclaim the colony, the other wanted the colony to remain isolated.

On Woden, we only had each other and our personal agendas. I'd wanted out. Cameron wanted community. Despite my best effort to remain aloof, we became friends.

Unfortunately, our friendship and his guidance had drowned with him.

Cameron also wanted me to make Community with the colony. I had no idea how; without him, his Community would reject me. And I'd fail Cameron's mission.

WSC wanted its colony back. If need be, it would use military force to take it. Then I'd fail WSC and the people of Endurance.

Everything had gone wrong.

My fingers ran over Huth's white fur, along her back to her head then her ears. She was Essal's life-giver and like Essal, she was dead.

My cheeks seem overly damp. I tasted a bit of salt on my lower lip. My vision blurred. I leaned forward, buried my face in Huth's fur, and sobbed.

I cried over Mom's leaving, Dad's death, my lost fiancé, the deaths of Essal, Huth, and, especially, Cameron. A dam broke deep in my chest. All the tears I'd kept inside for so many years flooded out. I cried because I'd been dumped on this planet and was on this stupid Woden. I cried for all the times I could have been with Jorge and my friends back at the habitat but I'd rejected them instead. I cried over my stupid, lousy life.

The tears came as if they'd never stop.

I'm not sure how long I sat there doubled over Huth before Nu Venia nudged me and said, "It is not good to sit thus."

It felt as if I'd awakened from a deep sleep, but instead of feeling refreshed, I was emotionally exhausted. "What?"

"Huth's fur will freeze to your pants and jacket, and you will be unable to free yourself." She sounded logical but devoid of emotion. I'd brought her back from her private world; now she was pressing forward with the rules of life. "There is need to butcher Huth and Essal before they become stiff."

What? She planned to eat them?

That was not going to happen.

I sat up.

"No, Nu Venia," I said obstinately. "We won't butcher Huth or Essal. We're not going to butcher another chovis for the rest of this trip. I don't care if that means we won't have anything to eat. We're not killing another chovis."

"Jessica, it is not acceptable to waste meat. Nothing on Akiane is wasted."

I knew Essal and Huth would have been honored to feed and nourish us. But I chose to honor them by not eating them.

"I don't care, Nu Venia. I'm going to bury them," I said.

"Bury?" she asked. "What is that?"

How could she not know? What did her people do with their dead?

I pulled my gloves out of my jacket pocket and put them on. "I'll show you."

I handed Huth to Nu Venia, picked up Essal, and headed toward shore. Nu Venia and chovis followed. We laid Essal and Huth side by side.

The ground was too frozen to dig and there wasn't a stone in sight. During The Storm, huge waves had watched the beach clean.

I got an ax from the pack and hacked at a large rock protruding out of the cliff until I had smaller manageable pieces, which I placed around Huth and Essal.

"This is a waste of good meat."

"Nu Venia, I don't care. It helps work out my anger," I said.

I chopped more rocks.

She watched for a while then got an ax and joined me. Together, we attacked large boulders, making them into smaller rocks. Aggressively beating at rocks really did help my grief and was more worthwhile than crying.

Once finished, we stood in silence.

"This is not permanent, Jessica," Nu Venia said. "When Loki returns, the rocks, Essal and Huth will be washed away."

"It doesn't matter. When I think about them, I'll remember them buried here, like this, not chopped up in stew."

"Chovis do not know the difference, Jessica."

"Nu Venia, it makes me feel better."

After a moment's silence, she said, "Makes me feel better too, Jessica."

"There was a lot I never told my father. I was so angry at him for making me leave my home and move to Woodlands, a town in the middle of nowhere." I still felt the resentment of leaving my cousins, who were my best friends. "I fought him every time he wanted to go camping—and yet, when I did go, I enjoyed those times alone with him. I liked learning about mushing dogs and winter camping. Turns out my father had been preparing me for Woden," I said.

"After Mom left, I never told Dad I loved him. Maybe somewhere, deep in my heart, I blamed him for not trying harder to keep her with us." His sad face drifted into memory. Tears returned. "He used to say he loved me, but I never said it back. After a while, he stopped saying it. On the last day we were together, the day he died, he said he loved me."

"Did you say it back?" Nu Venia said.

"No, too locked up. I couldn't say it. I just smiled and said thank you. Now he's gone and I can't ask him to forgive me for being such a bratty child. I can't tell him that I forgive him for taking me away from friends and family or that I loved him with all my heart. And still do." I wiped tears away.

"I too have been angry with Cameron," she said. "I did not want Woden. He would not allow me to stay behind." She stopped and took a deep breath before she continued. "If I had stayed at Endurance, I would never have known what happened to him."

"If it had just been the two of us, I would have died with him," I said. "Or I'd be here by myself, not knowing what to do. Either way, I'd be dead and no one would know what had happened to either of us."

"Not knowing, would have been worse for me. I would never have forgiven myself," she finished.

We alone but together.

"Nu Venia, I'm alive because of you," I said. "Thank you."

"Jessica, I am thankful for you."

"Because of Cameron, I'm finally able to forgive my father. I wish I had thanked him."

"Cameron held you in high regard, Jessica," she said.

"I don't know why."

"He understood who you would one day become."

"He saw the same in you." I meant it as encouragement. She didn't take it that way.

"In me, he saw what he wanted," she said with a hint of bitterness. "He saw things that are not possible. That was the reason I did not want to come with him." She paused.

"Being on Woden has been better than staying at Endurance as an outcast," she continued. "Cameron was the only one who wanted me. I tried to talk him out of Woden, but he would not listen. He said it was Holy One's will."

In a softer voice, she asked, "Is it Holy One's will that he is dead?"

"Sounds like you need to forgive both of them," I said. "We both need to forgive."

She sighed. "For me, it has been a long time since I have told Cameron how much . . ." She couldn't say 'love' either.

It surprised me how much we were alike, both broken.

We needed Cameron and were unsure it we could survive without him.

"With Cameron, I have been angry," she said. "Now I will never be able to tell him how I truly feel."

I started to place a consoling hand on Nu Venia's shoulder but caught myself in time. My hand dropped to my side.

"I'm glad we met," I said. "And I'm glad you're here with me now. I could not go through this by myself."

Of course, if I'd never come to Akiane, we wouldn't be out here in the first place.

No, that wasn't true. WSC would have sent someone else, and who knows how things would have turned out, though I doubted they could be any worse.

"I also hold you in high regard," she said. "I am glad not to be alone."

In our broken state, that was the best we could do.

I knelt next to the rock mound and placed my hand on it. "Good-bye, Essal. Good-bye Huth. You were both good friends. Keep an eye on Cameron. Don't let him be lonely. Tell him that Nu Venia and I miss him."

Then I softly said, "If you should happen to meet my father, please tell him I love him, and I miss him." I brushed away tears.

Nu Venia knelt next to me and placed her hand on the mound. "I miss you." She bowed her head and tenderly said, "Tell Cameron I love him and will always miss him."

I imagined Essal and Huth standing on the other side of the mound of rocks listening and wagging their tails before turning and leaping into the other side of life to find Cameron and my dad. They would be loyal for all of eternity.

Chovis gathered around us as if they understood. Maybe they did and appreciated the fact that we were not eating one of their own.

Essal's puppies sniffed the mound and whined. One climbed on top and lay down, displacing a few rocks. I picked her up and held her in my arms. Essal's other three puppies crowded around me. I picked each one up and held them close. They snuggled against my fur jacket as if I were their mother. They licked my face. I'd always hated being licked but now it was comforting.

I handed two of the pups to Nu Venia so they could comfort her.

Imos squeezed in between her and me to let us know that we were not alone. Imos had been a good friend to Huth and Essal and would be the next chovis to watch over us.

Nu Venia and I each placed an arm around Imos' neck. She licked Nu Venia's face, then mine.

It was reassuring to be surrounded by my new family.

The next morning we were awakened by chovis howls.

Thinking the tupilak had returned to finish us off, I was up and outside within seconds.

"Chovis do not warn of danger," Nu Venia said. "They welcome Nella's return."

"How do they know?" I squinted into the early morning light. "I don't see her anywhere."

"It is chovis way," she said. "We must hurry and pack before Nella arrives."

"Why?"

"Once she realizes Cameron is no more, she will lie down on the exact spot where he was dragged into the sea," Nu Venia said. "She will lay there until she dies or the ice melts and the ocean claims her."

"She's that loyal?" I asked.

"Chovis are that loyal," she said. "Leave the tents. Take food, water, fur bedding, and any gear we still have."

With one whistle from Nu Venia the last of our chovis took their positions. Many chovis had deserted us for the ocean. Even so, there were enough chovis from both teams to make one complete team.

The larger, stronger chovis stood directly in front of the sled. The slightly smaller chovis stood in the middle. Imos and lead chovis from the other sled, assumed their position at the head of the team.

While Nu Venia hitched the chovis in place, I loaded the last of our leather bags of food and water on top of the folded plastic boat still on our sled. Then I placed the furs on top of everything and strapped them down.

For the sake of space and her comfort, Nu Venia became the size of a young teen. She sat on the sled holding Essal's puppies, snuggling in one of the furs.

I stepped on the back and yelled, "Huk."

We met up with Nella near the same place where we'd lost Cameron.

Chovis stopped.

Somehow, Nella knew something was wrong and was carefully searching for Cameron.

Just as Nu Venia had said, Nella laid down in the exact spot where the tupilak had dragged him in. The ice had since reclaimed the whole, but we could see the markings.

I got off the sled and knelt before Nella and took her face in my hands.

"Cameron is not with us," I said.

She whimpered in concern for him.

"He wants you to take us to open water, then you can return to him."

She looked as if she understood, but didn't like it. She pulled away from me. I thought she might abandon us right then and there, but she got up and ran toward open water.

As I stepped on the sled, the team chased after her.

Nella allowed us two rest stops, but she would not let us make camp for the night. She wanted to finish as quickly as possible and return to Cameron.

It was well after dark before she stopped.

She barked once to say we had arrived, then started her journey back to her best friend.

Chovis and humans watched her disappear into the night.

We were alone and on our own.

Nu Venia and I unloaded everything and pulled the boat off the sled. Cameron had request it from Admiral Grossman just in case we need a boat for our return trip. As it turned out, we did. Now it would become our bed for the night.

Two paddles were strapped to one side of the boat. We undid the straps and placed the paddles to one side, unfolded the plastic boat, and found a long rectangular box.

Inside the box was an outboard motor with a solar panel and one lithium battery. We put the box next to the paddles.

The boat inflated into an orange 15-person motorboat with oarlocks on each side for to the paddles and an attachment for the motor in the back.

Food and water went in the bow. Furs were laid down in the rest of the boat, our fur sleeping bags on top, with more fur blankets on top.

After we were fed and watered, chovis and humans snuggled into the blankets and went to sleep trying not to think of the days ahead.

Chapter 13

Akiane Historical Chronicles
Father Joseph Striken

Akiane Date: Year 27
Endurance: One week later

GOD COMMANDS his children to love all people—friends, family, and enemies, as He loves them. Father Joe had, on occasion, wrestled with the loving enemies part. In his arrogance, he thought he knew how to love, while in truth, he had never truly known love, at least not until he'd adopted a child.

One week after Abir gave birth, two more children came forth in cocoons. The first mother, Alethea, kept her child. The second mother abandoned hers. Father Joe tried to find a mother to take it, but couldn't. He spoke to a few men he thought would make excellent fathers. They also declined his request. A couple of young girls excitedly said they wanted it, but their mothers said no.

Alethea never doubted that she should keep her child and was proving to be an outstanding mother, but even she had said no to taking on another cocoon.

"I'll be happy to let your cocoon share my child's nest while you make your own nest," she said.

126

Joe decided it was his moral obligation to keep it, resigned to the situation, and accepted Alethea's offer to help him.

She gently rolled her cocoon to one side.

He plopped his next to hers and started to leave.

"Father, you must roll the cocoon in the liquid," she said.

"Why?" he asked.

"To keep the membrane from drying out."

Why does she not do it? he thought. *Why must I?*

He tried to roll it without getting his hands covered in the liquid. It was not possible. His hands became sticky even before he started to make his nest.

No one had liked the idea of laying the cocoons on the ground with the dogs.

Three engineers devised a plan to build a nest for them. They used eight long, sturdy vines, which grew near each other, and braided them into a stand, then tightly weaved the rest of the vines into a basket. When bent, the vines leaked a milky substance, which kept the cocoon's membrane moist and nourished the child within.

Joe chose a spot near Alethea. He tried to separate eight vines to braid together. He was not good with his hands.

He had trouble untangling the runners from each other. As he worked, the sticky substance seeped out, which made the vines slippery and difficult to handle.

When he got one vine in place, the others slipped out of place.

The stand was supposed to be one meter high and straight, but halfway up, his sagged to one side. He didn't know how to pull the vines tight enough to straighten them. He took it apart and started over only to have it sag in another direction. Joe and his nest were hopeless.

It was impossible to stay clean with sticky liquid perpetually leaking. His hands, clothes, and shoes, even his hair was tacky. By the end of the afternoon, he was tired and hungry, ready to give up, and embarrassed to admit that it was foolish of him to have taken on the task in the first place.

The entire mess was proof that he'd made a bad decision. This was not God's will for him. He should have sought harder for someone else to take the thing. He'd given up too easily. He would return to his quarters, clean up, and talk to every member of the community until he found the proper person to care for the child.

"Alethea, it has become clear to me that I am not meant to be a parent," Joe said. "Will you continue to watch over this one until I find a suitable parent?"

She'd tied a wide ribbon around her head so her thick black curls would be out of her face and tumble freely down her back. Her smile reminded him of when he was tall, fit, and young.

* * *

It had been a boost to his pride when young women came to him sincerely believing God had told them they were to be his bride.

Father Joseph was too holy and dedicated to get married. He thanked them, and politely declined their offers. That had been so many years ago, a different life on another planet, in a different part of the galaxy where humility had been a bitter pill to swallow.

He had been on the fast track to becoming a bishop until he learned he'd been assigned to WSC Moon Base.

He'd contacted his bishop to ask him why he was being reassigned. He really wanted to ask, "Are you out of your mind?"

"You are the most qualified," the bishop said. "Moon Base is composed of multi cultures. We want someone who lacks prejudice and bias. We want cultural relativism, someone who appreciates the splendor of blending many cultures. You've lived and worked in many countries and have been successful no matter where you've been assigned. We expect no less of you now."

The bishop gave a similar argument when Father Joseph received new orders to join the settlers on *WSC Hawk.*

"Those on Moon Base are professionals. They're trained to get along. The settlers are civilians. There will be problems for many of them while adjusting to so many different cultures on one ship. We are in high hopes that you will be a great asset to the ship's counseling team."

When Father Joseph tried to object, the bishop promised it was only for the journey to the colony; he would be returning with *WSC Falcon.*

Joe prayed for many long hours, which turned into days, then weeks, in the hope that God would relieve him from his fate. Instead, God gave him peace to go. He deferred to his new orders and packed.

Deep in his heart, he'd known he would never return to Earth.

* * *

The day *Hawk* landed, he feared The Storm would be the climax of a very tedious trip. He prepared for death.

He not only survived but began a happy, fruitful life.

There had been moments of loss, doubt, and great discouragement, but none like today.

He'd made a mistake and he wanted out.

"I have a task that I must first tend to, Father." Alethea turned and walked slowly away.

"But Alethea," Joe called after her. "What about the child?"

"I'll soon return," she said. "You may turn both cocoons for me."

He didn't even want to do that, but he did it, anyway.

After a frustrating hour, she returned with Carlos, one of the engineers who helped design the nests.

"Father Joe," Carlos said with a slight nod of respect. "I hear you are in need of assistance."

"You come to care for the child?" Joe asked hopefully.

Carlos laughed. "Father Joe, I am here at Alethea's request to build you a nest."

Joe felt betrayed. He wanted to be in his quarters reading his Bible and praying!

Carlos remained clean as he worked. With the help of a long sharp knife, he cleared the runners from the stalks. In no time, and with little effort, the nest stood straight and strong. Joe was unsure how he had managed it.

As the foundation settled in place, the vines stopped oozing. Yet the vines in the basket continued to slowly leak. Carlos used tree sap to seal the outside of the basket so it would hold the liquid. Soon there was just enough creamy goo to fill half the basket.

"Here," Alethea said as she handed Joe his cocoon. "You must turn the child several times a day, Father."

"Why?" he asked.

"So the outside does not dry out," she said.

"How do you know this?" he said.

Alethea laughed. "Father, I have been caring for my cocoon for almost eight days. I have learned much," she said. "How old is yours?"

"It came this morning, early," he said. "I have to come every day?"

"Several times each day, Father."

He roughly took the thing.

It will interfere with my Bible studies and prayers, he complained to himself and plopped the thing in the liquid.

If I cannot endure the turning of the thing, how can I raise a child? Truly, I am not parent material. He feared for the welfare of the child and his future as a priest.

He again sought to be rid of it, and in desperation asked Alethea if she would please take it off his hands.

130

She smiled sweetly and shook her head. "No, Father, the duty is yours."

He feared she was right.

"Why did you take the child in the first place?" she asked.

"I thought it my duty."

"That is a poor reason," she said. "You are priest. Did you not first pray? Or did you act without consulting your God?"

"I forgot to pray." Joe felt a hint of shame. He who continually reminded others of the importance of prayer had not sought God's guidance before he'd acted on such an important decision as this.

In truth, it never occurred to him to pray. Perhaps in his pride he thought God would be proud of him. Now he didn't seek God's will for fear of what He might say. Joe didn't want to be stuck raising a child. As long as God had not spoken on the matter, there was always a chance he could get out of it.

"And have you spoken to Him as of late?"

Joe cringed at her question.

Perhaps he should pray. Perhaps in His mercy, God would relieve Joe of this thing and lead him to the one who would truly love and care for it.

Alethea continued, "So you took no thought or consideration for yourself or your beliefs?"

"Of course not," Joe said a little too defensively. "I knew it was wrong to just abandon the child."

"And you are the only one in all of the Community who was worthy of such a task?"

Joe stared at her in confusion. He had not thought himself worthy, but how annoyed he was. "No one else was willing," he said weakly. "I could not just let the thing die."

"Now that you've had time to think about it, your selfishness is objecting." The name Alethea was Greek for truth. And in truth, she had spoken.

131

Even though the words were spoken so as not to offend, it felt as if she was holding a mirror, forcing him to confront the reality of his true nature.

Because his speech was temperate and did not gossip or curse another, he thought he knew love. Joe's so-called love was his greatest pride. *Pride cometh before a fall.* He felt himself slipping off his self-made pedestal.

Again this mother, so full of compassion and wisdom, smiled angelically. "When you come, do not turn the cocoon and leave. There is a child inside who needs your love. You can turn the cocoon all you want, but it is your love that truly nourishes the little one."

A scripture reference came to mind: *Though I do all, without love, I am only a resounding gong or clanging cymbal.*

"I don't understand," Joe said.

"Sing, speak, read your Bible to the child," she said. "The cocoon itself is no more real than a rock. It is the person inside who needs you."

She began to sing a love song to her child.

After a moment's hesitation, Joe joined Alethea and they sang to their children together.

Father Joseph Striken's Personal Entry

Instead of pleading that God relieve me of the child, I have repented for my lack of love.

Now I speak to my child, about the day's events, and read children's Bible stories to her, or him. I have stopped calling my child "it" or "the thing." Instead I say, My Little Heart.

Alethea is an angel from God. With her help my heart has softened. Reading the Bible teaches me about God, but loving My Little Heart is helping me to understand the true nature of God.

Chapter 14

Rona Montgomery
Unbelievable

Akiane Date: Year 328
Endurance: Scientists' Quarters

RONA COULDN'T believe her eyes. She reexamined Olivia's files. It took several seconds for her brain to process the information but was she interpreting it correctly?

Lu muttered, "Ohmygod," and Rona finally realized the truth of what she was seeing.

Olivia had sent them a sequencing map of the retrovirus that she'd found in the fish. It wasn't defective like that of the colonists. It had the complete RNA— ribonucleic acid—with instructions. How was that possible? Where did it come from? How did Olivia find it?

Lu grabbed Rona's arm and shook it. "This is where the new protein comes from," she squealed.

"You don't know for sure," Rona said. "We must be cautious and not jump to conclusions."

"Even so, we at least have the *means* to find a cure," Lu said.

Rona knew she shouldn't get caught up in Lu's overly optimistic opinion but she could help herself. This was what they had been hoping for. If they were gong to find a cure, this was the first step.

Olivia left her work area to join Rona and Lu and plopped down between them. She placed a white plastic container on the floor.

Rona and Lu were grinning from ear to ear. "Thank you so much," Lu said. "You can't believe what this means to us."

"Yes I can," Olivia said.

"Where . . . how did you find this?" Rona asked.

"I found a fish breeding colony three days ago." Olivia spoke nonchalantly as if she'd found a really good novel that they should read.

She'd known for three days about the RNA, while Rona and Lu were in a frenzy trying to find a cure for a dying baby. Olivia knew about their research, and she'd waited *three days* to tell them what she had found!

"Why didn't you tell us sooner?" Lu scolded.

Rona had never seen her so upset. She didn't blame Lu; she was just as upset. How was it possible for anyone to be as inconsiderate as Olivia?

"I report to you now instead of WSC?" Olivia retorted.

"Olivia, that's not what Lu meant and you know it," Rona said. "A baby's life is at stake. She'll die without our help. If we'd had this information three days ago, who knows what we might have accomplished by now."

"Excuse me for not being at your beck and call," Olivia said.

"Fine," Rona said. "Do you have anything else to share or are you leaving so we can get on with our work?"

"You don't have to be so snippy," Olivia said.

Rona wanted to tell Olivia to get out, but Lu said, "Tell us what else you discovered."

Olivia smiled as one with a great secret. "The fry that come from a nest do not have the retrovirus, but their dams do." She held up her hand to stop them from speaking.

Lu couldn't help herself. "Proof the retrovirus is not passed on genetically to the next generation."

"But, we found fish that carry their young in a pouch like seahorses, or mouthbrooders, similar to, Ariidae . . ."

"What is Ariidae?" Lu interrupted.

"Sea Catfish. There are 143 species, which include 43 freshwater species," Olivia said, annoyed that she had to explain this to them. "Ariidae are mouthbrooders. The dam or sire, that's the mother or father, collect their eggs and carry them in their mouth until their eggs hatch and become baby fish, which are called fry."

"We know what mouthbrooders are, Olivia, and what a dam, sire, and fry are. What we don't know is the name of every fish in the ocean," Rona said.

Olivia's face contorted; she was ready with a comeback but Lu cut her off, "Olivia, what did you learn about mouthbrooders."

Her eyes darted between Lu and Rona trying to decide what to do. She turned to Lu and answered, "The fry of the mouthbrooders and the pouchcarriers have the defective retrovirus. Their parents' retrovirus is not defective. They and the nesters all have the missing RNA. Nesters are fish who make nests to lay . . ."

"Olivia!" Rona scolded. *Just how ignorant does she think we are?*

"The nesters' fry do not have the retrovirus," Olivia finished.

"What?" Lu and Rona asked at the same time. "How is that possible?"

"We think it's because the mouthbrooders and the pouchcarriers have continual contact with their eggs, which infects the eggs, but the enzyme is not passed on. We don't know why," Olivia said.

"And we don't know how the uninfected fry become infected. You interrupted our studies." Olivia took a deep breath. "But since you asked for my files, I thought you might also be interested in this." She handed them the container she'd brought with her.

Lu grabbed it before Olivia had time to change her mind and leave with it. She lifted the lid and her face lit up. She showed it to Rona. Her mouth dropped open. There were eight vials in the storage container. "Olivia, what is this?"

"Samples of the complete RNA."

This could be the clue they needed. Lu threw her arms around Olivia's neck. Olivia didn't like hugs. Rona expected her to explode into a tirade. Instead, she smiled and hugged Lu back.

It was as if Olivia was two completely different people and rarely anything in between. Rona never knew which person to expect, but when Olivia was nice, she was really, really nice. And when she wasn't, everyone ran for cover.

Olivia started to get up, but stopped. Most of the time she was in such a sour mood it was a surprise to see how pretty she was when she smiled. Now that she was happy she actually glowed.

"This really is the most amazing place, isn't it? There are so many mysteries to unravel and we're standing on the foundation of every research project related to Akiane."

Olivia laughed as if she didn't have a care in the world.

"I'm thinking of spending my entire career right here on Akiane."

She jumped up and hurried back to her studies.

Rona and Lu stared at each other, stunned at the mood change.

"Rona, what just happened?"

"I have no idea, Lu."

They should have done more extensive testing, but there wasn't time.

Rona and Lu used one vile of blood from the mother and one from the child, and separated white blood cells from the blood fluid to release their DNA. The defective retrovirus was causing cell degradation, which could be why the colonists were dying.

Lu placed a section of the sticky blob of DNA on a slide, added a drop of fish retrovirus, and locked it under a microscope. They watched the results on the holo-screen. The new retrovirus merged with the defective retrovirus, allowing mRNA to deliver its message. They watched in fascination as the retrovirus repaired its host's DNA.

It worked for both the mother and child's DNA. They ran several more tests just to make sure the first test was not a fluke. It worked every time. They needed to perform more tests on more subjects, but they didn't have more subjects or more time. The best they could hope for was that the tests they performed would be all they needed to save the child. It *had* to work.

Late that afternoon Rona and Lu returned to the path where they first met Qorow Low. They slipped in among the bushes where no one would see them.

"What if she doesn't come?" Lu asked.

"We decided to come here at this time every day for an update. She'll come," Rona said.

"But what if something happ . . ."

"She'll come, Lu. Let's talk about something else."

They did until they heard the leaves rustle.

Qorow Low asked them the same question every time.

"You have a cure?"

It wasn't difficult to know what she was thinking. She wanted to believe, but her fear kept her from truly hoping for the best.

"We can't give you any guarantees, but we do have something we'd like to try. We won't know if it will work unless we test it," Rona said.

"But it might work?" Qorow Low asked encouraged.

It was wrong to try to convince the mother to use her child as a test subject for an idea that had not been thoroughly studied. If they failed, WSC could recall them and they could lose their careers.

"We hope so," Rona said.

"Can we see Sharhr?" Lu asked.

Qorow Low opened her winter jacket and unstrapped her baby from her chest. She lowered her arms so her baby rested in her hands and Lu could examine her. The mother had come to trust them because they had made Community. Therefore, she allowed Lu to touch and scan her baby.

Her baby was blue-gray, barely breathing, and had lost nearly all her hair.

The first time Rona saw her, Sharhr had looked ill. Now she looked one breath away from death. She feared they were too late. No matter what they tried, the child would not recover.

Qorow Low studied her daughter's face. "Sharhr, my one and only love." She waited but no response came.

Rona decided the truth was the best course of action.

"It's doubtful this will work," she said.

Tears rolled down Qorow Low's face. She nodded. "I am with understanding."

"We need more testing," Rona said.

"Understanding is path to truth. Testing others will help you learn?" Qorow Low asked.

"Yes, and it will help us help your people," Rona said.

"You only have my daughter."

"Yes."

"You can test my beautiful daughter, but you must also test me," Qorow Low said.

"That's not a good idea," Lu said. "We don't know how it will affect you."

"There might be a cure, yes?" Qorow Low asked.

Neither Rona nor Lu had the courage to answer. Their training on Moon Base had not prepared them for this.

"You hope," Qorow Low said.

"Yes," Rona admitted.

"If it will not cure, why give it to her?" Qorow Low asked.

"If there is a very slim chance, we would like to try." *Even if it means our careers,* Rona thought. "But if she does not get better, we were hoping after her . . ." Rona couldn't say "death."

Qorow Low closed her eyes, and very softly said, "I am with understanding."

"Will you give us her body?" It was a difficult question to ask, but Rona knew it needed to be asked.

Qorow Low held her baby closer and bit her lip.

"If we can see what effect the serum has on her, it might help us to learn something," Lu said.

"How will you do such a thing?" Qorow Low asked.

Lu hurried to answer her. "We have medical equipment that will allow us to see inside her body without cutting her open."

"We will not harm her body," Rona reassured her.

"Can you do it here with me?"

"Our equipment is at our work area. You would have to come with us." Rona patiently waited while Qorow Low considered her request.

"You are truthful in wanting to help. But I am unable to make known our union," Qorow Low said.

"May we give your daughter the serum?" Rona asked.

"Also me."

"That's not a good idea, Qorow Low," Lu said.

"Understanding is path to truth. The more you test, the more you learn, yes?"

"Yes," Rona said.

"My beautiful daughter may not live, but I will," Qorow Low said. "Test us both or have no learning."

"We only have one syringe," Rona said.

"I will wait."

"Would it be all right if we kept Sharhr for observation?" Rona asked even thought she knew the answer. "It would help us with our research."

With great emotions, Qorow Low shook her head. "This is the only time . . ." She had trouble speaking. "I will try to bring her body to you."

"I understand. This is the only time you have with her. But if you are both to be injected, it would be helpful if you both stayed with us for a few days."

She held Sharhr against her cheek. "I cannot." More tears came. "He would not understand."

"He who?"

She buried her face in Sharhr's blankets and turned away. "No," she whispered. "I cannot."

Lu pulled out a second syringe.

"Where did that come from?" Rona asked.

"I prepared an extra just in case she might also want an injection," Lu said.

"Why didn't you tell me, Lu?"

"I didn't want to cause another argument."

Rona nodded. "I am with understanding."

Mother and child both received the serum.

When they had cured Vong, Lu injected his palm at the site of his infection.

The mother and child's infection had spread throughout their bodies, so Lu injected the serum in an artery in their necks, allowing the blood flow to carry the nanobots throughout their bodies.

Lu was ready, but Rona still wanted to wait until they'd gathered more information. Even so, she gave Lu the go ahead.

They would meet the following day at their usual time and take samples of Qorow Low's and her child's blood.

"I wish we could keep them overnight for observation," Lu said as they watched Qorow Low slip into the brush.

"Me too, Lu. Unfortunately, we can only do what we can do," Rona said.

"It will mean a lot if we can get the baby's body," Lu said.

"I'll be really surprised if we do get it," Rona said.

"Why?"

"Adumie."

"You think she'll tell him?" Lu asked.

"You know how difficult it is to keep a secret in a small community. She won't say anything, but someone else might."

"I'm going to check with Terzo to see what he found Dr. Beasley's medical logs," Lu said. "He's had trouble finding them."

Rona was in no mood to chase down a rabbit hole with Lu about some phantom medical logs.

They walked back in silence.

Chapter 15

Adumie
New Relationships

Akiane Date: Year 328
Endurance: Colonists' Quarters

BECAUSE OF the slow dying illness, Community no longer thrived as it once had.

Each individual family unit was descended from a particular settler who first came to Akiane. As each family unit grew to over 75 people and became too large for one room, they tore down the walls on either side so they could expand.

As they reached 200 that unit of people would split into three groups and take over the surrounding rooms near the original room.

A group of family units became a family cluster. All together family clusters made up Community.

The slow dying illness gradually reduced family clusters back down to one room. As Community reduced in numbers, smaller families decided to move in together.

At first, families stayed true to their units and gathered their personal things and cots together, leaving walking spaces between each group. It didn't take long for those individual family units to break down, too.

More families moved in, but there wasn't room for them to have their own separate space. Instead they were offered cots that had been emptied because of the illness. People mingled. Mere acquaintances became close friends. Cots were rearranged by friendship instead of family.

Community comforted each other over the loss of their loved ones. As a whole, Community cared for the dying even if the ill person was not in their family unit.

In the past, as members of a family could no longer perform their work duties, other members of that family would take over their duties. Now, Community helped with the workload without the division of families. For the first time, the people of Akiane truly had become a Community.

To Adumie's surprise, such relationships made Community stronger.

When Qorow Low's family unit moved in, she placed her cot next to Adumie.

Since this was not proper, he demanded—loudly—that she return to her family's area. He expected her to comply. She simply dropped her head in deference, but did not obey. He moved his cot, like a loyal chovis, she followed. Three times he moved his cot; three times she followed.

He ignored her, hoping she would eventually leave. She did not.

Adumie stayed away from the areas where she worked, so they would have little contact during the day. He came to his cot late each night expecting her to be asleep. She was not.

She would lie awake waiting for him. Her loving smile would spread across her face when she saw him. Without a word, he would lie with his back to her. As soon as her breathing changed and he knew she was asleep, he would roll over and watch her.

Her feelings for him were a mystery. His growing feelings for her became an even bigger mystery.

She was not pretty. Nor was she cute as her name, Qorow Low, claimed. She was not ugly, but she did possess something that Adumie did not have—peace.

As he watched her, her peacefulness drifted toward him. And for the first time in many years, his dreams were not disturbed by his sorrow for Petra.

In the morning, he woke to find her watching him. As soon as his eyes opened, she smiled.

One day, he smiled back.

Qorow Low had been so excited when her daughter Sharhr came forth from her cocoon alive. The child was sickly; it was clear she would not live long.

In her innocence, Qorow Low did not dwell on the inevitable. Instead, she rejoiced that she was able to hold her child and talk to her and love her, at least for a few days.

Every other child was speaking and walking within an hour of coming forth. For three whole days Sharhr got worse. On the fourth day, she spoke her first words.

She repeated said her life-giver's words, but not with the same clarity. "I uv oo."

Everyone cheered when Sharhr took her first wobbly steps on day five.

On the sixth night, Sharhr lay down to sleep and did not wake up. The following morning, her little body had deflated.

Grief caused Qorow Low to lie down as if she might never rise again.

Adumie feared her death. Who would greet him each morning with a smile? He feared without the light of her smile, darkness would again overtake him.

Adumie pulled his cot next to hers. His knees nearly touched her cot. He rested his forearms on his knees, leaned forward, and watched her intently. He wanted to remember every bit of her face, the gentle curve of her cheeks, the unforgettable shape of her nose, the soft sound of her breathing.

She opened her eyes just a little.

He smiled.

"Do not be angry," she softly whispered.

Adumie gently passed gloved fingers over Qorow Low's hair. He did not care that it was forbidden.

"It is not possible for one to be angry with you." He truly meant it.

She had become his closest friend. He ached to comfort her and hold her in his arms. Forbidden.

When Qorow Low joined Sharhr in death, Adumie's heart would once again be ripped open as when Petra had died.

Adumie had betrayed God by loving Petra too much. God punished him by taking her from him. She was one of the first to succumb to the slow dying sickness.

Now Qorow Low was dying, because, Adumie had once again loved another before God.

"Trying to say. Be angry with me; no one else." Her gentle voice was devoid of emotion.

His hand froze. "What did you do? Who should receive my anger?" He pulled his hand away.

"Explain," he said.

Pain seized Qorow Low, stealing her breath. Adumie would gladly have given her his breath, but he could only watch helplessly.

As her pain eased, her breath returned, but she wheezed as she spoke, "I brought Sharhr to off-worlders."

Inconceivable. She was the one person he thought would always stand with him, even if they did not always agree. He never thought that she would betray him. That was something Cameron or Jecidia would do, not Qorow Low.

"Why would you do such a thing?" he asked.

"Hole in my heart," she said. "Sharhr was the way of other children. Could not accept. Two off-worlders . . ." She was having difficulty speaking. "Hoped would heal."

"What did intruders do?" He was furious, not with Qorow Low, but with intruders' continual interference and lies of hope.

"Put something in Sharhr's neck. Said was nano . . .," she paused trying to remember the exact words, ". . . tiny machines made to heal."

"You did as any life-giver would in time of desperation," he said, perhaps a little too harshly.

He forced a smile to reassure her, so she would not see the true intensity of his fury.

She was not fooled. The face, which he loved, grimaced.

He wanted to be with her until her last breath. Now, he could not. He would deal with intruders. At least, there was comfort in knowing Qorow Low would not be alone.

No one in the Community died alone. Someone was always at their side, even while they slept, not just for their care, but to comfort.

It was something for which Adumie was grateful. Qorow Low would be made as comfortable as possible until she made the journey to the other side, where she would join those who had gone before her.

Jecidia was among those who had come to console but was not close enough to be intruding on Adumie's time with Qorow Low. That one never truly trusted Adumie as high priest. He stood in the shadows ready to express his disapproval of Adumie's leadership.

He did not want Jecidia to die, but in his case, his illness was taking too long. He had suffered more than any. Once tall and proud, he could no longer hold his size and had been reduced to a withered old man. Every aspect of life, from breathing to sleeping, was difficult for him. Still, he refused to give in.

147

Jecidia walked Endurance as if he were healthy and still high priest. He held his body erect as if he were still the size of a priest and not the size of a subordinate. He expected to be heard and listened to when he spoke, especially when his opinion contradicted Adumie.

Now he had come to pass judgment on Adumie's last moments with Qorow Low. As if in respect, Jecidia had stood to one side of Adumie's cot with his hands clasped behind his back. But now, he stepped forward to intrude.

"Sharhr would have died no matter what off-worlders did," Jecidia said, in defense of Intruders.

As much as he hated to admit it, the withered one was right. No matter how much Qorow Low lavished love on Sharhr, she could not have saved the child. Still, intruders had no right to interfere with their treachery of optimism.

Qorow Low was dying of grief because of those lies.

"But they may also be the cause of Qorow Low's death," Jecidia continued.

Adumie leaped to his feet. His cot skidded away. "What does he mean?"

She moaned. "I thought . . . ," she said. "I was with hope."

Adumie hated the way she shrank from him in fear. Her reaction stopped him from speaking words of harshness that burned on his tongue. A growl of disgust escaped from deep within.

How could Qorow Low risk her life thus? Because of her foolish faith she had allowed off-worlders to steal the last precious moments of her life—time that belonged to Adumie.

"Why would you do such a thing?" he demanded.

"If off-worlders cured my Sharhr, they would cure all," she said.

"Who did this to you?"

"Those of Earth warned me it might not work," Qorow Low said timidly.

"Then why do it?" Adumie asked accusingly.

148

"So they could learn."

"Who, Qorow Low? Who would learn?"

She shook her head.

"I want names."

She shook her head.

"The dark one, Rona, and the one who stands at her side, Lu," Jecidia said.

"The small one is her child or her subordinate?" Adumie demanded.

"I am unsure," Jecidia said.

"Not like us," Qorow Low said. "Do not show honor in size. All are equals."

"No, they are not like us," Adumie said. "Those of Earth have no respect."

From under the covers, Qorow Low's gloved hand reached out to him. "You must promise me," she said.

He shrank away. "What?" He did not mean for his voice to be so callous but his fury raged. "What must I promise?"

Adumie very much wanted to grant her last request but he had an ominous feeling that he was not going to like it.

"Give Sharhr and my body to Rona and Lu."

The thought was revolting. "Why do such a thing? Why would you ask such a thing?"

If he did as she asked, there would be no funeral, no last words spoken over her body. There would be no procession to bring her body to open waters where she would be laid to rest. She would never join those who had gone before. Most important: Adumie would never be able to join her in the afterlife.

"Please," Qorow Low pleaded.

In an effort not to upset her, Adumie again sat on his cot but he did not pull it closer. "Tell me. Why give Intruders your bodies?" How could he possibly do such a thing when he could barely say the words?

"So they can learn," she said.

149

Jecidia shifted his feet. "It is imperative that their bodies be given to the off-worlders." He might have said more, but Adumie silenced the withered one with a raise of his hand.

Adumie could not bring himself to say no to Qorow Low, nor could he say yes just to please her. She would never know of his final decision.

Jecidia would object. Adumie would deal with that one later.

Her expression knotted in pain. "I do not feel well. I feel my insides are changing," her voice was brittle.

"They have made you worse." A vile hatred rose in Adumie.

As if exhaling part of her soul, she let out a shallow sigh and closed her eyes.

"We must decide how to fulfill Qorow Low's request," Jecidia spoke softly so as not to disturb her.

Adumie knew what to do. He did not need this meddling one's advice. He rose to his full height. "Yes, something will be done."

Qorow Low's eyes fluttered opened. "Do not be angry. They want to help," she pleaded weakly. "Please, for the sake of Community."

"You were already ill and would have died before the fullness of your years. Now off-worlders have stolen away what time you had left. I will be without your company. You ask me not to be angry?"

"Adumie," she whispered. She was having difficulty keeping her eyes opened.

"It is unclear if she dies from the illness or is suffering from a broken heart," Jecidia said. "She might still live once she has grieved."

Adumie did not receive the words spoken as comfort. When Petra died, Adumie's heart seemed to have deserted him and had become hard as lava rock. Qorow Low had melted that hardness.

He felt his heart hardening once again.

Too weak to stay awake any longer, Qorow Low slipped into a deep sleep.

Adumie called to one of Qorow Low's family members, Melar.

She came quickly to his side.

"Stay with her," he said as he pulled his cot closer for her to sit. "Tend to her needs."

Melar bowed her head. "By my honor."

In a softer voice, he said, "Send word of any changes."

"Immediately," she promised.

Adumie left. He heard Jecidia shuffling behind him. His pace increased.

"What are your plans?" Jecidia's breath became shallow. He sucked in deep breaths between his words. Still he strove to keep up.

Adumie did not slow down nor did he answer the meddling one's question.

"I do not think it is a good idea," Jecidia said.

Many times Adumie had threatened to throw intruders outside in the snow and frigid temperatures and close the entrance doors behind them. Perhaps it was time to fulfill his threats.

Intruders wanted Akiane let them see what Akiane was really like.

"Adumie, if off-worlders die, Earth may avenge their deaths."

"It will take many years for an Earth vessel to return," Adumie called back. "There will be no one to avenge when we are all dead."

He left Jecidia standing alone, desperately trying to catch his breath.

Chapter 16

Rona Montgomery
Closed Doors

Akiane Date: Year 328
Endurance: Scientists' Quarters

RONA DECIDED she'd had enough.

She went to her bunk bed, pulled a pair of scissors out of her pack, sat on her bed, bent over, and started cutting.

Long black coarse curls fell to the floor.

Rona stood and scanned the thirty-six beds, set side by side in neat rows like kernels on a corncob with just enough room to walk between them. Most beds were neatly made, with all personal items properly stored in luggage and tucked underneath their beds. But there were those whose unmade beds were cluttered with combs, hairbrushes, toothbrushes, and sleepwear along with other personal items. Rona didn't understand how scientists could be so meticulous about research and be so careless with their personal things. At least the beds near her were well-ordered.

The bunk to her left was Jess', neatly made with her duffel bag on top as if awaiting her return.

Every morning, that duffle bag was a reminder that Rona had no idea where Jess was, what had happened to her, or even if she was still alive. If only she could call or send a message but without satellites orbiting the planet to transmit communications, it was impossible to speak to Jess. Rona could only wait, hope, pray, and wait some more.

With sixty-five men in the next dorm room, Rona couldn't dress as casually as she liked. Every morning she had to shower, dress, and brush her hair and teeth before she entered the living area.

The few men and women who had been distastefully relaxed in their dress code now adhered to the unwritten rules of appropriate dress to avoid verbal objections.

That was why she had decided to cut her hair. No electric plugs in the dorm rooms meant no hair dryers, which equaled to uncontrollable hair. Less hair meant less work.

"Maybe that wasn't such a good idea." Rona said to the disheveled image in the mirror.

"Rona!" Beth called as she intered the dorm room. "Oh, my." She ran to her friend. "What happened to you?"

"I had a moment of . . . of . . . insanity," she said.

"I'll say," Beth said.

"I'm tired of fighting with my hair every single morning."

"Give me those scissors."

Beth reshaped Rona's hair into a reasonably behaved Afro.

"You've done this before," Rona said.

"Four sisters and three brothers," Beth said. "We couldn't afford so many haircuts."

"I'm surprised your family was so large," Rona said. "I didn't think people had that many children anymore."

"Well, Mother wanted a large family and Father usually gave her what she wanted," Beth said. "Mother wasn't spoiled." She laughed. "Well, not much, anyway; he just loved her, a lot."

"Beth!" a voice called from outside the dorm room. "What's taking you so long?"

"That's Avil. I'll finish up tonight and I promise you'll look great." Beth handed Rona the scissors. "But right now you have to come outside. You're not going to believe this."

Beth ran out of the room. "Coming, coming."

Rona studied her image in the mirror. She liked what she saw. It was a good day to have a new haircut. It matched her new feelings of victory.

The first two months of her arrival had been a disappointment, but in six days she and Lu had made a significant breakthrough. They still didn't have all the answers, but each step was bringing them closer. They'd treated the mother and child, and met with them every day at the same time. Each day had brought small signs of improvement.

The blotches that had covered the sides of the mother's face had faded. The baby girl had spoken her first words and had taken her first steps. Good signs both were getting better.

Rona and Lu were so excited they could barely contain their joy. But because the mother didn't want Adumie to know just yet, they promised not to say anything to their friends, just in case they accidently spoke about it when someone in Community could overhear.

Each time they met, Lu took blood samples and immediately processed them. If things continued to progress, it was a sign that all was well. The mother could share the good news with her people and there would be a flood of happy colonists calling.

Rona expected she would be the last at breakfast and have to settle for whatever was left over. She stepped out of the dorm room and saw that everyone was gathered at the far end of the room at the bay door, it was closed—again.

She quickly joined the others.

The last time they'd awakened to find the bay door closed, it was in anticipation of the coming gravitation storm. Instead of an explanation as to what was about to happen so they could prepare, Adumie had closed and locked the bay door, trapping them inside. It wasn't until the earthquakes toppled over tables and shattered their breakfast that they understood what was happening.

They spent that terrifying night locked up, listening to the equivalent of sonic booms erupting from the nearby volcano, and half expecting the habitat to come tumbling down on them.

Spago did his best to calm nerves by explaining the sonic explosions and earthquakes. He reassured them the habitat had been built with self-healing material. It would survive The Storm and so would they.

The Storm ended.

The building survived.

Their nerves were still fragile.

Rona heard Lu say, "Please, not another storm." She was crying softly, leaning against Spago. His arms protectively wrapped around her.

Those two are certainly becoming an item, Rona thought.

Olivia was on the verge of hysteria. She was pacing, turning in circles, and clawing at the long sleeves of her blouse. "I can't go through that again," she cried.

Ever the white knight, Jorge stopped Olivia and held her in his arms. Her head rested on the middle of his chest.

Several women and men had experienced a panic attack during The Storm. Dr. Lesley gave them a sedative to help calm them.

This morning, he came prepared. He slipped through the crowd carrying a tray of glasses of water and a small box of white capsules.

"It's not my policy to give out tranquilizers indiscriminately," Lesley said, "but in this case, if anyone else needs one, let me know."

"Let's wait and see what's happening first," Gino said. "Take one only if you are truly upset."

Olivia had fought Lesley that first night, but this time, she took the pill, closed her eyes, took a deep breath, and relaxed.

Rona didn't want to go through another gravitational storm. That awful night she, like the others, feared they might all die. She'd hoped to be off this godforsaken planet before the next storm hit. She started to shake.

Maybe I need a tranquilizer, she thought.

Mathieu took Rona's hand. She leaned against him for comfort. She hadn't taken the time to get to know him while they were on *Britannia*. When she became depressed at the loss of her Genome Project, Dr. Mathieu Rutger became her psychological knight in shining armor. Through his counseling she got over Jorge, started working on the Canine Project, and to her delight, discovered a budding relationship with him.

"What's happening," she whispered.

"No one knows." Mathieu seemed nervous, until he looked at Rona and asked, "What happened to you?"

Rona blushed. "Oh, you don't like it!" Her hand flew to her hair.

"I love it," Mathieu said. "I'm just surprised. What inspired you?"

"I'll tell you later," she whispered.

Spago's crisp voice rose above the others. "There's nothing happening at the mountains," he said. "It's quiet. In fact, the volcano has once again become dormant. The last time there was plenty of evidence that a volcano was about to erupt. Now there's nothing."

"What if this is a different disaster?" Beth asked, her eyes wide with concern.

"It has nothing to do with the gas giant," astrophysics Bonga said. "The planet Loki has moved on, and there's nothing new, not a planet, comet, or anything astronomical happening out of the ordinary."

"Enough!" Gino's loud voice quieted all others. "Don't expect the worst. The colonists could have closed the bay door because of something any one of us did. They don't like us, remember."

"Maybe they found another chovis with a radio attached to its ear," a voice suggested.

"We retrieved all the radio tags from the puppies in the habitat," Lu said.

"They could be upset because Gino's taking too many rocks," Jorge said.

"Or Jorge for studying their algae," Avil suggested.

"It could be anything or everything," Gino said.

Lu's head pivoted as she scanned the crowd searching for Rona. Their eyes met.

Rona knew what she was thinking. This didn't have anything to do with radio tags. This was about the mother and child.

Rona nodded. Something had gone wrong or the colonists would be thanking them, not imprisoning them. A sick feeling of dread hit her. Maybe the treatment hadn't worked after all. She desperately wanted to find out. She needed to examine the mother and child to learn what had gone wrong. She had to fix it. She couldn't find a cure with her hands tied like this.

Fear clouded her thoughts. It would be almost two years before the next ship arrived and she would be required to report on her progress to her adviser at Moon Base.

Rona wanted something besides the research from the Canine Project to send to WCS. She wanted something substantial on the Pegasus Genome Project.

She really wanted to prove herself to . . . whom?

157

Her father? He was too far away and would never know or care what she did, or if she had succeeded or failed. No, not him. Then who? Adumie? Why would she care what he thought?

WSC Research Team?

She very much cared what they thought. They had believed in her and had commissioned her with an important project. This was supposed to define her professional career, not become a career-ending failure.

Lu and she were supposed to meet with the mother at their usual time. They wouldn't be meeting them today.

Would Qorow Low know why they weren't there? What if she didn't and thought they had abandoned her? What if she couldn't meet because she was 'dead, and that was why the door was locked.

"Let's prepare just in case there is a storm," Gino said. "It will give us something to do besides worry."

Rona and Lu exchanged looks. They'd promised the mother to keep her secret. Should they say something? Lu shook her head and walked with Spago to his work area to help him place his equipment on the floor. Rona stayed with Mathieu.

Tables were turned upside down. Chairs were laid on their backs. With some help, their cook, Vong, placed pots, dishware, and spice jars on the kitchen floor.

In the dorms, personal items were safely packed, bunk beds turned upside down and luggage placed on them.

The storage cabinet was too big to take apart and put back together so they left it as it was. With everything else taken care of, it would be easy to take the cabinet apart if needed.

Once finished, they huddled in groups in the middle of the bay area and waited, just as they had that long night.

During The Storm, Rona and Lu sat together with Jorge, Olivia, and Mathieu. This time, Lu sat with Spago and his team. Mathieu and Lesley joined Rona, Jorge, and Olivia.

Time lingered. Tension mounted. Nerves frayed. They spoke in whispers, as if talking too loudly might hurry the inevitable, but the inevitable didn't come.

Vong prepared a late afternoon lunch. A few offered to help, while the others righted the tables and chairs in the dining area.

They ate in silence.

Lu pulled Rona aside. "We forgot about our tests."

"I don't think now is the time, Lu."

"Rona, we should at least check on the centrifuge and properly save the samples from last night until we're ready to continue."

"You're right."

Lu opened the centrifuge and pulled out the first tube. She stopped and stared at it.

"Whose blood is that?" Rona asked.

Lu checked the label. Her head drooped. "The child's."

Rona took the vial from her. The blood had turned black.

"She's dead isn't she?" Lu asked.

"Yes, I think so," Rona said. "It wasn't our fault, Lu. We did the best we could."

"We could have done better if Olivia . . ."

"Stop," Rona said quietly. "This is not her fault either."

"But . . ."

"No, don't. Blame won't help. That little baby girl was too far gone and we knew it," Rona said. "Are all the samples like that?"

Lu pulled the other two vials belonging to the baby. "Yes."

"The mother?"

Lu hesitated. "I can't." She turned her head away and sniffed back a tear.

Rona pulled out one of the mother's vials. The top layer of plasma was clear, a thin layer of leukocytes, white blood cells. The bottom layer—bright red blood cells.

"Lu, look, the mother's blood is normal," Rona said in relief.

Lu whipped her head around, wide-eyed with surprise. "This is good news, right?"

"I certainly do hope so. We won't know for sure until we examine her," Rona said.

"Which we can't do if we're locked up in here." Lu's grief was replaced with anger.

"I'm betting she'll be all right, Lu," Rona said.

"So you think we're locked up because of the child?" Lu said.

"The baby died. I'm betting Adumie knows and is angry," Rona said. "I think we should tell the others. They have a right to know."

"Agreed."

"Well," Olivia said after they'd finished explaining the whole story, "Adumie said if we interfered again, he'd throw us out." She was surprisingly calm.

Rona wondered if the tranquilizer was still working.

"I guess being locked in here is better than being thrown outside," Olivia said.

Everyone agreed.

Rona sighed in relief. They didn't blame her or Lu. They were her friends and were scientists dedicated to research. They understood it was the colonists who were being unreasonable.

If only Adumie understood. As high priest, all his people faithfully followed him. Not one of them, not even Qorow Low, would challenge him.

If only I could gain Adumie's approval. She grimaced at the thought.

It was an unfortunate truth; Rona needed his approval. She'd gone behind his back hoping to earn his support through victory.

It was like the chicken and the egg. She couldn't have one without the other. But for her, both the chicken and egg were like sand slipping through her fingers, and there was nothing she could do about it.

And now, because of her, everyone was imprisoned in their living quarters. What if Adumie kept them locked up until the next transport arrived—in two years?

Chapter 17

Akiane Historical Chronicles
Father Joseph Striken Personal Entry

Akiane Date: Year 27
Endurance: 2 1/2 months after Faris' heart attack

THINGS ARE getting worse, Faris has not left her bed in weeks, not since the death of the first child born in a cocoon. Beasley says she has a bad heart. No matter what he does, his treatments are not helping.

I think she's dying of a broken heart because of the death of the newborn baby girl. No amount of my counseling has changed her mind. Not even the love of family or friends seems to be helping. The guilt is too great.

This happened to Faris once before when Harrie's puppies died.

Her father had the dog's life extended so she would live for the duration of the round trip to Akiane and back to Moon Base. She had been the only dog on the

162

planet. Yet, somehow, the dog unbelievably became pregnant.

To everyone's surprise, Harrie gave birth to a litter of puppies, each in their own cocoon. We had never seen such a thing and had no idea what to do. All the puppies died. Faris slipped into a deep depression.

She had dealt well with all that happened when we first arrived, Eagle exploding and Hawk battered by monstrous waves. Tragedy is a part of the dangers of space travel. Faris knew those deaths were not her fault, still she took every death personally.

The puppies' deaths were too much for her.

When Harrie became pregnant again, the possibility of the second litter dying dropped Faris into a deeper depression.
What she didn't know was that by some miracle of God, Little Harrie had dug up native vines that would save her litter. With the help of her nose, she showed me how to wrap the cocoons in the vines.

The possibility that those pups might live brought Faris out of her depression. She carried a rocking chair to the vines, sat, hummed, and waited for them to come forth from their cocoons.

If the second litter had died, I'm not sure what would've happened to her. By the grace of God, those vines saved the puppies and Faris' life.

I do not see a similar miracle rescuing her this time. The death of Abir's child weighs too heavily upon her. I fear this time she will not recover.

163

Chapter 18

Akiane Historical Chronicles
Fatimah's Personal Entries

Akiane Date: Year 27
Endurance: The day of Faris' death

FATIMAH REMEMBERED all too well the first time she had stood on the caldera's edge and stared out over the serene ocean. Just like the desert, the waters stretched to the horizon, but unlike the desert, the ocean horizon seemed to merge with the sky that came back rolling over her head.

On the other side the of rim, The Storm had melted years of snow, turning the land into a muddy mess. Fatimah was not looking forward to the trees budding, grass sprouting, or wild flowers blooming. She wanted to go home.

WSC Falcon had arrived after The Storm after *WSC Falcon* had exploded and *WSC Hawk* had been battered beyond repair. So many had died. The settlement had failed before it had begun. Even though it would have been a strain on *Falcon's* resources, Fatimah thought it best to take the remaining survivors back to Moon Base.

Unfortunately, the survivors of *Hawk* and the settlers on *Falcon* wanted to stay and colonize the planet, but they couldn't do it alone. *Hawk's* engines were ruined. Without a power source, there would be no heat to keep the last of winter at bay, no electricity for lighting or cooking. Their hydroponic produce would fail. The settlers could not survive without *Falcon's* engine as their new energy source.

Faris volunteered her ship and crew to stay and help the survivors, but only until the next ship arrived.

Fatimah was one of the few who disagreed, but she and the others deferred to their captain's final decision. The next WSC transport was to bring more settlers and supplies, and would take *Falcon's* crew home.

Fatimah knew in her heart they would never leave the planet.

Loneliness had weighed heavily on her. She missed her home planet. She would never see her friends and family again. Her sister had given birth to children that she'd met on interplanetary communication, but she would never get to hug.

Communications to WSC Moon Base were down because of the solar flares.

Like a wet wool blanket, disappointment wrapped around Fatimah and seemed to suffocate her.

In time, the crew became part of the settlement. Akiane became their home and Fatimah and Faris began their 29-year friendship.

* * *

WSC Falcon had been Fatimah's first assignment, Faris Assetti her first captain.

Sergeants and captains didn't become friends. So how had it happened?

In a sense, their friendship started long before they arrived on the alien planet, even before they'd left on their trek across the stars. Fatimah knew the day they met that she would never serve another captain with the same loyalty that she would serve Captain Faris Assetti.

Once they came to the realization that they had been abandoned by WSC, military rank mattered little, captain and sergeant first class became friends.

Fatimah remembered the official beginning of their friendship.

"Fatimah," Faris had called.

"Yes, my captain." Fatimah saluted.

"How many times must I tell you to stop that?" Faris scolded in good humor.

"At least one more time, ma'am."

"Well, then on my command, stop it."

"Yes, ma' . . ."

"Sergeant! I want you to go back to your room, change out of your uniform, and pack it away. You are never to wear it again. Do you understand?"

Fatimah stood and stared at her. "I don't . . . I won't know who I am if I am not in Space Force, ma'am." Tears of disappointment started to fill her eyes. She was the last still wearing her uniform. If she took it off, it would be an admission that the life she had cherished on Earth and on Moon Base was over. What would happen to her then? What was left for her?

"I will help you figure it out," Faris said tenderly. "I even have a dress you might like to wear."

"A dress, ma'am?"

"Please, call me Faris."

"I'm not sure I can, ma'am."

"Since I am no longer your captain, it is no longer necessary for us to be so formal," Faris said. "As friends, we should call each other by our first names."

"Yes, ma'am." Then it hit her, what her captain was saying. "Friends, ma'am?" It was shocking to learn that her captain wanted to be friends. It had been Fatimah's wish for years. But she had never dared to hope that her captain would feel the same.

"Yes." Faris laughed. "We've been friends for a while now. Today, I'm making it official. As my last official command, you are no longer my sergeant, but my good friend Fatimah. And as your friend, you shall never call me captain or ma'am again. Do you understand?"

The joy in Fatimah's heart spread across her face. "Yes, Faris, I understand."

"Good. Let's find you a dress and then we'll take a walk in the garden and get to know each other better."

Faris was ten years older, but as friends, they were equals. They stood in each other's weddings. They had shared good times, like the birth of a new child. And rough family times such as when Fatimah had walked out on her marriage before their first anniversary.

* * *

It had always been a military career for Fatimah until she met Amur. Still she made him wait two years before she consented to marry him. Even then she would not have gone through with it without Faris' encouragement.

Less than eight months into the marriage, she had buyer's remorse.

The new bride did not understand the rules of married life. Her only solution was to leave with no intention of returning.

Fatimah decided to walk and camp along the edge of the caldera. The winter years were just beginning, but temperatures were still tolerable since it had not yet begun to snow.

She doubted she would make it all the way around, but it would give her time to think.

She had spent most of her adult life in the military and was used to order, with everything in its place, her bed made every morning, her clothes picked up at night, not lying on the back of the couch or the armchair, or socks on the floor.

Socks, socks, socks were never picked up.

"How is it possible for a grown man to be incapable of bending over and picking up his socks?" she yelled in frustration. "Why do I have to do it?"

Compromise. Compromise. Compromise.

"Marriage is a compromise." She had heard over and over. Why was she the only one who had to compromise?

In the service, when someone said they would do something, they did it. None of this: *I'll get to it; I forgot; I was just about to do it.* Their last fight came after she had "taken care of it" before he did.

"Patience. Patience. Patience." So she was told.

She preferred shouting.

"Why did I marry him in the first place?" she shouted.

That stopped her in her tracks.

Ultimately, she decided, it was all Faris' fault. She had advised Fatimah to stop running from Amur but turn and face him, instead.

Fatimah resisted until Faris made her aware of how often she spoke about him. She could not stop thinking about him. He was in her thoughts as she went to sleep and when she woke in the morning. She almost got killed while hunting tupilak because she was not paying attention but thinking about him. If not for her hunting mates, she would have died.

She couldn't imagine life without Amur. Even now after leaving him, she wanted him on this walkabout with her. It felt good to be near him, touching him. In her entire life, she'd never been afraid of anything. Not seriously, anyway. Yet, he made her feel safe.

With each thought her anger lessened.

Unexplained emotions.

"He would be a good father," she told the child in her belly.

She was so used to following military orders, doing exactly what she was told, she'd forgotten how to be flexible. Even after so many years of not being in Space Force, her training was still deeply ingrained in her.

"Maybe it wasn't entirely all his fault," she admitted.

She turned at the sound of footsteps behind her. Amur was jogging toward her. He was coming for her. She braced herself for the next big fight.

His steps slowed. He stood in front of her and studied her face. "I've missed you," he said and wrapped his arms around her and held her as if he would never let go.

"I don't care how long this walkabout lasts, take me with you," he said.

"You came without gear," she said.

"I didn't want it to slow me down."

"There's really not much out here," she said. "I only brought what I needed."

"You will have to share."

"What if I don't want to?" She meant it as a joke.

He took her seriously and held her at arm's length.

"Then you'll have to watch me starve and die. I'm not going back without you." He stood, determined not to give in or be turned away.

Would he really rather die than live without her? Why not? She would rather die than live without him.

"I was just thinking of returning home," she said, hopeful that he would take her back.

His stance relaxed. "Well, that's too bad," he said. "I was looking forward to keeping you warm tonight."

She uncharacteristically giggled. "How about if you keep me warm in our bed instead." She moved closer and wrapped her arms around him. He enveloped her in his.

This is where I belong, in his arms, not camping in the cold by myself.

Were socks really worth fighting over? Maybe laughter was better. Maybe it was time for her to learn compromise, patience, and flexibility, and forget about socks.

She pulled away as her hand returned to her belly. "I have something I've been meaning to tell you."

With the help of Faris' wisdom, Fatimah never left again. She and Amur had a great marriage, with three boys and two girls.

Everything good in her life was because of Faris.

Now their friendship was coming to an end. And for the first time since she'd left Moon Base, she would be without her captain and her best friend.

* * *

After Faris Assetti won her fourth election as governor, it was decided not to hold another election. Faris tried to object, but she was so loved and respected, none would listen.

She seemed to know each and every person in the settlement by name. She remembered birthdays, weddings, and how many children were in each family. She was well organized and when a plan didn't work, she very quickly regrouped with a better plan. Faris would be their leader until she was too old to lead, or until her death.

Sixteen weeks after her first heart attack, Faris had risen from her bed and called a Community meeting. She announced that she was no longer governor. It was time for her to move on. She asked for an election so Community could choose their next leader. She returned to her bed.

A week later, when no one had submitted their name to run for office, Faris' final order was to appoint Fatimah as governor.

No one objected, except Fatimah. She didn't want the job, not that she was incapable, but to say yes was to admit that her longtime friend was dying.

Faris seem so small in her bed. Her ebony hair had turned white, her skin withered, and her eyes became hollowed.

Her husband, children, and grandchildren left the room so the two women could say goodbye in private.

Faris held Fatimah's hand. "You will be a great leader."

"I will never be as good as you." With the will of a warrior, Fatimah controlled her emotions. She knew as soon as she was alone, she would crumble. For now, she would be strong for Faris' sake.

"I remember how stiff you used to be," Faris said. "Such a soldier."

"Space Force," Fatimah corrected.

Faris attempted a smile.

"I doubt I would have changed if we had not been stranded on this planet," Fatimah said. "You taught me how to relax."

"Ah, but we were not stranded, we chose to stay and help the colonists," Faris reminded her.

Fatimah remembered how upset she had been at that decision. As time passed, she learned to love her new home and, despite the trials, she was grateful she had stayed.

"There is a box for you," Faris whispered. "It is here on the bed with me."

Kneeling next to the bed, Fatimah reached over her friend to take the box. She opened it and almost lost her resolve. Inside was Faris' captain's peaked cap, her medals, and her captain's eagle insignia.

Of all of Faris' memorabilia, the only thing Fatimah would have wanted was that which had brought them together, Space Force.

"No, Faris, you should be buried with these or you will be out of uniform."

"Fatimah, I will not be buried in uniform," Faris said. "I will wear a dress." She smiled.

"Even though we are no longer military, I want you to have these." Faris weakly, but lovingly, squeezed Fatimah's hand. "You have been my dearest friend. You will take my place and become a great leader." She attempted another smile as she closed her eyes.

"Goodbye, old friend. It has been an honor to serve with you." Fatimah released Faris' hand, picked up her box of memories, and stood. She wanted to stay until her friend took her last breath, but her family should be at her side for her last moments.

The warrior could no longer hold back the tears. It was time for her to return to her quarters to grieve in private.

Chapter 19

Akiane Historical Chronicles
Faris' Funeral

Akiane Date: Year 27
Day after Faris' death

WRAPPED IN yellow, her favorite color, Faris' body lay on a mat covered with gray moss. Pallbearers placed the moss mat on a sled, and a team of six chovis pulled her to the ocean waters as Fatimah, her family, and the priest walked with Faris' family. Every member of Community joined the funeral possession.

Chovis that were not pulling the sled walked quietly along side. Sensing the somberness of the moment, they did not playfully wrestle or chase one another.

It was a reasonably easy walk across the caldera. The snow and ice had melted, the mud had mostly dried, and spring flowers were blooming.

Each mourner picked a flower to take to the beach.

When they reached the rim of the caldera, the pallbearers unhitched the sled and carried it up the stairs that had been carved into the rim. At the bottom of the other side, they hitched the chovis back to the sled and continued on.

174

As the procession reached the beach, the priest began to sing:

I remember well my afflictions and my wonderings;
my soul is not saddened.
Each new morning brings Allah's compassion.

It was so like the priest to insert Allah's name instead of God, as if to hide the fact that he was singing a Christian song.

The first flute started slow and low. Then, one at a time, two flutes, a tambourine, three cornets, and one guitar joined in. The tempo became festive, celebrating Faris' life.

Voices began singing:

I ride high the winds of dawn,
I journey beyond the horizon;
I follow the course his right hand directs.

Fatimah had to admit it was the *aghniat rayiea* (perfect song) for Faris who, against the odds, had always persevered.

Yet the joy of the song could not override the emptiness in Fatimah's heart. *Kanat tarqud 'afdal sidiyq laha lilraahati.* (She was laying her best friend to rest.) She would miss her friend's wisdom and advice, their laughter, and the blending of their lives and families.

I remember well my afflictions and my wonderings;
my soul is not disappointed.
Each new morning brings Allah's mercy.

A slight breeze and gentle ocean swells lapped at the beach, welcoming Faris to her new home.

When the singing came to an end, each was left to their thoughts. The ceremony consisted of people remembering Faris' influence on their lives. Some memories were sad, some funny, all were heartwarming. Faris was much loved and would be missed.

The priest Father Joe spoke last: "I remember when the fish seemed to have vanished from the ocean. Faris planned to take a shuttle and a small crew to fly over the ocean to learn where the fish had gone and hopefully bring back enough fish to feed the Community. I insisted on being a part of the expedition.

"I don't think Faris liked the thought of me, a Catholic priest, coming along. But I would not be deterred. To tell you the truth, I wasn't looking forward to the trip either, but I felt that I was supposed to be on that shuttle, so I forced myself to go."

A soft laughter rose from the crowd.

"We got caught in a rainstorm so bad we feared we would not make it back." The priest paused as he remembered. He turned to look behind him at the yellow bundle lying on the beach.

After a moment, he turned back. "The shuttle got water-logged. It didn't have the power to gain the altitude we needed to fly back at top speed and return in one day. We could only skim slowly just above the water. It took us a week to return."

"Adryel named the trip Woden after a Norse god of war because we had just been at war with a hurricane-like rain storm. By God's grace, we survived." Again Father Joe paused and dropped his head. Everyone waited as he controlled his emotions. "There are no more Wodens in Faris' life. She is peacefully at rest."

Fatimah remembered that trip. She did not want her captain to leave without her but Faris had left her in charge, so she obediently stayed behind. She remembered how that storm raged and how quickly it had intensified. She feared the worst when the shuttle did not return as scheduled.

She couldn't sleep or conduct her duties. Each morning she sent out a search team, but they returned each night having found nothing. Several times a day, she climbed through *Falcon's* top hatch to stand on the ship where she could get a good view and watch for Faris' return.

176

What she remembered most was the relief and joy of seeing that little shuttle slowly gliding toward Endurance.

"We did return," the priest continued, "with fish and worms that looked a lot like leaves. Both were great eating. That was one of the best weeks of my life. All of us on the shuttle became good friends, but Faris became the closest. I cannot imagine a day without her." He stopped and wiped his eyes. "I'm grateful for every day God granted us our friendship." He moved to stand with her family where he received many hugs.

It was time for Fatimah to speak but she was too overwhelmed. Words wouldn't come.

Many private thoughts and memories rumbled in her head, none of which she wanted to share. She still couldn't believe that she and Faris would never again take long walks at daybreak, or tell each other stupid jokes. Faris would be forever absent at future combined family dinners.

She kept expecting Faris to sit up. *Why does she not sit up? Sit up. Sit up, before they put you in the water. Please sit up.*

Family and friends filed past to say their last good-byes and place wildflowers on Faris' body. Soon she was covered with them. Flowers gently slipped from the pile onto wet sand.

Fatimah's last pleasant memory would be of her friend covered in a blanket of flowers. *Faris would have liked it.*

Pallbearers lifted the mat. More flowers slipped off as they waded into the water and let go of the mat. Water rocked Faris as if she were a sleeping baby. Soon waves pulled her into the outgoing tide and took Faris out to sea. The moss kept the cot from immediately sinking, but eventually seawater soaked the moss taking Faris away.

She didn't sit up.

Fatimah stared at the ocean and thought, *lqad dhahabat hqana. kayf la yakun dhalik shyhana eindama la yabdu hqyqyana?* (She is really gone. How can it be true when it does not seem real?)

She heard footsteps and for a moment she expected Faris to be walking toward her. Instead, she it was Fintan.

"Fatimah," Fintan's unwelcomed voice clawed into Fatimah's sorrow.

No matter how clean he looked, the butcher always smelled of tupilak meat. Faris had been a petite North African woman who was unintimidated and expected respect. Fintan had towered over her, but Faris could stop his verbal attack with a look.

Fatimah gave him the same look and said, "Am I not allowed to mourn the death of my friend, Fintan?"

He took no notice. "There are issues that must be settled."

She was determined not to give him the satisfaction of an argument. *What would Faris do?*

Fatimah had a flashback to when they first started the settlement. Thanks to The Storm, the fantasy of building utopia had been replaced with the realization of how difficult it would be to start life over on an alien planet.

People became frustrated and scared they had made a mistake. That was when the fighting and unreasonable accusations started.

But it was too late. *Falcon* had been decommissioned.

Faris listened and responded with understanding. She always managed to smooth things over. Fatimah would follow her example and do the same.

"As in?" she asked softly.

"Some of us want an election," Fintan said.

Fatimah remembered Fintan's father, Connor, a jolly Irishmen who had planned to start a horse ranch, but like so many other settlers' big plans, it never came about.

Connor was an excellent butcher of tupilak, but a little bit of his heart was saddened that he never got his horses. He often spoke of them, remembering the greats by name.

As much as loved his family, Fatimah thought he loved horses more.

His sadness was overturned when his first-born son, Fintan was born.

Connor passed on his talent for butchering tupilak to his son, as well as his love of horses, but unfortunately not his good humor. Fintan became an angry, bitter man because he was a butcher unable to fulfill his father's dream of having a horse ranch.

Everyone had an opinion, but Fintan often loudly declared his for all to hear and was glad to speak for those too timid to speak for themselves. A small group of people gathered behind him as he spoke to Fatimah.

Others stood nearby, listening. Fatimah couldn't tell if they agreed with him or if they were just curious about the conversation.

'Abaq hadiana (Stay calm), she told herself. *Remember, Faris would politely listen, then just as politely, reason with him.*

"Are you already dissatisfied with my leadership after only a few hours, Fintan?"

He didn't hesitate. "Fatimah, we think it is time for a change."

"Why did you not speak up when Faris offered an election?" She tried to remember Faris' example of never raising her voice, which Fatimah found difficult. "Fintan, the time to make your feelings known would have been at the last Community meeting. You could have said something before I was appointed, but you have waited until the day of Faris' funeral, while I am in mourning. Why is that?" Her voice began to rise.

She had always found Fintan an unreasonable man. Faris knew how to handle him. Fatimah did not, nor did she care to.

Fintan showed no such control. "I say it is time for a change."

Fatimah had planned to be governor for no more than a year, then resign and call for an election.

"Which of you would like to lead in my place?" she asked the small gathering.

Some stared at her in defiance while others turned away. No one spoke or came forward.

"What of you, Fintan?"

"Do not think you can hijack this election, Fatimah," Fintan said. "It will proceed whether you agree to it or not."

"Fine. Have your election, Fintan. But what happens if no one comes forward? Will you become our leader?"

Fintan stepped back as if confused by the question.

Fatimah stood her ground. "What am I to do when no one chooses to run? Stand by and do nothing?" She wanted to scream. He might not back down with a look; they might stand eye to eye, but he was not a trained fighter. *I can easily bring him down,* she thought.

Fintan's confusion turned to thoughtfulness. In his small mind, he had not considered who would become the next governor. He only wanted Fatimah out.

"No? Then allow me to do my job," she said.

For what seemed like less than a second, she thought she had gotten through to him, then his back hunched, his fists tensed as if preparing for a fight.

"Plan for the election," he snarled, "or we will take matters into our hands."

"And do what, Fintan? Throw stones at mothers for not having control over how their babies are born?"

That was the real issue, babies born in cocoons.

"Do something or we will."

They stared at each other like two chovis snarling over a large fish. This disagreement was not about dinner. It was about the survival of newborn children.

"I speak for the good of the Community," Fintan said.

'Abaq hadiana (Stay calm), Fatimah tried to remind herself. "The Good of the Community?" *No I will not remain*

180

calm. Lays lhdha al'ahmaq. (Not for this fool.) "What about the lives of innocent children?" She took a step closer. "Beasley said the planet is changing us. How can you allow a child to die just because you do not like the manner of its birth?" she yelled.

"A cursed child has no right to live," he yelled back.

She took a step closer. "Do you now speak for your God?" It felt good to yell at him; it helped to air her frustrations and grief.

Fintan did not answer.

"Is that the kind of God you serve, Fintan, one who would kill innocent children? If so, He does not deserve your worship."

"I worship a God of love," Fintan shrieked.

"Then you are the one cursed, for you know nothing of love," Fatimah roared, "and you know nothing of your God." She took another step and was now within his personal space.

Fintan's resolve waned. "I will not stand here and be insulted by the likes of you. Deal with the problem or we will deal with you," he said in a threatening voice.

But Fatimah saw the coward in him.

Fintan and his companions left.

Turn tail and run, she thought. *You are nothing more than hot air.*

And so it had begun. Community was reverting back to when they had first started the settlement.

If not for Faris, the settlement would have been a failure. She had been right to stay, but she had wanted more than a settlement. She wanted a community of people who worked together as one, not as individuals. After all she had accomplished, Community seemed to be reverting back to mistrust and fear.

Now it was real. Faris was dead. She was never coming back. And the cracks of mistrust were appearing in the

Community's foundation. Faris' body had not reached the bottom of the ocean, and Fatimah had already failed.

Still on the Beach

Fatimah impatiently waited for everyone to leave so she could be alone on the beach with her thoughts, but the priest stayed.

She never understood Faris' relationship with the Catholic priest. He was often at family gatherings, and even attended the last day of *Ramadan*, their holiest day of celebration.

Fatima learned to tolerate him. He took the hint and did not force their relationship.

Now he was standing by her side. If he thought to become her confidant, Fatima was not interested.

'Iidha kan sayatrakni liwahadi faqata. (If only he would leave me alone.)

"I have no need for your comfort or counsel, Priest."

"You are not Faris," he said.

"Nor do I have need of your keen observation. I have had enough criticism for this day."

"That's not what I meant."

"You were Faris' counselor. You are not mine."

"Faris and I were friends. I have always hoped you and I could become friends."

"And your first act is to tell me of my failure to govern?"

"That is not what I meant."

"Enlighten me, Priest."

"You cannot govern like Faris because you are Fatimah. You must govern as Fatimah."

"What is that supposed to mean?"

She stopped and stared over the ocean, wishing he would leave her alone.

"Faris had her moments of doubt," he said, "though she never showed it."

"But you can see mine. Is that what you are telling me, Priest?"

"We had many conversations over her indecisions, but she always managed to find solutions to her problems."

"And I don't seem to be able to do that?"

"It took time," he continued.

She turned to him. "We seem to be having two different conversations. Say what you mean, Priest."

"All of her life, Faris had been trained to be captain of a spaceship. She was captain of *Falcon* for 12 years, then she was governor of Endurance for 27 years. She was used to making command decisions and having her orders carried out for most of her career."

"Becoming governor was a change in name, not in authority," Fatimah said. "Whereas, I was trained for combat and have no leadership skills."

"You find solutions to problems in a different way, Fatimah."

"Faris was the problem-solver, Priest, not me."

"Faris did not solve problems; she made command decisions and expected people to do as they were told."

"I do not understand."

"Fatimah, when we first landed, for eleven years the only meat we had was fish and dog. I'd say we were all pretty tired of it. We were fast becoming vegetarians. You gave us our first taste of tupilak."

"Tupilak. Yes, a beast worthy of calling a warrior. I remember the first time I saw the sea creature," she said. "An animal as large as a bull leapt out of the water with the grace of a dancer but charged with the ferocity of an army."

"I remember how good it tasted. Better than manna from heaven." The priest laughed. "Blasphemous, I know, but I have hopes that God will forgive me. It had been such a long time since any of us had tasted meat that good."

"Adryle asked if he could cook it. I had never eaten barbecue before." She paused as she contemplated her next words. "Community learned much from each other, especially acceptance and love. Now, we seem to have lost it."

"Perhaps we no longer need a mother to tell us what to do," the priest said. "Perhaps what we need is a wise woman to help us find new ways to solutions to help overcome old problems."

Fatimah intently considered his words. She had been too focused on her grief. Too focused? It would take time to fully grieve her friend, but she was governor. She would have to grieve on her own time while learning how to become a leader. It might be best to heed the advice of the priest, after all.

"You're a problem-solver," the priest said.

"My solution would be to leave Endurance and start over with more reasonable people. Let the rest fight it out for themselves."

"Fintan and his associates are not the majority. They do not speak for the entire Community," the priest said.

"Faris was trusting and believed there is good in all. I do not trust as easily, nor do I hold to such beliefs in the basic goodness of people. As you say, Priest, I am not Faris."

"Fatimah, would you really leave?" He seemed worried that she might follow through on her threat.

Unsure herself, she turned back to the peace of the ocean. "Priest, I am from the desert where there are no trees to obscure the horizon. Here, I live in a terrarium. No matter which direction I walk, I am stopped by a stone wall."

"I remember how you used to go camping outside."

Fatimah laughed. "I have had many camping trips and eventually walked all around the caldera. I forget how many trips it took, but I remember the freedom I felt. Strange, I know, for one who joined Space Force." They walked along the shore together. "Even though I was trapped in a spaceship, I could look out the window and see stars. I could see the universe."

"Then you got stuck here and lived your life on just one planet," the priest said.

"At first, I resented staying here. Outside walks taught me to love my new home planet. In some ways the ocean still reminds me of my lost desert. Nothing obscures my view of the horizon.

"At sunset the desert turned golden. Here, the ocean reflects the ever-changing colors of Kahair setting." She paused. "I fell in love, married, and had children. My family is my best accomplishment. I would not return to Earth even if I could."

"But you're tired of living in a terrarium."

"Yes, I am tired of being inside for seven years of winter. An occasional walk outside is no longer enough for me."

"Where would you go? How would you live when Akiane freezes?" he asked. "What does your family have to say about moving?"

"Ah, Priest, you have found my Achilles' heel. I have spoken to no one, but you. *'Iinah hulm 'akhshaa 'anah In yatahaqaq abdaan.* It is a dream I fear will never be realized."

Chapter 20

Rona Montgomery
New Discoveries

Akiane Date: Year 328
WSC Stanza: Eatery

THERE WAS a collective sigh of relief when the bay door shushed open and fresh air swept into the room.

Instead of one of the colonists freeing them, a woman dressed in a WSC Space Force uniform stood in the doorway with a crew of Space Force men and women standing behind her.

"Good morning," the woman said. "I am Commander Osgood and I have come to escort you to *WSC Stanza* for your journey back to WSC Moon Base."

"I don't understand," Gino said. "What is this about?"

"I have not been given an explanation," she said. "My orders are to oversee the packing of your equipment and delivery to all of it and you to the ship. You are to pack your personal items and bring them with you. Just outside are three shuttles to take you to *Stanza*."

"We've been on Akiane for less than two months," Gino said in astonishment. "You're not due to arrive for another two years. How is it that you're here so quickly?"

Commander Osgood smiled broadly. "Folded space technology has improved while you were away. We can now make fewer jumps, but travel further during each jump," she said, "which has turned out to be a good thing for you." Her smile disappeared. "Just what did you do to piss these people off?"

After their luggage was stored in their new rooms, the scientists immediately gathered in *Stanza's* Eatery, the lounge area, where off-duty personal and guests gathered to relax. They sat near an observatory window and waited for Gino to return from speaking with the captain.

"Adumie has banished us from his planet," Gino said as he sat down. "It is as you feared, the child is dead and the mother is dying," he said to Rona and Lu.

Rona stared out the window, but she didn't see the blue-green planet below nor did she see the storm brewing. Her only thought was, *I failed.*

"I'm sorry." It was the only thing Lu had said in the last 17 minutes.

It was the longest Rona had ever known her to be quiet, except when she was concentrating on work. Even then, she often spoke her thoughts out loud.

Lu was always moving, running, constantly chattering about something. It was unusual for her to sit quietly, lost in her troubles. She had been so quiet Rona had forgotten that they were sitting at the same table.

"It's not your fault." Rona's voice sounded far away and unemotional. "I'm team leader. The final decision was mine."

She didn't have the energy to be more upset. All she wanted to do was lie down in the darkness of her room and not come out until they reached Moon Base.

"But I pushed. I should have listened when you said no," Lu said apologetically. "I was too impatient."

187

Rona's gaze turned slowly from the window to Lu. She had buried her face in her hands as if crying. But there were no tears. Perhaps Lu also lacked the energy to express her true feelings.

"It doesn't matter anymore, Lu. What's done is done." Rona's career was over. Everything she'd worked so hard for all of her life was lost. The best she could hope for now was a job in a commercial lab near her family's farm where she would live for the rest of her life.

The scientific communities on WSC Moon Base and Earth had been waiting for new scientific discoveries from the alien planet in a different part of the galaxy. They'd hoped that the new discoveries would shed light on old theories. Now there was nothing to send them.

None of the Pegasus Projects were finished; they had barely started. Therefore, there was nothing conclusive to report on anything. The Akiane Research Project was null and void. The money and time that had been wasted in training, equipment, and personnel was staggering.

All of it for nothing, all because of me, Rona thought.

She turned and stared out the window.

If things weren't bad enough, it had taken *WSC Britannia* six years and seven months to reach Akiane. During that time, WSC had improved folded space technology. It only took *WSC Stanza* one year and fifty-two days to reach Akiane.

Rona let out a long slow sigh of defeat. In less than a year and three months, she'd stand before her project advisers and explain how she was responsible for everyone being exiled from Pegasus Colony.

She imagined standing before the committee. Her knees would feel like jelly. Would she even have the words to speak or would she stand with her head bowed as the board reprimanded her?

"Perhaps I was overstepping the grand plan by taking matters in my own hands?" Rona spoke her thoughts out loud.

"What did you say?" Lu asked.

Rona shook her head and slumped in resignation. "I was thinking about Adumie."

"Rona, why?" Lu asked in surprise.

"I'm just wondering if . . ."

"If God wants those people to die? Certainly not," Lu said. "That might be what that high priest thinks, but Rona, you can't live your life by the misguided beliefs of others."

"Lu, I failed." The words slipped out of her mouth and fell hard on the floor.

"We've had a setback, that's all." Lu almost sounded believable.

Rona wanted to believe. "But . . ."

"But nothing, Rona. You're not a missionary sent on some holy mission. You have a PhD in genetics, microbiology, and a number of other fields. You're a scientist. That's your calling. That's what you're supposed to be doing."

Lu's words were difficult to take in.

Rona sought comfort from her lukewarm cocoa.

Lu took a long deep breath, stared out the observatory window at Akiane, took a sip of her tea, and said, "I wonder if things would have been better if we'd gone to the other colony."

Most of the scientists sat in silence.

Though Lu had spoken softly, everyone had heard, turned and asked questions.

"What did Lu say?" Beth asked.

"Something about another settlement?" Avil asked.

"What other settlement?" Gino shifted around to face Lu.

"Yeah," Rona said, "what other settlement?" She sat back and stared, totally confused. "If there was another settlement, how do you know about it?"

"It's in the logs," Lu said.

"What logs?" Gino asked.

"The one Terzo recovered." Lu seemed surprised that no one knew what she was talking about.

All eyes turned to Terzo, sitting two tables over.

"Terzo, why is this the first we've heard of it?" Gino demanded.

"You never asked," Terzo said. "No one ever asked what I was doing. I didn't think anyone cared."

"We thought you were building another virtual game for us to play," Avil said.

"Why would you think that?" Terzo asked.

"Because you were always coming up with something new," Mathieu said. "That's one of the things we love about you." Several others agreed. "You keep us from being bored."

Rona remembered how he had started with the games on *WSC Britannia*. Since they were not online, Terzo tweaked them to make them more interesting. Then he began creating his own games. It was something he'd always wanted to do, but never had the time to pursue.

It was Terzo's turn to stare at them in disbelief. "I thought you were satisfied with the games I'd built."

"We were, but we thought . . ." Mathieu stopped.

"Well?" Terzo asked.

"Here is a clear case of a failure to communicate," Gino said. "Explain to us just exactly what you have hacked into, my boy."

"It was Lu's idea," Terzo said sheepishly. He was not one who liked the limelight.

"Lu?" Gino turned everyone's attention back to her. "Why all the secrecy?"

This was becoming a regular habit for Rona and Lu, being the center of attention. Only this time, to Rona's relief all the attention was centered on Lu.

"I t-told R-R-Rona." Lu sat up straight and nervously stuttered.

"When?" Rona tried hard to remember, but couldn't. It wasn't like Lu to shift the blame, so why now?

"T-t-t-the day J-J-Jessica l-left, remember?"

Rona remembered that day. It had felt as if she had just come from Jess' funeral instead of watching her leave on a trip she might not survive. "Lu, Jess had just left. I was in no mood for one of your adventures."

She didn't mean to sound angry, but a new fear gripped her. They were leaving the planet. What about Jess? How could Rona have forgotten her? What if Jess came back and they were gone? What would Adumie do with her?

"Enough," Gino said quietly, "we don't need a rehash of the past. Let's stay on topic. Lu, why did you and Tech Terzo hack into the colonists' private logs?"

"Oh no!" Lu and Terzo said together.

"We didn't read private logs," Lu said.

"I only hacked into military logs," Terzo said. "They are public record."

"I'm not accusing you of anything. I just want to know why you thought to read the logs?" Gino said.

"I didn't trust the colonists, at least not that High Priest Adumie," Lu said. "I didn't believe in his reason for sending Jessica on that Woden quest while the planet was still frozen. We had no idea what would happen to her." She caught her breath as she suddenly remembered. "We don't even know if Jessica survived the gravitational storm."

"Lu." Gino stopped her before she got lost in her own thoughts. "Stay on topic. The captain has given Jorge permission to join the search for Jessica. I'm sure they'll find her."

As if on cue, Jorge walked into the Eatery with his head down.

No one dared ask him how things went.

Jorge stood next to the observatory window to look down on Akiane and shook his head no.

Everyone understood.

The thought of Jess being dead was too horrid to accept. Rona feared if the search team didn't find her before *Stanza* left, Jess would be stranded on Akiane for the rest of her life. For Rona, the trip home would be unbearable.

"Stay on topic, right," Lu said, returning to the conversation. "Adumie said he made Jessica go on Woden because of the first Woden where Father Striken and Captain Assetti had gone on some quest to explore the planet."

"That's not what happened," Terzo said.

"What did happen?" Gino asked.

"Captain Assetti, Father Striken, and several others went on a fishing trip," Terzo said.

"A fishing trip?" Olivia asked.

"All the fish had left the area," Lu said.

"What?" Olivia exclaimed. "When did that happen?"

"When the ocean thawed soon after The Storm," Lu said.

"Does that happen every time?" Olivia demanded. "That would explain what we found."

Now they were talking about fish. Rona wanted to know about the other colony. Where was it? Who were those people? Did they also have the disease or were they healthy? Did they have a cure?

"Olivia, stay on topic." Gino scolded.

Oh, thank God for Larry Gino, Rona thought.

"I'm sure Terzo and Lu will be happy to help you and anyone else who wants access to the logs. But for now, we need to know about the other colony," Gino said.

Olivia started to object. Gino scowled. Olivia's face contorted in disapproval. According to Olivia's philosophy on life, her needs came before all else, but she did defer to Gino's authority. She sat back in her chair.

"I'll be quiet as long as I get to read those logs," she said.

Rona was glad Gino was able to rein her in when so many others couldn't.

"Agreed," Gino said. "Lu, go ahead."

"Well, the captain and the others took a shuttle to learn what had happened to the fish," Lu said. "They were supposed to be back in a couple of days with a load of fish to feed the colony, but they got caught in a storm, not the gravitational storm. This was after that storm, but it was similar to a hurricane and it delayed their return."

"They named that storm Woden, which was the name after the Norse God of War," Terzo said. "It took them a week to return. During that time, colonists thought they'd died in the storm."

"There was a big celebration when they returned safely," Lu finished. "Adumie lied about Woden."

"Or," Gino said, "the colonists may have exaggerated events, which eventually turned into a legend that no one could live up to."

"Maybe." Lu didn't sound convinced. She liked her version better.

"I'm sorry, Lu." Jorge said without turning from the window. "I was there when you tried to tell Rona, but I didn't want to listen either." He rested his head against the glass.

"That's okay." Lu smiled. "I'm the one who should apologize. The two of you were missing Jessica, but I was only thinking about the logs. I should have waited a few days and given you time."

Rona wanted to scream, *What about the colony? Where is it?*

193

"Lu thought there might be more to Woden than the colonists were telling Jess," Terzo said. "I was so bored, I welcomed something new to do. The computers are all in good working order, so it wasn't as if you needed me." He paused and blushed. "I mean, I like programming games once in awhile, but . . ." His blush deepened.

"But you're not here to entertain the rest of us," Gino said. "We understand."

"Well if you thought it was a thankless job," Mathieu said, "then you're wrong. Your games kept us from going stir crazy during our voyage and, as you noticed, while we were locked up. We're thankful for that, believe me."

There was a round of applause and several hardy thank yous.

Terzo's face turned crimson beneath his smile.

Rona fumed and could no longer contain herself. "The other colony," she growled.

"Yes, what else did the two of you learn?" Gino asked.

"Well," Lu said, "we did start with the captain's logs, then we continues after she became the first governor of the colony."

"Those logs ended when she died," Terzo said. "We continued on with the next governor's logs."

"We wanted to know what happened to the colony," Lu said.

"We read some military and some historical accounts for almost 30 years of the colony's beginnings, which ended soon after the colony split in two." Terzo gave a guilty shrug. "I'm sorry if is was wrong to read them."

Gino shook his head. "They didn't write those logs just for themselves. The colonists wrote them for those who came after them," he said. "Now tell us. What did you learn?"

"The colony had a disagreement and split in two," Lu said.

"What was the disagreement about?" Gino asked.

194

"Ironically, it was about babies being born in cocoons."
Lu's face lit up, she opened her mouth to launch into the
story, but stopped by a look from Gino. "Stay on topic," she
said.

Gino nodded.

"Anyway," Terzo continued. "There might be another
colony out there somewhere. We just don't know where.
The governor's logs stopped. The only ones after that were
from Father Joseph Striken's personal entrires."

"But, I have found some other logs you might be
interested in," Terzo said a bit mysteriously.

"What?" Lu asked excited at the new prospect.

"I found Dr. Even Beasley's medical logs."

* * *

Jorge continued to stand at the window. He was
listening to the conversation, but his thoughts were on
Jessica. The captain had ordered a radar search for Jessica's
camp. He'd hoped they would pick up her camp's heat
signature, but so far they had not been able to find her.
Because of *Stanza's* schedule, they might have to leave
without her.

The captain's voice came over Eatery communication's
system. "Dr. Krause."

Jorge's ears perked up.

"Report to launch Bay 4 immediately."

Instantly, Jorge turned around and ran out of the
Eatery.

Chapter 21

Jessica Hewitt
Realization

Akiane Date: Year 328
On the Boat Somewhere on the Ocean

THE DAYS dragged. It was like being on the bridge of the spaceship, with nothing to do but stare at a radar screen—no books to read, no music to listen to, no videos to watch. I couldn't even stretch my legs. All I could do was watch the screen just in case something appeared that could be a threat to the ship. Nothing ever appeared, not even space junk.

I was back in the same mind-numbing situation—sit, steer the boat, and scan the horizon for land, of which there was none. Sit, stare, scan, repeat...repeat...repeat...

Blue sky melted into a blue ocean. Now that the snow and ice had melted, my entire world was blue.

If I ever felt insignificant, this was it. I was a drop of water in a vast ocean with no idea where I was. We were heading south, which meant nothing. It was more likely we were going to miss Endurance altogether, cross the equator, head north on the other side of Akiane, and not realize it until we reached the south pole.

My only consolation—the trip wouldn't last that long. We'd die of hunger or thirst first.

Don't think about it, I reminded myself.

Perhaps we should have stayed on that island. We'd have had plenty of fish to eat and water to drink. In six years, summer would end and winter would return, the ocean would freeze, and we could have walked back. We'd have seven years of frozen ocean to find Endurance. But this way, in this boat, we'd only last a few days at the most.

The certainty of the hopelessness of our situation was settling in. We were going to die at a snail's pace.

As long as we had fish, we wouldn't freeze to death. There was something in the fish that kept us warm. But if our supply ran out and we couldn't find more fish, we'd go to sleep one cold night and, thanks to hyperthermia, we'd never wake up. Which was better than starving to death.

Don't dwell!

The itch in my right palm was becoming progressively worse, as if it was on fire. I wasn't sure how much longer I could endure it before I was ready to cut my hand off.

I pulled my gloves off and inspected my palm. It was completely red. There was something coagulating just under the skin, an infection. To my horror, I feared I might have to actually cut my hand off to save my life.

"Jessica, what is it?" Nu Venia asked.

"I don't know." I poked the infection. I was considering lancing it open and squeezing as much of the infection out as I could. But it hurt too badly. I'd have to ask Nu Venia do it for me.

But would she? Touching was forbidden.

She leaned in and forcefully grabbed my hand, and yanked it toward her with such force she pulled me off my perch.

I hit the tiller causing the boat to made a sharp left 90-degree turn, unbalancing both of us. We went tumbling into the boat. Imos and the puppies barely had time to get out of the way.

I jumped back onto my seat, situated Kahair over my left shoulder, and corrected our course south.

"Sorry," she said.

"That's okay, Nu Venia." I held my palm up for her to see. "I have an infection from when I cut myself, but I don't remember when it happened."

She moved closer, held my wrist with her fur-gloved hand. "How is this possible?" She sounded both worried and shocked.

"What are you talking about?" I asked.

"It is forbidden to hold hands." She said as she held my hand. "You did not hold mine. You must have held Cameron's hand. But why would he do such a thing?" She sounded as if we had betrayed her. She wasn't making any sense.

The only time Cameron had taken off his green gloves was when he was preparing a meal or tending to chovis' paws, or fishing. Just before he died, he had taken his jacket and gloves off preparing to catch fish, but he had never touched Nu Venia and certainly not me.

"I, ah, I don't . . ." Then I remembered. He and I had held hands. "Yes, it was when the tupilak had Cameron. Neither of us had our gloves on. I was trying to save him by holding his hand. I was trying to save his life. That can't be forbidden, can it?"

"When you held his hand . . .," she began. "Ah, . . ." She stopped. Her dark maroon skin seemed to pale. Something was seriously wrong.

"What?"

"Your palm." She took her fur gloves off. With her thin green gloves still on, she gently, almost lovingly, passed her fingers over the infection.

"Something bit me," I said. "I remember now. It was when I was holding Cameron's hand. Something small must have gotten in between us and it bit me. That was why I let go of him. The bite surprised me and I involuntarily jerked away and he slipped out of my hands."

"You were not bitten," she said. "Cameron transferred his essence into your palm."

I whisked my hand out of hers. "What are you talking about?"

"You have Cameron's child." Her words were spoken with reverence.

"What? No. I only held his hand. I never had sex with him. I'm not pregnant," I forcefully objected.

Pointing to my palm, she said, "Cameron's essence."

"Nu Venia, what are you talking about? I don't understand. I can't get pregnant from my hand."

Understanding crossed her face. "You are different."

"Evidently."

"Show me your left hand," she said.

I pulled my gloves off and showed her.

She held my hand, closely examining it, then said, "Different."

"Different how?" I asked.

She took her green gloves off and showed me her palms. They looked as if someone had taken a meat tenderizer to them.

"What happened?" I thought she's had an accident or maybe someone had abused her.

"I was born this way. All of us are. Your palms are not the same."

"No," I said, a bit mystified.

"Then how do you exchange essence?"

"Essence?" I asked. "I don't know what you mean? On Earth, essence is a scent, a fragrance. What is it on Akiane?"

She lifted her hand up, palm facing me. "This is why we wear gloves at all times, so we do not exchange essence by accident. It is by another's essence that one is able to bring forth a child," Nu Venia said. "It is forbidden for a child to have two parents. A life-giver gives birth by herself.

"Cameron knew you would not let go of him and I would not let go of you. Both of us would have been pulled into the water with him. He did what was blasphemous to save our lives. He gave you his essence because he knew the sting to your palm would surprise you and you would let go." She was overcome with emotion. "This is now all that is left of him." She cradled my hand in hers.

I too *might* have been overwhelmed with emotion if I had understood what she was saying. But my hand burned something awful and I wanted it to stop.

"Well, I'm not pregnant. I can't get pregnant from my hand. So what am I supposed to do about this?" I pulled my hand out of hers.

It was a long time before Nu Venia said, "You cannot have a child?"

"Not from this. I have a really bad infection, and my hand is burning up. I'm desperate. I want to cut this thing out and throw it in the ocean."

"No! It is all that is left of Cameron."

"Cameron? What about my hand?"

She slapped her bare hand over mine, palm to palm.

I tried to pull my hand away, but she held on tightly.

"Nu Venia, what are you doing? Won't you get in trouble for this?"

"It is all that is left of Cameron. You cannot throw it away. Do nothing. I will receive." Closing her eyes, she seemed to recede into herself. She tilted her head back, concentrating.

No, not *concentrating*; she looked *satisfied!*

What was she doing? I tried to yank my hand out of hers, but she held on too tightly.

I felt the infection slip out. She released my hand and examined at her palm.

I examined my hand *it was normal.* It no longer itched or burned, nor was it red. All that was left was a slight cut in the center of my palm.

Nu Venia examined her hand. "I think I expected Cameron to live forever," she said sadly. "I thought he would always be with me. I lost hope when he died." She closed her hand and placed it over her heart. Then she placed her other hand over it. "I now have him back. He is no longer completely dead." With grateful tears in her eyes, she said, "Thank you."

I thought I'd failed Cameron and Nu Venia by letting him die. Now I felt proud that I help save a part of him. The thought brought new hope that helped eased the pain of losing Cameron.

"It is strange," Nu Venia said.

"What is?" I asked.

"The course of events."

"How so?"

"Cameron was priest, the last of his line, and now his line will live on with me."

"What do you mean, 'last of his line'?"

"There are some who are different; they cannot bring forth life."

"What do you mean by different?" I asked.

"Every once in a while, a child is unable to bring forth another. When they die, their ancestral line dies with them," she said.

"Life-givers are female and those who are different are males," I said. "And men can't have children by themselves."

"Cameron's line will not end, but will continue with me." Tears streamed down her face, but they were not tears of joy. "This is something that should not be." She dropped her head. "No one will ever listen to me now."

She pulled her green gloves back on, then her fur gloves, turned away from me, and lay down as if her world had come to an end.

"I'm still confused, Nu Venia, why are you so unhappy?"
She didn't answer.

"Nu Venia, I know you miss him, and I know it's important to grieve for a lost loved one, but we have to survive. I can't do this without you. I need your help."

No response.

I secured the motor so it would stay on course, then I scooted to Nu Venia.

"Nu Venia!" I shook her hard. "I need you!"

Nothing.

I kicked her leg with the flat of my boot. I didn't kick hard. I just wanted her to come back to me.

"Nu Venia!" I yelled.

She rolled over to face me and yelled, "I have two life-givers."

"Okay," I said, "what does that mean?"

"Two," she said it as if she'd just confessed to murder. "I have two. Now so does Cameron's child."

"If that's supposed to clear things up, it doesn't," I said. "I have two parents."

She'd retreated back into her private world as if she hadn't heard. If she became lost, I might follow her into my own depression. I was not about to lose her now. I shook her so hard she popped up, threw off her blankets, and became larger than me.

Even though I knew she and Cameron could change sizes, it still surprised me when it happened.

"Are you trying to intimidate me, Nu Venia? I'm trained in hand-to-hand combat. I can take a man twice my size," I said. "How would you like to go for a swim?"

Her anger decreased, which was good. I doubted I could have taken her. If she wanted, she could easily have thrown me overboard. She became smaller than me, a sign she was inferior, or maybe it was a sign that she was losing her will to live.

"Stay with me, Nu Venia, I'm not going to let you sleep until you tell me what's going on."

She became thoughtful, as if something had just dawned on her. "You have two parents?" she asked as if I'd just told her my deepest darkest secret.

"Yes," I said. "Every human being has two parents."

She frowned. "This is truth?"

"Yes, of course."

"All off-worlders?"

I scratched my head. "All off-worlders, everyone on Earth, Mars Colony, Europa Colony, even WSC Moon Base," I said. "Every living human being, who has lived and died since the beginning of time, has had two parents. No one can be born without two parents."

Suddenly, we were the same size and once again equals.

"I am learning things are different between your people and mine," she said.

"Yes, I've come to the same conclusion," I said. "Things on Akiane are very much different from everywhere else."

"It is an abomination to have two life-givers on Akiane," she said with great shame and embarrassment.

I finally understood what she had been trying to tell me.

"It's not the touching that's forbidden, it's having a child with another person that is forbidden," I said.

"Indeed." She held up a gloved hand. "This is why were wear gloves. So one does not accidently exchange essence."

That was not what I was expecting. "But then . . . but who . . . what we just did . . ." I clasped my hand to my chest.

"Was wrong," she said. "It is abomination to give one's essence to another. Something Cameron did only to save your life and mine."

Essence was the equivalent of sperm?

"Cameron and I were both barehanded," I said. "Why did he do it?"

"To-make-you-let-go." She said each word slowly as if speaking to me in another language and by saying the words slowly, I would understand.

I did understand. "He did the unthinkable to save my life," I said. "Both our lives." My hand dropped to my lap.

"Indeed."

"Nu Venia, two women cannot exchange essence. Only men have sperm and they must give it to a woman so she can give birth to a child," I said. "If you don't exchange sp—, essence, how do you have babies?"

"A life-giver decides to have a child and a child comes," she said.

"That's it? She has a baby by herself just by willing it? That's not possible," I said. "There must be more to it than that."

She shrugged. "I do not know."

"Just like the chovis?" I asked. "You have babies by yourselves?"

How was that possible? The colonists had only been isolated from Earth for no more than 328 years. I was no biologist, but I knew that wasn't long enough for such an evolutionary change. Throughout Earth's history, many communities of people have been isolated from the rest of humanity. None of them become something else other than human.

"How did that happen?" I asked. "How did you change?

"It has always been," she said.

"Not when you first landed on Akiane," I said.

"No, Jessica, of course not. The first settlers from Earth were as you. But with time, we changed. A few at first, then all." She was quiet for a bit. "The first to be different were rejected by the others. It was thought if each person stayed with their family and didn't mingle with the others the problem would go away."

"And one does not exchange essence with another family member," I said. "As time passed, the rule stuck, not just within families, but to everyone." Then something dawned on me. "Nu Venia, you said Cameron was a man, yes?"

"Yes."

"Nu Venia, a woman cannot give birth to a boy by herself," I said. "A woman can only give birth to a son if she receives sperm from a man."

She was unconvinced.

"do you know of any life-givers who have been able to have a child together?" I asked.

She thought about it. "I am unaware of such a thing happening."

"That's because it doesn't happen," I said. "Here, on Akiane, a life-giver can become pregnant when she desires a child. That child can only be a girl. A life-giver cannot have a male child unless she joins with a man. The sperm, or essence, from a man can produce either a girl or boy. A life-giver cannot have a male child by herself."

She stared at me. "This is truth?"

"This is truth. How many men are there in Endurance?" I asked.

"Because of the slow dying illness there are now more men than life-givers." She thought for a moment, then asked, "Cameron had two parents?"

"Yes."

"Why did I not know?"

"You said his life-giver died soon after he was born," I said.

"She could have told me before she died."

"When did Adumie begin to call you an abomination?" I asked.

"Always," she said then she understood. "Cameron's life-giver did not want the same shame for him." She became angry. "Jessica, Adumie is male," she said none too kindly. "That means he has two parents. Why does he treat me thus?"

"He might not know," I said. "I'll bet you, not many of the men know. Their parents might have kept it a secret because of their shame and to protect their child. You know what that means don't you, Nu Venia."

"What?"

"There has been a lot more exchanging of essence than people have admitted to."

She growled.

"And how many men are sick, that you know of?"

I waited while she calculated.

She shook her head. "Besides Jecidia, very few. What does that mean?"

"I don't know. But Rona and Lu might be interested in that bit of information," I said.

Nu Venia took in a gasp of revelation.

"What?" I asked.

"Those of Earth, it is not sin to have a child with another?" she asked.

"No, it is not." I chuckled lightly.

"But you do not do it as we do."

"No, Nu Venia, we don't."

"Jessica, how do you bring forth a child?"

That was a question I never expected to be asked by an adult, and yet, there it was. I couldn't just ignore it. I'd been pushing her to tell me the truth; now it was my turn. I very awkwardly explained the difference between men and women, and how humans have sex and women conceive a child.

Nu Venia's eyes widened in disbelief. "You like it?"

"Yes, very much."

"What is it like?"

I smiled, remembering good times. "Nu Venia, that's like asking what it's like to jump out of a plane with a parachute."

"I am without understanding."

"You have to experience it to understand," I said. "Do you know what changed your people?"

Profound guilt crossed her face. "Jessica, it is the fish."

The same fish that I'd been eating all this time?

Chapter 22

Jessica Hewitt

Akiane Date: Year 328
On the Boat Somewhere on the Ocean

WHERE WAS I? Why was I rocking? Was I sleeping in a rocking chair? I was confused and groggy and having trouble focusing. With great effort, I pulled myself from a deep sleep, sat up, took stock of the situation, and to my even great disappointment, remembered.

We'd been on the water for three days and had become bored searching a blank horizon for land.

Nu Venia had leaned against the boat's side with her arm draped over the gunwales. After a while, she rested her chin on her arm, closed her eyes, and fell asleep.

Good, I'd thought. *She'll be well rested when it's her turn to steer.*

As the star Kahair moved across the afternoon sky, his warmth felt good, relaxing. I had trouble keeping my eyes opened. I remembered thinking, *I'll close my eyes just for a second.* Now I wondered, *How long had that second lasted?*

I'd awakened slumped over the steering arm.

Nu Venia had slipped off the gunwales and was curled up in her fur blankets.

Only Imos and Essal's puppies remained in the boat. The other chovis had decided to answer the call of the ocean, but before they left, they tore into our fish supply and ate all of it. We had none left to ward off the frigid nights. It wasn't cold enough to freeze the water, but it was cold enough to freeze us.

Shining brightly, Kahair was moving toward the western horizon, announcing late afternoon.

It was as if an artist loaded his paintbrush with pink, yellow, and white paint, and whisked his brush across the sky to form long wispy clouds. It seemed like a lazy and peaceful late afternoon.

But those cirrus clouds foretold of a coming storm.

I looked over my shoulder.

In the southeast corner of the sky, rising from the horizon, were ominous green-gray storm clouds. That was why the ocean was rocking back and forth. It was already feeling the effects of the storm that was headed our way.

The little motor refused to turn over. Kahair had been shining brightly and should have charged the lithium battery, but for some reason it wouldn't start. We should have had enough power to last us well into the night. I tried again and again.

If only I knew what was wrong, then I realized, *it wouldn't matter. I didn't know how to fix it.*

I sat back in defeat.

We'd gambled that we'd find land and lost.

No matter how large or small the storm, it would capsize us.

Even without the storm, we wouldn't survive the night. Without fish to keep us warm, hypothermia would set in before the storm overtook us. Either way, we wouldn't be waking up in the morning.

I had failed everything and everyone. I failed to convince the people of Akiane that they were a WSC colony.

I failed Cameron, who truly believed I was the savior of his people. He was so wrong.

In my defense, I never wanted to be anyone's savior; it was too much responsibility. Becoming a savior takes commitment of one's entire life and soul. It was certainly more than I wanted to give. I'd never been able to commit to anything, mostly because I didn't know how. When I did try, I failed miserably. Just ask my ex-fiancé.

In Space Force, I didn't have to think or be responsible for anything. I just did what I was told: when to go to sleep, eat, work, and relax.

If I couldn't save Nu Venia or myself, how was I supposed to save a planet of people?

I gave up trying to start the motor and snuggled into my fur bedding. I leaned against the edge of the boat and watched the darkening sky. The storm was brewing in the far south, but in the western sky, Kahair painted another incredible starset and the promise of a new day. He lied.

There would be no more new days for us.

I thought of Cameron and his God. What if Cameron was right all along and his God was real?

This might be the time to pray.

"Cameron said you had a mission for me. Do you?" I waited for some sort of response. None came.

"If you do have a mission for my life, now would be the time to do something about it."

Nothing.

"God, if you're there, I really don't want to die out here like this."

I waited.

"So this is it," I said. "After everything Akiane has thrown at me. This is it? She's won? And you don't care?"

There wasn't much to say after that.

I lay on my back. *One wasted life ending in one pathetic death.*

Stars began to appear. One lone star seemed to move stealthily across the sky.

What is that? I wondered.

Nu Venia moaned, thrashed, and wrestled with her blanket. She was having a nightmare.

As I moved to untangle her, she settled back into a restful deep sleep. Her nightmare was over.

I considered waking her, but what would I say?

"Just wanted to let you know, we'll be dead before morning. Nice knowing you. Good bye."

Would she want to know?

Hell, I wouldn't want to know.

What difference would it make if I did wake her?

Let her sleep.

I got comfortable and closed my eyes.

Later That Night
On the Boat Somewhere On the Ocean

I heard it growl.

A tupilak, twice the size of a polar bear, blacker than night, a bright pink nose with a black spot on one side and two fiery-red-demon eyes, was trotting across the surface of the water toward me.

The boat rocked back and forth in rhythm with its steps. It stopped next to the boat and leaned over me. Water dripped from its fur like rain. Its hot breath swished over me like gusts of wind. The sound of its growl grew louder than thunder.

One massive paw rose, dripping with water, and slammed down in the middle of the boat, causing it to shake violently. The other paw slammed down, just missing me.

The tupilak grinned. Its white teeth sparkled in the deep night. Bright red drool drenched my face—Cameron's blood.

211

It opened its mouth and roared, declaring it was the king of the ocean. From the depths of its belly I heard the voices of those it had eaten.

A light shone across my face.

Something pressed against my neck. "Got a pulse. She's alive."

"Got a pulse here, too. Nu Venia's alive."

"Cameron?" I whispered. He'd come for us.

Did Nu Venia know? Was Nella with him? Essal and Huth?

The tupilak was playing with me by tapping my face?

Water in my mouth. *I was drowning.* Didn't taste salty. *Already dead?*

More tapping. *Tupilak taunting me.*

"Jessie." Tap. Tap. More water. "Jessie. Wake up."

Water dripped over my face into my mouth. It tasted good. Strange.

My eyes fluttered open. Closed against the rain.

"Jessie! She's waking up. Jessie."

I forced my eyes open and tried to focus. Bright lights. Difficult to see. Blinked—couldn't focus.

Something important was happening, but I couldn't tell what.

I saw blond hair. An angel? Was death that quick and easy? Was I in Heaven? Why was it raining in Heaven?

Tried to speak. Words froze in my mouth.

"What did you say? Jessie?" A man's voice—familiar—such tenderness. Cameron? No, it didn't sound like him? Dad?

More tapping—like someone was—was trying to—to wake me.

"She's coming around." The voice sounded relieved. "Jessie, wake up."

The face focused. I recognized that smile, those dimples, the crinkled nose, and his freckles.

Jorge?

"Not dead?" My throat felt raw.

"Far from it." Jorge let out a relieved laugh. He held me close and sobbed. "I thought we were too late. You're so cold."

"How?" I croaked. "Find?"

He spoke into my hair. "The ship came two and a half days ago. Adumie kicked us out. We've been on *WSC Stanza*. Captain Leopold sent four shuttles to search for you. He let me tag along." Jorge pulled away, beaming. "I can't believe it's really you."

"How?" I wanted to know how he had found me in the middle of a vast, empty ocean.

"We didn't know where you were. We've been flying in circles. I thought we'd never find you." His voice choked at the words. "We had to return to the ship because of the storm. I was standing in the Eatery staring out the window, when the captain called. Their radar had found you in a tiny orange boat."

He gave me another big hug.

"Trans?" I was unable to say transport. "Two years?" We hadn't been gone that long, had we?

He released me. "Technology advanced while we were away. It only took them a year and 52 days to get here."

I'd be home in a year and three months? My heart leapt for joy. Then it sank. I'd survived Woden. That meant I had to finish Cameron's mission.

"Nu Venia?" I weakly asked.

Jorge called over his shoulder. "Nu Venia. How is she?"

"Cold, not hypothermic." A woman's voice said.

"Imos?" I asked.

"Imos?" Jorge asked, questioning. "There's no one else here."

"Chovis."

"What? Jessie, what are you asking?"

"Chovis?"

His eyes dated around. "There's a dog and some puppies."

"Alive?"

Jorge looked at me as if I was confused.

I asked more urgently "Alive?"

"Ah, I don't . . . Hey, how's the dog and puppies?"

"Alive," another voice said.

"Don't leave. Take them." I forced the words out.

Tired.

Wanted to sleep, but I couldn't leave Imos and Essal's puppies behind.

"Yeah. Okay," Jorge said. "Someone get the dog and puppies on the shuttle. We're taking them with us."

"Right," the voice said. "But we need to hurry; that storm is coming in fast."

I almost drifted off, but there was something I was forgetting.

Jorge started to pull me to my feet.

"No." I resisted. "Have something . . ." I swallowed to clear my throat. ". . . for you."

He eased me back down. "Can't it wait?"

I tried to shake my head.

"Okay, sure," he sounded reassuring, but I could tell he was worried about me.

My hand flopped toward the research backpack, but I couldn't reach it. Jorge pulled it closer and opened it for me. My arm was heavy, and my hand was weak. I couldn't grab hold of the plastic container or pull it out.

My finger tapped the container. "Algae. Red line."

He pulled the jar out and held it up to the shuttle's light.

"I don't think so." He squinted at it with wonder. "Looks like worms to me."

Chapter 23

Akiane Historical Chronicles
Father Joseph Striken

Year 28
Endurance: One year after Faris' Death

THOSE WHO listened to Fintan ostracized the cocoon children. Joe adopted three more children who had been abandoned. As time passed, it became clear that cocoon-born children were like any other children who laughed, cried, played, and loved.

As the cocoons hardened, children kicked their way out, just like the pups. There was much celebration among those who accepted the children, and anger among those who did not. Surprisingly, the children came forth healthy, the size of a toddler with skin in various shades of maroon. Their eyes and hair were black as night. Each child immediately recognized the voice of the one to whom they belonged. Within an hour they were walking and talking.

"Normal" and cocoon-born children played well together. They taught their parents there was nothing to fear.

Tensions eased among most adults, and they slowly learned to accept the cocoon children. But not Fintan, who no longer had the support to follow through on his threat of an election. He became a walking, smoldering volcano waiting to explode.

Babies came in batches. There might not be any births for weeks or months, then several would come within hours of each other, as parents held their breath during each pregnancy.

Then nine babies were born within 35 hours of one another. Three were born the normal way. The other six came forth in cocoons.

One of the mothers was an unmarried seventeen-year-old, who declared she had never had sex.

Fintan didn't believe her.

Of the nine born, only one cocoon had been abandoned.

Fintan dragged his wife out of the birthing area, forcing her to abandon their child. He then rekindled his cry: "Children born in a cocoon were not human, but a curse from God. And that curse was taking over their children because they were not listening to God's warning to repent."

Though he couldn't say what they were to repent for.

When asked why it took so long between cocoon births, Beasley could only guess. The parents who had been born on *WSC Hawk* all had normal births. Cocoon births came from parents who had been born and raised on Akiane.

"There is something on the planet that's changing us," Beasley concluded. "Eventually all of our children will be born in cocoons." His explanation was longer, but it made little sense to most people.

Father Joseph Striken's Quarters

Joe heard a soft knock on his door. He opened it and stared in shock at the woman standing in his doorway with a cocoon in her arms.

216

"You never expected to see me at your door did you, Father Striken?" Fiona asked.

"I . . . ah . . . no. I'm not sure if it's because you are Fintan's wife or because you're holding a cocoon. Is it yours? I mean . . ."

She laughed softly at his confusion, but there was no merriment.

"Yes, it is mine. May I come in?"

"Oh, yes, of course." He stepped aside. "But shouldn't you be making a nest?"

"I am told I have time," she said.

"Why are you here?" he asked. "I'm sorry, I don't mean to sound rude. It's just that . . ."

"You're surprised."

"Yes."

Her face contorted. "He tried to drag me away from my child. I know Fintan can be difficult. He can also be a most loving and considerate husband." She stopped and caught her breath. Joe thought she might start crying; instead, she became defiant. "I will not let him keep me from my child."

"You left him?" Joe asked in. He never understood what this gentlewoman saw in Fintan. Nevertheless, he was sure of their love and had never imagined that she would walk out on him. Certainly his imagination had never covered the possibility of her coming to him for counsel.

"Yes." She pulled a handkerchief out of her pocket, blew her nose, and composed herself.

"And you have come to me. Why?" he asked.

She turned her attention to Joe's four children playing at the far end of the room. "They've grown so fast."

Two of his girls were only a year old, but they were the size of five year olds. The other girl and boy were several months younger.

Joe remembered the days when his life and living quarters were well ordered. But like the area where his children were playing, everything about his life had

217

become disordered. Yet, he'd never felt so alive, and had become comfortable with the disorder.

"Father Striken, is it true your children came out of their cocoons as toddlers?" Fiona continued.

"Yes, cocoon children seem to age faster than other children. Beasley has an idea as to what is happening, but the explanation is a bit complicated."

"Yes, Fintan has been ranting about it." Tears formed in her eyes.

Joe thought those tears were for the loss of her husband.

"I'll miss my child being a baby," she said.

He saw that her eyes were red and swollen from crying, but she held herself with the determination of one who would not be defeated.

"That is not why I have come, Father Striken."

Joe guided her to a chair. She carefully placed her cocoon on her lap. He pulled a chair next to her and sat down.

"Then why?" he asked.

"You have three girls."

"Yes. I am sorry to say, their mothers didn't want them. This last year has been," Joe leaned back in his chair as he sought for the words, "life changing."

"They will need a mother. There are things only a woman can teach them."

Joe considered her words and thought he knew where she was headed. He knew his girls would need the guidance of a woman.

Alethea was the first mother to keep her cocoon. She had taught Joe how to love his cocoons instead of treating them like objects. She also did her best to encourage women to keep their children. Most listened, but he now had three girls and one boy from those who had not. He often wondered how many more children he would have to care for.

As helpful as Alethea had been, she had suggested he might need more than one woman to help him raise his girls. He thought those words came from one who feared she might carry the full burden of being his only adviser.

Joe tried his best not to ask too many questions or favors of her.

Now he realized Alethea was giving him good advice from the Bible in the book of Proverbs: *Plans fail for the lack of counsel, but with many advisers they succeed.*

His oldest daughter, Abigail, walked to Fiona and handed the woman her doll.

Fiona graciously accepted the doll, saying, "Thank you, my dear."

The girl placed her ear on the cocoon and listened. "He laughs." Abigail giggled, then returned to her sisters and brother.

Joe did not rush Fiona. He knew from experience it was best to give the one who came for counseling time to gather their thoughts. He settled in his chair and waited patiently.

Fiona returned her attention to him. "There is an empty room next to yours. I plan to move in, and with your permission, help you raise your girls."

Joe leaned forward in surprise. "You want us to become a family?"

"Of sorts, yes."

He knew that God's ways were often mysterious, and would become logical when one understood the full plan. But he and Fiona joining forces? What good could come of that?

Fintan's anger toward Joe would only increase.

Could the Community survive more turmoil and division over a priest and a married woman becoming a family?

And yet, he couldn't abandon Fiona and her child just because it was inconvenient for him.

"I'm an excellent cook," Fiona said hopefully.

Joe snorted. "The quickest way to help a man make up his mind is through his stomach, yes?"

Slightly self-conscious, Fiona said, "I had not thought of it that way, but yes, I did hope to bribe you. I will be raising a child by myself. There are several people who would be glad to take me in and help me, but I don't want charity. And I don't want anyone trying to convince me to return to Fintan."

"I'm a priest. It's my business to preserve the sanctity of marriage." *Why did God make things so difficult?* Joe wondered. *Because the journey creates character. Because He wants me to trust Him.* "I'm an excellent eater when someone else is cooking. And as of late, I learned the value of cleaning up after others."

"Well, that would be a change." Fiona sniffed.

"How so?"

"Fintan would not so much as pick up his plate once he finished eating."

Joe sighed, and said, "I remember what a great guy he once was. What happened, Fiona?"

"Lazard. Once it was learned Blood Vine milk could be fermented, Fintan became obsessed with turning it into the best liquor he could. But when he started drinking heavily, he became just like his father."

Joe had known Fintan and Fiona's parents. He'd christened Fiona and Fintan when they were born. They both came from good, loving homes.

"I don't remember Connor being mean," Joe said.

"According to Fintan's mother, back in Ireland, Connor loved his whisky, but it made him mean."

"I was on the ship with him," Joe said. "I never saw him take a drink."

"He gave it up for a free trip to start life over on a new world. He never took another drink. From then on, he was a dedicated husband and beloved father. Until Lazard.

Creating the drink was something Connor and Fintan could do together," she said. "It wasn't until after his father died that Fintan began to drink heavily and became mean."

"And now Fintan is following in the worst of his father's habits," Joe said.

Tears of desperation came fast. "Father Striken, please, he will make me give up my child. He is so furious. I've never seen him like this. I fear he might kill my child."

"You're seeking sanctuary." Joe made up his mind and would trust God with the rest.

She hunched her shoulders. "I guess I am."

"If he comes for you, I'm not sure I have the means to stop him."

"You're a priest. No matter how angry he is with me or you, he will not defy you," she said. "Besides, since I left him for my child, I'm not sure he will take me back even if I wanted him to. His pride will not let him."

"Do you think he would do harm to any of the other cocoons?"

"Before all this started, if you had asked me such a question, I would have been insulted. I might not have slapped a priest, but in my heart, I would have wanted to. Now." She couldn't face the thought of the possibility of what her husband might do. "After the first cocoon births, Fintan wanted to destroy the Blood Vines so no more children could be fed by them."

"Yes, I remember," Joe said. "By God's good grace, chovis' needs won out over the fear of cursed births."

"He begrudgingly left the vines alone. God works in strange ways, Father," Fiona said sorrowfully. "Even Fintan understands the importance of Blood Vines for chovis to survive."

"It might be prudent to have Fatimah place guards around the nesting area. Just to be safe." Joe didn't want to offend Fiona, but at the same time, he didn't want any harm to come to hers or anyone else's child.

Fiona covered her face with her hands and wept.

Joe's children stopped playing, looked at Fiona, and started crying. He hurried to them. "Do not cry, do not cry."

When one child was unhappy, they suddenly all became unhappy. Even though many parents had assured him this was normal, it bothered Joe that their moods could change so quickly.

"It's okay," he said. "Fiona needs your love and comfort, not your tears."

Abigail was the first to stop crying. She rubbed her nose on the sleeve of her dress and stood. She walked to Fiona and placed her head on Fiona's knee. "Don't cry. Daddy will make it all better."

Her sisters and brother joined her as they also patted and hugged Fiona.

It was reassuring to see how easily children forgot their sadness and became a comfort.

There had been many days when mayhem reigned, one didn't want to eat, another didn't want to get dressed, or take a bath; they cried and fought with each other and with Joe. The days of frustration made him question if God knew what He was doing. What purpose could there be for a priest to be a parent?

Thankfully there were far more days of love and laughter.

As his children gathered around Fiona, they brought a spark of healing in place of rejection. They gave her love in place of tears and brought a radiant smile to her face.

Perhaps God knew what He was doing after all.

"Seems my children like you," Joe said as he sat back in his chair.

Fiona laughed through her tears. "There is nothing like the love of a child to make things better." She gave each one a hug and kissed the tops of their heads.

"Then it is settled," Joe said. "Welcome to the family."

Fiona beamed. "Thank you, Father Striken. I'm not sure what I would have done if you had said no."

"Please. Call me Joe," he said.

"I'm not sure I can. Maybe in time," Fiona said.

"Then we will settle on Father Joe."

With a smile, she said, "I'll try."

"Good enough," he said. "Perhaps there should be some discussion to clarify the boundaries of our family arrangement. But before any final decisions are made, your child needs a nest."

Fiona's smile evaporated. Her hand passed over her cocoon. "To have a child presents many unknowns; but to have an alien child, for cocoons are alien to us, present us with completely new unknowns that are totally unfamiliar to any of us."

"We will learn together, not just you and me, but as a Community. With God's help all of us will come around, even Fintan."

"Nice sentiment, Father, but I do not see all of us accepting these children," she said. "Old prejudices are too set in place. Some of us are reconnecting with our religion. But instead of uniting us in agreement, fractions have formed. Some are understanding but some are becoming radicalized and are demanding that those who are different be rejected." She spoke in disappointment. "As if we have some disease."

"Prejudice spreads evenly over different religions, as does acceptance," Joe said.

"There are those on both sides who think separation might be best," Fiona said. "You might also be surprised to learn it is only the Hindu who are in full agreement. All 26 of them welcome the cocooned children and their mothers with open arms."

Joe shook his head in wonderment. "Perhaps all of us could learn a little about acceptance from them.

"But your nest," he insisted. "You do have time, but not as much time as you may think. Cocoons dry out, which is why they need a nest and need to be turned often. My nests are still standing. You can use one of them."

"Father, you have more than one nest?"

"I adopted four children who came close together. A nest works best when it holds one child at a time. So when I had two children given to me close to the same time, I needed two nests. Thankfully, I did not receive all four children at the same time. So yes, I have more than one nest, which are reusable. I care for them as I would any plant, so they're ready at a moment's notice."

"Children," Joe called their attention to him, "would you like it if Fiona lived next door to us and we become family?"

They squealed in delight.

He stood. "Then let's take her to our nests and place her cocoon in one of them."

"Can I help turn it?" Abigail asked.

"Me too?" the others chimed.

With a glance, Joe consulted Fiona.

She stood. "I would be delighted to have your help."

Chapter 24

Akiane Historical Chronicles
Father Joseph Striken

Akiane Date: Year 28
Endurance: Blood Vines—Same Day

"THE NURSERY is growing," Fiona said.

"We now have 17 nests among the Blood Vines," Joe said. "Though not all have children in them."

Joe's children left his side and ran to play among the vines.

He noted how peaceful the area was.

The three original designers, Carlos, Lenard, and Kitty, were giving instructions to the new parents on how to build their nests. Alethea was offering advice on how to care for cocoons to Mollah, the teenage mother.

Then he saw Fintan and his friends.

Why must there always be a snake in the garden? Joe thought.

Mollah was the youngest female to become pregnant and who adamantly declare that she had never had sex, but had spontaneously become pregnant.

Beasley believed her, saying that she was of the second generation born on Akiane, which increased the

225

probability of the biological change. "Chovis have puppies even when they do not mate. It seems it will be the same for our women."

Once again, comparing a human to a dog did not go over well. But it did encourage the revival of the belief that cocoon children were cursed. This time Beasley did not defend his words or apologize to those offended.

As Joe and Fiona approached the nursery, he heard Beasley shout, "Get over it. This is the way of things from here on. A day is coming when all of our children will be born in cocoons. We need to prepare for it, not stick our heads in the mud. Women will be able to have children with or without a partner." Those words earned him a black eye from Fintan.

If Fatimah had not been there, Beasley might have received a more severe beating, but the next blow came from her.

Joe hurried to join the group just as Fatima's fist slammed into Fintan's nose. He heard the crunch as Fintan cried out in pain.

Some who had witnessed the incident were furious, but there were just as many who were smiling.

"Got what he deserved," someone said.

"Are you all right?" Joe asked.

"She broke my nose," Fintan accused.

"That I saw. What I don't know is why?"

Blood seeped between Fintan's fingers.

"She didn't want to hear the truth," he said in a muffled voice.

Fatimah had a temper, but Joe knew she wouldn't hit someone without cause. There had to be more to the story.

"What truth?" Joe asked.

"That God has cursed her and her family for not believing in Him," Fintan said.

226

"Why did you say that?" Joe asked, losing all patience. He'd had all he could stand of this man. "Your own wife has had a cocoon. Does that mean you too are cursed by God?"

"I took measures and kicked her out." He lied.

Joe felt his fist curl and was severely tempted to finish what Fatimah had started. He closed his eyes, tried to relax his hand, but his arm tightened instead. He'd never hit anyone in his entire life. But then he'd never been so angry with anyone in his entire life.

He took three deep breaths hoping to calm down. It wasn't working. Joe turned and saw Fiona standing behind him. In shame, his anger vanished. *Forgive me,* Lord. He was so very thankful that she had not heard his thoughts.

"Fatimah broke my nose," Fintan loudly complained.

"Let me see," Beasley said, rubbing his own bruised cheek. "Move your hands, Fintan."

Fintan resisted.

"Let me see it," Beasley insisted.

Fintan's hands dropped away.

"Give me something for the pain before you . . . Aaaahhh."

Beasley adjusted his nose, which made the pain worse. Fintan pulled away and didn't see the good doctor's self-satisfied smile. His assistants tried to hide their smiles.

Fiona whimpered in concern.

Joe couldn't believe it. *What happened to "cause no harm"?*

One of Beasley's assistants handed him a roll of surgical tape. Even with all the miraculous advancement in medicine, sometimes the old ways were best. Especially when the patient refused to remain still.

Fintan tried to leave.

Beasley stopped him.

"Let me see it, Fintan," he said, "I need to tape your nose in place."

"I'll be needing no more of your help, doctor," Fintan shouted, yanking his arm away. "I'll be taping it myself."

"As you please." Beasley placed the tape in Fintan's hand. "Someone should be in the med labs if you need help later on."

"I'll not be needing help from the likes of you." Fintan growled as he tenderly touched his nose.

The man's eyes were watering in pain.

Fiona handed her cocoon to Joe as she went to Fintan.

At the sight of his wife, bully Fintan suddenly became a little boy. His cries of pain came freely. "Fatimah broke my nose. He made it worse." Fintan moaned and pointed to Beasley.

Beasley blushed with shame when Fiona glanced his way. She shook her head in reproach, but a slight grin creased her lips. Beasley's blush turned to surprise. She wasn't angry. Fiona was a woman who understood her husband and still loved him.

Beasley's smile started to broaden. Joe jabbed him in the ribs. If Fintan saw what had just transpired between them, he would have gone into such a fury that Beasley would have gotten more than a broken nose.

"Come." Fiona's arm wrapped around Fintan's shoulder. "I'll take care of you," she said with the sympathy of a loving wife. She gently wiped blood from his nose, took the tape from his hand, and led him away.

Joe feared they might make up, which would mean he'd lose her help and probably her friendship. *How selfish of me,* he thought. *It would be best for their family.*

Then he remembered, Fintan wouldn't take her back unless she gave up their child. Fiona would never do that.

Once out of *earshot*, Joe asked, "What precipitated the incident?"

"Fatimah's teenage granddaughter, Mollah," Beasley said. "Fintan has been carrying on about her having a child out of wedlock, as if that's never happened before. Fatimah lost her patience."

"Something must be done about him," Joe said.

"Well, Joe, short of hanging him by his toes, I don't know what that is," Beasley said.

"I was thinking more along the lines of prayer."

"Let me know how that goes." Beasley said sarcastically, and left with his team.

Joe knew how much Fiona wanted to care for her cocoon herself, but he also knew the child couldn't wait.

And so begins our new family, he thought. *She will tend to her husband and I will tend to her child.*

He gently placed the cocoon in his nest and began massaging the vines. Life-giving milk started flowing. His girls ran to watch as Joe turned the cocoon to moisten its membrane. He did it slowly as Alethea taught him so as not to disturb the child within.

"I want to see," Daniel protested. He was too small to see over the edge of the nest.

Alethea picked Daniel up so he could see.

"Do you have another child, Father Joseph?" Alethea asked.

"No, this is Fiona's child," he said.

"I heard she left him. She is a most courageous woman and loving mother," she said. "Does not Fintan understand, that by his reasoning, his own child is cursed?"

"He believes we must purify ourselves by prostrating before God and begging His forgiveness," Joe said.

"Father Joseph?" Alethea raised an eyebrow.

"I don't believe that." He lifted his hands in denial. "Only a pagan god would ask for such a sacrifice."

"Beasley warned us that change was inevitable, yet we did not believe," she said.

A group of serious looking men entered the area. They strategically stationed themselves around the nests guarding them.

"Fatimah fears more trouble," one of the men spoke to those in the Blood Vines. "She has sent us to stand guard. There will be someone here at all times as long as we are needed."

Soon more people arrived. Joe estimated 30 men, women, and children.

Daniel wiggled free. As soon as Alethea set him down, he ran toward the new arrivals.

Alethea caught her breath in fear of more trouble.

The guards hurried to greet the newcomers.

Joe braced himself for another confrontation. Just because guards were here by Fatimah's request did not mean they were welcomed. The new arrivals might be more of Fintan's "friends."

"Daniel, come here," he called, but his son kept running to meet one of his friends.

Joe needn't have worried.

Everyone was smiling. They carried blankets, baskets of food, and jars of Lazard for drinks. Soon there was a spontaneous picnic to celebrate and welcome new cocoons and their parents with love, support, and acceptance. They came with the assurance that everyone together formed a Community and together they would figure out the new chapter in their lives.

Same afternoon in Fatimah's quarters

"Maybe you can forgive, Priest, but I refuse to let the likes of him insult those I love." Fatimah paced her room, each step was as intense as her fist hitting Fintan's nose. "I know it's unbecoming of a leader, but I don't care."

Joe had left his children in the care of those celebrating and had set out to find Fatimah. He found her alone in her living quarters.

"I do not care what Allah or your Jesus preaches. No one calls my granddaughter a whore," she yelled in frustration as she slammed her fist in her palm.

"It is difficult to believe a woman can have a child by herself," Joe said, in an attempt to explain Fintan's point of view.

Fatimah stopped pacing, faced him, and growled.

He raised his hands in truce. "Beasley has corroborated the truth of your granddaughter becoming spontaneously pregnant. Somehow this planet is changing our children. He thinks it has something to do with the fact that there are more girls being born than boys. He says if there are not enough men, then women will have to have children on their own."

"So you believe because science says it? How spiritual of you, Priest." With the defiance of a soldier, she stood ready to do battle.

He again raised his hands in surrender. "How many more noses do you plan to break?" Joe asked. "You are aware that I am not in agreement with Fintan, yes?"

A slight grin softened Fatimah's face. "Several more noses would satisfy how offensive Fintan has become." She continued to pace. She stopped in front of a wall and released a slow sigh of frustration. "Unfortunately, it would not be the honorable thing to do."

"Breaking a few noses *would* be satisfying," Joe said.

She spun around. "What?"

"Fatimah, I may be a man of the cloth, but I'm not as holy as I'd like to be."

Their hearty laughs eased the tension in the room and helped Fatimah relax.

"I suppose neither of us are what we wish," she said.

"What do you want to do?" Joe asked. "I mean, besides physically abuse people."

"The soldier in me wants to fight, to stay and prove to those like Fintan that they are wrong." Her voice quivered.

"But?"

Her entire body slumped.

Joe knew more was coming.

"There are those who do not wish to fight or stay," she said. "They, like me, are tired of living indoors. Our children and grandchildren do not know what it is like to live outside. We wish to show them."

"Not live in Endurance? Come winter years, you would freeze to death." Joe had lost his good friend, Faris. Was he about to lose Fatimah as well? Now he wished *he* had slugged Fintan.

"No, we have found land at the equator where the temperature is such that the ocean does not freeze and weather is more habitable. We will still have winters, just not as severe."

"Why was I not told of this?"

"It was thought that it would be best to keep it quiet and tell as few people as possible."

"Why, Fatimah?"

"We didn't want Fintan and his friends forcing us to leave before we were ready."

"And you thought I would leak your plans? Do you think so little of me?"

"Joe, no." This was the first time in 30 years that she had used his first name. She had never called him anything but Priest. At first it was meant as an insult because he was not *imam khatib*, a Muslim priest, but as they became friends, "Priest" had become a term of endearment.

"I couldn't bring myself to tell you," she said. "I knew you would be disappointed, and I feared you would not come with us."

"So why are you telling me now?"

"A few of us have already moved there."

"Yes, I've notice the absence of a few people," Joes said. "I thought they might be fishing."

"They are preparing a building large enough for all of us to live in while we build our individual homes," she said.

"That was the original plan," Joe said. "We were to live in the ships while we built our city, then we would build our homes. Instead, we built a garden and still live in *Falcon*. What makes you think your plans will be any different?"

She shook her head, took a deep breath, then looked him in the eye. "It is hoped that we have learned from our mistakes. They have planted Blood Vines and built nests. Crops have already been planted. Living quarters are being built that will last through the upcoming Storms."

"Does Fintan know?"

"He found out and is unbelievably pleased. He's even helped load the shuttle with supplies." She chuckled.

Fintan knew, but Joe didn't. He felt slighted, even lied to by omission.

When she first mentioned the move, he thought it would be years away. "How long have you been at this?"

"The idea was explored while Faris was alive, but I'm the one who has recently implemented it."

"What?" How could this happen without his knowing?

"Some of the younger generation have wanted to start over," she said. "A few years ago, they consulted the data from probes sent out to search for suitable places to live when we first landed. With Faris' permission they started exploring."

"Fatimah, why didn't Faris say something to me then?"

"I don't think Faris thought they would go through with it. And at first, they didn't, not seriously anyway. But recently, the trouble over the children happened." She shrugged. "Faris would never have agreed to the split, but now that she has gone, the plans have become more serious."

"When will the final move happen?"

"A matter of months." Fatimah sat next to him. "I want you to join us."

He leaned back. "I had not thought to ever leave Endurance," he said. "There will have to be much thinking before I can make a decision."

"And prayer?" Fatima asked.

He nodded. "Yes, prayer is definitely needed."

This was his home. Did he really want to leave? What would be best for his children? He couldn't abandon Fiona. They had just agreed to join together as one family. She might have left Fintan, but she would never move to another settlement. She would never leave her husband behind like that.

Joe doubted there would be much prayer. His heart had already decided.

Chapter 25

Jessica Hewitt
Reunion

Akiane Date: Year 328
WSC Stanza: Sick Bay

I BOLTED straight up, breathing heavily. Where was I? A room. Light green walls. Another dream?

What monster would jump out of the corner and attack? I waited. Nothing came.

The bed and blankets felt real. No fur.

Maybe I had died and this was Heaven. Why was I alone?

Maybe this was Hell and my punishment was to spend all of eternity locked up in a small green room by myself.

Then I remembered. Nu Venia, the chovis, and I had been rescued. We were on a ship.

A weight-lifting sigh of relief escaped my lips. The pounding of my heart settled. My breathing slowed. I was no longer lost. I was safe on a WSC transport. I was in a bed with clean sheets, blankets, and a pillow. None of it was fur and none of it smelled like chovis. I was safe, alive, and toasty warm, headed back to Earth.

Earth. I'd never be cold again. And would never, never, ever leave her again.

I slowly lay back and drank in the realization I'd been rescued and I was going home. I closed my eyes and smiled.

Thinking of Earth made me terribly homesick. What would it be like to be hot and sweaty, lying on a sandy Baja, California beach instead of being afraid of falling off an ice floe, or stepping through precarious melting ice, or being attacked by a sea monster, or having the ice-encrusted ocean explode all around me.

What would it be like to safely play in the Pacific surf with only sharks and rip tides to worry about?

I was going home.

My family and friends would never believe the adventures I'd had. When we gathered for family reunions, I would be the military cousin with the alien war stories. All the children would gather around wide-eyed, intently listening while their parents nodded their heads at how easily I made up my sci-fi tales. Some of the most important events of my life could hardly be believed. If I hadn't lived them myself, I might not believe them.

But those family reunions were far into the future.

The first thing I wanted when I got back was homemade ice cream. When I was a child, my favorite homemade ice cream was from a shop in St Paul, Minnesota.

It took me a moment to remember. It wasn't an ice cream shop. It was my backyard.

Mom mixed the ingredients. Dad pulled out the mixer and poured the mixture in it. I pushed the button and watched through the clear top as it slowly churned into ice cream.

Sometimes Mom and Dad turned on music and danced on the back patio. Sometimes we played chase, card games, or board games. We always ended the evening eating homemade ice cream.

The happy memories faded.

We stopped making ice cream just before Mom left. Once, Dad and I tried to make it by ourselves but it didn't taste the same. Dad said he must have forgotten something. I think it was because it reminded us too much of Mom. We never made ice cream again.

"Ah, you're awake." Rona stepped through the door with a huge smile.

She held the door open as Jorge entered carrying a tray of food. I smelled a steaming cup of hot chocolate. On the tray was a plate of food with a silver cover to keep it warm.

It was good to see Rona and great to see Jorge. I couldn't count the times I was sure I'd never see either of them again.

Was I smiling too much? That smile began somewhere deep inside and seemed to end somewhere beyond my face.

Jorge looked intently at me. His dimples came, followed by his smile. I thought he was going to hold me in his arms and kiss me—then he glanced at Rona. His eyes slowly came back to me and his smile faded.

So did mine.

Rona beamed as she practically skipped to my bed, bent over, and gave me a surprisingly tight bear hug that made me gasp for breath. I hugged her just as tight. Her hair smelled of rose petal shampoo and a hint of perfume. Most importantly, she didn't smell of chovis. I wondered what I smelled like?

After placing the food tray on a shelf along the wall, Jorge gave me a warm, lingering, welcome back hug. I didn't want to let go. What if this was a dream? He might disappear into a misty whiteout. Then I'd have to face the reality that I was still lost and dying. Or maybe I was already dead and this was an afterlife wish.

"Welcome back." Jorge kissed me lightly on the lips then straightened.

I blinked several times, just to make sure they were still there. This was not a dream. The nightmare was finally over. I exhaled a long sigh of relief.

"How long was I gone," I asked, "and what ship is this?"

"You've been gone for almost a month," Rona said.

"We're on the *WSC Stanza*," Jorge said.

"Where's Nu Venia?" I asked. My voice was surprisingly weak and soft. I coughed to clear my throat.

Jorge brought me a glass filled with ice cubes in ice-cold water. I almost laughed.

"Jorge, got anything warmer?" I said.

"Yeah, right. Sorry, Jessie," he said and traded the water for a cup of hot cocoa.

I took a sip. "Aaaa. Now this hits the spot." Another sip. I didn't have to wait for the drink to warm me. I was already warm. Instead, I savored the flavor of chocolate.

"I was afraid we might never find you, even after you were safe on board. Last night I had a dream that a tupilak had eaten you," Rona said.

"I don't want to think about tupilak," I said. "I just want to enjoy the warmth and the bed. Can I have another blanket?"

"You were so cold. How long were you on the water?" Jorge pulled a blanket from the overhead storage bin.

"That would have been our fourth night," I said. "We wouldn't have survived another night if you hadn't found us."

"How did you survive three nights?" he asked.

"Fish," I said. "There's something in them that kept us warm." According to Nu Venia, there was also something in the fish that could physically alter my body's biology. Should I say something? I was too afraid of the answer.

"Olivia will be happy to hear that," Jorge said.

I didn't care about Olivia or her fish. "Rona, how is Nu Venia?"

"All is well," she said. "The doctors haven't given any indication to the contrary. She woke a few hours before you."

That was a relief. We'd both survived. "When can I see her?"

"You might want to finish recovering first," Rona paused.

"You're not going anywhere without breakfast." Jorge retrieved the tray. "You hungry?"

"Famished." I was more than ready for something other than dried meat, dried fish, and frozen vegetables.

Rona raised the head of my bed and moved a portable table over my lap. Breakfast! There was nothing better to ease homesickness than a good, old-fashion country breakfast of eggs, bacon, hash browns, and a thick piece of toast slathered with butter.

That's not what I got.

Breakfast was *junk pizza*.

My mouth instantly watered. With that first bite of cheese, tomato sauce, pepperoni, sausage, onions, bell pepper, mushrooms, and anchovies, I knew I was home.

I got one whole slice finished, before Rona could no longer contain herself and blurted out, "Zhoa's dead."

That stunned me. I'd expected I would die, but not someone who was safely back at the habitat.

"What happened?" I asked, suddenly losing my appetite.

"He got an infection from the tupilak, a retrovirus," she said.

"How?"

"He cut himself while he was butchering one of them," she said.

"I was there when that happened." Was that really only a month ago? It felt as though it had happened to another person. "But Mathieu, Lesley, and Vong were also there. Did they get sick?"

"The doctors, Lesley and Mathieu, wore surgical gloves and masks," Jorge said.

"Zhoa and Vong teased them about that. Maybe all of them should have dressed like surgeons," I said.

"It was the cut that let the retrovirus in. It started as a rash. Lu and I gave him an ointment. Lesley gave him antibiotics. Nothing helped," Rona said.

"Zhoa died during the gravitational storm," Jorge said. "We think the fear of the storm increased his adrenaline, which accelerated the infection."

I would have believed a volcano, lava, or quakes getting them, but a retrovirus? People didn't die from retrovirus anymore.

Rona sniffled. "Vong started to get the same infection, but thanks to what we leaned from Zhoa's autopsy, Lu and I were able to save him."

Jorge draped a comforting arm around her shoulders and pulled her close. She rested her head on his shoulder.

I knew it. While I was gone, those two had become a couple. Well, I couldn't blame him—out of sight, out of mind. Even so, I'd only been gone a month.

He had kissed me for the first time, just before I left for Woden. He declared undying love and promised to wait for me. I spent the entire trip thinking about him.

Once Rona regained her composure, they casually moved apart. They were trying to be discreet until they found the right time to break the news to me. Perhaps I'd save them the trouble and let them know I knew.

"Lesley and Mathieu did the autopsy," Rona spoke rapidly, barely taking a breath. "It was the retrovirus. Lu and I found it in the chovis and tupilak. Olivia found it in the fish. The colonists also have it. We think the tupilak get it from the fish and give it to the hunters, butchers, and cooks who continually handle raw meat barehanded, but the children are also ill, which makes no sense."

"Is it contagious?" I asked.

"No." She shook her head. "It's not supposed to be contagious and it's not supposed to be passed down from parent to child."

"Then how do the children get it?" I asked.

"The colonists wouldn't let us examine them, so we don't know," she said.

The door opened and Mathieu came into the room.

It was barely noticeable, but Rona caught her breath. A mysterious grin that passed between them said he and she had a secret only they knew.

But when his attention turned to me, Mathieu's expression changed to one of concern. "I thought Cameron was Nu Venia's father."

"I thought the same thing when I first met them. Actually, Mathieu, she was his guardian," I said. "Long story."

"Well, they must have been more than that, because she's pregnant," he said, "and it happened recently."

"Oh, I did that," I said without thinking.

The silence was so profound one could have heard a pin drop all the way back on Earth. Jorge took a step away from me in shock. Rona was wide-eyed. Mathieu tilted his head as if he was trying to imagine what might have happened between us.

I burst out laughing.

"Not to worry, I'm female all the way through with all the right body parts. Let me start at the beginning." I told them about the transference of sperm by holding hands.

"That's not possible," the men said simultaneously.

"Well, that might not be exactly true." Everyone's attention turned to Rona.

"Lu and I also took a sample of DNA from Nu Venia's child," she said. "And before you object, it was her idea. She asked if we could tell if her child was healthy. Her child is perfectly fine, no retrovirus. Except . . .."

"Except what?" I asked.

"The child's is yours and Cameron's. There's nothing of Nu Venia in the child."

I wasn't sure I really wanted to know, but I asked anyway. "And that means?"

"You're the mother of Nu Venia's child."

Chapter 26

Jessica Hewitt
Revelations

Akiane Date: Year 328
WSC Stanza: Sick Bay

"BUT NU VENIA?" I asked.

"Is the surrogate mother," Rona said.

"Rona, did you tell her?"

"Jess, I didn't know what to say. I didn't even know how it was possible."

"But now you know."

"But I don't understand it."

"What have you learned from the other colonists?"

"For the most part, they avoid us as if we gave them the retrovirus," Rona said. "But one mother, I guess it doesn't matter if we keep her name secret any more. Qorow Low came to us and asked for our help to save her child."

"Did you save her child?" I asked.

"We thought we had, but unfortunately, no," Rona said. "Lu and I took blood samples from her and her child, but she wouldn't allow us to give them a physical examination. We tried treating them and they were getting better. We don't know what happened to the mother. But we're fairly certain the child died, which is why we were banished from Endurance. No one else ever let us get near them."

"That's because they're embarrassed," I said.

Rona seemed perplexed. "Why? Embarrassed about what?"

"Because the colonists can have children without a partner," I said. "They're no longer humans like us. Somehow this planet changed them."

Jessica explained in detail Nu Venia's explanation about how babies are born on Akiane.

"I've examined Nu Venia," Mathieu said. "As far as I can tell, she's fully human and capable of becoming pregnant the old-fashioned way. Of course I didn't think to examine her hand." He thought for a moment. "I can't imagine how it's possible for her to get pregnant from holding hands."

"That's why touching is forbidden," I said. "I'm telling you, they reproduce without a partner." I held up my hand. "Nu Venia got pregnant when we held hands. That's not the old-fashioned way."

"Jess, it's not that I don't believe you, I just don't see how it's possible," Mathieu said.

"So how is it possible?" Jorge asked.

"Parthenogenesis," Rona said.

"Okay," I said. "What is that?"

"A Komodo dragon is a perfect example. If there are no males present, she'll lay eggs anyway."

"As in cloning?" I asked.

"In cloning, a female reproduces an exact copy of herself. In parthenogenesis the mother's chromosomes will double and create a full genome complement half from the mother and the other half as if it came from the father. She does not exactly copy herself." The more she explained, the more excited she got, and the less Jess understood.

"If all of it comes from her, how is that not cloning?" I asked.

"It's difficult to explain," Rona said, as if I wouldn't understand, which I didn't. "At first, Lu and I thought the problem was from many years of inbreeding. Then we thought years of cloning had produced gene degradation. But from what you've just told us, after more than 300 years of parthenogenesis, their DNA is . . . well, tired."

"Why?" I asked.

"Humans weren't meant to duplicate themselves, Jessie," Jorge said. "We're designed to reproduce."

"I don't think it's this para whatever. If that was the case, there would be more men in the Community," I said. "But there are so few boys born that when one is born, there's a big celebration." I said. "I think there are more colonists secretly holding hands and making babies and some of those babies are boys. That's why boys are so rare. They don't tell their children they have two parents because they believe it's a sin to hold hands."

"Why do you think that, Jessie?" Jorge asked.

"Because they can't have a male child without a father," Mathieu confirmed. "And together, a man and a woman produce a healthy child. And that child might not have the retrovirus."

"However they do it, these people made an evolutional change, which is impossible to do in the amount of time they've been on Akiane. The change happened too quickly. It wasn't natural, and now the process is falling apart." The possibility of a new biological discovery was diminishing for Rona as reality set in. "They're dying because of it."

"We need to do something," I said. "They honestly think they're not supposed to have sex," I said. "Any child born of two parents is considered an abomination and an outcast."

"Lu and I lost so much time studying dogs when we could have been studying colonists," Rona said.

"Chovis," I corrected. "Why were you studying them in the first place, Rona?"

"It was better than doing nothing," she said.

Mathieu placed a hand on her shoulder. She placed her hand over his. Jorge didn't notice.

I was unsure what to do. Should I tell him they were a couple? For now, I decided to stay on topic.

"What did you learn about the chovis?" I asked.

"Most of them are female, but every once in awhile, a male is born," she said.

"I've got news for you. If there's not a male around, chovis also reproduce by themselves," I said. "Kind of like your worms, Jorge."

I remembered how he used to get excited when he was talking about worms.

Which was why I expected more of a reaction out of him than, "Huh?"

"Still, the colonists are not exactly like the chovis," Rona said. "The male chovis mate with an average of five bitches, then leave the area. Lu and I followed every puppy that became an adult male. We have several recordings, some as long as 45-minutes."

"Forty-five minutes straight?" Jorge asked in disbelief.

"Yes, 45 minutes, one bitch after another," Rona said. "Once finished, or maybe I should say, once the males become bored, they leave the habitat and don't come back."

"Maybe they come ashore somewhere else," I suggested.

"We attached a radio tag to every male puppy we found. We followed their signal into the ocean where we lost contact with them." Rona shook her head. "They come back as tupilak."

"Excuse me?" I asked.

"Adumie and some of his friends brought two dead tupilak to our room. Each had radio tags on their ears. The colonists thought we purposely put the tags on them."

"But you didn't," I said.

"No," Rona said. "I'd never even seen a live tupilak."

"Well, I have," I said. "Not a pretty sight. And just like the old Inuit myths, tupilak attack people, drag them under

246

the ice and eat them. That's how Cameron died." I grabbed a napkin from my tray to wipe the tears that came so easily.

"We wondered what had happened," Jorge said.

Rona kept talking, "The tupilak DNA matched exactly with two of the male chovis we had been following. They jumped in the ocean and swam off as chovis but returned as tupilak." She was excited again. "That's how we learned the tupilak and the chovis are the same animal."

The tupilak that had taken Cameron had the exact same nose as Addle because it was Addle. She left us for the ocean, grew into a tupilak, bided her time, and then took her revenge on him.

"That explains why chovis don't eat tupilak and tupilak don't eat chovis," I said. "They're the same animal and are not cannibals."

I wasn't sure if Jorge was listening because his thoughts were elsewhere.

Rona's excitement faded. "If only we knew how the colonists changed, but it's too late. Now that we've found you, we're heading back to WSC Moon Base." She realized what she'd said. "Don't get me wrong, Jess, I'm overjoyed that we found you, but now I'll never learn how all this happened."

"Nu Venia said the fish changed them," I said.

"It's not the fish." Jorge spoke slowly. His mind was processing important information. When realization dawned, he brightened. "Not by themselves anyway. I think the worms did it."

"What worms?" Mathieu asked.

"Yeah, what worms?" I asked.

"The worms you brought me," Jorge said.

"I didn't bring you any worms," I said.

"You did. You gave Olivia and me each two jars full of them," he said.

247

I vaguely remembered him saying something about worms while on the boat, but the rescue was as foggy as a dream that lingers for a short time and then slips away.

"I gave you algae from the same red line we saw when we first flew over Akiane in the shuttle," I said.

"The red line isn't algae, it's worms," he said.

"That's a lot of worms," I said.

Despite the gravity of the situation, I couldn't help smiling. Jorge had come to study biodiversity of a snow-covered alien planet. He'd hoped to find worms. He'd found them, and I helped.

"Olivia told us how, on Earth, marine life gathers to eat plankton," he said.

"Akiane's marine life gathers to eat worms," I said. "I've seen it."

"Rona said the retrovirus in Zhoa and Vong was missing parts of its RNA, and that's why their bodies reacted to the retrovirus the way they did," Jorge said. "I think the worms carry the enzyme the retrovirus needs to function properly."

"I don't understand," I said.

"RNA polymerase is the first of several steps RNA uses to copy DNA strands to make new, complementary RNA molecules," he said.

"I still don't understand."

"A retrovirus rewrites its host's DNA, but a retrovirus needs RNA polymerase, the enzyme, to start the process. In this case, the code also contains the worm's DNA. Though I'm not completely sure what that means," Jorge said.

"I do," I said.

"Explain," he said.

"I was listening when you told me about worm characteristics," I said. "And just like the worms, the colonists can reproduce with or without a partner."

Jorge smiled proudly because I knew the answer but his smile turned into a mixture of shock and amazement when I said, "And just like worms, the colonists can change sizes. I've seen Nu Venia and Cameron do it."

They reacted as if that was the strangest thing we'd just been talking about.

"You must have noticed how much larger she is now than when you first saw her," I said. "When we left, she was the size of a child. Now she's a full-grown adult, and she's pregnant. You think that happened in just a month's time?"

"We didn't really see her," Rona said. "We were so sad that you were leaving. I barely remember who was with you."

"I saw her when I followed you for . . .." He stopped before he said our first kiss. " . . . our last cup of tea together, but I too barely remember her or Cameron."

"Even so," Mathieu said, "it seems that the fish and the worms have a symbiotic relationship."

"And the colonists got caught in the middle," Jorge said.

"This is all theory," Rona reminded them. "We have to do the research to prove it, which we can't do because we're leaving."

"Don't give up just yet, Rona. We have those logs Lu mentioned," Mathieu said.

"What logs?" I asked.

"That's one of the things we came to tell you, Jess," Jorge said. "The captain has new orders for you. You have a whole new colony to meet."

"What?"

Chapter 27

Jessica Hewitt
Conference Call

Akiane Date: Year 328
WSC Stanza: Captain's Ready Room

I FINALLY finished breakfast, but of course it was cold by then. Still, cold pizza was better than chovis stew. And no matter the century, pizza never goes out of style.

There was a soft knock at my door. A private entered and told me that Captain Leopold requested my presence. The private waited outside my room while I took a shower and dressed. It was my first real shower since I'd left *Britannia.* I'd dreamed about this day, but now I couldn't enjoy it.

The bridge was like any other—lots of people at their stations with buttons to push and monitors to watch.

The bridge's first officer rose from his chair and faced me. "Welcome to *WSC Stanza,* Lieutenant Hewitt."

Every head turned toward me with proud smiles, admiration, and a few thumbs up, then as one, they stood at attention.

No one stood at attention for a lieutenant. With as many times as the captain came and went, they didn't even stand for him. I thought someone else had entered the room, but no, they were standing for me.

Why were they honoring me? I felt embarrassed, out of place, and totally confused.

"There was a lot of cheering on the bridge when we heard you were safely on board," the first officer said.

"I, ah," I didn't know what to say. "Thank you."

The crew and I were the same age, but they were fresh and green. I was, not older, but well-seasoned. We stared at each other. Were they waiting for me to say something? Was I supposed to impart some kind of wisdom? I didn't have any.

The first officer tactfully rescued me. "The captain is waiting to debrief to you. Everyone, back to your stations."

The private fulfilled his orders and walked me across the bridge to the captain's ready room door and pressed a button on the doorframe.

From inside the captain said, "Enter."

"I'll be here when you're ready," the private said. "I'll escort you to your new quarters." He moved to one side of the door and stood at attention.

"I'd like to visit Nu Venia after the captain is finished debriefing me," I said.

"As you say, Lieutenant."

Unlike Captain Norris, who had remained in his chair and expected me to stand at attention, Captain Leopold came around his desk and greeted me with a handshake.

"Good to have you on board, Lieutenant Hewitt. I do hope we're making your stay a pleasant one."

"Sir, yes, Sir," I said.

"At ease, Lieutenant."

"Yes, Sir, thank you, Sir." I relaxed my stance.

He smiled, walked back behind his desk, and sat down. "Sit."

I sat across from him.

"First business at hand, I've briefed Admiral Grossman about the discovery of the new colony," he began. "You'll be pleased to know that the admiral is ordering you to make first contact with the colony."

Pleased to know? I had a flashback of when I'd stood before Captain Norris and he gave me orders to make first contact with Pegasus Colony. I'd begged and all but cried to be released from those orders. This time I was curious enough about the new colony that I *wanted* to go, but first I had my own request.

"Sir, may I return to Endurance first?" I asked.

"That is for the admiral to decide. But I'm under the impression that High Priest Adumie doesn't want you or Nu Venia to return. The admiral has granted his request." Captain Leopold's smile vanished.

"Between you and me, Lieutenant, I think the admiral has lost interest in the old colony. I'm sorry. I don't have the authority to grant your request. I can see about an audience if you wish to speak with the admiral yourself. "

"Yes, Sir, I would."

After my debriefing about Pegasus Colony, Woden, and how I was recovering, the captain politely dismissed me.

The private informed me my quarters were next to Nu Venia's.

As I entered her quarters, Nu Venia jumped to her feet.

The first question out her of mouth was, "When do we return to Endurance? I am uncomfortable on this ship and I wish to return home."

"I don't know," I said. "Admiral Grossman is undecided what to do with us." That wasn't exactly a lie. I still hoped that I could change his mind. I just wasn't sure how I was going to do that.

Nu Venia moaned in discouragement as she sat down.

I joined her on the couch. "There is good news."

"What?"

"My friends have learned of another settlement."

"Jessica, I am without understanding."

"I'm not altogether sure myself, but there are some historical logs that mention how a large group of people left Endurance and started a new settlement," I said.

"Yes," she said. "There was a disagreement. Some were tired of living in a building. They wanted freedom of outside."

"Do you know what happened to them or where they went?"

She shook her head. "They were never heard from again. It was assumed all had died."

I couldn't help smiling.

"What?" Nu Venia asked.

"If I had known that when I first arrived, I would have held it over your head and we would never have gone on Woden."

"Cameron would still be alive."

"You would still be angry with him, Nu Venia, and we wouldn't be friends."

"One cannot remain in the past, one can only move forward," she said.

"Indeed."

We visited until the private returned and escorted me to the conference room where the admiral requested my presence.

Admiral Grossman's face was waiting for me on the ship's communication monitors.

I wasn't any more enthusiastic about talking to him now than when we first met. Even though I'd learned a lot and was grateful for having gone on Woden, I'd never thank him for it. I couldn't stand his smug, self-satisfied smile for sending me on Woden in the first place.

Keep your feelings to myself, I commanded myself.

WSC Stanza's conference room was much like the conference room on *WSC Britannia.* One six-sided table, which sat twelve people, a large overhead com-screen at one end of the room and one smaller holo-screen on a side desk. Admiral Grossman's pasty white face with his fake smile was on both screens.

He also stood on a round platform under the larger screen. I guessed the other platform was for me to stand on.

Moon Base must have perfected holographic imagery across space. That wasn't in *Britannia's* conference room.

Our transmissions were sent across the Milky Way through a series of relays set in place by *WSC Eagle* as it trekked across space to Akiane more than 300 years ago.

Over time, those relays had become old and slow. *WSC Britannia* traveled the same route as *Eagle*, and stopped to replace each relay, which had added an extra 11 months to our trip.

Some relays had been badly battered by small asteroids, and a couple were barely functioning, which was why it took so long for messages to travel between Akiane and Moon Base, and why the radio message requesting me had been garbled.

Each time a relay was replaced, the technicians would test not just the new relay but all those previously installed. One time we had to backtrack because a relay didn't respond. A medium-sized asteroid had crashed into it and destroyed it. That added an extra five weeks to the trip.

I'd been annoyed at the delays. But now, speaking to the admiral, I was glad *Britannia* had taken the time to update WSC communication systems. Instead of years, it only took twenty minutes for his transmissions to reach me, and twenty minutes for my responses to reach him, which made for a lengthy conversation.

When someone started speaking, the transmission began recording and transmitting. But if the monitor on the other end had not been activated, an image would appear and wait to be turned on.

Which was why the admiral's image was waiting for me. He'd sent his first message.

"I wonder what good news you have for me today," I said.

My words would not be transmitted until I stepped onto the platform or commanded the computer on. Once I did, I'd have to keep all my snarky comments to myself. Otherwise, every word I said would be transmitted back to him.

Mental reminder to self: *Keep mouth closed.*

I sat at the desk and commanded, "Computer, speak."

Admiral Grossman's image began speaking. "Welcome back, Lieutenant. I never doubted your abilities."

Right.

"Sir, thank you, Sir." I spoke even though I knew he had more to say. But my face and response was now on its way to the admiral's monitor. He would know I was listening to his little speech and would be prepared for my return comments.

"It will be good to have you back on Moon Base once your mission is completed," he said, as if he planned to greet me as I disembarked from the transport.

I doubted we'd ever meet in person, which was fine with me.

"*WSC Stanza* has been ordered to delay return by 72 hours."

Here it comes, my next unpleasant assignment.

"You can forget about Pegasus Colony."

"What?" I couldn't help myself. "Sir, you ordered me on Woden. I risked my life for those people. If I don't go back, everything I'd just endured will have been for nothing. I have vital information for them, Sir. Information that could save lives."

The admiral continued speaking, "Your new orders are to investigate the new colony and inform them that we are sending personnel to make official diplomatic contact.

Once you have made all the necessary arrangements for their arrival, *Stanza* will return you to Moon Base."

"No, Sir, " I said. I didn't hear the rest of his speech. I kept talking. "I have to return to Endurance. I know why they're dying. I have answers, Sir. Well, almost. But Dr. Rona Montgomery and her colleagues are close to finding a cure because of the information I brought back to them. We can't abandon those people now."

We finished at the same time.

I waited, none too patiently, for his response to my outburst.

"You have your orders, Lieutenant," he said.

What? How could he? Unfortunately, I couldn't tell him what an old fool he was, not without getting into a lot of trouble. He could order the captain to throw me in the brig where I would stay for the entire trip back—to my court-martial.

His fake smile was now a frown. He was receiving my second outburst.

Then came the response. "I want you to make first contact with the new colony, Lieutenant," he said.

"But Sir, it's important that I return to Endurance first. I went on Woden because of them. You ordered me to go for the sake of pubic relations, Sir." I'd been here before, in a conversation just like this, just one month ago when I pleaded not to go on Woden. Now I was pleading to return to Endurance, and once again, he wasn't listening.

"The whole point of Woden was to gain the right to speak to the colonists and now I have it. I know I can convince them they're a WSC colony, just like you wanted. Sir, you can't abandon them now." I kept talking, hoping that he would listen.

"*WSC Stanza* is not there for your convenience." That was a threat. I had to follow his orders or pay the consequences. Then his fake smile returned. "Lieutenant, maybe this new colony will be more cooperative. You have your orders," he said again with more emphasis.

His image disappeared and was unwilling to continue the conversation.

Three more days and I'd be done. I'd introduce the new colony to WSC and they would welcome us with open arms. If all went according to plan, in three days I'd be heading back to WSC Moon Base, retire, and be back on Earth where I could forget all of this.

If all went according to plan.

I had a long history of things not going according to plan. Something always happened.

It would be just my luck that this time things *would* go according the admiral's plans, and I'd never fulfill Cameron's mission.

No matter how carefully I tried to make things right, stuff always happened to throw my life out of whack.

Maybe it was time I stopped being the victim and took control.

I'd follow orders, but I wasn't going alone.

Akiane Historical Chronicles
Fatimah's Last Day

Akiane Date: Year 28
Endurance: 7 months after Faris' death

WITH MIXED emotions, Fatimah walked through Endurance. Memories of the past 28 years flooded over her and tumbled into her thoughts.

The day Captain Assetti decided to stay and help the settlers was the day the bottom had dropped out of Fatimah's life. Despite the promise that they would eventually return to Earth, she knew she would never see her family again. She had thought that was *'aswa yawm fi hayataha* (the worst day of her life).

Now she could not conceive of returning to Earth, or not being a Community member. But today was the last time she would walk through the gardens of Endurance, the home she had helped build. She would once again say goodbye to friends she would never see again.

Happy sounds of children laughing diverted Fatimah's attention. They were in a small play area made of rocks that ranged from small to the size of a boulder, all of which were placed for the enjoyment of children. It had been her youngest son, Khalid's favorite play area. He and his friends had chased each other around and over the rocks, and had climbed the boulder as if it were the highest mountain in the land.

As she watched the children, she noticed something familiar in one of the boy's hands.

"Arty, what do you have?" Fatimah asked.

"I didn't steal it," Arty said defensively.

The children stopped to watch the conversation, worried that they too had done something wrong.

"No, of course you didn't," she said. "May I see it?"

The boy jumped off the rock and gave her the toy.

She turned it over in her hand. It was Khalid's toy spaceship. His father had carved it out of stone for him. Now a grown man, he was too old for toys.

"Where did you find this?" she asked.

"It was sitting on top," he said, pointing to the boulder. "I think someone forgot it. I didn't mean any harm."

"No, of course not." The day before she'd seen Khalid holding the toy, trying to decide what to do with it.

Shuttles were transporting people and the necessary equipment needed. Luggage would multiply the trips. It was decided that each person could take only one container filled with personal items. A toy was not essential. Khalid must have decided to leave a bit of himself behind.

She handed the toy back to the boy. "I believe this is now yours, Arty."

His mouth dropped open. His eyes were wide with delight.

"Really?"

"Yes. Have fun with it, Arty. And when you are older, pass it on to another."

"Yes, ma'am." He ran back to his friends flying the spaceship over his head.

A little girl, who had been watching, smiled sweetly at Fatimah. She brushed long strands of hair out of her eyes.

"Come here, Twila." Fatimah took a gold rose hair comb from her tight curls.

259

Before Space Force, Fatimah had worn her hair in the traditional braids of her tribe. But braids were too much work to maintain, therefore her tribe held a ceremony for the cutting of her braids before she left for Moon Base.

As part of the official declaration of independence for World Space Coalition and its Space Force, Faris and Fatimah let their hair grow out and braided it. Faris kept her braids, but Fatimah soon decided she liked her hair short and wore her hair combs only as decoration.

The girl obediently came to her. "This is for you." Fatimah showed her the hair comb.

The girl carefully took it. "Oh, it's beautiful." Little fingers delicately touched each rhinestone.

"Would you like me to put it in your hair?"

"Oh yes."

"Turn around."

Twila obeyed. Fatimah ran her fingers though the girl's hair, pulled it into a ponytail, and attached the hair comb so the roses were on top of her ponytail.

"There." Now Fatimah was leaving a piece of herself behind.

Twila's fingers carefully ran over her head to the hair comb. She turned and threw her arms around Fatimah's neck. "Thank you."

She hugged Twila back, then rose to leave.

Building Endurance and the struggle to survive had united everyone into a Community from which so much had been accomplished.

Fatimah remembered how pleasantly surprised she had been when they had overcome their military and civilian differences. Believers set aside their differences and joined together in what they had in common.

They decided to turn *Falcon* into their living quarters. *Hawk* became a hydroponics farm and work areas for different projects.

She thought back to how the Community learned to work together, each using his or her skills while gaining new skills to improve their chances of survival. She smiled as she remembered how some had struggled with tasks such as fishing, cleaning fish, gardening, shoveling snow, and building the dome. Eventually even those jobs became specialized.

They had a weeklong celebration once the dome was finished. On the last day, they christened it Endurance because they had endured much, and had persevered.

Endurance became the Community's oasis in the desert of a frozen world, while the harsh seven-year winters toughened them.

Fatimah remembered the shock when Captain Faris' female dog, Harrie the Spitz, gave birth to puppies born in cocoons. They'd learned so much from the death and survival of Harrie's first two liters. Unfortunately they did not heed the doctor's warnings, or they would have been better prepared for when humans began to deliver cocoons.

One little three-year old boy named his dog Chovis. No one knew where he got the name. It didn't take long for the three-year-old to become confused and decided to call every dog chovis. The name stuck and dogs became chovis.

Though WSC had provided the colonists with DNA to raise livestock, Fatimah's biggest disappointment had been that they never built domes specifically for livestock. It would have been nice to have birds, more variety of dogs and cats, and meat other than fish, tupilak, and chovis. Maybe those domes would be built at their new home.

Almost thirty years later, they still had not built their city. Now if the city was to be built, it would not be with the help of Fatimah's hand.

Since Faris' death, the dome had closed in on Fatimah. She felt stifled. When the idea to move and build in open space resurfaced, she suddenly realized how much she hated living in an enclosed area and how much she missed being outside.

Khalid had spent his whole life growing up in a terrarium, and yet he loved being outside. When he was 15 years old, he learned how to fly a shuttle and began to study *WSC Eagle* logs sent to *Hawk* about Akiane. For the next two years, he explored the best places, and found an island 50 kilometers in diameter right on the equator.

Ocean waters didn't freeze and winter temperatures were tolerable. He believed the Community could build a town and live outside.

When the eager 17-year-old first mentioned his idea to his mother, she suggested he present it to the Community.

They were both surprised at how many people liked the idea, but there were just as many who were loyal to Endurance and didn't want to move. No one wanted to split Community therefore the idea was tabled.

The disagreement over children being born in cocoons reignited the idea of becoming two settlements. The new island was given serious thought, explored, and declared suitable. Khalid and his brother, Griffin, along with a building team, moved to the island and proceeded to make it habitable.

As if he had the authority, Fintan made it clear that once they left, they would never be welcomed back. He wanted no communication between the settlements. That was the most difficult part about the move, leaving the others behind.

This was Fatimah's last day at Endurance and why she was taking her last walk. She wanted to find the priest for one final good-bye.

Which made this *al'aswa aljadid fi hayat Fatimah mutarjim.* (the was worst day of Fatimah's life)

Akiane Historical Chronicles
Father Joseph Striken

Akiane Date: Year 28

Endurance: Fatimah and Father Joe's last visit

"SOMETHING HAS happened that I never expected to happen," Joe said. "I have become a father."

He and Fatimah were sitting on rocks near Fiona's nest. Fatimah used to visit him while he was caring for his cocoons and had on occasion relieved him of duty. Now she kept him company while he relieved Fiona.

Caring for a cocoon was not an easy job. It needed constant turning, day and night. And his four children also required constant supervision. Therefore he and Fiona took turns watching his children and her cocoon. This day he had his two older girls while Fiona and his two younger children made bread together.

"But you have always been a father, Priest," Fatimah said.

"A priest, yes, but now I'm a father of children." His blissful smile seemed a permanent fixture on his face. "It's not only a whole new way of life. It's a whole new way to love."

Fatimah frowned. "I thought you considered all of us your children, even those of us who do not believe as you do."

They'd had this conversation before, but Joe was so excited with his new role in life, he enjoyed repeating himself. Fatimah indulged him and with each repetition, they learned a little more about each other.

"I was never the same after my first child and my capacity to love has only increased as I gave birth to my other children. I never planned to be a mother. I never even planned to marry," she said.

"So many plans were lost," he said. "Yet far better plans have replaced them."

"So many new plans were realized," she agreed.

Joe thought Fatimah had never looked more radiant than at that moment as she thought back over her life.

"We never forget our first love, do we?" he said.

Her eyes focused on him. "Do you regret being a priest and never getting married?"

Joe closed his Bible and placed it on his lap as a sly grin creased his face. "Do you regret leaving Space Force and getting married?"

"A part of me will always be a soldier."

"And I will always be a priest."

She shook her head. "Guess this means you won't be getting married."

"Why, when I have friends like you to advise me?"

"Love and discipline, Priest, love and discipline."

"The love I understand, but discipline?" He watched his two older girls playing chase in the vines. "I can't imagine spanking my little ones, to force them to obey." Just the thought of such an act pained him.

Fatimah had an easy laugh and a beautiful smile, something Joe had not seen for some time because of the seriousness of the past few months.

"You are being too tender hearted, Priest. Does your Bible not speak of disciple?" she asked. "The parent sets the boundaries of what is appropriate. When the boundaries are tested, you must decide if the battle is worth fighting for or if giving is more appropriate. Understanding the difference prevents unnecessary disagreements and will save you from losing more battles than you win."

How times had changed. Until recently, he would never have confided in Fatimah. She had been so closed and distant. She had not approved of his friendship with Faris. Now he was almost as close to her as he had been with Faris.

"Wait until you start pulling your hair out," she said. "You'll understand. The trick is to forgive and love despite their imperfections. Discipline helps them get over their imperfections." She paused. "If only we could discipline grownups."

"I think I'm beginning to understand the depth of my emotions. Sadly, I don't just mean learning to love my children." He shook his head in disappointment. "I never thought I could . . .." His jaw clenched. "Hate is too strong a word, but I am strongly upset with those who are willing to reject a newborn just because they're different."

"I know," Fatimah said. "Because of this division . . .." Her unspoken words hung between them.

He lifted his head and watched her. "I expected you to speak of it sooner."

She didn't directly answer him. "Those who are unwilling to accept the new change in our children are making it difficult for the rest of us."

"I don't understand," Joe said. "Why move up the timetable? I thought you were going to wait a few more months."

"Parents are encouraging their children to bully the cocoon-born," she said. "Fintan is to blame."

"I had hoped the birth of his child would change him," Joe said.

"Having his own cocoon only intensified events. After the fuss over the other children, his pride was too great," she said. "He had to take a stand."

"My children have had to deal with bullying," he said. "It is an unfortunate opportunity to teach love and forgiveness."

"They do have a good teacher."

He smiled mournfully. "My children seem to be better at it than I."

Abigail used to play with Fatimah's granddaughters. Even though they were slightly older, she wanted to be just like them. Their hair was braided; Abigail wanted her hair braided. Fatimah taught Joe how to braid Abigail's hair.

Soon after, her sisters, Lydia and Madeline, wanted their hair braided. Joe braided their hair to match their big sister's braids.

His youngest, David, did not want to be left out. He wanted his hair braided like his sisters. He told David little boys didn't braid their hair.

David wanted to be just like his sisters and wanted his hair braided.

In truth, Joe didn't want to braid another head of hair. Three heads were more than enough.

"David you are named after a great king. Kings don't braid their hair," Joe said.

It didn't help. David cried big tears of disappointment and refused to be left out.

That was the first time Fatimah reminded Joe that some arguments were not worth winning.

"If you want peace, Priest, braid the boy's hair."

Joe worked out a schedule so he didn't have to braid everyone's hair on the same day and braided David's hair.

"I have noticed how you are more peaceful and agreeable now that you have children, Priest," Fatimah said.

"I don't pretend to know all there is concerning our Lord's love, but thanks to my children I am continuing to learn. They are experts at teaching patience."

Fatimah nodded. "That they are."

"I had no idea how demanding a child could be, Fatimah. I never fully understood how a parent could become so frustrated with them."

"Children think they are the center of the world," she said.

"They have no regard for how I am feeling." He grimaced. "If I am sick or if another is in need of counseling." He paused as his face softened. "And yet, they have great capacity for affection, like hugs of comfort not just for me, but for others as well. They keep no record of my wrongs."

"Children do have the capacity to teach us many things," Fatimah said.

"I have indeed learned much," he said. "But I do not think you have come to counsel me on my shortcomings."

Sadness returned to her face as her shoulders slumped.

Joe looked over the field of Blood Vines and at the new cocoon nests, the parents caring for them, and the guards watching over the area.

Vines were becoming uncontrolled. Paths needed daily trimming. Here and there vines clustered creating rolling mounds of leaves. Vines wrapped around each other to form what looked like a leafy tree trunk. A few of those "trunks" reached the ceiling and sent runners along the glass ceiling. Runners reached out from between "tree trunks" to wrap around each other to form "bridges." Bridges thickened as runners grew out of them from every direction. Mounds, trees, and bridges grew among and over each other making a wild mess.

Among the mess were main pathways, with trails to each individual nest, but no one seemed to mind that the Blood Vine Nursery had become known as "jungle."

"I fear for the trouble that will come when more children are born in cocoons. I suspect your little family may be growing soon," Fatimah said.

"Perhaps I should start a few more nests, just in case," he said, half joking, half serious.

267

"What will you do with so many children?" she asked.

Joe worried about the prospect of raising more children. As much as he loved his four, how many was too many?

Fatimah smiled mischievously. "I see you raising a monastery of little priests. What will their parents say when they realize what you are doing?" She teased.

His shoulders shook with mirth. "If they didn't want their children raised Catholic, they should have kept them."

Fatimah laughed so hard she almost slid off her perch.

"That will teach them."

Their laughter settled into an awkward silence.

"I have come to ask for your decision. Will you accompany us?" Before he could answer, she quickly added, "Please say yes."

"This is unbelievable, Fatimah. I can't imagine you not being here," Joe said. "It's a small Community. I hear Fintan is already gloating as if your moving is his victory, and all our problems will leave with you."

"I am asking you, Fiona, and your children to come with us."

"Fiona and I have discussed it," Joe said. "But as much as we'd like to go with you, we're staying. Despite what Fintan says, there will be more children. Who will care for all those who are abandoned if we leave? Who will teach new mothers how to care for their cocoons?"

"Who will teach them to build their cocoons?" she asked.

Joe had never been able to successfully build one.

In a low voice he said, "I was planning on kidnapping the original designer, Carol, to help us make new nests."

This would be the last time they would laugh together.

"Do you think they will always be so cruel?" she asked.

Joe shook his head. "Not if Beasley is correct. Once every child is born in a cocoon, they'll have to accept the truth, even Fintan. How long before you leave?"

"My family is already there," she said. "I waited until the last day, because I could not." She stopped. Waited. Then continued. "I will delay if you are coming. Otherwise I leave in a few hours."

Tears filled Joe's eyes. He had thought about it for a long time, but had waited until the last possible moment before he made his request. "It might be best if you take my children with you."

"Joe?" Fatimah asked in surprise.

"Children need love. But they also need to know they're safe. At least they will never be bullied again."

"No, you are their father," she said. "I believe Allah has given them to you. So those who remain can witness true love firsthand. I will not take your children."

He couldn't help it. Joe let out a choked sigh of relief. Was he giving in too easily? Should he press the point? He would have been willing to give his children up for their best chance, but how he would have ached with loneliness. He didn't have it in him to argue the point.

Fatimah smiled impishly.

"What?" Joe asked.

"You said you are having difficulty loving those who refuse to understand changes."

"Yes?" He knew where she was headed but didn't want to hear it.

"When we leave, you will be left with all those you do not like," she said. "How will you deal with that, Priest?"

"With great difficulty," Joe said with a heavy heart. It would be his greatest test yet. It was far easier to suffer such trials when one had friends like Fatimah to stand with him. "At least Fiona will be here to help me."

"I think you will learn much, Priest," Fatimah said.

"Unfortunately, so do I." Joe used his sleeve to wipe his nose and tears from his face, something he'd learned from Abigail.

Akiane Historical Chronicles
Father Joseph Striken's Personal Entry

Akiane Date: Year 29
Endurance: Nine months after the others left

FATIMAH AND the others have been gone less than a year. It seems so much longer.

I still expect to see Fatimah walking around the dome. Sometimes I have a thought that I need to tell her. Usually, it's something new about one of my children. Then I remember I'll never be able to share another thought with her or Faris again. I often think about them and I pray for them daily.

Beasley was correct. The change in birthing has finally arrived. For months, all of our children have been born in cocoons.

The Blood Vines have become the official nursery. Except for a select few, and much to Fintan's chagrin, Community has finally accepted this as the way of life.

Our children are no longer being abandoned. Some parents were hesitant at first. I was called in just in case, but after we talked, they decided they wanted to keep their child. It has been such a blessing to see the change in hearts.

Although there is much sorrow and shame in the way the others were shunned and encouraged to leave, now they're greatly missed, and would be welcomed back, but we have no way to contact them because we don't know where they are.

They took all the shuttles during their move. We don't have the means to search for them. Much has been lost with their leaving. It will take time to recover, for people to forgive themselves for their hardened hearts, and to forgive the instigator who caused the trouble in the first place.

Fintan has been ostracized and has become more disagreeable than ever. He yells at everyone and tells them of the disaster they are bringing upon themselves. The only two people who are willing to speak to him are Fiona and I.

It is difficult not to yell at his bullheadedness. How I wish he had left and the others had stayed.

Fiona frequently reminds me that Fintan needs love just like everyone else. It amazes me that she still loves him. She brings their child, Lily, along when she visits him. She thinks he's softening.

It's true that he does not yell as loud or as often at her and his daughter. He sits quietly and watches his little girl play with her toys. And he's starting to respond when she tries to interact with him.

Fiona promises that if they do make up, she will not abandon me. She plans on moving him in with her— next door to me.

I'll be greatly surprised if that happens, and will consider it one of God's greatest miracles. I know I shouldn't be cynical, and nothing is impossible for God, but it's difficult for me to believe in Fintan's change of heart. It's even more difficult for me to pray for his heart to change. I want him to disappear from our lives.

I must confess, in the deepest part of my heart, I pray he never moves in with her. That would mean Fintan would become a member of our family.

If that does happen, I will be the one who will need much prayer.

I have asked Fiona to pray for the softening of my heart.

She smiled, and said, "I already am, my friend."

Chapter 28

Jessica Hewitt
The Other Colony

Akiane Date: Year 328
The Other Colony: Persephone

BEGRUDGINGLY, NU VENIA came with me to the other colony. I understood.

Cameron had done the same thing to me when he dragged me on Woden. He didn't have the words to explain what I would gain from the trip. Even if he'd tried, I wouldn't have listened. Cameron may have been the youngest of the three of us, but he was certainly the wisest. Too bad I didn't understand that sooner. I could have learned a lot from him.

I convinced Nu Venia that she should be the ambassador for her people to their long-lost relatives. If the new colonists were as disagreeable as those at Endurance, they might be more receptive of me if someone from their own lineage stood at my side.

Nu Venia feared she would be the reason they'd be unfriendly since the original settlers had split under negative terms. What those terms were, I didn't know. She wouldn't tell me.

273

WSC Stanza didn't have the means to contact the colonists or prepare them for our arrival. They weren't expecting a visitor from Endurance and certainly not one from Earth.

Because we didn't know what kind of greeting we'd receive, Captain Leopold ordered the shuttle to remain on land just in case we needed to make a hasty retreat. Two armed guards accompanied us. They were to stay close to us until they were assured of the situation.

As we flew over the colony, it was obviously apparent how different the two colonies were.

Endurance was a dome where people lived like a bubble boy in his sterile environment, unable to enjoy the outside world.

These colonists here were far more creative. They'd settled inland, on a small continent the size of Australia, among hills covered by the same palm-like trees we'd seen at Endurance.

They'd cleared an area far inland near a large river and far way from threatening Storm waves. They built their town on either side of the river and built three swing bridges to connect the two sides.

As far as we could tell, there were no volcanoes or hot springs in the immediate area.

Their town was larger than Endurance, but it was spread over several hills and was built into and on the hills. Instead of lava, they used wood as their building material.

There were paths and stairs leading up the hills and swing bridges connecting buildings on top of the hills.

On the principal hill, sat an extra-large, two-story log cabin. Elaborate stairs curved back and forth along the hill leading to smaller buildings built along the way and continued to the log cabin.

Crops were planted on graduated terraces carved into the hills. Livestock grazed in meadows between the hills.

Colonists were outside enjoying the day, working in their flower gardens or crops while children played. All stopped and watched as we flew overhead.

"Sergeant, where is the equator?" I asked one of our armed guards.

"We are flying over it, Lieutenant," he said. "Winters are milder here than on the rest of the planet."

That explained why everything was already green and flowers were blooming. Back at Endurance the caldera was a muddy mess from melted snow and volcano ash. It would be a long while before the ground thawed and wild flowers bloomed.

"Nu Venia, why didn't your people settle here?" I asked.

"The first settlers did not understand the severity of The Storm. After twelve years in space, they wanted to be outside." She paused. "They would not have landed where they did had they known they were about to be swept out to sea by huge waves."

"Why not move to a more suitable place after the gravitational storm passed?" I asked.

"*Hawk* was unable to fly," she said.

"In other words, nothing turned out as they planned," I said.

"Just so."

By the time we'd flown over the town, landed, and walked across a meadow, a crowd had cautiously gathered. Children hovered behind their parents.

A large orange and white cat sauntered across our path, ignoring us as cats do throughout the universe. Birds chirped from nearby trees. Flies and bees buzzed by. Dogs ran alongside children. We saw horses, camels, and cows, grazing in an open pasture. We saw sheep, goats, and llamas roaming the hills. Deer, moose, and antelope grazed nearby.

"Nu Venia, where did all these animals come from?" I asked.

"I do not know, Jessica. I have never seen anything like this before," she said. "Our ships brought dormant seeds for the planting of crops and DNA for stock, but we didn't build a dome for animals. We planted seeds and stored DNA. We were supposed to build domes for stock, but we never did."

"And over time, you forgot."

"Just so."

Their dogs were not chovis. I saw shelties, chocolate labs, and Tibetan mastiffs just to name a few.

At Endurance, everyone ran from us. Here, once they got over the shock of seeing us, everyone welcomed us. They waved as they hurried to greet us. Children left their parent's side and ran toward us.

As soon as they reached us, they spoke all at once. A few of the little ones raised their arms, wanting us to pick them up. Others had stopped to pick colorful bouquets of wildflowers that they excitedly presented to us. Our guards moved in closer to protect us and refused the flowers handed to them until I reminded them we were guests and it would be impolite to reject gifts. Soon we were all carrying a child and a bouquet of flowers.

All except Nu Venia, who had two reactions. At first she shrank from little hands reaching out to touch. Then she become overwhelmed by how full of energy and bright eyed the children were. They ran, squealed with delight, and excitedly danced around us.

"How is this possible?" she asked softly. "These children are happy and healthy." Tears gently rolled down her cheeks, which she quickly tried to wipe away, but they kept coming. She managed to get the tears under control just as the adults joined us.

"Welcome."

"We are honored with your visit."

"Come meet Vawynn."

They treated us as if we were long lost relatives they had not seen in centuries—which we were.

Unlike those at Endurance, these people were all different shapes and heights. Their hair was blond, red, brown, and cut in different lengths. Their eyes were different shades of blue, black, and hazel. Their skin was light to dark, some with a hint of maroon. There was no conformity here.

People in Endurance were dressed from their neck to their toes. These people were dressed for spring with skirts, shorts, sleeveless blouses, and sandals.

"They welcome us even though they do not know who we are." Nu Venia was taken aback. "They do not fear or mistrust us."

"Nu Venia, they live life as it is meant to be lived," I said, "without restrictions."

The crowd became so large we were unable to continue walking.

"It is good that you have come," one said.

Like their children, adult faces shone with welcoming smiles.

"So pleased to meet you," another said.

"It has been too long since we have greeted another from Akiane."

They had no idea that I was from a different planet from the other side of the galaxy.

"Enough, enough," a laughing voice said. "Give our guests room."

The crowd parted to allow a tall slender woman who moved with the grace of a ballerina. She had warm reddish-brown eyes, and long copper hair that hung in waves down her back. She was a little taller than us, and except for her light maroon skin, she didn't look like the people of Endurance.

Nu Venia took a step back in embarrassment. She was completely different from the rest of her people. Her eyes were yellow with green specks, dark maroon skin, and white hair. Now she felt inadequate next to this lovely woman.

I too felt inadequate. My California tan had long faded on the journey to Akiane. And after a month of camping, my short brown hair was shabby. I'd lost a lot of weight because of Woden and was far too thin.

"I am Vawynn." As a sign of welcome, she bowed elegantly. She stood before Nu Venia and reached for her hands.

I held my breath, afraid of Nu Venia's reaction.

Vawynn did not wear gloves. As far as I could tell, her palms were smooth like mine. She could not pass or receive essence with hands like that. These were Nu Venia's people, but they looked more like earthlings than those at Endurance.

"I am Nu Venia from Endurance."

"I hoped that's who you were. We have long since wanted to make contact, but were unsure if we would be welcomed."

Nu Venia stiffened at Vawynn's touch, but since she was wearing her gloves, she didn't object. She politely smiled so as not to offend our hostess, but she didn't relax until Vawynn had released her hands.

Vawynn turned to me.

Before she reached for my hands, I said, "My name is Jessica. I am not from this planet. I'm . . .," *How to explain?* "I am from Earth."

Murmurs swept though the crowd. It was difficult to tell if it was a negative response or one of happy surprise.

"I know you think we abandoned you 328 years ago." I paused. *Should I give the same speech I gave to those at Endurance or start over?* "Our absence was not intentional. We honestly thought everyone had died."

"Why would you think that?" Vawynn spoke with the confidence of a leader. She held herself aloof with her head tilted slightly to one side. Her arms were crossed over her midsection as if protecting herself from us—from me.

So Nu Venia was a welcomed guest, but I had to prove myself—again. Perhaps we should have gotten to know each other before I dropped the bombshell.

When I first arrived at Endurance, I was full of the fear of failure. One stern look from Adumie and I cringed. Not today. Cameron would want me to hold my head up and stand with the confidence that we were equals, because we were equals.

To my surprise, I felt confident. "Because we never heard from you," I answered her.

"Why come now?" Vawynn asked.

"We received a message from Endurance that a colony was here. World Space Coalition immediately sent a ship. I've been here for almost two months and have just learned of your town. I've come on behalf of Earth. Nu Venia is here on behalf of the people."

Vawynn's arms dropped to her sides as she accepted my explanation. She reached for my hands. I reached for her. "On behalf of Persephone, we welcome you," she said.

"Persephone? Isn't that the name of a goddess?" I asked.

"Yes," Vawynn said, "the Goddess of spring." She raised her hand and waved it over her town. "Winter does not rule as strongly here as it does over Endurance. Here, spring comes earlier and stays longer."

I was so used to being rejected by the people of Akiane. Now, I couldn't completely let my guard down in spite of the warm welcome. Vawynn might have had a hidden agenda.

I needn't have worried.

Chapter 29

Jessica Hewitt
Vawynn's Woden

Akiane Date: Year 328
The Other Colony: Persephone

I'D INTENDED to stay at Persephone no more than an hour or so. I had plans to do battle with Adumie and somehow win him and his people over. First, we would cure them and then have them loving the fact that they were a WSC colony.

Our tour of this small town was now leaning into hour three.

Vawynn didn't walk, but strolled. The same happiness that made her face glow also sang in her voice.

As we *slowly* toured the town and climbed stairs, she stopped at each home and introduced each person by name. Each family had a story to tell of their ancestors. Many insisted we come in and sit.

Thankfully, Vawynn politely declined.

I tried to politely move us along, but the tour continued.

A crowd followed with us.

Vawynn explained how genetic engineers designed their animals to stay small so they could be herded into barns to protect them from the worst of winter. With time, animals become winter-tolerant and were able to stay outside all year long. The "barns" were turned into community buildings.

We visited newly planted crops.

All of it was interesting, but I was running out of time.

While we walked, Vawynn and Nu Venia bonded, slowing my plans to less than a snail's crawl. When their conversation turned to babies, my ears perked up.

We'd come to the Blood Vines, which had not been allowed to grow into a jungle as in Endurance; these vines were neatly cropped and were without nests.

"Are your children not born in cocoons?" Nu Venia asked.

"We have not had a cocoon born child for over two hundred years," Vawynn said.

"But you still have Blood Vines," Nu Venia said.

Vawynn smiled. "We still make Lazard."

They both smiled.

Nu Venia, Cameron, and I drank Lazard as part of our celebration at having survived The Storm. It was the Lazard that had loosened my tongue. It wasn't that I was drunk; it was more like I couldn't stop talking. I wasn't sure that I ever wanted to drink Lazard again. I didn't know what other secrets my tongue might let loose.

"We no longer call them Blood Vines, they are now Lazard Vines," Vawynn said.

"Is that all you use the vines for?" Nu Venia asked.

Vawynn easily laughed as one without a care in the world. "We do have other uses for the vines. We still spin thread for cloth, and weave baskets but let them dry before we use them."

"But there is nothing like a good drink to warm the tongue and speak one's heart," Nu Venia said.

"Perhaps we should celebrate the reuniting of our people over a drink," Vawynn said.

Those who followed in our wake all agreed that it was a good idea.

"Perhaps we should save the Lazard for later," I quickly said. "Unfortunately, Nu Venia and I are on a tight schedule."

Nu Venia became serious. "My people are sick and are dying."

"The retrovirus," Vawynn said.

Nu Venia stared at her in disbelief.

"Explain," I said.

"The fish carry it," Vawynn said.

"You do not appear to be sick," Nu Venia said. "Do you not eat fish?"

"We eat fish, but we wear gloves when handling them," Vawynn said. "Cooking the meat renders the retrovirus harmless and safe to eat."

"You must also butcher tupilak with gloves on," I guessed.

"Tupilak?" Vawynn asked. "What is tupilak?"

These people have never seen a tupilak. How was that possible?

"The sea creatures that look a lot like monstrous chovis," I said.

Vawynn shook her head. "What is chovis?"

"Dogs," I said. "Didn't you take some with you when you moved here?"

"There was not room in the shuttles to bring anything but people and what each could bring with them," she said. "All our animals have come from the genetic samples that were provided for us from Earth."

"Shuttles?" I asked. "You have shuttles?"

"We were a large group. We had to use all the shuttles or it would have taken a very long time to make the move. Those at Endurance told us never to return. Therefore we dismantled the shuttles and made equipment such as saws to cut wood used to build Persephone," Vawynn said. "Until this day, we have not seen or spoken to anyone from Endurance or Earth, until you arrived."

"I am very sorry for that," Nu Venia said. "We are a people who have not yet learned from our mistakes." Her voice sounded harsh as if she was preparing for an argument about the past.

"It was a long time ago," Vawynn said. "On this day, we make a new start." I wasn't sure if she'd missed the anger in Nu Venia's voice or if she was politely ignoring it.

Once she realized all was well, Nu Venia relaxed.

A small child tugged at Nu Venia's fur pants. "Do you have any children?" she asked.

Nu Venia's hand went to her belly. "Not now, but soon. You do not birth cocoons. How do you have children?" she asked Vawynn.

Vawynn's laugh was as free as a bird in flight. It floated around us, then pulled us into her joy. "I only know of one way in which to have children."

Nu Venia turned to me for an explanation.

"They have sex," I said. "Their children, all of their children, have two parents."

Nu Venia's eyes widened in surprise, then narrowed in disgust. I thought she was going to lose her breakfast over the horror of what these people had done. Right then and there, the way in which the people of Persephone gave birth could have ended any hope of unity between their two cultures.

It would also end any hope of saving Endurance. This was not a good time for Nu Venia to have a melt down.

"Nu Venia," I said in an effort to calm her before she said something damaging. "It's okay." But what could I say that could satisfy her without reinforcing the fact that she and her people were the ones who were not normal.

"What is happening?" Vawynn became distressed. "How have I offended?"

Nu Venia seemed rooted where she stood. Her head swayed from side to side as if everything she believed was crumbling and her brain was having difficulty handling the avalanche.

"My people have been living far too long under false beliefs," she said. Her gloved hand covered her mouth. She took a deep breath in an effort to keep her anger at bay.

Vawynn became more distraught. She took several deep breaths. Her face lost composure. Her lovely voice turned to sobs. "What is wrong? What have I done? Why is Nu Venia troubled?"

Several people in the crowd also became distressed. The smaller children began crying.

The guards closed in for our protection. I raised my hand. They halted.

"All that we have believed is wrong," Nu Venia cried. "We have tried to survive by conforming. We have refused to change. Now we DIE." She paced back and forth as she spoke. "We have tried to survive without moving forward. We refuse change. *We die.*" She stopped and turned to Vawynn. "Your people left because you were unwilling to conform, *and you are thriving.*" She trembled under her emotional stress.

Vawynn stepped toward Nu Venia as if to comfort her, but was unsure of the problem. Since she didn't know what to do, she stepped back.

While Nu Venia was having her moment, I was having one of my own.

Ever feel like slapping yourself in the forehead because you've realized you're an idiot for being shortsighted?

Cameron would have seen it.

Everything needed to help Endurance survive was here at Persephone.

Without touching her, I stood directly in front of Nu Venia, forcing her to stop pacing. "I . . .." She was unable to speak. "I . . .,"

"It's all right," I said. "Everything will be all right."

"How? Jessica, how?"

"The truth," I said. "Once we know the truth, everything will become clear. Then we'll know what to do. Isn't that what Cameron taught us? Learn the truth, gain trust, and make Community."

My words did not stop her tears, but she nodded as she calmed down.

Cameron was right. Community first. But there wasn't time to go on Woden and drink Lazard with Vawynn. Nu Venia's people would not survive that long. Admiral Grossman wouldn't agree to another Woden and I certainly didn't want to endure that ever again.

I had been resenting touring Persephone. I had wanted to hurry it along. I didn't realize that this was Vawynn's form of Woden, so the three of us could make Community.

Nu Venia and I needed to know how these people were able to beat the retrovirus; but, to do that, she first needed the truth to tear down false beliefs. Not just the truth about how babies were born, but why Vawynn's people did not have the same illness as Nu Venia's people, and why they were so happy when Nu Venia's people were so very miserable.

I turned to Vawynn.

"Nu Venia's people no longer have children as you do."

Vawynn frowned.

I continued, "The retrovirus from the fish has changed them. They do not have sex, the women have the ability to have children by themselves."

"How is this possible?" Vawynn asked.

I motioned for Nu Venia to take off her gloves. She held up her hands for Vawynn to see.

Vawynn reached out to touch Nu Venia's hand. I stopped her.

"Touching is forbidden," I said. "Nu Venia's people can transfer their genetic essence through the palm of their

285

hands. That's why they wear gloves at all times so they don't accidently, well trade essence."

"Is this true?" Vawynn asked.

"Yes," Nu Venia said. "Retrovirus comes from cleaning fish and tupilak barehanded. It changed the palms of our hands and gave us the ability to continually become infected. We pass the retrovirus to another simply by holding hands. In so doing, the retrovirus also took with it a bit of our essence, DNA."

"I'm told the retrovirus cannot be passed from parent to child," I said. "Yet, the children at Endurance all have the retrovirus. Yours do not. Why?"

"The retrovirus was in our hands, too," Vawynn said. "We continued to pass it on to our children when we turned our cocoons in the Blood Vine milk. We transferred the retrovirus from hands to the milk and the milk fed the retrovirus to our children."

Nu Venia sucked in a breath of shock. "What did you do? Did you make special gloves to turn the cocoons?"

"No, we made tongs," Vawynn said. "When we stopped touching the cocoon with our bare hands, we stopped transferring the retrovirus to our children. Within two generations, we no longer gave birth to cocoons. I will give you many pair of tongs for your children."

This time Nu Venia's tears were of joy and relief. "My child will not be sick?" Even though Rona had already said her child was healthy, Nu Venia would have re-infected her child once she put it in a Blood Vine nest. Now she was assured her child would live a long and healthy life.

Vawynn's angelic smile returned. "Your child will never be sick. We will teach your people how to make tongs so none of your children will be sick ever again," she said. "In time, your children will no longer be born in cocoons."

Nu Venia turned to me. "There is no shame in having two parents." She was so overcome with emotion she was having difficulty standing. I helped her sit on the ground before she fell.

She grabbed my jacket with both hands and held on as if I was her life jacket.

"I am not abomination," she whispered.

I knelt before her and said, "No, you are not."

"I am normal."

"You are normal." I gave Nu Venia her first hug since she'd become an adult. Instead of cringing, she hugged me back as if she would never let go.

When we parted, the tears were still there, but her face shone with joy.

"Everything has been a lie from the very beginning." Nu Venia's tears dried as she continued, "I refuse to live any longer under the shame Adumie has pronounced over me. I am not shame. My child is not shame." With determination and resolve, she stood. "We return victorious from Woden. We will tell them of Persephone. If they do not listen, you and I will leave them to their fate."

"Persephone welcomes any of you who wish to join us," Vawynn promised. "But if permissible, I welcome the opportunity to visit Endurance."

"It is time to let Endurance die and move on." Nu Venia spoke with firm conviction. "I will leave those who will not listen. Let them die with their lies."

She specifically meant Adumie.

I was not comfortable with Nu Venia's decision.

Cameron would not have approved. His mission was to save his people, all of them, including Adumie. He would not have wanted anyone left behind. But who was I to argue with Nu Venia? What if she was right? Maybe it was time to let Endurance go and move on.

And yet, deep in my heart, I knew there was a better way. Cameron would want us to find it.

I would not let him down.

Chapter 30

Jessica Hewitt
Closed Doors

Akiane Date: Year 328
WSC Stanza: Conference Room

ADMIRAL GROSSMAN wore his Space Force khaki uniform for me, but for Nu Venia, he was dressed to impress with his Service Blue uniform and his medals arraigned over his left breast. She didn't notice or care.

I wore my blue dress uniform. I doubted he cared.

Nu Venia dressed the same as everyone in Endurance, wearing her loosely fitted green satin-like blouse and pants. Both were made from strands of thread from Blood Vine stalks.

Instead of standing, Nu Venia and I sat at the desk with the smaller monitor.

The admiral's smile was pleasant and less fake than usual. "Nu Venia, it is good to finally meet you, I have heard so much about you."

I had no idea what he'd heard. I'd not said anything.

"I'm sorry to hear about your father's death. What was his name? Carmen?" If he was trying to be compassionate, he was failing. He had no idea what he was talking about.

"Sir, his name was Cameron," I corrected, trying not to let my frustration be heard. "And he was Nu Venia's charge, Sir." Even though I knew how long it would take for my words to reach him, I continued, "Admiral, Nu Venia has a request."

I'd warned Nu Venia beforehand not to say anything she didn't want the admiral to hear. We waited in silence while he droned on about the original purpose of the mission, and history of events.

He stopped talking. He'd received my transmission.

His expression changed. "That's right. Cameron. My apologies." He didn't bother to hide his annoyance at my having corrected him in front of her.

"Yes, I know Nu Venia wants to return to Endurance, but that is not going to happen. It is my understanding that she is not welcome there."

Where was he getting his information?

As if he'd heard my thoughts, he said, "I have spoken with Adumie." That explained why it took him so long to contact us. He'd been bonding with Adumie.

They were two peas in a pod. I had no doubt they got along just fine. Each had his agenda and neither cared what the other wanted. But in this case, they both arrived at the same place, which was for Nu Venia and me to give up on Endurance.

"Actually, Lieutenant, I find it appalling how you are using this poor girl for your own means while she's grieving over her charge's death."

I stared at the monitor as I searched for a response, but was too stunned to speak.

"I'm beginning to understand Adumie's request that you not return to his dome."

I understood all too well.

Adumie never planned to honor his people's tradition of Woden. Which meant he was willing to condemn his people to death, but why?

And what about Nu Venia? Did this mean she would never be able to return home?

"I think it would be nice for Nu Venia to come to Moon Base for a visit." The admiral's fake smile returned.

Nu Venia turned to me and was about to say something. I kept my eyes on the monitor and placed my hand on her knee. She composed herself and turned back to the monitor. I removed my hand.

"If she prefers," he continued, "Captain Leopold has offered to shuttle her back to our new colony, Persephone. I'm sure she'll be much happier there. Then you *will*," he emphasized "will" so I would not miss his meaning, "return to us, Lieutenant, where you will be rewarded for your excellent service."

A reward was not what he had in mind for me.

"Off," he commanded. Our monitor went blank.

"That's it? There's nothing we can do?" Nu Venia jumped up. "Is there nothing else we can do?" Her despair just about broke my heart.

"Apparently not. Both of them got what they wanted, to shut us down," I said. "We've hit the final wall, and I fear we might not be able to find another door to open or a window to crawl through."

We had everything, all the pieces, that we needed to save the people of Endurance. All we lacked was the means to get there.

During my debriefing with the admiral, I asked the captain for help, but he was under orders.

"I wish I could, I honestly do. But Adumie has cut off all communications," he said.

The admiral was suddenly too busy to answer my request for another audience. He said we'd have plenty of time to speak when I returned. In truth, he never planned to speak to me again. More than likely, he'd send me back to Earth without a word.

Nu Venia and I sat in the ship's Eatery for our final meal together, but we were too upset to talk or eat. The waitress came by three times to ask us what we wanted. Each time, I merely shook my head. We'd not seen her for a while.

"The captain will not return me to Endurance?" Nu Venia asked.

"Not without permission from the admiral, and the admiral doesn't care about Endurance now that he has Persephone in his pocket," I said.

" 'In his pocket?' I am without understanding," she said.

With a half-smile, I said, "It's an old Earth saying. It means the admiral has what he wants and has moved on to other projects."

Nu Venia stared out the Eatery's observation window.

I remembered sitting in the *Britannia's* Eatery looking down on Akiane and feeling just as rotten as I did now. I'd dreaded being ordered to the planet mostly because I dreaded being a failure. And after everything that had happened, I'd failed anyway.

"What about me?" she asked softly.

"You can come back to Moon Base and plead your case to anyone who will listen," I suggested weakly. "I'm sure the world media will be interested. And once they hear your story, they'll make the admiral comply."

She shook her head, just as I knew she would. "All will be dead by the time I return," she said.

"I know," I said. "Moon Base is a wasted effort."

"I could return to Persephone." Her eyes pleading for hope as if my decision would be the final answer. "Vawynn will help me."

"Of course she would if she could," I said. "But they don't have a means to cross the ocean to Endurance."

"Jessica, she said they have shuttles."

"Which they disassembled 300 years ago, Nu Venia. Even if they still worked, not one knows how to fly them."

"Is there nothing we can do, Jessica?"

I passed my hand over my eyes then through my hair. "Without the admiral's permission, no, there's nothing we can do." I leaned back in my chair. "It's over."

"Adumie has won," she said.

With a discouraged nod, I agreed, "Seems so."

Gino sat at our table.

He nodded to Nu Venia. "My name is Larry Gino."

Instead of extending his hand in a greeting of welcome, he laced his fingers together and rested them on the table.

Nu Venia politely said, "This is a good day to meet a new friend." But she clearly was not interested in talking to anyone. She stared out the window instead.

If she thought that would make Larry leave, she was wrong. I knew from personal experience, he was not easily put off.

I'd used that same tactic when he tried to befriend me while on *Britannia*. When he didn't leave, I left. He never did get the hint. Larry could have been a good friend, but I hadn't been interested.

He'd leave me alone for a few days or weeks; once he left me alone for an entire month. I thought he'd finally given up, but one morning, while I was eating breakfast, he sat down and started talking. I left my half-eaten meal and walked away.

Not polite of me.

Larry was much like Cameron. No matter how rude I was to him, he was never offended. I knew I owed him an apology, but now wasn't the time.

"I don't mean to stick my nose in, but it is a small ship, and little stays secret for very long," Larry said.

"I guess everyone's talking about our predicament." I sighed.

"There's that." He shrugged.

"It is thus at Endurance." Nu Venia faced him as she spoke. "There is little effort to hold secrets. Words are freely spoken and repeated to any ear that listens."

Larry usually came with a friendly smile and lots of small talk. Today, he'd not come with either. This time, there was a reason for his visit.

"What do you have for us, Larry?" I asked.

"There might not be anything either of you can do about the admiral, but Vawynn might be able to help," he said.

"Larry, if you had been listening," I began.

He waved a hand at me, just like my father used to when I was too frustrated to listen to his advice. What he wanted was for me to listen.

"Yes, yes, I know," Larry said.

"Okay, Larry. What?" I said.

"You're thinking from inside the box," he said.

"Inside the box?" Nu Venia asked.

He smiled.

"Larry?" I asked.

And just like my father he explained a simple concept that I should had thought of myself, but was unable to because I was too wrapped up in my own little box.

"Jessica my dear, you cannot change your admiral's mind, but Vawynn might be able to."

"What?" Now he had our attention.

"How?" Nu Venia asked.

"My dear, you represent the admiral's failure. Sorry, I mean no disrespect."

"Your words do not offend," she said.

"Vawynn represents the future, one in which the admiral wishes to succeed," Larry said. "If she requests an audience with him, he would not only have to speak to the leader of Earth's only galactic colony, he'd welcome it. It would be a historic moment for him."

"Great for public relations," I said. "Larry Gino you are a genius." I gave him a great big hug and a big kiss on the cheek.

"I do have my moments," he laughed.

Chapter 31

Jessica Hewitt
Vawynn

Akiane Date: Year 328
WSC Stanza: Conference Room

"WELL DONE, Lieutenant," Admiral Grossman said. For the first time his smile was actually genuine. "It is a pleasure to meet you, Vawynn." To prove that he meant it, he wore his white ceremonial uniform with all his medals and stars proudly displayed.

Nobody cared, least of all me.

Vawynn wanted to stand before the admiral. Therefore we stood on the holo-podium.

She stood straight-backed, head held high, the fingers her hands neatly laced in front of her. It was a similar pose of a rigid military officer, but she was relaxed and at ease.

Admiral Grossman stood with his legs supporting his bulk as he enthusiastically leaned toward her. "Lieutenant Hewitt tells me you are as eager as we are to re-establish the relationship between our worlds."

Those were not my exact words. They weren't even close.

With the grace and elegance of a master diplomat, Vawynn bowed her head and said, "It is an honor to be reunited with our home world."

"Well, Lieutenant, you have completed your assignment," he said, finally satisfied with my efforts. "You can return and we'll send an official ambassador to Persephone." He straightened, pleased at how things were progressing.

I should have been happy. That's what I'd wanted, to go home. So why wasn't I happy?

He anticipated my response and said, "Endurance is no longer your concern. Your mission has been completed." For the benefit of Vawynn, his smile stayed the same, but his eyes narrowed. He didn't want an argument in front of her. He wanted total obedience. "It is time for you to return to Moon Base."

If I left now, I'd be deserting Nu Venia in her hour of need. She'd be a woman without a home.

Even if she could return to her people, they wouldn't understand how she became pregnant with Cameron's child. They would forcefully remind her that touching was forbidden and no one has a child with another. They really wouldn't understand when they learned I literally had a hand in her carrying his child.

She'd be like the woman in the Bible who got caught in adultery. I didn't think they'd actually stone her to death, at least I hoped they wouldn't, but they would turn their backs on her, of that I was sure.

Nu Venia was welcomed at Persephone, but it wouldn't be the same. She wouldn't be able to save her people and she'd have let Cameron down, all of which wasn't her fault.

She'd try to deny her guilt by saying her people got what they deserved.

But I knew all too well what guilt was capable of doing to a person.

It would eat at her and would affect her relationship with her child. How could she tell him about Cameron and how he sacrificed his life to save his people, only to have her walkout on them?

Nu Venia's only recourse was to never speak of Cameron. That too would eat at her.

Dad never spoke about Mom after she left. He thought he was protecting me, but it drove us apart. It ruined our relationship for years. I spent my whole life thinking their divorce had been my fault and that he resented me for it. Thanks to Cameron, I realized as much as Dad loved me, he never stopped loving Mom. His and my relationship would have been so much better if we'd known how to communicate.

I couldn't let the same thing happen to Nu Venia and her child. But how to make the admiral understand?

"Admiral," Vawynn said, "those at Endurance are my people. You have the desire to reach out to Persephone and reunite our worlds. My people have the same desire to be reunited with those at Endurance, but we do not have the means to travel over the ocean. May my first request of our new relationship be to ask for your help to reunite my people?"

Oh, she was good.

We waited.

Behind the admiral's smile was a face that had turned red with fury. I almost burst out loud laughing but I stopped when I heard Vawynn catch her breath in surprise. She'd lost her composure and reached her hand toward his image.

"Admiral," she exclaimed.

I caught her arm and gently pulled it to her side.

"No," I whispered. If she acknowledged his fury, everything would be lost.

She looked at me.

I smiled broadly.

She understood, regained her composure, and smiled.

The admiral was too angry to notice. "I understand your need to meet with your people, but *Stanza* is scheduled to depart in 32 hours," the admiral said. "I doubt there is enough time." As his anger grew, he turned purple.

As much as I disliked him, I truly did not want him to have a heart attack over this.

"I have another request," Vawynn said.

Oh no, I thought. We'd not discussed any other requests. Was she about to blow the whole deal?

"It is my understanding that you originally sent scientists to study Akiane and her people, but now your scientists are returning to your Moon Base," she said. "We at Persephone would be most interested in your people staying with us."

She was a genius. How could the admiral say no?

"It would help our two worlds to become better acquainted. What do you think, Admiral?"

When the admiral reappeared, he was considerably less purple. If he said yes to her last request, he'd get what he wanted, but he would also have to grant Vawynn's first request, which would be a win for us and a defeat for him.

He should have seen that reuniting Endurance and Persephone would be a political win for him. Maybe he did, but he wanted it on his terms, not mine. It would mean he was not in complete control of the situation; I was.

With Larry's help, the admiral had been outsmarted and he didn't like it.

"Excellent idea, Vawynn." His words were strained. It must have caused him great pain to say them.

To our surprise, the admiral started laughing. It wasn't a pleasant sound. It was more like an evil chuckle.

"How do you plan to save those people, Lieutenant? I've read the reports. Those people have bad DNA. What are you going to do, Lieutenant, give them yours?" His laugh became more robust and disconcerting.

He stopped laughing, his coloring improved, and his eyes widened. "I can see the headline: *Young Lieutenant Single-handedly Saves Pegasus Colony with her DNA.*"

We'd pushed him too far, and he'd lost it.

"Hell, why not have *Stanza's* entire crew donate their DNA? Better yet, I'll order them to do it." He snickered at the silliness of his idea. "You'll collect so much, there will be enough DNA for both colonies."

I was stunned. He was acting like the idiot I thought he was.

He was still in good humor when he said, "You give them healthy babies and they'll listen to anything you have to say. They might finally agree to become a colony."

Then his anger returned with more intensity. He wanted complete obedience, without question. "Do you see how foolish this sounds? As for public relations, I'll take care of them. Trust me."

Trust him? If the truth got out that an entire colony of people died, I would become his scapegoat. I'd be the one who had insisted on abandoning them. And I'd be the one in the brig for most of my life, while he received the sympathy of having listened to my bad advice.

With a tight smile and a harsh voice, he said, "*Stanza* is scheduled to leave in 32 hours. There will be no more delay."

"I am most appreciative of your patience," Vawynn said with a slight bow of her head. "And may I say, you are a brilliant man, Admiral Grossman."

Her words made me turn my head in surprise and exclaim, "What?"

She reached out and held my hand. I immediately regained my composure.

"May I say, those of Endurance and Persephone are most grateful for your orders to save children and their parents," she said.

She was dazzling, stroking that old fool's ego, but she was right. The admiral's rant had been brilliant. He didn't mean one word of it, yet she used his words to our benefit.

Give those at Endurance fresh DNA to save their children—even if High Priest Adumie wouldn't listen, the life-givers would. Mothers with healthy children would force him to listen.

I leaned into the screen. "Sir, you are brilliant, Sir!" And I meant it. "But instead of DNA, what the colonists need is fresh sperm. The men of this crew will be so proud to tell their family and friends they helped save Pegasus Colony. They in turn will tell the rest of the world. Imagine the PR, Sir. You'll be a hero." I didn't mind him taking the credit if it got the job done. With him in the limelight, the digital media might forget about me. "I'll speak to Captain Leopold and Dr. Montgomery right away, Sir."

"Computer, off," I commanded. I wasn't going to waste time waiting for his reply. I knew exactly what he was going to do as soon as he heard our last transmission. He'd scramble to get to the captain. He'd be 40 minutes too late.

I jumped up and headed toward the captain's ready room. After all, he had requested my presence immediately after I talked to the admiral for a debriefing. All I was doing was following his orders.

I told Captain Leopold what the admiral had said. He closed his eyes. A soft moan escaped his lips. He knew exactly what I was doing. I was asking him to ambush the admiral.

After a moment of contemplation, he said, "This may be both our funerals."

"Yes, Sir."

"Tell your people to prepare for visitors," he said. "On your way out, send my first officer in."

I stood. "Thank you, Sir. From the bottom of my heart, thank you."

I ran to Rona's quarters. I was still with her when the commander's voice came over the ship's com explaining the need for DNA and sperm and requesting volunteers to donate.

Admiral Grossman rescinded the 32 hours deadline for the return trip to Moon Base. He claimed the window of opportunity was all wrong. I imagined him snarling orders.

He was the admiral, and I was a lowly lieutenant. He wasn't about to let me have the upper hand. He couldn't take back his comments about the crew giving DNA, but he could shorten the time needed to finish the job.

We now had 26 hours. He wanted 18 hours, but the captain said he had been preparing for 32 hours, time he needed now that he had to off-load scientists and their equipment to Persephone.

But the admiral wouldn't listen.

"Sir, 26 hours!" I complained.

"It's the best I could do," the captain said.

"Thank you, Sir."

Rona, Lu, Lesley, and Mathieu collected the first sperm samples, from the crew. Once the first batch was ready, we headed for Endurance.

Lu and Lesley stayed behind to draw as much blood and receive many sperm samples from the crew as possible. They would refrigerate and process them at Lu's new lab at Persephone.

Spago, Gino, and a few others volunteered to stay and help. They wouldn't have time to get everything from all 862 crewmembers, but they would have time to get more than enough for all the life-givers at Endurance to have at least two maybe three children.

The captain ordered all personal items and research equipment from *Stanza* to Persephone. Everything got packed and sent except for Larry Gino's things and my duffel bag.

There was a knock on my door. I opened it and found Larry Gino standing there.

"I believe I'm getting old," he said. He didn't appear older than the first time I'd met him.

"How so," I asked.

"I think that gravitational storm did me in. I was afraid I'd never see my family again," he confessed.

"But I thought this was your last great adventure," I said.

"It was and has been, but it's time I return home, Jessica."

"Have you told Spago?"

"I tried, but he's not listening," he said. "He'll have to face up to it soon enough. I'll enjoy our last few hours working together. And you? What are your plans?"

"Me?"

"I hear we'll be returning together."

"Yes, I guess we are," I said. "I'd like to apologize for the way I treated you on the voyage here, Larry. This time, we'll have plenty of time to get to know each other."

I'm not sure what I expected, but his response was not it.

"Have you told anyone? Like Rona or Jorge? Nu Venia perhaps?"

"I don't know how I'm going to tell them."

"Jessica, are you sure you want to leave?"

"Well, I have to, don't I? I've been ordered to return. Besides, Earth calls me home. I can't imagine not returning."

"Home. That's what everyone desires, isn't it?" He patted me on the arm. "Just make sure you answer the call to *your* home."

He left me standing in the doorway with no idea of what he was talking about.

I looked over my orderly little cabin. My duffel bag, with everything I owned in it, sat on my bed. I should have unpacked. But there was too much to do. *I'd have plenty of time once the ship launched,* I reasoned.

Going back to Earth was what I'd been working toward. I'd left Earth hoping to find myself and start life over when I returned. Well, I'd found myself, and now it was time to go home.

I was about to fulfill the admiral's order. Endurance would become a colony, and Cameron's mission to save his people would be accomplished.

It was time for me to return to Earth.

I closed the door, walked away, heading for the shuttle bay area, dreading tearful goodbyes.

Chapter 32

Jessica Hewitt
Victorious Return

Akiane Date: Year 328
Endurance: Commons Area

ENDURANCE WAS meant to be a shelter, a protection from harsh winters, a place to raise families. It was a place for the future Community to thrive and expand. It was not meant to be a place of hopelessness. But something had gone terribly wrong.

When my friends and I first arrived on Akiane, all those weeks ago, we were told to stay by the entrance until someone came to escort us to our new living quarters.

High Priest Adumie had not been happy to see us.

Jecidia and Cameron would have been more welcoming, but the high priest wouldn't let them.

On my second arrival, Nu Venia and I returned victorious with Vawynn at our side.

Vawynn wanted to prove that her people were healed so we stopped along the way to pick up five adults, seven teens, four children, and two babies. They walked behind us. Behind them came the scientists.

The few people who were in the garden stopped what they were doing when they saw us, then quickly ran off. No doubt to tell Adumie that we'd returned with strangers.

Evidently, no one told the chovis we weren't welcome. They ran to greet their two-legged friends. Scientists knelt to greet their four-legged friends with hugs and received licks of welcome.

Imos proudly walked at my side. Essal's puppies trailed behind her. I wondered who would take care of Imos after I left?

Nu Venia, of course.

Imos had already attached herself to both of us. After I was gone, they would take care of each other, and Imos would become a lifelong companion to Nu Venia's child.

The real question was who was going to watch over me after I left?

We made our way through the garden without incident.

What was once a well-manicured habitat, now, for lack of gardeners, had become a jungle. Because of The Storm's latest visit, trees leaned, some had toppled over with their roots exposed, and boulders placed for their aesthetic beauty had been tossed to one side. It would take a lot of work to get this place back in order.

Perhaps it is best to abandon it for Persephone, I thought.

I knew Adumie wouldn't relocate. He'd rather die than give up. I wondered how many would stay just because he was their leader?

We entered the main building and headed to the Commons area where Nu Venia said important Community meetings were held.

This day would be an historic Community meeting.

"What is your father's name?" Nu Venia asked.

"Lloyd," I said.

"Lloyd it is."

"Is what?"

"The name of our child," she said.

"*Our* child?"

"I carry him, but he comes from you and Cameron."

"Why not name him after Cameron?"

"Cameron is of the old ways. Because of him we are walking toward a new beginning," she said. "Lloyd will be the first child born both of Akiane and Earth. He will be the first from Endurance who will not be infected by the retrovirus."

I thought about it, then said, "Lloyd. I like it. My dad would be proud."

She placed her hands on her stomach and said sadly, "When a man-child is born, there is much mourning. My people will say this man-child is a punishment for having Cameron's child."

"Why?"

"A man-child cannot bring forth the next generation, Jessica."

"So they are outcasts?"

"Jessica, no. We mourn the end of a family line, but we honor the man-child by raising them as priests," she said. "Our child will not be given to the priests because I will raise him myself."

"Are all men priests?" I asked.

"No," she said. "As some grow older, they choose not to remain as a priest."

"Are all priests men?"

"No. There are women whom the Holy One has chosen to serve Him."

"Nu Venia, remember our conversation on the boat? A woman cannot bring forth a man-child by herself. She must have a man to mate with."

She froze. "That would mean...?"

"That would mean, all your men have two parents. Won't that be an interesting topic at our Community meeting?"

Without a word, she started walking again. I couldn't tell from her expression what she might be thinking.

"Speaking of which, how do we call a meeting?" I asked.

"Not to worry," she said. "There will be attendance. And on this day, lies will be exposed."

Nu Venia walked with her head held high. Her maroon face flushed with determination. She was no longer that little person who tried to hide her existence. We were the exact same height, a sign we were equals and partners on a mission. Cameron would have been proud of her—of both of us.

News traveled fast.

As we walked into the main building, many colonists were already there.

I understood what Nu Venia meant when she'd said, *"All would attend."*

Those who'd seen us in the garden had not run to warn Adumie; they'd run to tell the others that we'd returned.

As we entered the Commons area, there was the hum of whispers and looks of amazement, curiosity, and far too many faces filled with disdain, and fear.

The first time I walked into the Commons area, I was impressed by the size of the room, and the large murals of the history of the people of Akiane. The murals began with the tragedy of their landing, their settlement in the caldera, the building of Endurance, and finally a happy community of people.

The last mural was unfinished, as if the happiness had suddenly come to an end.

This time I saw murals that were faded and paint that had cracked. Among the murals were holograms of their ancestors that no longer worked. The military could repair the holograms and search computer files for new photos, but the murals would need professionals to repair them.

307

Jecidia was the last to enter the room. He walked slowly, leaning on the arm of a friend. He motioned to be seated at Adumie's table. Once settled, Jecidia whispered something to his friend, who bowed his head in compliance and quickly left.

Adumie sat with his head down, lost in thought. He seemed a decade older and more weary of life than when I last saw him.

Slowly, as if awakened from a bad dream, he began to notice the commotion in the room. Wonder spread across his face as he realized Jecidia was sitting at the same table with him. Then he noticed the many people who were also in the room.

I smiled at the astonishment when he eyes settled on those he'd banished from his planet. But that was nothing compared to his fury when he focused on Nu Venia and me.

He rose like a warrior ready for battle. "Why return?" he demanded. "You are not wanted here. Your admiral gave his word you would never return."

"He's not as trustworthy as he pretends," I said.

Nu Venia stepped forward. "We return victorious. We have made Woden. You cannot deny us." Though she didn't yell, everyone easily heard the self-confidence in her voice.

Adumie's eyes widened, his upper lip stretched thinly into a snarl, his chest expanded, and his hands became fists. He was ready for battle.

"You never expected to see us again, did you?" I asked.

Adumie searched for Cameron.

"Cameron is not with us," I said. "He was taken by a tupilak and is no more." My emotions might have once again risen, if not for Nu Venia's announcement.

"I carry Cameron's child," she said with great pride.

I was not expecting her to say that. I thought we'd ease into it and tell them in a month or two.

She refrained from explaining my part in the matter. That bit of information could be saved for a later date.

308

The room vibrated with wails of anguish from 200 colonists. One might have thought Nu Venia had just confessed that we'd cannibalized Cameron.

Adumie paled, but recovered quickly.

Several people shouted: "Blasphemer!"

Others pounded their fists on tables or in the air. Anger and revulsion filled their eyes, faces, bodies, and voices.

"Cameron would never do such a thing."

"Without Cameron, Woden has failed."

"Go back to Earth."

"Leave us."

"Your kind is not welcomed."

"Depart and take the abomination with you."

Since they didn't want to hear the truth, the logical thing would have been to leave them to their intolerance.

But I'd not come for logic. I'd come to honor Cameron.

He wouldn't give up on them, and I wouldn't disappoint him.

It was a little intimidating with so many people yelling insults at us. It seemed that most had something to say, but not quite everyone. A handful of people, including Jecidia, sat in silence. *What was he thinking?*

If he were still the leader, he'd have treated us with respect. Nu Venia said he'd been sick for a long time. Even though he had trouble walking and breathing, he refused to give up.

Nu Venia remained calm. She stood unashamed and unintimidated.

Adumie's voice rose and silenced all others, "Intruder's words spoken will not be listened to."

People nodded and murmured their agreement.

He had given me my opening.

"Ah, but I'm no intruder. Cameron gave his life fighting a tupilak, so Nu Venia and I could return victoriously from Woden." I proudly raised my voice and said, "Nu Venia and I have earned the right to be heard."

Attitudes didn't softened. No one acknowledged our right. They didn't deny us either.

To my surprise, Nu Venia took over the conversation.

"Is it because Cameron is not here that you will not listen, or is it because you believe I am abomination?" Nu Venia stared at them, daring them to confirm or deny. "It is only by Adumie's word that you believe I am abomination. Has anyone asked how he obtained such information? Did he witness the act? If so, why didn't he stop them? Why has he never named the other guilty party? Who is my other parent, Adumie? Tell us."

The weight of every eye turned on him, and for the moment, they forgot Nu Venia carried Cameron's child.

Adumie's voice cracked as he spoke. "This one does not lie about such importance."

"No, I don't believe you do." Nu Venia walked toward him. "I believe you told the truth. I do have two parents."

"What deception is this?" he asked suspiciously.

"Deception is not from me," she said. "What deception do you hold? Why expose Petra after her death? Why not bring her before Community while she lived? Why shame her after death? Why shame me?"

He stared at her wide-eyed, not understanding what she meant.

I had no idea where she was headed. This was not on our agenda.

"You have no right," Adumie rasped.

"No right?" Nu Venia snapped. "You accuse Petra and me and you say I have no right? This is my life. Who has more right than me?"

I never thought Nu Venia could be so confrontational. I wanted to stop her. An argument between her and Adumie might not go over well with the Community. But she'd already started. If I tried to stop her now, it would only make things worse.

Adumie stumbled as he sat down.

The crowd watched in silence, not sure where this was headed.

Nu Venia took several rapid steps toward him. "Who is my other parent, Adumie?" she demanded.

A swish of breath exhaled from the crowd. Something was wrong, but they didn't know what.

Jecidia was the only one who didn't react. He sat quietly listening and thinking.

Adumie heaved if he'd been slammed in the chest.

Rona turned to me for an explanation, but I had no idea what was going on.

"Nu Venia?" I asked.

"I am no abomination," Nu Venia yelled at Adumie.

Then she turned to Rona and said, "Tell him. Tell all of them. I am no abomination."

Chapter 33

Rona Montgomery
Victory

Akiane Date: Year 328
Endurance: Commons Area

RONA FROZE, unsure what to do. She had no idea what Nu Venia was talking about. No one had said anything about an abomination.

She'd come with the desire to save people, but it looked like she'd walked into an insurrection.

How does one overcome so much hostility?

With hope, Rona realized.

That was what she wanted to pass on to the colonists. Hope.

Suddenly Rona found herself speaking. "I have good news," she said with a shaky voice. She swallowed hard and kept on speaking before she lost her nerve. "I have the cure for your illness."

No one noticed. They were too engrossed in the argument between Nu Venia and Adumie.

Maybe she was wrong to speak up. Maybe this wasn't the time.

I finally have the answer, but not the means to reach them, Rona thought. *They need to listen. It's time to stop the blame and guilt. But how do I get through to them?*

Jess was at her side.

"Great idea. Divert the conversation before we get thrown out again."

She pulled Rona forward.

"Quiet!" Jess forcefully bellowed like a sergeant yelling at her troops.

Rona had never seen Jess like this. She was no longer her usual frustrated self. She seemed to have evolved into a self-confident leader.

"Do you have more horrible news for us?" one shouted back.

"Listen. LISTEN!" Jess shouted louder.

They quieted.

"Please listen. We're not here to harm you. Our doctors and scientists have discovered how to make your people well," Jess said.

They became confused, but silent.

In a much softer voice, Jess said, "Now listen to Rona. She has something important to tell you."

Jess escorted Nu Venia out of the way.

Rona was again standing in front of a group of people explaining the retrovirus. The last two times people had listened, but they were scientists and her friends.

These people were a hostile crowd. If she failed, it was all over. Rona needed them to listen and believe her. Otherwise, she couldn't heal them. A trickle of sweat ran down her back. She felt as if she were standing at the bottom of an impossibly steep cliff.

Rona took a deep breath and started up that cliff. "I know why you're dying."

"Why?" a voice yelled.

"Because you do not exchange essence." As soon as she had spoken, she knew she'd taken the wrong turn. Rona cringed and braced herself for a fight.

It was more than they could stand.

"You came to turn us from the Holy One!"

"We do not listen to lies!"

"You come to destroy us!"

"Get out!"

"Get out!"

"Get out!"

The cacophony of voices grew by the second.

That was it. One sentence and Rona had lost them. She took a step back just as Nu Venia took several angry steps toward them.

"Stop it," Nu Venia yelled. "Stop it!"

Rona continued to move away until she felt a hand at her back stopping her retreat.

"Stand your ground," Jess whispered in her ear and gently pushed her forward toward Nu Venia.

"Stop it," Nu Venia repeated louder. "Jessica and I have returned from Woden. By your own custom you must listen to us and to those we bring with us."

"We only hear lies," someone growled.

"Indeed."

"Just so."

"Lies."

Vawynn stepped forward. She pulled her hood off so everyone could see her. She was one of them, but she didn't look like them. She was not as tall, she was thinner, her eyes were green, and her hair hung down to her waist. But most importantly, her skin shone a light shade of maroon.

"Where do you come from?" someone asked in awe.

"Who are *you*?" asked another.

"My name is Vawynn," she said. "I am of your blood. I am from the group of people who left Endurance in the year 28 to start a new settlement."

She had their full attention.

"All was strange for us when we first arrived on Akiane. We did the best we could with what we knew. Your people chose one path, my people chose another," Vawynn said.

She took her gloves and jacket off. A friend came forward to take them from her.

Her arms were bare. Her blouse was low cut in the front and back. As she slowly walked among them, she stopped so they could get a good look. Her skin had no signs of the slow dying sickness, and her palms were smooth.

"I was born on Akiane," she said, "Yet, I do not have the illness. Rona speaks truth. Because we have two parents, there is no sickness among my people. Look and see that we are healthy." She motioned for her friends to come forward.

They too took off their winter coats, revealing skin devoid of sickness.

They and Vawynn walked among the colonists. "My people and I are healthy," she repeated several times. "All of us. All ages. Men and women."

Those of Endurance examined their relatives with a mixture of emotions. Some believed, while others stubbornly thought it a fabrication. Most stared at Vawynn as if she were a goddess.

Perhaps she is, Rona thought. *Perhaps, she's the metaphorical magic wand needed to win this battle.*

"The Holy One has indeed blessed you and yours," one woman said.

"You say having two parents is an abomination, but all of our children have two parents and are born healthy. Would God give good health and long life to one who is evil, and give disease and death to one who is pure?" she asked.

"You are saying we are evil?"

"No, I am saying, God loves all," Vawynn said. "It is simply a matter of how our children are born."

315

Her "goddessness" vanished.

"Throw them out."

"Throw them out!" the crowd echoed.

If this woman can't reach them, what hope do I have? Rona grimaced.

The old man sitting at the table with Adumie rose to his feet. The room immediately quieted. Everyone waited as he laboriously shuffled toward the off-worlders and stood in front of Rona.

She stepped back, fearful of the trouble he might cause.

If he throws us out, what then? she wondered. *Should we try again or just leave?*

Vawynn had invited the entire scientific crew to Persephone where they and their research were welcomed. Perhaps she should just go and forget about Endurance.

The thought crashed into her brain with a resounding *NO!*

The old man stood between Rona and Nu Venia. He faced his people, and said, "This one has made Woden."

To Nu Venia, he said, "Speak."

Nu Venia acknowledged him respectfully with a slight bow of her head. "Jecidia."

To his people he said, "Listen." Though he spoke softly, that one word was obeyed.

"For years we have prayed for divine healing. We hoped that this illness would leave us and no longer kill. But there has been much disappointment," Nu Venia said. "Prayer has not been answered in the way we hoped."

"In what manner should we expect an answer to prayer?" someone said.

"I think we have been expecting the wrong answers." Nu Venia sighed heavily.

Adumie once again found his voice and rose to his feet.

"You believe these intruders are an answer to prayer?"

His anger had not subsided despite Jecidia's command. His nose flared, his eyebrows scrunched, and he shook with fury.

"They bring death, and you think they are an answer to prayer?" he demanded.

"What is wrong with you?" Olivia rushed forward to take over the conversation. "We're not responsible for this illness. But we could cure it if you weren't so pigheaded."

Rona flinch. *This is the end of the conversation.*

"How dare you," Adumie began, but Olivia cut him off.

"How dare *you*," she screeched. "You would rather let your people die than admit you're wrong."

"Olivia, be still." Jess tried to gently pull her back.

She whipped her arm away. "I will not. They need to listen."

"I will not listen to the likes of you," Adumie bellowed.

"Olivia," Rona said. "Stop it. You're making things worse."

"No, I'm not. He is." Olivia's voice echoed off the walls "You think you're so high and mighty," she continued. "You are not."

Jorge tried to grab her, but she squirmed out of his grip, and took several defiant steps toward the big man. She tilted her head back and with her hands on her hips, stood boldly before him.

Compared to her, Adumie was a giant.

It reminded Rona of a picture of a mouse standing completely unafraid of an eagle swooping down upon it.

In a different situation, Rona might have thought it funny.

"You threw us out! For what? Because Rona and Lu tried to help you? How stupid is that?"

"Olivia, stop it," Jorge said.

She didn't.

"You accuse us of stealing, but you maliciously destroyed our equipment. You locked us up like animals.

You sent Jess and two of your people on a suicide mission to prove their worth. Now you refuse to hear the truth. And you call yourself a man of God. Where I come from, you're no better than a criminal."

"How dare you!" A vein in Adumie's neck throbbed. His eye twitched.

Jorge and Mathieu grabbed Olivia by her arms, lifted her off the floor, and carried her out of the room kicking and screaming.

Still, Olivia would not shut up. She fought like a wildcat.

"He needs to be told the truth," she shouted.

Adumie shouted in turn. "Do you see what these people are like? Do you see how they cannot control their own?" He spoke with arrogant amusement.

From down the hall, they heard Olivia's last words, "And who controls you? All your lies, your willingness to allow your people to die, who do you answer to? God! That's who. One day, you will answer to God."

Rona could still hear her yelling, but now she was cursing in Dutch, her native language.

Whatever headway we might have made is now gone, thanks to Olivia. Rona had never been so embarrassed.

Vawynn and her people moved to stand behind Nu Venia, Rona, and Jess.

"That one speaks the same lies as you," he said, pointing to Jessica. You come not to heal, but to take what is ours." Adumie growled. His eye had stopped twitching, but the vein in his neck continued to throb.

Jess did not flinch at his words, or turn from his gaze.

Could Jess undo Olivia's damage? Rona wondered. *No. It's up to me.*

Rona took a deep breath, took one step forward and said, "Olivia's passion is real. Our desire to help you is just as real. We don't want you to die." She paused, waiting for someone to object. No one did. She continued, "We have the means to heal you and your children, but we can't unless you let us." To her amazement, they were actually listening. "Maybe God didn't answer your prayers the way you wanted, but what if He has a better plan?"

Nu Venia joined Rona. "Adumie, the off-worlders not only bring healing, they have reunited us with our lost family."

Vawynn joined them.

"It is time we listen and learn," Nu Venia confirmed. "We must change our ways if we are to survive." She placed a hand on her stomach. "We must do this for the sake of our children. Is that not what Assetti and Stricken did. They returned from Woden with new life so we could survive on Akiane. These people do the same. They bring to us new life so we can live. With their help, we will live for generations. How can healthy children be a curse? Should we not welcome those of Earth, and those who were lost to us, with open hearts for the sake of our future, for the sake of our children?"

"Do not listen to her," Adumie cut in. He stood hunched over. His legs wobbled. He swayed as if he might topple over. "She speaks not for God." His voice was weak and breathless. He pointed at Nu Venia as if his finger might bore a hole in her. "That one is abomination."

Nu Venia did not waver under his finger, his accusing stare, or his damning words.

"You want the truth?" Rona said. "The fact that Nu Venia has two parents saved her life."

Adumie's anger changed to shock. "I am without understanding."

"I will explain." She turned to his people. "Who among you is not ill?" Rona asked the people of Endurance.

To her surprise, more than two-thirds of the people stood.

"How many of you are men?" she asked.

More than half raised their hands.

"This is proof," Nu Venia said. "See how many of you are men? You are a man because you have two parents. All who are healthy are healthy because you have two parents. Why have you never spoken of it?"

"None of us have two parents," one said defiantly. "Our parents would not keep such truth from us."

"Yes, all," Nu Venia said. "You parents did not speak truth so as not to shame themselves or you."

"You might not have known the truth that all of you have two parents," Rona said in a compassionate voice. "I'm sure some of you did know, but were afraid to say something because you were ashamed. On this day, the shame ends."

There was a long moment of silence. And just as Rona was starting to believe the colonists would never change, someone said, "I thought I was the only one."

"This one believed the same."

"And this one."

"How many of you standing have healthy children?" Rona asked.

"None," one said. "We did not want our children to die of the illness. We birthed no children."

"Just so," several agreed.

"If you would have had children with another, all your children would be healthy." Then Rona had a thought. "How many of your parents come from the same family?"

A swish of shock passed over the entire group.

"We would never," one said.

"One does not exchange essence within one's family," another said.

"Qorow Low told me you once lived in family groups, each in one large room, each a small community. But all together you are one Community," Rona said.

"This is truth."

"You were taught not to exchange essence within your family," she said.

"Indeed."

"That's good," Rona said. "It's unhealthy for the child if parents come from the same family, but it is healthy to exchange essence between different families." She paused to let this bit of information sink in. "But somehow the 'do not touch' in the family translated into the rule that no one in the Community should ever come together." She paused for effect. "See how many of you are healthy? This is proof. Soon the only ones of you who will live will be those with two parents."

From out of the crowd, a tearful voice spoke what was in everyone's heart. "This one desires to have children who are healthy and strong."

"Mine is to watch my children grow up," another said.

"This one wants my children and my children's children to have healthy."

"Do you hear what off-worlders say? Do you see Vawynn and her people?" Nu Venia said. "Adumie, the sharing of essence will save us."

"It is time to listen, Adumie," Jecidia said. "It is time for change."

Adumie closed his eyes and turned away.

Chapter 34

Adumie
Truth

Akiane Date: Year 328
Endurance: Commons Area

ADUMIE HEARD only silence. His people were waiting to see what he would say.

He didn't know what to say. Everything Adumie had believed was not exactly a lie, but neither was it truth. One does not change with the flip of a switch. It takes time. Now was the time to pray, contemplate, listen, and wait for guidance. But everything was changing whether he liked it or not. And it was changing faster than he could control.

Adumie crumpled into his chair.

"I am no abomination," Nu Venia softly said. "Yet, you shamed me and my life-giver. You never mention who my father is. Why is that?" In a pleading voice, Nu Venia asked, "Who is my father?"

"I am your father," Adumie said just above a whisper.

He confessed his greatest sin. There should have been shouting, demanding he was no longer wanted as high priest.

Instead, the room was completely silent. No movement or whispering, no angry accusations.

He dared not lift his eyes to see the faces of horror. He watched Nu Venia's feet, as they came toward him.

She knelt before him. "You are my father?"

There was nothing to say. All those years he'd pointed an accusing finger at her, now the accusation pointed back at him. He closed his eyes and turned his head away.

"There is no denial from you?" a woman angrily asked.

"You stood as leader?" another asked. "A blasphemer?"

With a heavy moan, Adumie's shoulders wilted. The burden was too great for him to carry any longer.

"Why?" Nu Venia asked. "I don't understand. This one is your daughter. Why treat me thus?" The pain in her voice stabbed as a knife slicing through his heart.

"I wanted, I wanted." He stopped. He tried to collect his thoughts, but they didn't make sense, not even to him. How could he express himself to others, to Nu Venia?

For the first time, Adumie looked into the mirror of his soul. He did not like what he saw. How could he have treated his own daughter with such contempt? His own daughter. What kind of man was he? No wonder God did not answer his prayers.

"Why not tell the truth?" Nu Venia asked.

"Petra feared the shame it would bring upon me."

"She cared not for the shame it would bring upon me? Did you not care? Why would you do this to me?"

He could not bear the hurt on her face. "This one has behaved badly." Tears. He knew exactly why he had behaved badly. He had been ashamed of his actions and too much of a coward to claim Nu Venia as his own.

She had been a constant reminder of his failure. He had believed his love for Petra had been sin. Her death was his punishment.

Now he realized he should have loved Nu Venia as much as he had Petra.

His entire life was one long catastrophe because of the lies. If only he had known the truth—it was better to love. Now he had lost the right to love and be loved.

Nu Venia rested her forearms on his knees, and took his hands in hers.

His initial reaction was to pull away, but since they were both wearing gloves, they could not exchange essence.

The last person who had touched him was on the day he held her mother, Petra, in his arms 14 years ago. It was only fitting that the next person who touched him was his daughter.

"Do you not hear what is being said?" It sounded as if she spoke with forgiveness. How could she so easily forget all he had done?

He did not understand the question. "What?"

"You are male. Only two people can bring forth a male child."

A feeling of dread overcame him at the realization that he was about to be pronounced an abomination. All those years he had accused her of being unacceptable, now he too was unacceptable.

He could not dispute the truth being spoken.

"We have all believed lies. It is time to forget the past and walk in truth," she said. "It is time we listen to Rona and allow the off-worlders to help us."

Adumie bowed his head and said, "I have wronged you. I am repentant."

Nu Venia turned from Adumie, stood, and stepped away.

She was abandoning him. He raised his head to watch her leave. Instead, he saw a ripple pass through the crowd of off-worlders as a vision entered the room.

Leaning on Melar's arm was Qorow Low. Her maroon face was no longer pale. The blotches along her hairline were barely noticeable.

When their eyes met, she released Melar's arm and walked toward Adumie. Melar sat down at the same table as Adumie.

The fear that Qorow Low was dying had been his greatest trial, but she had not died. She stood before him.

How?

He did not care how. The one who gave joy to his heart still lived.

Everyone in the room seemed to fade away. They were the only two left.

Adumie rose to greet her.

"Why so sad?" Qorow Low asked.

"This one thought all was lost," Adumie said. "I did not know what would become of this one when you, the one who has taught me love, was no more."

"This one is not leaving," she said. "There was such grief at the loss of my first child I thought to die."

She motioned to Jecidia. He came and stood next to her.

"After you left, that one and I talked." She turned back to Adumie. "This one must finish grieving, but I will live because of the cure off-worlders bring us."

She placed her gloved hand on his chest. "We have become a dying people for lack of truth. How can we become a Community if each stands alone? It is time we overcome our fears and become one family made of many friends, no longer separated by family units, but one Community of people united in love and understanding."

He was unable to respond or think clearly. It was too confusing to grasp the meaning of what she was saying. There had been too many years of wrong thinking, so much shame and guilt over secretly loving another. Now those from another world, those he thought were enemies, told him love would save his Community. How was this possible?

Qorow Low was so beautiful. His green-gloved hand reached out to her. His fingers moved into her hair; his palm rested against her cheek. He wanted to take his glove off, but it was too deeply ingrained in him: *Do not touch.*

He remembered where he was; they were not alone. He pulled his hand away, and took a step back. It was too late.

Everyone in the room had seen and knew how much his heart ached for Qorow Low.

Twice his heart had been ripped open because love had been denied him. Now he questioned everything he believed and had only two choices: let his people die or go against everything he believed to save them.

Love was not a sin. How could such warmth and joy be wrong? Love was a gift from God. He wanted to hold Qorow Low and never let go.

One does not touch, his brain shouted.

The Holy One had given her back to him. He drank in her beauty, her radiant smile. He didn't care what the others thought. He wanted to hold her and never let her go.

He pulled her close. She didn't resist. They wrapped their arms around each other. She placed her head on his chest. He rested his cheek against her head.

Generations of mistaken beliefs unraveled the walls around Adumie's heart and disintegrated.

Chapter 35

Rona Montgomery
New Revelations

Akiane Date: Year 328
Endurance: Commons Area

RONA WAS stunned at what she'd just witnessed.

Then she heard a man quietly say, "This one has feelings for another." He was looking at one woman in particular. "But I have not had the courage to express my feelings."

The woman sobbed in relief. "This one also has feelings," she said.

Both were standing among those who were healthy because they were born of two parents.

He walked to her. They took their gloves off. He took her hand in his and held it against his chest. She leaned against him as he wrapped his arm around her and rested his cheek against her head.

"I can hear your heart beating," she said.

"I can hear you breathing," he said.

Their breaths synchronized.

After a few moments, they separated.

"We will have a healthy child together," he said.

"Just so." She beamed.

In front of everyone, they had exchanged essence. Several people seemed shocked, but no one objected.

Rona was relieved that they were both healthy. The chance of their child being healthy was excellent.

"This one has been critical of Qorow Low's feelings," a woman said. "I have been accusing of one who did not deserve it. I ask forgiveness."

"Forgiveness is gladly given, Mercener," Qorow Low said. Then she turned to Adumie. "Do you hear?"

Adumie nodded. "This one also asks forgiveness."

"For you, there is nothing to forgive. But there is much love," she said. "It is time to forget lies and live in truth."

He attempted a smile, but instead of looking happy, he looked pained.

Some colonists were not as accepting of the new attitudes; they still looked suspicious.

"Let's begin at the beginning." Rona thought it best to take charge and better explain things before more people decided to exchange essence and things got out of hand.

She cleared her throat, and said, "I made a serious mistake when I tried to heal Qorow Low's child. I didn't have all the information I needed and I acted too quickly."

As the team leader, she felt it was only right that she took full responsibility for the child's death. "Qorow Low, I am gravely sorry your child died."

Qorow Low smiled. "You come to heal, but first you must learn." She swayed. Adumie held her steady; another quickly brought her a chair. Together they helped her sit. Adumie sat next to her.

Once she'd caught her breath, she hoarsely said, "My child would have died even if you had done nothing. I never thought to have so much time with my sweet little one. You gave me more than I hoped for. If that one's death has given you understanding, then she did not die in vain."

"I believe your child was a great help in my understanding. Both of you have been." Rona would have preferred an intimate conversation with the two of them, but there appeared to be no secrets within the Community.

At least not any more.

"My sorrow is eased" Qorow Low respectfully nod.

Adumie shifted uneasily in his chair. Evidently, he didn't completely agree with her, but he refrained from speaking his thoughts.

"One of our people died of the same retrovirus that is affecting you," Rona said, addressing the colonists. "Another became ill." She pointed to Vong. He bowed. "I treated him and he has made a full recovery.

"During my research, I learned that every fish, tupilak, and chovis has this retrovirus, and so do all of you. Now I realize that it is not as harmful to you as it is to us. Over the years, it has become normal for you."

"If this is truth, then how is it we are still ill?" Jecidia swayed slightly as he spoke.

"My guess is, over the years, there are more of you who traded essence, sperm, than you thought," Rona said. "That continual joining of healthy DNA must have slowed down the problem, but for those who continued to have children by yourselves, things eventually began to fall apart."

"This one is without understanding," Mercener said.

Rona began, "The retrovirus is incomplete so it cannot work properly. We have found a worm that lives in your ocean. It has what you need so the retrovirus *will* work properly and not be harmful to you or to your children."

Rona felt a sense of relief. They were listening to her. But she thought it best not to go into too many technical details, it would only confuse the situation. It was more important for them to believe her.

"We have learned from Vawynn that you pass the retrovirus to your children when you turn your cocoons. You leak the retrovirus from your palms into the Blood Vine liquid."

Nu Venia held up a pair of tongs. "With these, we can turn our eggs without infecting our children."

"Yes," Rona said, "but you get the retrovirus from handling raw meat and fish with your bare hands. If you wear gloves you will not become infected in the first place.

"For centuries you've mostly had children without a partner and have been reusing the same DNA over and over. Humans were never meant to reproduce like that. After such a long time your DNA is breaking down. That's why you and your children are dying. It's not the retrovirus. It's the way you're giving birth to your children. But the problem can be fixed if you are willing to allow your children to have partners when they are adults."

"Our DNA is bad?" a voice asked.

"No, it's tired," Rona said. "That's why Vawynn's people are healthy. First, they stopped reinfecting themselves, and second they have children the way nature intended babies to be born. They have two parents who mixed their DNA to form a new chain of healthy DNA that produces healthy babies."

Rona paused before she continued. "In time, you and your children will no longer be infected by the retroviruses, and your children will stop being born in cocoons. I know this is confusing. To tell you the honest truth, it confuses me. But I promise you our team will continue to study your situation. It may take a long time, but we will figure this out. For now, this is the best answer I have for you."

Mercener asked, "If we exchange this sperm you speak of, we will become well?"

"Your children will be healthier, but those of you with only one parent will continue to be sick," Rona said. "You need to be healed from the effects the retrovirus that started centuries ago. Those of you who have two parents don't need to be cured. You need to follow your parents' example and continue to have children together."

"This one is unwilling to exchange essence with another," Mercener said. "I have been raised not to."

"This one wishes not to."

"Nor this one. It is too strange."

"We thought you might feel that way. I do not expect you to change your ways just because I tell you to, but if you want your children and your children's children to survive, you will have to allow your children to touch," Rona paused. "Until then, the men from *WSC Stanza* are willing to give you sperm."

The colonists gasped.

Rona quickly continued, "They will not touch you. But they do want you to have healthy babies." She unzipped the refrigerator pack that hung over her shoulder and pulled out a small vile. "Many of the men in the crew from the ship orbiting above have donated their sperm to help save your Community."

She held a vile up for everyone to see and twisted it around in her fingers. "This is sperm. It's not labeled. No one knows whose sperm this is. The children will be wholly yours. The men who are staying on Akiane have not given their sperm."

"Why not?" Mercener asked suspiciously.

"We didn't want any of our men to wonder who might be their child," Rona said. "We want you to know that we make no claims on your children."

"You would do this for us? Even after all we have done?" Mercener began to sob.

"That was a misunderstanding," Rona said.

Mercener bowed her head. "I was the one who destroyed your equipment. My intention was to drive you away. This one is repentant."

"From the time you first arrived on Akiane 328 years ago, there has been much misunderstanding between you and WSC, even between your two settlements," Rona said. "It is time to put all of that behind us. We accept your apology, and please accept our apology for not being here when you needed us."

"This one accepts for her people." Mercener's voice was filled with blissful emotion. "I want my children to survive." She took her green glove off and held out her hand as she walked toward Rona.

Rona extended her free hand motioning her to stop.

Mercener halted. "Are you rejecting me? You do not forgive as easily as you say."

"Please, no. Giving life to a child takes an incredible amount of energy," Rona said. "If you are already sick, giving birth may accelerate your illness."

Mercener's hand dropped to her side. "You offer false hope."

"I'm offering you more than just having healthy children. I also offer you a longer life. I want you to watch your children grow up and have their own children," Rona said. "I also want you to have healthy DNA."

Silence. Had she gone to far? Did they think her promise was too good to be true?

"You first need to be healthy enough to have children," Rona said.

"You have a cure?" Mercener asked. "How is this possible?"

"You need the cure I spoke of earlier," Rona said.

"Where do we get this cure?" Jecidia asked.

"From fish in combination with worms."

Mercener backed away. "You wish to heal us with worms?"

Another woman stood and pointed to Qorow Low. "Only this morning, that one was on her death bed."

Qorow Low turned in her seat to face those behind her. "This morning, yes. But now, I feel much better."

"My original treatment took time to work on Qorow Low. That's why she got worse before she got better. I'm not sure if she is completely healed just yet," Rona said.

"What I offer you now comes from the medical logs in *Falcon's* computers. When your people first landed, they too became ill, and many of them died. They found a cure but didn't realize the effect it would have on future generations." Rona paused. "We want to stop the affects of the retrovirus. Therefore this treatment is only for those who are ill. Those of you who are well do not need to eat it."

Rona again paused. What she was about o say will either seal the deal or end any chances of curing these people.

She replaced the sperm vile, pulled out an other vile, an held it up for all to see.

"This holds fresh DNA. I'm hoping to give all who are ill a shot of this after you have eaten the meal Vong has made. I'm hoping that together they will repair your DNA."

"I will accept whatever you have to give me," Qorow Low said to Rona.

"No." Adumie objected. "I will not have it. That one will only steal more life from you."

"If this one does not try, you will lose me sooner." Qorow Low tried to smile through her pain. "When this one is healed, then we will have much time. We will have children together."

"You want to exchange essence with this one?" Adumie's eyes opened wide, his mouth dropped but he didn't seem disgusted.

"Of course I do." Qorow Low lovingly smiled.

His face softened as he smiled. "Honor fills this one's heart."

"Actually, Qorow Low is already on the road to good heath," Rona said. "Her child died because she was too ill. Thankfully, Qorow Low is not as sick any more. The worms should reinforce her healing. And if you will let me, I'll keep a close watch on her to make sure she is okay." To the room, she said, "My medical team will do our best to stay in touch with you to see how you are progressing."

Vong moved forward. "I made a cereal-like meal with raw fish and worms."

"Why raw?" Adumie asked.

"Heat stops the retrovirus from working, making the cure useless," Vong said. "Rona says it must be raw or it will not work."

Vong had come with two self-propelled carts holding a large vat of his meal and over 200 bowls and spoons so he would have enough for all who wanted to eat.

He filled a bowl then asked Adumie, "Would you like to feed her?"

Adumie was still doubtful and started to object.

Jecidia waved a hand. "Qorow Low might become ill again if she does not try."

"He's correct. What we originally gave her was an experiment," Rona said. "Since then I've read Dr. Beasley's notes. He said this is the cure."

"And I read your cook's logs in search of this recipe," Vong said.

"I must try. But this one is too tired to feed herself," Qorow Low said to Adumie. "Your assistance is required."

Adumie accepted the bowl and affectionately fed his love.

Everyone seemed to lean in, in anticipation, as they watched Qorow Low take her first bite.

"This is good," she said, surprised.

Vong beamed.

"One must not ask Qorow Low to eat if this one is unwilling to partake," Jecidia said. "Is there a bowl for me?"

"There certainly is," Vong said.

Jecidia's legs shook violently. His arms fluttered in an attempt to keep his balance.

Vong caught him before he fell over. Melar ran to help Jecidia to his chair. The atmosphere in the room became strained.

Vong realized what he'd done; he'd not only touched Jecidia but had held him in his arms.

"I am so sorry," he said, mortified at his transgression. "I didn't mean to offend you. I was just trying . . ."

"It is all right," Jecidia said with a bit of a laugh. "If not for you, this one would have fallen on his face." He grinned weakly. "Most undignified."

"I suppose that would have been embarrassing." Vong chuckled in relief.

"Indeed."

Vong filled a bowl for him, but was surprised when the man sitting next to Jecidia came to receive the bowl.

"I have become weak," Jecidia said. "This one has volunteered to be at my side when I am in need of help. His name is D"Aray."

"I will see that he eats each bite," D"Aray said. "He can be a bit difficult at times."

Jecidia grinned naughtily.

The colonists watched Jecidia as he took a tentative taste.

The crowd held its breath.

He stopped and looked around the room at his people. He pursed his lips, dug into the gruel with his spoon, opened his mouth wide, and shoveled it in.

Jecidia eyes glistened. He swallowed. "Better than I thought," he said to Vong. "You made this?"

"Yes."

"You have done a fine job," Jecidia said approvingly.

Vong smiled with pride.

"D"Aray will also have a bowl," Jecidia said.

D"Aray accepted his bowl and ate.

"I will have another bite," Qorow Low whispered.

Adumie gave her another spoonful.

The crowd seemed to like this, and began speaking to each other.

Mercener stood in front of Vong. "I will eat."

"Wait," Rona said. "I want to run tests to see how the retrovirus works. Qorow Low has already helped us by giving a little of her blood so I was able to program my HMS to her physiology. I should have tested Jecidia and D"Aray before they started eating."

With an expression of worry, Jecidia stopped eating.

A buzz rose from the crowd. "Blood?" several asked.

"No, I don't need your blood any more," Rona assured them. "But I do need a record of your progress. It helps us know if our cure is working. It also helps us to make adjustments if we need to."

Jecidia frowned. "This one does not understand."

"I'll check your progress with this." Rona held up a Hand Held Medical Scanner for everyone to see.

"Are you in need of another checking of me?" Qorow Low pulled her sleeve up.

Rona held the HMS against her arm until it beeped.

"There, it's done," she said.

Everyone stared, not completely convinced.

Rona turned to Jecidia and asked, "May I?"

He nodded.

"Please pull up your sleeve," she said. "I promise not to touch you with my hand, only this device will touch you."

He pulled his sleeve up. Rona placed the HMS close to his arm. When it beeped, she stepped away, typed his name in, and pushed a few buttons, then said, "Thank you. It worked perfectly."

She stared at the scanner, pushed a few buttons, and said, "Jecidia, you have a heart condition."

The words came out before she realized it.

Jecidia's illness had made him susceptible to the retrovirus, but the fact that he had two parents and had healthy DNA had slowed the impact of the retrovirus.

How many others are having similar problems, she wondered.

336

Suddenly, she and Lu had a whole new research project. They were about to become very busy.

"Heart condition?" Jecidia asked.

She'd already introduced so much to these people, now here was something new.

Rona smiled as if everything was under control. "Let's deal with the retrovirus first. If you'll allow me, tomorrow, I will run some more tests and will find a cure that will help you feel amazingly better."

Jecidia smiled, nodded, and said, "Tomorrow."

D"Aray raised his sleeve. "This one is next."

Rona took a reading and labeled it with his name.

"Mercener, would you prefer to wait and see if the meal works for the others before trying it yourself?" Rona asked.

Mercener stood, uncertain. She looked at Qorow Low, then at Jecidia. "I have already lost so much." She was overwhelmed by her emotions. "I want to be healed," she pleaded. "I want to have healthy children." She pulled her sleeve up and held her arm out to Rona. "Please."

Rona took her HMS readings. "Thank you."

Vong filled a bowl and handed it to her.

Mercener bowed her head as she received it. "Thank you."

"You're welcome," Vong said. "I truly do hope you get better and have many children."

More people came forward to be scanned, then get their bowls from Vong.

As Rona had suspected, the majority of the people wanted to see if the "cure" worked before they ate, which was a good thing. It would provide a more controlled group for testing.

A few people wanted to take bowls to those who were too sick to attend the meeting. Vong volunteered to go with them. Rona gave him a second HMS and showed him how to use it. He took it and one of the carts, and followed the others. Malar took his place and handed out the bowls filled with meal.

Rona couldn't help smiling. Her first thought was, *WSC will be pleased that the Genome Project is finally underway.* But the thought that warmed her the most was, *Lu and I don't have to return to Moon Base just yet. We're staying and will help heal the colonists.*

This was far greater than a Nobel Prize.

"Good," Qorow Low said, as she finished, and smiled sweetly.

Adumie wrapped his arms around Qorow Low and held her tight. "How long will it take?" he asked Rona.

"I don't know. Her blotches are already fading. If they continue to fade, then it worked. But the more information we gather, the better we'll be able to understand what exactly is happening. Some may heal faster than others. For some, it may be too late." Rona's eyes darted around. "We need to run tests and keep watch on everyone. I wish I could be more confident, but we have never done this before. All we can do is wait and see."

"Would it help if you took these readings from all of us?" Adumie asked.

"Yes it would," Rona said, surprised.

"So be it," he turned to his people. "All will be scanned."

He turned back to Rona and rolled up his sleeve.

This was the victory Rona had hoped for. She should try a few at a time and study each outcome, then make adjustments and try again. But Rona would not say no to anyone who wanted to try.

These people need hope, she reasoned. *And now they have it.*

In the next few days, she'd know one way or the other if it worked, and if the hope she'd given them was warranted.

Chapter 36

Jessica Hewitt
Leaving or Staying

Akiane Date: Year 328
Endurance: Commons Area

WHO UNDERSTANDS what is happening on Akiane better than me? I thought. *The new ambassador wouldn't understand the dynamics of two separate colonies.*

Adumie wouldn't understand WSC or its military structure. Everything around him was changing. He needed someone who understood and was willing to help with the changes and it had to be someone he could "trust."

Would the new ambassador also have to endure Woden? Who would be willing to make it with him or her? My guess was no one.

I'd already survived Woden. There was no need for another to do it. I was already a part of the Community. But if I left, I'd take my Community membership with me. The new ambassador would have to start from scratch.

I doubted the Community would completely reject someone new, but I also doubted he or she would be fully accepted. I wondered just how passionately that person would seek to understand these people.

What I'd accomplished had not been for a new ambassador; it had been for me. It was my responsibility to finish what I'd started.

Admiral Grossman's original orders clearly defined that I was to convince the people of Akiane they are a WSC colony. I still had the paper those orders were written on. I had not received papers for my new orders. So, technically, I was still under the original orders.

A cold hard realization swept over me. My job wasn't finished. If I didn't complete my original assignment, everything I'd just accomplished will have been for nothing.

Neither Cameron nor Adumie would be satisfied until the home they loved was repaired.

There weren't enough colonists to bring the gardens under control or to clean up after The Storm or make repairs to the main buildings in the habitat. The offer of gardeners, engineers, and construction workers from *Stanza's* crew would go a long way in public relations between Endurance and WSC.

Without anyone noticing, I quickly exited the Commons Area to speak with the captain from one of the shuttles.

When I returned, I knew Adumie was not ready to have this conversation. His full attention was focused on Qorow Low.

I sat next to Jecidia.

"Endurance is in need of many repairs," I said.

He sighed heavily. "Perhaps after all are healed, we can begin. It will take time."

"I have a proposal."

"Indeed?" he asked, truly interested.

"I have spoken to the captain and asked if some of his military personnel could help with repairs," I said.

Jecidia stopped eating, leaned back in his chair, and gave me his full attention.

"He has agreed," I said. "One hundred men and women are coming, well, 98 workers and two cooks, are on loan for as long as you need them. They will take orders from you."

"From me? " he asked. "Why me?"

"I think Adumie has his hands full with Qorow Low, and I am unsure how he will respond to more off-worlders," I said.

"This one will also have his hands full with healing," he said.

"If not you, then who?" I asked.

"Nu Venia," he said. "She has made Woden. She has returned victorious. She has understanding of your people."

I sat back in my chair surprised, but it was the perfect answer.

"Nu Venia it is," I said.

"These on loan, where will they live?" Jecidia asked.

"They can stay in the same area where my friends and I lived," I said. "I know it will take time for your people to get used to them being here."

"With time will come trust," he said.

"Just like Woden," I said. "Trust makes Community."

"Just so," he said.

"Just so," I agreed.

"What will happen to your people?" Jecidia asked.

"Vawynn has invited them to live in Persephone, but they will come back to check on you and your people," I said.

"You will live with them?" he asked.

"I plan to return to Earth with the ship." My words sounded hollow.

He shook his head. "I do not believe you are finished here."

"What do you mean?" I asked.

"That is for you to decide," he said.

"Now you sound like Cameron."

"That one learned much from our long walks." He smiled.

I smiled. "It's time for me to go. I have completed my orders. WSC now has two colonies. The people of Akiane are reunited. Cameron would say I'd done all of this. I'm not sure I deserve the credit. He's the real hero, he and Nu Venia. I only helped."

"Such accomplishments would not have been possible if the Holy One had not brought you to us," he said.

He wanted me to stay.

I needed to return home. Everything I'd endured had been for that one goal.

I stood. "It's time I leave."

He smiled. "Indeed."

I walked away.

When I reached the exit door, I stopped and turned to look around the room.

Three groups of people, those from Earth, Endurance, and Persephone were mingling.

They bowed as they introduced themselves, and started getting to know one another. Those of Endurance brought mugs of hot tea and snacks. People were smiling, talking, and laughing. They were communicating and would become one large Community.

I had completed my orders and Cameron's mission. They didn't need me anymore.

The private who had been my escort while on *Stanza* approached carrying two duffel bags, one over each shoulder. A commander walked at his side, also carrying a duffel bag.

The private acknowledged me, dropped the duffle bags at his side, then announced to the room of people, "I'm sorry to interrupt, but Captain Leopold is preparing to leave. We need to shuttle everyone back to Persephone."

He paused as if finished, then said, "The captain has decided to leave two shuttles and two pilots, one for each colony."

An enthusiastic cheer of surprise rose from the crowd. Now both colonies had the means to continue building relationships.

"Lieutenant." The commander saluted me.

I saluted back.

"This is Commander Bishop," the private said. "Once the civilians have been transported to Persephone, the commander will oversee the troops who are coming to assist Endurance."

"Commander, see the older gentlemen sitting at that table?" I said pointing at Jecidia.

"Yes, ma'am."

"Introduce yourself to him; he will see to your living quarters." I pointed to Nu Venia and said, "Have him introduce you to her. She will discuss work details with you."

"Lieutenant." He walked off.

It felt funny giving orders to a commander and have him following them.

He introduced himself to Jecidia.

Jecidia motioned him to sit, then called Nu Venia to join them.

"It is time," the private said to me.

This was it. Time to leave. I took one last look. What did I really have on Earth? The past. Something I could never get back. All my life, I wanted to return to the memories of a happier time when things were right, before Mom and Dad began fighting. Nothing was the same after she left. Things would never be the same.

On Earth, I had old memories. What did I have here?

Nu Venia and her child—the future.

The Community—an opportunity to watch it grow and solidify.

Rona, Lu, Olivia, and a number of others—friendship.

Jorge—a possible future with him?

If I left, I'd miss out on all of it. I'd never meet Nu Venia's child, Lloyd, named after my father. Who would tell him about his namesake? Little Lloyd carried some of my DNA and was a product of two worlds. He would become a constant reminder of Woden and Cameron. What would he be like? Who would he become? We could chat from Earth but I would never really get to spend time with him or truly get to know him.

The memories I'd acquired on Akiane are far better and happier, than the ones I'd left on Earth.

If I stayed, I'd be a part of history, which meant my name would go down in the history books of two worlds. That wouldn't be so bad?

Imos sat at my feet. Essal's puppies wrestled nearby. This would be the last time I scratched her behind her ear.

Jorge joined me.

The night before we were supposed to have dinner and a quiet evening alone, but I'd ruined it by telling him I was leaving. He didn't take it well. He left before dessert.

This was our last moment together. Or was it?

Maybe it was time to let go of old memories and make new memories?

And just like that, I knew what commitment was. I knew I would help these people who were once defeated but now had a future.

In my imagination, I saw Cameron walking through the Commons Area with Nella, Huth, and Essal at his side. His chest swelled, beaming with pride. And then he was gone, no doubt going to find my father to let him know I'd turned out all right.

"Lieutenant?" the private was politely trying to get my attention.

"Guess this is where we say goodbye," Jorge said.

"Private," I said. "Tell Captain Leopold I'll be staying."

344

He had suggested that I stay, but I'd declined. Evidently, he was right.

I'd never seen Jorge smile like that before. He was absolutely luminous.

"Yes, Lieutenant," the private said. "Where shall I send your things?" He picked up one of the duffel bags at his feet.

Now, I was going to disappoint Jorge, again.

"Keep it here," I said. "I'll be staying at Endurance."

Jorge's face fell.

"Yes, ma'am, the captain said you might decide to stay. In which case, I am to give you this." He handed me an envelope.

"Who is this from?" I asked.

"It's from the admiral."

My stomach did a flip-flop. What trouble was I in now?

"The captain convinced the admiral that you were the best person to be ambassador to Akiane. These papers relieve you of duty. You are no longer in Space Force." He handed me another envelope.

"He also said I'm to be your assistant" the private said with a grin and handed be a third envelope.

"I didn't know I needed an assistant," I said.

"It's a big job covering two colonies, ma'am."

"Whose idea was it for me to have an assistant?" I asked.

"A good assistant anticipates his ambassador's needs." He shrugged.

"You could be right, Private. Why don't you store our duffel bags to one side. We'll deal with them later. Then go get a cup of tea and introduce yourself to someone. Make a friend."

He saluted.

"I'm an ambassador. No more saluting."

"Yes, ma'am."

"Private, what is your name?"

"Charlie Harrison, ma'am."

345

I extended my hand. "Nice to meet you Charlie, I'm Jessica."

He shook my hand. "Nice to meet you, Jessica."

I pulled Jorge out of the way of our friends filing out of the commons area.

"I can't leave Nu Venia," I said. "I'm going to stay here with her."

"What about me, us?" he asked, clearly disappointed.

"The whole purpose was to gain trust and build community between WSC and the colonists. But I didn't make Woden alone. Nu Venia and I did it together. I need to stay here and help her finish Cameron's mission."

"Can't you do that from Persephone?"

"No. There are things you don't understand."

It would take time to explain the seriousness of Nu Venia carrying Cameron's child. The Community was changing, but it would take time for them to adjust to her having his and my baby. We needed to explain how that happened and my part in it. I couldn't let her deal with that by herself.

Jorge shook his head and turned away. "I should have said something while we were still on *Britannia*. At least we would have had that time together." He started to walk away.

I grabbed his arm with one hand and placed my other hand on the side of his face.

"I'm not staying only for Nu Venia, I'm also staying because of you," I said. "I'll make time for you. I promise."

"What about tonight?" he asked hopefully.

"Tonight Nu Venia and I and ah, and my assistant, I almost forgot about him, need to decide where we're gong to live. In the morning, you send a shuttle for me, and we'll spend the day together.

"All day?"

"All day."

"I'll be here at dawn." His dimples deepened and his freckled nose crinkled his joyfully smile returned.

"You could at least let me wake up before you come for me."

"Okay, I'll be here five minutes after dawn."

"Fine," I relented with a laugh. "I'll be dressed and ready, but you'd better bring breakfast."

He kissed me. How could I have forgotten that kiss?

When the kiss was over, I reluctantly let go and watched him walk away. It reminded me of our first kiss and how I had left him standing alone as I started on my journey for Woden. Now I understood how he felt.

But I was a woman on a mission I fully intended to complete, and I could only do that at Endurance.

Fortunately, there would be plenty of time to enjoy life.

Something I hadn't done in a long time.

I never wanted to set foot on this alien planet. I mean, why would I? Winters are seven years long. Every eleven years there's a gravitational storm that literally rocks this world.

I didn't know if I'd ever leave. Maybe I never would. I left Earth to find myself, so I could return and start my life over. It seemed I'd "found myself" 27 light years away from Earth, and had found the perfect place to start over.

Jorge stopped, turned around, stared at me for a full minute, waved, then ran to catch up with the others.

I'd found everything I'd ever wanted on this alien planet, including my heart.

The End

Thank you for being a fan and taking time to finish People of Akiane Trilogy. If you enjoyed it, please consider telling your friends and posting a review on your preferred social media. Word of mouth is an author's best friend and much appreciated.

If you think you don't know what to write, you do. What you would say to a friend is perfect for a review.

Phyllis Moore MythRider

Why MythRider? Because there is more than one author named Phyllis Moore. But I'm the only MythRider.

Follow Phyllis Moore MythRider at:
Email: PhyllisMooreMythRider@gmail.com
Blog: MythRider.WordPress.com
FB: Phyllis Moore MythRider
Goodreads: https://www.goodreads.com/phyllis_moore